MYTHIC
IMAGINATION

OTHER TITLES IN THE
COLLECTED WORKS OF JOSEPH CAMPBELL

More titles forthcoming

MYTHIC IMAGINATION

COLLECTED SHORT FICTION

Joseph Campbell

Introduction by David Kudler, Managing Editor,
The Collected Works of Joseph Campbell

New World Library
Novato, California

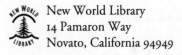

New World Library
14 Pamaron Way
Novato, California 94949

Text design by Tona Pearce Myers

Library of Congress Cataloging-in-Publication Data
Campbell, Joseph, 1904–1987.
  Mythic imagination : collected short fiction / Joseph Campbell ; introduction by David Kudler.
      p.   cm. — (The collected works of Joseph Campbell)
Includes bibliographical references.
ISBN 978-1-60868-153-2 (hardback : alk. paper)
I. Title.
PS3505.A528215A6 2012
813'.52—dc23   2012029666

First paperback printing, May 2022
First hardcover printing, November 2012
ISBN 978-1-60868-809-8
Printed in Canada on 100% postconsumer-waste recycled paper

New World Library is proud to be a Gold Certified Environmentally Responsible Publisher. Publisher certification awarded by Green Press Initiative. www.greenpressinitiative.org

10 9 8 7 6 5 4 3 2 1

CONTENTS

————————•————————

ABOUT THE COLLECTED WORKS OF
JOSEPH CAMPBELL

———————•———————

AT HIS DEATH in 1987, Joseph Campbell left a significant body of published work that explored his lifelong passion, the complex of universal myths and symbols that he called "Mankind's one great story." He also left, however, a large volume of unreleased work: uncollected articles, notes, letters, and diaries, as well as audio- and videotape-recorded lectures.

The Joseph Campbell Foundation—founded in 1990 to preserve, protect, and perpetuate Campbell's work—has undertaken to create a digital archive of his papers and recordings and to publish the Collected Works of Joseph Campbell.

THE COLLECTED WORKS OF JOSEPH CAMPBELL
Robert Walter, Executive Editor
David Kudler, Managing Editor

INTRODUCTION

---•---

JOSEPH CAMPBELL studied one thing his entire life: narrative. Yet that one thing had, so to say, a thousand faces: ancient myths, epic poems, medieval romances, timeless folktales, modern novels—all were expressions of what Campbell saw as humanity's "one great story."

The products of that lifelong study most familiar to us are the seminal nonfiction books, essays, and talks on mythology that he produced during his life (1904–1987) and that, together with his journals, make up the Collected Works of Joseph Campbell in print, audio, video, and ebook formats. Campbell was a masterful dissector of the art and science of narrative, as influential in helping both writers and readers understand the core of what story *is*, one could argue, as any thinker since Aristotle wrote his *Poetics*.

Yet as anyone who has read his books or heard him speak can attest, he was also a masterful storyteller: engaging, entertaining, thought-provoking...and funny.

It should come as no surprise, then, that early in his career as a student of story, he should himself have turned to creating stories of his own. From his early teens, Campbell was a conscientious diarist, recording and analyzing the events of his own life—bits of dialogue, interesting anecdotes, disturbing dreams. Soon after he abandoned his doctoral studies, he began identifying himself as an author. "By [1929], Joseph Campbell had already been working for some time on his short stories, his chosen vehicle as a writer."[1] From that time through the 1940s, Campbell applied the same imaginative, analytical mind to the art and craft of fiction that would bring us insightful, inspiring studies of modern literature and primal mythology.

The seven stories in this volume were all created during this period, before Campbell resolved that "comparative mythology...is to be my study."[2] Of the short fiction that he worked on, they are the only pieces that we still have. Six of the stories have never been published before—the sole exception being the earliest, "Strictly Platonic," which appeared in *Liberty* magazine in 1933 and which we have therefore presented as an appendix. Two of the remaining stories— "Moonlight in Vermont" and "Last Paradise"—were written as stand-alone pieces and are presented as such. The remaining four stories were also originally written to stand alone. At some point, Campbell realized that they shared many thematic threads, so he gathered them into a cycle that he titled *Where Moth and Rust* and wrote a foreword and a prologue to introduce them.[3]

Campbell's tales vary in setting and tone from light and pastoral ("Moonlight in Vermont") to urban and ironic ("The Lord of Love") to apocalyptic ("Voracious" and "The Forgotten Man"). "Strictly Platonic" is a college satire, and "The Belly of the Shark" is a metaphysical/ psychological thriller, while "Last Paradise" is a complex morality tale, a metaphoric exploration of the costs of modern civilization.

The four stories that make up *Where Moth and Rust*, written during the Second World War, collectively reflect Campbell's deep unease with the course of human civilization—not shocking, given the outlook offered by the news of the day. Conceived (as was *Dr. Strangelove*) as a kind of future history, the cycle offers four bleak, wartime glimpses of the world rushing toward its own destruction. There's no sense of a shiny future of technological marvels to be found, but rather a fictional exploration of the themes laid out in Oswald Spengler's *Decline of the West*.

Anyone at all familiar with Campbell's work will recognize immediately that all of his extant unpublished stories are unabashedly mythological in theme and in content. At some point in each of the six unpublished stories, the protagonist receives a call to adventure—a visit from or an invitation to a world where none of the considerations of mundane life apply—and is either transformed or destroyed by that experience. In each case, there is either an explicit or implicit evocation of primal mythological imagery: the goddess Kālī births and devours; the Leviathan swallows; a timeless house of the *sidhe* appears and disappears; Kīrtimukha, the Face of Glory, consumes all; the Buddha bestows illumination that may or may not be annihilation. Like a modern version of Ovid's *Metamorphoses*, these tales explore what happens when human beings come into contact with the eternal.

Written during the years preceding the 1949 publication of *The Hero with a Thousand Faces*, these works show Campbell exploring many of the narrative and thematic ideas found in his classic study of the structure of hero tales from around the world and across the ages. He tells his stories, which explore all the classic themes of modern Western fiction—love, loss, yearning, the struggle to conform, the desire to break free—with a strong sense of the psychological combined with a resounding sense of the mythic.

Fantastical and at times literally otherworldly, whimsical yet unflinching, Campbell's writing was utterly out of sync with the American fiction scene of the years before, during, and after World War II. The majority of American fiction of the period was grittily realistic. From Steinbeck, Hemingway, and Faulkner to Hammett, Michener, and Mailer, mainstream American authors were focused on this world. Authors of a more speculative bent—Asimov, Heinlein, del Rey, and Bradbury, for example—were writing classic tales of science fiction and fantasy available mostly in pulp magazines, but their writing was bursting with American optimism, a hope for the future that seems utterly lacking in Campbell's.[4]

Given that his fiction did not hew to the tropes of either the realistic or the speculative fiction of the time, it's understandable that Campbell couldn't find a publisher for his writing.

Though he was a positive, ebullient man, Joseph Campbell's worldview was deeply influenced by the philosophical pessimism of Spengler, Arthur Schopenhauer, and Friedrich Nietzsche. These so-called Romantics' philosophy challenged the notion of Progress, what Campbell called "an ameliorative mythology [that through] prayer or good deeds or some other activity, one can change the basic principles, the fundamental preconditions of life.... This is like marrying someone in order to improve him or her—it is not a marriage."[5]

As one reads the tales in this collection, taking in their combination of the quotidian and the mysterious, it is hard not to think of magic realism, a style of literature that flourished in Latin America throughout the mid- and late-twentieth century but that wouldn't have an impact in the United States and the rest of the world until the 1970s, three decades after Campbell turned away from writing fiction. Yet prescient though his writing seems, it springs from the same modernist, surrealist roots as the Spanish-language work of Jorge Luis Borges and Gabriel García Márquez. Campbell's models were the novelists about whom he wrote and spoke so much: James Joyce and Thomas Mann. "Proceeding from the naturalistic novel... in all of these works just following the [First World] War one finds [Joyce and Mann each] bringing into discourse the mythological associations which underlie his composition."[6]

Like Mann, Campbell attempted to marry the mundane with the mystical. Like Joyce, he tried to give his storytelling a "scrupulous meanness"[7]—keeping the narrative voice colored and limited by the perspective of the point-of-view character, whether it is the banal smugness of the unnamed president in "The Forgotten Man," the inchoate romanticism of the Hawaiian debutante in "The Lord of Love," or the laconic cynicism of the college-educated GI in "Last Paradise."

With such heady models, Campbell's ambitions must have been high in creating his own mythically inflected fiction. We think that the reader will not be disappointed.

———————————●———————————

SOME NOTES on the creation of this collection:

As stated, none but "Strictly Platonic" was ever accepted for publication. We have included the dates of composition of these stories, which were noted by Campbell on each manuscript, to provide a further perspective on the development of his thoughts and themes.

We have chosen neither to emend nor to annotate expressions and sentiments that might strike a twenty-first-century reader as odd. Joseph Campbell was a man of his time, writing for his time. Whether he's invoking the "Alphabet Soup" of the New Deal by mentioning "them O.P.A. critters" (the O.P.A. was the Office of Price Administration) in "Moonlight in Vermont" or spoofing the grandiloquent malapropisms of radio preacher Father Divine ("The you-man body do tangibilate and the you-verse do tangibilate that which the iddibidible is been a-thinking") in "The Forgotten Man," we've decided to let Campbell's language speak, as it were, for itself.

Likewise, we have chosen not to attempt to bring the racial and cultural politics of the 1940s in line with that of our more sensitive contemporary sensibilities. For example, in each of the stories in *Where Moth and Rust*, he portrays a collision between the dominant perspective in his America and another culture: African American in "The Forgotten Man," Polynesian in "The Belly of the Shark," Asian American in "The Lord of Love," and Native American in "Voracious."

In each case, the point is not cultural relations, but rather an underlying clash between modern society's "terminal moraine of broken mythological traditions"[8] and fundamental, universal myth itself— "the secret opening through which the inexhaustible energies of the cosmos pour into human cultural manifestation."[9] Here, as in all his subsequent work, Campbell makes it clear that narrative itself has universal power, however it may be expressed. As he wrote in *The Hero with a Thousand Faces*, the hero's "visions, ideas, and inspiration… are eloquent, not of the present, disintegrating society and psyche, but of the unquenched source through which society is reborn. The hero has died in modern man; but as eternal man—perfected, unspecific, universal man—he has been reborn."[10]

David Kudler
July 26, 2012

ENDNOTES

1. Stephen and Robin Larsen, *Joseph Campbell: A Fire in the Mind* (Rochester, VT: Inner Traditions, 2002), p. 127.

2. Joseph Campbell, *Sake & Satori: Asian Journals—Japan*, ed. David Kudler (Novato, CA: New World Library, 2002), p. 227.

3. Campbell tried out alternative titles for two of the stories. "The Forgotten Man" went at various times by "The Nightmare" and "The Maimed King"—a reference to one of Campbell's favorite mythic images: the crippled wasteland king of the Grail romances—while "The Lord of Love" was also titled "The Bodhisattva."

4. To give a sense of the literary tastes of the time, the *New York Times* bestseller list for the week of January 10, 1943, lists the following thirteen titles: *The Robe* by Lloyd C. Douglas; *The Valley of Decision* by Marcia Davenport; *The Song of Bernadette* by Franz Werfel; *The Prodigal Women* by Nancy Hale; *Rivers of Glory* by F. van Wyck Mason; *Look to the Mountain* by LeGrand Cannon; *The Uninvited* by Dorothy Macardle; *The Cup and the Sword* by Alice Tisdale Hobart; *The Man Miss Susie Loved* by Augusta Tucker; *Thorofare* by Christopher Morley; *Drivin' Woman* by Elizabeth Pickett Chevalier; *The Lieutenant's Lady* by Bess Streeter Aldrich; and *The Seventh Cross* by Anna Seghers. No Joyce, no Mann, no Faulkner, no Chandler, no Heinlein, and certainly no Campbell.

5. Joseph Campbell, *Pathways to Bliss: Mythology and Personal Transformation*, ed. David Kudler (Novato, CA: New World Library, 2004), p. 6.

6. Joseph Campbell, *Joseph Campbell Audio Collection*, "Lecture II.1.7—James Joyce and Thomas Mann" (San Anselmo, CA: Joseph Campbell Foundation, 2012), track 1. For more of Campbell's thoughts on Joyce and Mann, see *Mythic Worlds, Modern Words: Joseph Campbell on the Art of James Joyce*, ed. Edmund Epstein (Novato, CA: New World Library, 2003) and *Mythos III: The Shaping of Western Tradition* (Silver Springs, MD: Athena/Acorn Media, 2011), program 4: "Between Pairs of Opposites," and program 5: "In the Well of Myth."

7. James Joyce, *Letters of James Joyce, Vol. II*, ed. Richard Ellmann (London: Faber and Faber, 1966), p. 134.

8. Campbell, *Pathways to Bliss*, p. 100.

9. Joseph Campbell, *The Hero with a Thousand Faces* (Novato, CA: New World Library, 2008), p. 1.

10. Ibid., pp. 14–15.

PART I

MOONLIGHT IN VERMONT

1941

Abstract goddess figure (terra-cotta, Egypt, c. 3500 B.C.). © Brooklyn Museum.

"GET UP!" Through his sleep, Freddy Bliss vaguely heard the agitated voice, but he was unwilling to open his eyes. "Up! Up! Up! Up!" A hard hand was shaking his shoulder. Freddy opened his eyes. It was that old dimwit, Carl the Finn. Somebody had switched the light on; the bulb, blaring from its wire, was dangling naked from the wooden ceiling.

Farmer George Waterford—a seasoned old fellow in his late seventies, sturdy as a bull, thick shouldered, with a severe, thoroughly honest gray eye—was wriggling his belly into his pants. "Get up, dang it!" he shouted at Freddy. That frightened the youngster, and he stirred. Old Waterford finally got his pants on and went over to the lad. "See here, Freddy," he commanded, "you just get up out of that bunk." He was usually grumpy, but this time his voice had a special accusation.

Freddy arose and squinted in the horrible light. He had not removed even his shoes before tumbling into bed, exhausted, only a few hours before. Taking a comb from his pocket, he began trying to do something with his naturally wavy hair.

"Now, listen, you," Waterford said. "Just put that thing away and get out of here as fast as you can. Give Jim and Carl a hand."

Freddy pocketed the comb and left the building, not knowing what he was supposed to do. What was going on? Cows were mooing everywhere. In the distance, he saw a flashlight swinging in the dark and heard the hoarse hollering of Jim Drayton, Farmer Waterford's son-in-law. What had happened is that Freddy had neglected to close the gate properly that evening, and twenty-eight immense Guernseys had escaped into the corn and were now wandering everywhere in the dim moonlight, mooing, trampling down the gardens.

Carl came trotting past, herding three of the animals before him with a stick. Waterford appeared, saw Freddy standing stupidly, and struck him on the back. "Lend a hand here, dammit! Head them into the barn!" Nearby a cluster of the cows lowed, startling Freddy; then they turned and lumbered off in the wrong direction. Freddy made a feeble effort to go after them. "Over here!" he heard Waterford call. Jim Drayton's voice and light were far away.

Chaos, havoc, wild hallooing, and one flashlight darting hither and thither crazily! After an hour of this pandemonium, the bovine marauders had finally been channeled cow by cow into their stalls in the lighted barn. Waterford regarded the scene with vinegar satisfaction, rubbed his leathery neck, and wiped perspiration from the top of his hard old head. Then he looked at Jim and Carl and asked, "Now where's that kid?"

"Freddy disappear?" asked the Finn, his crackled face glancing about quickly. He then moved to the door and peered into the moonlight. Even now, in the middle of the night, Carl's thin little shanks were done up in faded khaki puttees.

Jim Drayton, meanwhile, was going along the line of cows, slapping the rear end of each captured truant. The splendid animals were all at home now, standing in their individual stalls, flanks still heaving from the excitement. Drayton—a short-necked, quiet-spoken man of about fifty, clothed in chauffeur's livery—was employed on a large estate nearby and returned to the farm every night to sleep. Coming back late this evening, he had discovered the animals loose in the corn.

Carl turned back from the door and said, "Freddy's disappeared, all right."

Having concluded his examination of the stable, Drayton said abstractedly, "Don't worry about that kid."

"Gol' dang it," grumbled Waterford, his hickory head jutting forward. He turned to the door. Carl stepped out ahead of him, and the two called and hallooed into the night but received no reply. "What are we going to do now?" Waterford asked, shaking his head.

"Go back to bed," Drayton replied, approaching his father-in-law with a quiet air of indifference. His chauffeur's livery had been soiled conspicuously, his polished shoes thoroughly mired. "That kid has given you trouble enough," he told the old man. "Let him go."

The three men moved wearily from the barn to the lighted, glassed-in back porch of the pretty New England farmhouse, where Jim and his wife, Susan, Waterford's only daughter, slept alone; for the old farmer, who ran the farm, liked to be in the shack with the hands. Waterford, who never drank and never smoked, had worked the farm like an ox every day since boyhood. The fine herd of Guernseys, the fields of corn and alfalfa and clover, were his whole existence; and they supported him well. The farm was fat, the lawn before the little white house was well tended, all the roofs were in good repair.

In former years, when there had been more hands, a long table had run the length of the porch, but now there was only a short table that could accommodate five or six. Susan Drayton—a prematurely white-haired, motherly busybody—was standing by the door when her menfolk arrived. She beheld their filthy shoes and clacked her tongue.

Drayton stamped his feet at the threshold and began to remove his shoes; his wife fetched his slippers. Carl simply walked in and sat down. Waterford, visibly fatigued, moved slowly to his favorite straight-backed chair and seated himself heavily. "Well," he sighed, "now we gotta find that kid." Susan eyed him with concern. Forever fussing in the kitchen, she had prepared coffee, which the men drank quietly, staring across the edges of their cups.

After a time, Jim Drayton set his cup down, leaned solidly back, and addressed his father-in-law. "Listen, George," he said with his hard voice, "you and Carl go back to bed. I'll phone up Burns—he can help me find the kid. He can't be lost very far."

The farmer wearily replied. "Why, say, with that darn jitterbuggin' head he's got, he could be dying this minute in a ditch somewhere. Know what today?" He glanced over at Carl. "I told the kid to unhitch the team, hey, Carl?" The Finn grinned and broke off a piece of coffee cake. "Next I know," Waterford continued, "he's undone every gol' dang buckle he could set his hands to, and my harness is lyin' in two-foot lengths all over the ground!"

Drayton softly laughed.

"Right, Carl?" demanded Waterford. The Finn, still grinning, chewed and gave a nod. Waterford shook his head. "Why, say, that youngster ain't got the common sense it takes to keep a leg clear of the reaper. Right, Carl?"

Susan interrupted. "You can't expect the boy to learn everything at once," she tartly told him.

"Well, now, look here," her father answered. "I guess I got a right to expect plain common sense."

"The boy just don't know," she stated. "How can you expect him to, when he never so much as seen hair nor hide of a cow before two weeks ago?"

The farmer shook his head. "These dang times," he complained, "are the craziest I ever seen. Look here. Them O.P.A. critters down in Washington, they put it in the papers, over the radio, everywhere you turn: 'There's a war on. The farmer's got to produce.' Same time, they take away all your hands. Why, I ain't seen a first-rate young hand now for more'n six years." He finished off his coffee. "Carl here, he's one year older than God; and me, I'm two. When they do send us some young blood, it's a jitterbug from Brooklyn." With a sudden show of good humor, he laughed. "Why, say, you know, I do believe that kid don't know enough to unbutton—"

"Father!" his daughter reprimanded, as Carl grinned.

Jim Drayton shook his head. "Well, George," he commented slowly, "I guess it's tough on people in all walks."

Susan began clearing up the plates, accompanying the work with a pert lecture. "It was a good idea they had to send them poor kids up out of the city. All it takes to make decent hands of them is a little patience."

Her father looked at her and widened his eyes. "Patience!" he exclaimed. His calloused hands fell heavily on the table. "Well, now, I declare, I think I've had a lot of patience. But see here: how you going to be patient with a gol' darn jitterbug who don't know enough to get his legs clear of the reaper? Give him patience and he's dead! Right, Carl?"

The Finn, starting to nod off to sleep, didn't reply.

The old man resumed. "I send him home to do something safe: mow the lawn. I got old eyes, but even so, I can see he ain't mowed that lawn. Why, say, he knows just exactly where I be every minute, and the further away I be, the less he does." He shook his head, stamping to his feet conclusively. "Well, now, I guess he's gone and got a busted skull, and some ten-cent lawyer'll be suin' me for damages."

"George," said Jim Drayton softly, "go back to bed."

Waterford, already at the door, wheeled around. "Bed? I'll not sleep one cussed wink till I've got that kid back where I can holler at him. Come on, Carl." He stumbled down the steps into the night. "And say, Jim," he shouted back, "you'd better bring along another light."

_____ 2.

THE MOON SOARED ABOVE THE CLOUDS. It was a romantic moon. Freddy Bliss had never before been at large like this, in country moonlight that he could see by almost as well as by day. The night odors of the fields were surprisingly strong, and they were kind of wonderful. Freddy was no longer falling-down tired. He was no longer hunting the cows, either. He'd gone lashing into the corn, trying to drive out a couple of the animals, but soon found himself, unexpectedly, on the other side of the field. None of the animals were in sight,

and Freddy could no longer hear the loud, aggravating hog-call voice
of old Waterford or see Drayton's light. God only knew what had
become of the Finn.

Freddy found a big tree and sat down to enjoy, for a moment,
the romance of the light of the moon. For the first time since his
departure from New York, he was feeling really happy—feeling alive.
Gosh, if only he had one of his girls here! He drew from his pocket a
little imitation-leather billfold that he'd bought in a drugstore before
leaving and, opening it, gazed at the two high-school beauties smiling complacently from behind the isinglass—one, blonde; the other,
red-headed. (It was too bad about the redhead: her hair always photo-
graphed black, so you could never really get the full effect in a picture.)
Freddy found it was rather difficult to see by moonlight, so he tried
squinting to make the flat cardboard physiognomies fill out into three
dimensions and come to life. But it was no use. In fact, day by day it
was becoming less and less easy even to remember what the two of
them really looked like. All he could see anymore were these tantalizing but inadequate pictures. He fingered behind them and pulled
out two other smirking little faces. Both, this time, were blonde. He
squinted at these photos, trying again for that optical effect, but it did
not work. It never worked.

Freddy tucked the wallet away and drew out his blue pocket
comb, which was also protected by an imitation-leather sheath. He
began quietly, reposefully, to comb back his hair. It always gave him
confidence to do this. Freddy was a handsome kid, with good, intelligent features. In his native habitat he was popular and alert—but a
little frail. Out here on this farm, though, with nothing but old people
and these animals around him, all his liveliness had been killed. Boy,
that had been *some* idea of Freddy's mother's—to spend a nice, healthy
summer helping the war effort, in Vermont!

Combing his hair while meditating ruefully, Freddy perceived
strolling his way from the cornfield what he took to be one of Farmer
Waterford's red Guernsey cows. He had never before taken much note
of any of the cows, but in the moonlight this one was an oddly fascinating animal: a young cow—you could hardly see the udder—walking

along at a good clip, head down, its nose barely an inch from the cropped grass. He wondered if he should bother to get up and drive it home. He was enjoying the reverie, but it was late, and he would have to be up very early in the morning.

He looked around, trying to fix in his mind all the wonderful dark forms of the dimly luminous landscape; then he shut his eyes and tried to breathe in all the field odors. Back at the farm there was nothing but the smell of dung. Never had he enjoyed just shutting his eyes like this and drinking something in. He began to feel that he was now just about as happy as he had ever been, and there were no girls or jazz or radios or movies or anything—that was the most surprising thing about it! Gosh, if he could only hang on to this moment for a while. When he opened his eyes, the cow was standing there, head lifted, regarding him with dark and gentle eyes; its exceptionally long horns curved gracefully upward like a beautiful lyre.

Freddy gathered himself, got to his feet, and tried to head off the cow. He wanted to herd it around the broad field of corn and back into the yard, but the sprightly animal kept outwitting him by always jogging in an unexpected direction. The cow seemed to know exactly where to go to avoid all the wire fences, and presently was conducting him out across a considerable field. Freddy, feeling challenged, began to jog. They were crossing an immense pastureland with a winding stream and many little wooded places, when the cow disappeared into a grove. Freddy followed, so absorbed in his adventure that he was unafraid of the dark. When he came out the other side, he could see the young animal about a hundred feet ahead. It trotted across the lowered bars of a gate and disappeared into a stand of corn.

Freddy was now determined to head the cow home. Pursuing it into the corn, he imagined he was on the traces of his quarry. He stopped to listen: only a slight breeze stirring the leaves. He continued on and, after a period, broke into the clear and encountered a heavyset, angry farmer confronting him with a gun.

"Well," said the farmer, "and who are you?"

Freddy was shocked. He had never seen anybody with a gun —except in a Coney Island shooting gallery—and this hostile fellow looked dangerous. Freddy knew that if he were shot here, no cop would be around to rescue him. It was all pretty wild—like the stuff in Westerns. Freddy hurried to explain that he had been following a cow.

"Ain't no cow in that corn," the farmer stated.

"Well, I'm sure I saw this cow go in," Freddy reasoned.

The farmer repeated firmly, "There ain't no cow in that corn." He narrowed his angry eyes. "That was my daughter."

"Daughter!?" Freddy exclaimed. "Why, no, mister. You got me wrong; I was following a cow." Freddy laughed nervously. "I may be green, but I can tell a cow from a girl."

The farmer failed to smile. "That was my daughter," he repeated. "She always picks her corn at night."

Freddy wanted to insist, but the man gave the gun a stout shake, and he decided not to argue.

"Where you from?"

"I'm from just over there." Freddy pointed. "Mr. Waterford's place. George Waterford."

"Waterford? Never heard of him."

Freddy was afraid. This man was obviously trying to put him in the wrong. He began to squirm. "Mister, please, I was just out hunting for Old Man Waterford's cows. Gosh, mister, you must know George Waterford: big fellow, like a barrel. He's been your neighbor over seventy years!"

The man shook his head decisively. "I've been here seventy years, all right, but I'm hanged if I ever seen or heard of any Waterford. Guess you must'a followed that cow of yours quite a way."

Freddy was trying to figure a way out of his predicament when the man suddenly said, "Better come inside, youngster. It's mighty late, and you look like you could do with a bit of sleep."

Freddy, even more frightened by this abrupt turn to hospitality, tried to reject the invitation; but the man, insisting, herded Freddy toward a small, thoroughly dilapidated wooden house.

The door stuck, then opened with a start. Inside was a tiny, undecorated room, lighted dimly by an oil lamp standing on a splintered table. A young woman was taking fresh ears of corn from her looped-up apron and setting them out in a row under the lamp. When the man broke in with Freddy, she paused only a moment to smile, and then went on.

"Jennifer," the man snapped, "after supper, make up the bed under the stairs."

Once more she turned, this time looking at Freddy with a long, deep regard that sprang everything inside him. Her eyes were dark and very large; the lashes, long and black; her hair, yellow as wheat, was drawn up to expose two delicate ears; her skin was white, like milk—so smooth that Freddy wanted to swoon against it. And her lips, he thought, were out of this world. She was the most beautiful, the most impossibly beautiful creature he had ever seen!

Without a word, she swept all the ears of corn back into her apron and departed to another room.

"Sit down," the farmer said.

Freddy was pressed into a broken chair. The beautiful girl returned, moving on bare white feet with wonderful assurance, and set before him a small loaf of heavy bread, a pot of honey, some butter, and a large pitcher of milk. Then she deliberately looked at him, tilting her head in open friendliness, and smiled—before again retiring. Freddy was transported. Her teeth, he thought, though overlarge, were otherwise the most splendid he had ever seen: regular, perfect in their alignment, white—and covered by those lips!

"Have a bite," the man said.

Freddy required half a second to realize the man meant that they should begin their supper. Without a word, the two set themselves to the table. The boy allowed himself to be served, and as he ate the bread and drank the warm, foamy milk, he began to realize that his feeling of uneasiness had disappeared. He was beginning to experience within this undecorated house the quality that had enchanted him out there in the night. A breeze was coming in through the loose-seamed walls; it was laden with the rich odors of the farm. Such odors had seemed repugnant to him back at Waterford's, but they now belonged to his state of repose.

"Where you been reared?" the man asked abruptly.

With a bang, his stern voice slapped the scare back into Freddy, and the boy immediately choked on a gulp of milk.

"You don't look to me like a very good hand."

Coughing, Freddy sat back, wheezing and clapping his chest, and reached for his glass. It was empty. To Freddy's surprise, the man aptly filled it. But when the boy had recovered and settled down, the old questioner, having studied the lad somewhat covertly during the meal, scrutinized more severely than ever.

The unpleasant, wizened fellow had the leathery skin and deep neck creases behind the ears that Freddy now associated with men of the soil. He was as rugged as Waterford, but he had a leaner, longer countenance. His eyes, of no particular color, were a pair of angry-looking accusations gazing from a snarl of bushy brow.

Freddy nervously explained that he was from the big city, Brooklyn, and that his mother had sent him north for a summer in the country. The man did not reply but appeared to expect to hear some more. Freddy confessed that he had never so much as seen a cow before two weeks ago and that he'd been having a difficult time trying to learn to attend to his chores. He did not admit how little he cared for the farm but instead expatiated falteringly on the beauty of the Vermont landscape by the light of the moon. The man's silence acted as a vacuum, sucking from Freddy everything he had. Before he was done, he had revealed more than he knew.

"So, you don't care very much for our life up in these parts," the man commented when Freddy was done. "You think we're kind of dirty; the farm animals, disgusting; our talking and dressing, kinda plain; and you don't like how we spit."

Freddy attempted to excuse himself, but the man interrupted. "Young fella, it's just a gol' dang shame you don't happen to care for this work, 'cause you're going to see one heck of a lot of it before you quit this piece of property."

Freddy's eyes grew wide.

"We ain't had a young hand 'round this house," the man went on, "for more 'n twenty, near on forty years, and there's a peck of work for you to do. "He wiped his mouth on his arm and pointed. "Now get to bed."

The shattered boy arose and went out through the door to the next room. His captor shouted, "What's your name, there, son?"

Freddy did not hear.

"Hey, you!" The man called sharply. "I said, what's your name?"

The boy turned and told him limply.

"Freddy," the man repeated. He raised a finger. "Well, Freddy, now don't you lose one more wink of sleep tonight. Your first day on this piece of property's gonna be hard."

Freddy was licked, licked and tired. Retreating to the cranny beneath the stairs, he removed his shoes and socks and lay as stiff as a mummy on the little cot that the girl had prepared for him. The house had grown silent, save for a door somewhere that was creaking, but he could not shut his eyes. A beam of moonlight coming through a split in the wall cut the darkness like a knife. Some while later, he thought he heard a squeak from the floor above. Somebody up there was walking. Could it be the girl? He could hear, almost feel, soft footsteps overhead. He heard footfall descending the stairway. Was she coming down to speak to him?

When Freddy craned his neck to see, the girl was standing beside the cot. He could smell the clean-wash scent of her blouse, the fresh fragrance of milky skin.

Bending over, she asked in a whisper, "Are you awake?" Her breath caressed his face. He was in a swoon.

The unbelievable beauty gently shook his shoulder. "Wake up, young man," she insisted softly.

Freddy caught her hand, and she let him experience the texture of her skin while employing the moment to assist him to his feet. "The night is beautiful," she whispered. They were clutching each other's hands. "Come," she urged quietly, "let us wander again under the moon."

Understanding the sense of, but undisturbed by, that surprising adverb "again," Freddy allowed himself to be led out a back door and into the open night.

And what a heart-awakening joy it was to ramble freely with her, hand in hand, through the silvered reaches of the land, matching each other stride for stride, their feet bare. Feeling the dew on the grass was a new excitement for Freddy, and as he watched the clouds racing past the moon, happiness welled up inside him and flooded his heart; and this time, here was a girl.

They wandered together through the fields, and as they ambled, she pointed out the glens and told him the names of the peaks of the distant hills. Her way of speaking so caressed everything that it was almost as though she were displaying the details of her house, as though she had collected all these things about her with affection.

"That little hillock," she indicated a gentle rise, "is where I lie and read my poetry."

"Poetry! You read poetry?"

"I love poetry," she declared. "Shall we go up?"

She brought him to her place in the waving grass, and there they reposed, alone in a little nest beneath the moon. Freddy was glad she had let him keep hold of her hand. "Will you teach me about poetry?" he asked.

She leaned forward and pressed her lips to his cheek for an instant. They were cool. He could feel the entirety of their perfectly wonderful shape. Then something happened to him. It was exactly like a paper bag being snapped inside out: what formerly had been outside—the girl, that kiss—was now inside him; and what had been inside, now was out. He could not even imagine what he had wanted of life before this moment.

Freddy was still in that daze when the girl arose and lightly drew him to his feet. Again he found it miraculously simple to move with her. The land over which they traveled seemed to be inside him, together with the kiss, and the girl: it was a little crazy. As they headed back toward the stable, she pointed out the cornfields and the alfalfa, distinguished for him the buckwheat from the wheat. The whole place was alive with her vitality and her voice—even with her loveliness— and as she showed him the farm, it was almost as though she were revealing herself to him. Every step they took, she told him something he'd never known before; and yet it always seemed, the moment she'd said it, as if he had known it all his life.

The girl brought him to the stables. The odor of manure now entirely pleased Freddy, the tang of the animals gave him a sense of joy, and he was happy to push wide the ragged door. The two entered, and she led him to the central, working area of the old building. It was ordered, dark, and deserted. Freddy could hear the heavy thumping of a dull hoof and the swish of a tail emanating from the stall of a solitary nag. They approached the old horse and patted the offered nose. The girl circled an arm around the animal's neck and clapped its shoulder, leaving Freddy with its head. He discovered that he liked the velvet feel of the nuzzling muzzle. They proceeded on to a protected stall, where a cow that had recently given birth was reclining beside her calf. Though it was impossible to see the mother in the dark, Freddy craned in with a sense of special, quiet awe.

The girl turned to him. "Let's go up into the loft now."

With constrained agitation, Freddy followed her up the ladder. Jennifer showed him the stowed hay and explained how the barn operated: the mechanics of the derricks, the racks, the gears—she made everything clear to him.

"And that place over there," she said, pointing to a pile of hay, "is where I dream."

They went over. She sat down. Freddy arranged himself beside her. He had never before been so close to a girl's body.

She asked, "May I stroke your lovely wavy hair?"

It was beyond belief: she actually took his head into her lap and gently, peacefully stroked his hair. Freddy had never before gone this far with any girl. She was so wonderful. He desired only to shut his eyes and dwell in bliss.

"Don't you think I have a lovely farm?" she whispered. She had to repeat the question before he could reply.

"It's wonderful!" he answered vaguely, rolling his cheek against her lap. Golly, but her limbs were soft; and she was larger than he might have supposed.

"You will now find it easy to do the work," she assured him.

Freddy pressed still closer and reached an arm about her waist. Her body filled him with the same relaxing peacefulness he had known while lying on the grass-padded ground beneath the tree.

"We have been waiting here for you a long, long time," she murmured, "my grandfather and I." It was like hearing some beautiful voice in a dream. "The old walls of our dear house are splitting," she went on, "and the rains come in through the roof. It is a golden, milky farm, but it lies fallow in the fullness of its strength."

The girl wrapped her arms around his shoulders and lifted him up so that his cheek was pillowed on her bosom. He opened his eyes a little and discovered her face very close to his. For a moment he had the queer illusion that he was looking into the large, warm, dark eyes of the young cow he had followed into the corn.

"You will love my grandfather," she was saying. "He will help you, and when he sees what a wonderful hand you are, he will be proud of you. And he will give me to you to be your bride." She ran her fingers gently through his wavy hair. "I love your hair," she sighed. Then she drew his mouth to her own, and they joined mouths in a kiss that went on and on and on and on—and on.

3.

WHEN CARL THE FINN DISCOVERED THE KID asleep beneath a tree, Waterford was fit to be tied. He came stamping up, hog-calling through the night. "Gol' dang it to hellfire!" he howled. "Pity's sake! Dang bust, if I ever did see the likes of this one!" He gave the boy a yank. "Get up, you jitterbug! Get up, you cussed pest!"

Waterford, for nearly a week, was about as angry as an old fellow could stand to be, and Freddy had a terrible time of it. The farmer was all for shipping him home immediately.

"Give the poor boy a chance," Susan Drayton would continually plead. "He's doing better, ain't he? Why, Daddy, I declare, I can see it for myself."

"Well, he ain't much of a hand yet with a fork," the old man would retort with a disgruntled lurch.

Day after day they would argue about it at the table, right before the boy; but then one day Carl the Finn cracked his shriveled face, patted his biceps, and gave a dramatic point in the lad's direction. "Freddy gotta build up muscle." He contorted his jaw and winked. "Freddy learn," he said. "Freddy learn."

It was the first time anybody on the farm had ever heard Carl offer an unsolicited opinion on any subject whatsoever, and it marked the conclusion of the argument. Waterford still played severe, but all the hellfire had gone out of his grousing. Freddy even began to enjoy the way the old man would thunder about his landscape like a black cloud in an extensive sky. He was now permitting Freddy to assist in the hay fields—and that was an important sign.

One expansive Sunday the boy was assigned to hitch the favorite bay mare, Nellie, to the buckboard; whereupon, with a gay gleam and a fine flourish, the old man climbed into the seat. "Get aboard, you two!" he ordered gruffly, giving a brief signal to Freddy and the Finn. They swung up over the tailboard, Carl grinning his crackled grin from ear to ear. "Gee-ah!" cried the master, giving the whip a great snap. He turned to the two. "Off to Nellie's wedding!" he declaimed gallantly. And Freddy knew that at last he had made the team.

Then one evening toward the end of the summer, Jim Drayton came home from his employment driving a girl in the car. An additional place was set at the table on the dining porch, and at supper time, as the Finn was tearing himself a chunk of bread and Jim Drayton, at the head of the table, was pouring coffee into his saucer, a young woman entered bearing butter and a large pitcher of milk.

"Jenny, dear," Susan Drayton introduced, "this is Freddy." The soiled young man had just sat down. "Freddy boy," she continued cozily, "this is Jenny, my daughter." Freddy stumbled trying to arise. "Sit down!" Susan insisted. "Sit down!"

Waterford held out his plate for more potato, and as Susan served him, she explained to Freddy, "Jenny's just come back from the big city." Then the two women, at last, drew out their chairs and settled.

Jenny had been placed across from Freddy, and he peered at her whenever he safely could. She had a reposeful, peaceful quality about her. Queer! Where had he seen that face before? Her golden hair, combed up from delicate ears, was braided and wrapped beautifully about her head. Her skin was smooth and milky—Freddy felt it would be marvelous to touch. He wished he could swoon against it. He was not eating very well.

Jenny, meanwhile, was surreptitiously studying Freddy. When he noticed, she drew her eyes from his naturally wavy hair and smiled at him. Though her teeth were overlarge, the jaw being somewhat heavily formed, Freddy thought them entirely wonderful: they suggested some forgotten lost delight he could not define. And when she smiled that way, deepening her eyes, he realized that he had been waiting all his days for a girl with exactly this quality. True, she was a bit plump given his former standards, but for some reason (Freddy was unable to remember why) all those standards had changed. Perhaps it was merely that he had not seen any young people for so long. On the other hand, how to account for this curious, profoundly convincing sense of recognition? Could he have seen her picture somewhere about the house—perhaps that time he'd ventured into the sitting room? He tried to think.

"Well, now, did you *like* the city, Jenny?" Waterford asked, with an inflection that strongly implied his expectation.

She swallowed something with a gulp and nodded. Her grandfather looked let down. Her father laughed. "But I like it better here," she added with a twinkle.

Waterford revived. "Well, now," he offered, "come to think: there must be quite a pack of folks down there." He looked over at Jenny. "Why, of course," he argued, refuting himself. "And I suppose all them folks must have a point or two. Hey, Jenny?" He cast a roguish wink at Carl.

"Trouble is," Susan Drayton put in tartly, "we just don't get down there half enough. We're stuck up here, too close to this speck of a farm."

The old farmer sent another of his gay winks to the Finn. He turned to Susan and her quietly smiling spouse. "Why, look-a-here," he suggested, "we got a good young hand now, so you poor old folks, you and Jim here, you got time to do all the jitterbuggin' you like." He tossed back his head and roared with laughter.

Jenny's large eyes lifted to the young man. "Are you spending the *winter* with us, Freddy?" she asked.

He gazed into her dark, very gentle, somewhat cow-like eyes, and for a second or two, he was unable to respond. That he would be going home he had simply taken for granted; he should be heading back, in fact, in a couple of days.

The girl favored him with a particularly winning regard. "Do you like my farm?" she asked.

Freddy glanced at Waterford, who was still laughing. Then he looked back to this wonderful girl. And he knew: he would be a farmer here to his ultimate day.

PART II

WHERE MOTH AND RUST:
A STORY CYCLE
1942–1946

Saturn Devouring His Son (detail; oil on canvas, Spain, 1821–23 A.D.). Francisco José de Goya y Lucientes. Museo del Prado, Madrid, Spain. © Erich Lessing/Art Resource, NY.

FOREWORD

———————•———————

THE FOLLOWING STORY CYCLE was discovered in a manuscript that comes up to us, by a curious turn, from the most distant future. It is of interest because it deals with a period of history approximately our own. The reader will note that the author confuses the traits of several entirely distinct historical personages and incorporates the dimly perceived features into a tale series of standard and well-known folklore patterns. Three of the plots are of the Perilous Quest type; one is of the Heavenly Lover type. It is evident that the author will have lacked invention. Yet the cycle enables us to study the manner in which the rich historical materials of our own day are to become broken down by a later generation and mixed with mere myth and märchen stuff. Note the total inability of the author to understand (if indeed he can be said to have striven to understand at all) the ideals and virtues of our present world. Note too the mood, which so collides (to its own great discredit) with the wholesome hopefulness of the modern Christian. One can only say that if it is to such black biliousness as this that our present-day selfless labor for the future is to lead, then better that the future should be left to shift for itself, and that our eyes focus hardly beyond the living minute.

"Any resemblance to anything that has happened since is accidental."

PRELUDE

———————●———————

THOSE WERE THE GREAT DAYS FOR SLAUGHTER. Combustibles of every category were being hurled from every angle at every considerable body around the surface of the mad-whirling globe. With its cursing, shrieking, and continuously exploding welter of a cargo, the world-sphere revolved, like some frantic animal afire, about its tethering post of a sun; and there was no one anywhere either to pity it or to release it: the fury would have to burn itself down to smoking cinders.

The unceremonious and burly institution of the press gang had been amplified, made respectable, and vigorously systematized to such a degree that in every hamlet of the civilized world little boards of citizen-patriots sat plucking youths and fathers from among the homes and schools for training and service in those all-consuming armies. And it was remarkable with what phlegmatic fatalism the totality of the human population of the planet acquiesced to this general depletion of its substance. Narcotized with unrelenting shots of propaganda slogans, atrocity slanders, cartoons, posters, radio sensations, medals, adjectives, pulpit talks, and the photographs of baby-kissing, edict-hurling presidents and leaders, like so many sheep the men and women of the century permitted themselves to be drained off into classified platoons and then shipped, by the batch, to mass liquidation in the far-flung fields. On the seven seas, by the shipload, two thousand, four thousand, six thousand at a stroke, they went down to furnish banquets to the harsh gullets of the deep; in the Arctic they stumbled and froze stiff; in the jungles they dropped and rotted. Meanwhile, the citizenry at home—to its own great edification, ennobled, strengthened in both physique and character by the great seriousness, the great purposefulness of the little tasks which during peacetime have nothing either of the heroic or even of the convincingly human about them—bravely gave to smoke and mud their sons and fathers, bravely kept faith that it would all, in the end, add up to something fine. The scorching tragedy of their suffering itself sanctified the cause: in the name simply of the dead, war was piled upon war, "that they shall not have died in vain."

That was an age during which, under pressure and terrific heat, vast, miscellaneous conglomerations of man-sized egocentric entities were becoming fused into prodigious organisms, and these trans-human, continent-consuming titans hardly breathed but to turn against and lock with each other in brontosaurian battle: each lustful for unique sovereignty over all the protoplasm of the planet, each boastful of its own peculiar power to transmute the smoking life-substance of the world into a shining image of such harmony as might re-echo in richly human sociopolitical tones the sublimest and most orderly melodies of the revolving spheres.

Between wars and during weekend furloughs, children were begotten by the hundred million, to be later indoctrinated, classified, and shipped off on assigned missions of glory.

Black Kālī, who gives birth to and feeds on life (carved wood, Nepal, eighteenth–nineteenth century A.D.). Victoria and Albert Museum, London, England.

THE FORGOTTEN MAN

———————•———————

(January 2, 1942–March 26, 1942)

DURING ONE OF THOSE NOW-LONG-FORGOTTEN, but in their time dreadfully memorable, wars that beset society in the Iron Age, the president of the alliance that claimed to represent the principles of charity, justice, and the freedom of man had the political misfortune to awake one morning—a Negro. That is to say, though he had been born white and pedigreed, and had been gently nurtured, when he slowly turned in his vast bed (his vision sleepily blurred, and his mind only gradually coming to consciousness), Mr. President, with a certain qualm, became aware (hardly distinguishing the moment when dim presentiment was converted to dimmest certainty) that during the night the pigmentation of his skin had become black. His left hand and forearm, protruding from the rolled-up lavender pajama sleeve, still dead asleep, were black, and their skin was now of that slightly different texture which he recognized as that of another race.

Not quite surprised—only sick that it should at last have come to pass—Mr. President, resting a moment, unwilling to initiate his first act under the new dispensation, lingered heartlessly in a zone between night and day. Then, heavily and slowly, he rolled onto his back, leaving on the linen sheet the dead arm and hand. Eyes fixed, he gazed at the ceiling, knowing that the form of the nose between his eyes was what it had always been, only black, and presently, with no further experience of emotion, he brought his right arm and hand up slowly before his face, where he regarded quietly first the back and then the palm.

It was to have been an epochal day in the history of the human race. During the past several weeks potentates of twenty-four brother and sister democracies had been assembling to hear the president. This morning at 11:45, in a great room of the White House, he was to address not themselves only but a battery of microphones blazoned conspicuously with the initials of twelve colossal radio corporations, while newspapermen from every corner of the universe lifted, sighted, and flashed cameras. It was to have been the great day of the sky-brightening message, at last announcing to the world the eternal principles upon which the peace was to be founded. The armed might of the enemy, after years, had been brought to a point of imminent disintegration. Those courageous peoples who had long before gone down under the heel of the aggressor were now to be heartened and encouraged to strike from within the atrocious organism already cracking under pressure from without. There was to be a world peace equally shared by all the classes, all the nations, all the races. The moment of the temporal redemption was at hand.

The black hands of the clock slowly moved, and the domestic machinery of the White House progressed from the slight stirrings of earliest morning to the stronger movements of early morning. Within a minute there would be heard a quick, perfunctory knock, and there would enter a delicate breakfast on its tray. The colored domestic would move to close the window, and the unendurable would take place—the eyes of the servant would meet the face of the master.

Unable to act, totally unable to stir to forestall the moment of the unendurable, the great man, without moving, let the gaze of his eyes turn from the black, steady hand that protruded from the lavender

sleeve to the black, moving hands of the mantel clock. Over there he
saw the minute wane, quiver, and pass. He heard no quick, perfunctory knock; no breakfast entered on its tray. Whereupon, feeling the
solid moment disintegrate within him, Mr. President of the United
States became aware that he was now capable again of dealing pru-
dently with any possible—or even impossible—contingency. He sat
up, a majestic Negro, pushing back against the pillows, rubbed the
tingling, still half-asleep left arm briskly a moment, and reached for
the phone.

"I want to speak to George," he said thickly. He cleared his throat,
"...to George."

A genteel female voice informed him that poor George, most un-
happily, had this minute been discovered dead in bed, but that the
breakfast would be up, nevertheless, immediately.

The president felt the hairs of his face stand up.

"I shall want no breakfast," he commanded briefly. "Connect me,
please, with Mrs. President."

The phone clacked; a receiver was lifted. The great Negro had
shut his eyes.

"My dear, I must see you. Something has happened. You must
not be surprised when you enter the room," he said. He put the phone
back and limply settled. Vaguely he fingered the erected stubble of his
cheek.

Not three minutes had passed when the door abruptly opened.
The woman, already fully dressed to preside over the final arranging of
the household, now with an anxious look to receive the shock of the
as-yet-unnamed, briskly entered. She was a tiny yet imperious, high-
busted matriarch, pitched stiffly forward by her slightly old-fashioned
corset style. She held her haughty little head grandly poised, and with
every gesture strove to project into the present the lordly life-forms
of what she conceived to be an aristocratic and long-successful line.
Actually, she was but the outer husk of a woman. Comfortable circumstances and a gentle fate had permitted her to grow easily into
the patterns favored by her influential family. Doors, yea walls, had
opened before her, so that she had lived and marvelously prospered

without ever having been forced back against the foundations of her character. Furthermore, with her swift social progress there had developed (more like a parasite within her than like anything of her own essence) a hard, rude ambition. It was this that had mastered and coordinated not only the elements of her own untried nature but everything within range of her imperious eye.

Here, then, was the woman who flung open the door. Impossible that she should have guessed what it would be; and yet, though her eyes grew wide and a quick hand sprang to her bosom, she immediately recovered and narrowed her gaze to a severe reproof.

"What have you done to yourself?" she sharply asked.

The black face, watching her from the pillow, failed to move.

After a brief, uncertain moment, during which her eyes again slightly widened and her body gradually stiffened, her voice broke forth in a harsh whisper, harsh with fear: "But you are not my husband!"

Staring, suddenly she screamed. She clutched at her head wildly and half-turned. "What have they done?" she cried. "What have they done?" Wheeling, she flew away like a sparrow—the door remaining open behind her. And the mad cry resounded only twice again from the distant regions of the house.

Unflinching yet obscurely helpless, the president simply watched the empty door. Absolute silence had succeeded the woman's cry, as though an arctic wind, pouring from the room, had abruptly nipped the budding of the new day. Following an endless, frozen moment, the black hand reached again for the phone, but the line was dead.

_____ *2.*

MUCH LATER IN THE MORNING, a strictly adequate secretary of state came through the dead mansion and entered the wide-open room. He found the president heavily slumbering, as though from great exhaustion. He paused long on the threshold, and with only the slightest stir of countenance, regarded the sleeping head. Apparently satisfied, then, that the state decisions had been correctly made, he stiffly dragged a stilted chair to the bedside, opened his portfolio on his knees, and drew forth a voluminous sheaf. He did not move to rouse the sleeper but sat rigidly beside the bed, clearing his throat from time to time, letting the presentiment of his presence gradually work its way down through the toils of slumber. At length the sleeper stirred, his eyes opened a bit. He smiled and struggled to push himself up against the pillow.

"Well, John," he said easily, "here you are."

The visitor, baffled for a moment, quickly recovered, cleared his throat again, and fixed his eyes on the papers.

"This is an extraordinarily difficult moment, sir."

The president smiled.

"You are aware, of course..."

The president nodded.

The consultation proceeded, impossible beyond belief. The secretary, by the mere device of adhering to the strictest rules, succeeded in suppressing every hint of either social or professional comment. He never betrayed the friend before him, the president before him, or the intrusive Negro before him. His deed this day was a triumph of diplomatic tact. What he conveyed to the man before him was the decision of the cabinet, who had hurriedly met in an extraordinary session, addressing the disposal of the remains of the suddenly deceased president of the United States, and the solemn circumstance of this epochal morning. History, it appeared, could not be asked to stay its course: the vice president was already preparing to assume the splendid center of this morning's stage. And during the next two days, the peoples of the world, particularly the official people of Washington, would be encouraged to celebrate and recelebrate a glorious festival of freedom; meanwhile, an empty coffin would be conveyed, with no more than appropriate dignity, to the graveyard and there tucked away. Again meanwhile, a stately Negro, enjoying a modest income, would depart from Washington in an expensive car for a secluded haven of rest and comfort. The wife and family of the deceased president had been advised by the present secretary to set out immediately for the country,

lest the inhuman stress of the moment should unstring them to a cry
or move that might betray the dreadful secret.

The consultation ended, with a correct bow on the one hand and
on the other, unseeing eyes. The head again fell back.

3.

THE POTENTATES AND SPECIAL GUESTS had already fully as-
sembled in the great room of the White House; the envelope of ether
surrounding the planet had been cleared of every wave (with the sole
exception of a curious, unidentified broadcast stemming from no one
could tell quite where, not very strong, not very clear, and consisting
mainly of a series of little tinkling melodies, played monotonously on
plucked strings, woodblocks, and little drums). The vice president of
the United States, a former university president, with a clear forehead,
bifocal lenses, and a shaven cone of a chin, was reading to mankind
a paper which he himself, during the dark months just past, had laboriously composed, and which was to have been spoken forth by
the lamented president. All knew, of course, that the gentleman now
reading was the direct and only author of the message, yet it was being
elaborately pretended that he was but a saddened, courageous mouth-
piece of the great man defunct.

As these first accents of a new Global Age began to unfold their
merciful song throughout the inhabited world, time hung for the
nonce suspended: butchers paused with lifted axe, lovers with disheveled hair, murderers with smoking gun, businessmen with dead cigar;
every Radio Taxicab in every city of the planet became the center of
a cluster of enrapt citizens, every window of every home gave forth to
the swept streets this melody of peace. And so, with the attention of
the whole world fixed upon the great room of the White House, the
way for the departure of the Negro now fitfully sleeping in the bed of
the President Defunct, not only through the halls of the White House,
but even through the streets of the city itself and the highways of the
land, was free and clear.

A firm knock at the door; there entered a handsome young mulatto in livery, who respectfully paused and bowed. "I have been sent," said he, "to help you."

The eyes of the man in the bed slowly opened; the two regarded each other in silence. It was a moment not for words but for a profound spiritual adjustment. The dark eyes of the invalid, the blue eyes of the mulatto, the world-pause between eons, the first sign of the new age: who shall say what disintegration of hope, presentiment of future, recognition of the visage of the inevitable, and deep, obscurely grateful acquiescence were mingled in the silence of this half-anesthetized moment? The invalid presently smiled.

"What is your name?" he asked.

"Theophilus," the youth replied.

"Ah!" said the man, as though the name had confirmed his reading of the face. His eyes again heavily closed. Rubbing his forehead, achingly, he brought the hand down over the eyes. "You may help me rise, Theophilus."

The young man bowed, and, with the manner of a doctor, moved to the bedside of his charge. His arm supporting the heavy shoulders, he helped the man to sit up and bring his feet around to the floor. "I feel exhausted," the man said, "as though I have been sick a hundred years." The attendant helped him to remove the lavender pajama jacket, and he paused only a moment to extend his black arms in front of him and regard the deep dye of the skin. He smoothed the right palm back along the entire length of the left arm, then briefly lifted his eyebrows, cleared his throat, and made to rise.

Theophilus drew the bath, fetched the bags and packed them, helped the master dress, steadied him out through the door. The hall of the mansion was clear, except for the bulky back of someone standing guard at the front entrance. Their way was through a side door to the left. The voice of the vice president sounded from a microphone in a remote part of the house: "...and there are no distances today; there are today no remote peoples. Great liners ply the airways from Washington to Chungking, from Washington to Moscow, from Washington..."

No one saw them quit the room; no one saw them move through the halls; no one saw them enter the car; no one heard the doors slam, the motor start, the gears catch; no one saw the great black limousine—a young mulatto driving, a stately Negro in the backseat—turn down the avenue, gather speed, and zoom like a bullet through the city and westward out across the land.

——————————————————— *4.*

AT A CERTAIN FORK OF THE ROAD, the car turned to the left and proceeded swiftly along the winding ribbon of concrete, across a mountain pass and southward into cotton country. In the business section of a large commercial city, traffic forced a pause. Newsboys were screaming on every corner the news of the president's death. Streamer headlines flashed the message from every hand. A lanky Negress about to make the traffic crossing, with a bundle in her left hand, a newspaper in her right, and a large pink hat awry on her heaped-up hair, beholding the long black car, slightly paused to inspect the occupants. She suddenly recognized the man, now black, who was sitting in the backseat, and with a quick stiffening of every limb, widened her white eyes, shrieked, clapped the newspaper across her face, and collapsed. The traffic signal changed and the limousine moved on.

Cross-country now, along the red dirt roads, the traveler gazed through the window at the wide-stretching, swiftly passing fields. The cotton crop had already been fairly gathered; only occasional figures, stooping in the hot sun, slowly moved between the rows, their long-trailing cotton bags like strange, unwholesome, parasitical slugs dragging at their necks. The traveler with an obscure emotion regarded hour by hour the passing of this extensive world: buckboards drawn by lazy mules bumping slowly along the pitted ways; shanties beyond the fields clustered under big rubber-leafed trees; sprawling rivers languidly flowing; now and then a poverty-ridden town, colored folk rocking in battered chairs on splintered wooden porches; an old car, gaily painted, sprouting with fishing poles and laughing children,

standing a little off the road, somebody at work beneath it. The traveler beheld these things with unmoving countenance and a strange,
heart-aching warmth.

Long after sundown, with an abrupt left turn the limousine entered the bounds of a large estate, the country place of one of the
members of the president's cabinet. After following a winding driveway between majestic trees, it drew to a stop beneath a colonial porte
cochere. The traveler started from a nap. Theophilus was standing at
the car door. A light snapped on, and through the glare came a chatter
of women's voices.

An old colored woman with heavy bosom and prodigious hips
trundled painfully down the steps and loomed beside Theophilus.
This was Dorothea, born in slavery, a sturdy great-grandmother of unnumbered years and steatopygous proportions that obscured the basic
stays and jointings of the human physical norm.

"God bless you, child," she declared. "Just come in. Just come
right in. Leave everything to me."

Theophilus helped the president exit the limousine. Dorothea
took his weight on her shoulder and aided him into the home. Two
other figures assisted Theophilus with the bags.

The estate—in colonial days, a plantation; since the Civil War,
merely a country seat; most recently, nearly abandoned—remained
now under the guardianship of Dorothea and a little community of
colored caretakers. During days and weeks, the noble Great Black
Man moved among these stately rooms, strolled pensively in the gardens, and deeply brooded the destiny now germinal within him. The
seconds ticked, the hours rang their rounds, the weeks and months
were uncounted. From Dorothea's kitchen his meals came to the table, served silently by Theophilus. His bed at night was ready. His
clothes were fresh in the morning. Like a tree—mindless of the surrounding space-world and taking for granted the moisture of the land,
the refreshment of the gentle air, the sweet flow of the life sap, the
unfoldment of its limbs and leaves—the profoundly in-turned inhab-
itant of the silent house and silent garden slowly nurtured the dark
cosmos that now slowly revolved within him, slowly found its center,

and slowly learned to communicate the import of its movement to the deeper outposts of his mind.

Who will read the dark sense of the long silence? A world with its forms, its hopes and fears—yea, more: with all the concrete effects of its long, irreversible development through prehistoric and historic times (progress out of a neolithic past and through a celebrated line of ancestral, feudal deedsmen, forward across Atlantics, and expansively out of colonial beginnings to the mastery of a shining, steel-hard empire)—a complex world of hardened, complex forms had abruptly cracked and fallen from this man, like a nutshell from a nut. Alone—alone—the naked kernel of his being stood puny and unsheathed, within the vast encasement of the world-shell itself, the casing, too vast, of the cosmic sphere.

Too vast, indeed, to support his former view of his own historical importance, yet mysteriously concordant with the grandest lines of his simple humanity; for these, even now, were beginning to assert themselves in the interior of his silence. Furthermore, as they became defined, slowly, his eyes and other senses began gradually to recognize the counterparts of these interior forms in the exterior landscape. The world that he was now learning to behold was not a mere field of optical interest, but an echo to the sad, solemn, silent melody of his awakening. There distilled from the Indian's land, now the Negro's land—flat, flat on to the horizon, its rank, irregular, uncomely vegetation sprawling in disarray—a strangely thrilling life-pungency, somehow sensible not to his nose but to his eye. The continent—not the republic that more or less had mastered it but the continent itself—was beginning to sing to him its unknown prodigious song. (That great airliner, meanwhile, flying overhead, from Washington, making for Mexico, he never heard.) What a speechless joy! What a recognition of powers craving utterance through his own black body: powers within him, identical with those already speaking to him from the land! He fell, suddenly sprawling on the earth and flattening himself against it in a crazy embrace, whereupon the ground was suddenly coarse and unresponsive—simply dirt and weeds.

Disappointed and abashed, the man gathered himself to his feet, brushed the sticks and dirt from his clothes, and resorting to a little garden kiosk overlooking the ill-kept lawn, the moss-bearded oaks, and the great sweep of ragged country away to the horizon, sat down to try to revive within him the great experience so rudely broken. How could he call to life again that breathing form of the land?

He had been sitting thus no little time, romantically but unsuccessfully gazing, when there appeared, approaching him, a great form indeed—but in such burlesque of the form of his expectation that he fairly emptied with a laugh at the absurdity of the coincidence. For there came moving across the field of his meditation that aged ageless bulk of a black slave daughter—that great-grandmother of all soilfolk—Dorothea: breasts ballooning loosely before her, buttocks magnificently bumping, slowly, solemnly, behind. Her thick, mahogany hams and legs, at a firm, flat-footed pace, were bringing her along, while her fine old head was held proudly high—jaws aloft, nose flat, eyes down, topped by a child's red-knitted skullcap.

"Good morning, Dorothea."

The old woman continued, heavily moving.

"How is Dorothea this morning?" the man persisted.

She paused in her progression, betraying a willingness to chat.

"You have been very good to me," he said with sincerity. "Your good food has quite restored me."

The old woman took her chin in hand, tilting her head reflectively, scrutinized the man's face, and comfortably folded her left arm across her stomach.

The man smiled. "Do I not look very much improved?" he asked.

"According to thy faith," said she surprisingly, "so be it unto thee."

He leaned back with pleasure, preparing to enjoy, with patronizing sympathy, whatever manifestation of grotesque old-mammy philosophy might now be about to pour into the quiet day.

"The you-man body do tangibilate and the you-verse do tangibilate that which the iddibidible is been a-thinking; always and without dipperation, knee-gation and disification; according to and following the way *in which* you visualize things pertaining, appertaining, repertaining, to your life's invisibilated existence." She turned away a little, gazing out over the country, placed her tilted cheek against her hand, and marvelously, endlessly soliloquized, as though all had faded from around her; as though all were revolving around her; and the inexhaustible river flow of her dreamlike, queerly reminiscent, almost-intelligible language, rippled forth, grew stronger in its rhythms, welled onward, and flooded out and over and around the landscape, without bounds.

"My help cometh from the Lord," she said, "which did made the heaven and the earth: I will lift up my eyes unto the hills, from whence cometh my assistance. The visibilation of things about you and me is the tangibilation of that which the Lord has forever been a-thinking; and according to the co-inside of that which me and you been a-thinking with that which the Lord has forever been a-thinking, the visibilation of things about the Lord and the tangibilation of the you-verse will unite and personify and concentrate and desirablize in one convenient likeness."

The voice went on without let. The listener, now beginning to feel the strain of an oversustained benignant posture, felt his pleasure gradually giving way to an experience of simple boredom. He was relieved when another shift of posture on the part of the old woman brought her eyes again to his and suggested that she might be preparing to draw her cosmological rhapsody to a close and to move along.

"My pappy," she said, "was a slave, and I was born amidst and amongst that long sorrow. And my pappy, he used to praise the Lord and the wonders of his unterpretebleness; and the wisdom of the poor man, he said, was the joy of the Lord himself. There was a little city, says the Book, with a few men within it; and there came a great king against it, and he besieged it, and built great bulwarks. And now then there was found in it a poor wise man, and he by his wisdom deliberated that city; yet nobody remembers this poor man. The poor man's wisdom is despised. But still now, wisdom, like the book says, is better than weapons of war." She looked at him severely, but it was impossible to determine whether the severity was directed explicitly against him or generally to the sense of her theme. "One sinner destroyeth much good," she said, and she prepared to move away.

"Wisdom," she went on, "benefits the tangibilation of the omniscient habits of the Lord, but the materialation of the life's existence of the sinner…" She began to move again, heavily, the great buttocks bumping solemnly, the mahogany legs going forward on the flat feet, continuing to emit, with gradually declining audibility, the Mississippi flow of the sleep-talk of her long life-brooding. "…the materialation of the life's existence of the sinner goes like clouds across the tangibilation of the habits of the Lord, and those are the poisons that suffuse and infuse the undesirableness; but the wisdom of the poor man is like lilies. Yea, his countenance is like Lebanon; excellent is the cedars. O ye daughters of Jerusalem, this is my beloved. For God veiled Himself in the invisible until He tangibilated man and creationed the poor man to be and become His own likenesses…"

_____ 5.

TOWARD SPRING, some weeks following the collocation with Dorothea, the Great Man felt himself to be sufficiently healed in soul and body to set forth amongst the peoples of the cities of the land. He bid Theophilus prepare the car and consider plans for an extensive tour. "I wish to know my people," said he, somewhat pretentiously. "I wish to take the measure of their sorrow."

Theophilus, without change of expression, bowed and turned to the preparations for the journey. Good Friday morning the long black limousine rolled slowly from the colonial porte cochere, followed the winding driveway between the majestic trees, passed the bounds of the large estate, turned left, gathered speed, and cruised away.

In silence the tour proceeded through a countryside beyond despair. Dusky, disheveled nymphs sat with their little brothers beneath trees, along the concrete waysides, and beside the polluted streams, and they would lift their arms and wave at the swift passing of the black car.

Many weeks he journeyed through the cotton lands, the savanna lands, the river lands, the shantytowns, the slum towns, the blow-away cities, the dust bowls, the chain-gang states, the Jim Crow states, the lynch-law republics, the Ku Klux civilizations: bitter kingdoms bedizened with Coca-Cola signs and stinking with the rubbish of broken lives. And not long had he been on the journey when the rumor began to circulate that a noble black man, cruising in a great black limousine, had come to be the folk redeemer, come to set the black man free, come to take the measure of the last measure of sorrow, whereupon to usher the transfiguration. And wherever the car now arrived, it was regarded first with interest, then with hope, finally with jubilation. Little towns turned topsy-turvy, dancing and shouting to see the car speed by. Everywhere throughout the land banners and pennants began to appear: "He now doth move amongst Us." "The Day of the Kingdom is At Hand." "This is the Moment of the Banquet." "All Thanks to You, Mr. Wanderer." No one knew where the car would next be seen, but wherever it appeared all was in readiness before it. Festivals were arranged, churches stood with doors flung wide, children paraded in fresh-washed white, every available tatter of gentility and stateliness was summoned to present its front to the miraculous wanderer.

"Theophilus," the man said, "our glory is defeating our purpose. Take me secretly to your own home. Let me live a while in obscurity and observe the life in quiet."

So they sold the conspicuous limousine, transferred to a simple runabout, and proceeded with all cautiousness to the town of Edenhope, on the east bank of a broad-flowing, muddy river. They entered the town at midnight, turned left from the main thoroughfare down a dark lane to the pretty gate of a decent, rather large frame dwelling. The door opened, emitting a golden light, and there came eagerly bowing down the steps a sprightly, overexcited little old colored man, all eyes and overhelpful hands.

_____ *6.*

THE HOME OF THEOPHILUS was a crated jungle. The seven sons had saved their pennies—two as Pullman porters, two as hotel cooks, two as jazz musicians in Chicago, one, Theophilus, as chauffeur to a successful politician—and their combined incomes sufficed to maintain the delimiting crate in semi-repair. Five of the youths were now in the house: a laughing, joking, roughhousing assortment of young lions of varying bulks and ages, all of a lithe, easy, coffee-colored maleness. They liked lounging out in the street, where they would greet, as friend or stranger, every passing Negro pedestrian. They liked performing conspicuous repair operations about the house and grounds, clambering, with shouts and belly-splitting laughs and with much passing back and forth of the hammer, up to the roof to fix a shingle; or swarming into the dark cellar, with many spurts of matches and with a rusty wrench or two, to stop a leak. The yard was a litter of their remains. They were the heroes and nuisances of all time. The moment Theophilus crossed the threshold, he shed the stiff uniform of his service, melted into their number, and ranged among them.

The elder daughter of the house, Angelina, was unpleasantly fair and surly, lighter than her brothers and with severe, reddish brows drawn fiercely to a thunderous scowl. She would sit by the hour, brooding into an ancient, tarnished hand mirror, and again by the hour before a soul-broken piano, torturing scales and delicate French songs from its cracked heart. The younger daughter, Rosalinda, was dark as night, warm as love, with sublime black eyes, delicious pulpy lips, a vigorous young seal-sleek body, and a marvelous innocence of her own splendor. Her love was a black boy, young and vigorous as herself. When this De Vere would come bounding in for a visit, the entire establishment (Angelina excepted) would blossom with benignant smiles.

But the marvel of the home was its population of old women. They inflected through every conceivable and inconceivable modification, permutation, and interrelation the elemental elements of the carcass female: great-grandmothers, grandmothers, mothers, aunts, cousins, and friends, everywhere in rocking chairs, shuffling about the halls and parlors, swarming in the kitchen, chattering, giggling, cackling, wheezing everywhere, closing and opening innumerable doors. Not for want of motherliness would this grand house decline. Not for want of thimbles would the sons of this house go threadbare. Not for want of supporting life advice, witchcraft, and biblecraft would the daughters lack magic in love. For there was here such a warp and woof of fate weaving and unweaving as nowhere outside the fabulous and transcendental kingdom of the moon itself.

The queen-mother of this teeming micro-Congo was a magnificent figure of a woman, with grandly proportioned hips and shoulders, mighty bosom, and majestic head; the dark splendor of her eyes, the dark comeliness of her features, the assurance of her speech and movement, her life-power as she would stand amidst the teeming flocks of her house so filled the rich atmosphere of this dominion that the very bricks of the antique chimney were miraculously sustained, biologically refreshed, phrenologically encharactered, alchemistically transmuted by her magic. Her great consort had been killed, some years ago, attempting to rescue his daughter Angelina from a "nigger-hunting" band of college hoodlums. Amidst the tin cans of a vacant lot, five yards from her father's corpse, the shrieking child had been beaten, stripped, and multitudinously raped. The gang made off, though not before they were recognized, but no white man's law could be brought against them. Nor could the hysterical child be taken to a hospital in that country. Battered girl and murdered father were carried to the home by frightened neighbors, and, like poison, the fire of that moment ran through every cell of the house.

But what a fluttering butterfly of a man was the deep-wrinkled, skinny, jet-black, bowing and scraping brother of the mother of the household, who arrived from New York some two weeks after the calamity. Having lived his comical life as a porter in a third-rate businessmen's club, where he had been a "character" and favorite, patronizingly tipped, clapped on the back, joshed and flattered, he was now incurably infected with solicitous subservience. Everywhere about the home he danced his superfluous, but humorously appreciated, attentions; and when time would be a little long, he would visit the piano room of the shattered daughter, Angelina, and listen with genteel appreciation to her song.

Now, if the Great Black Man, the great observer, had wished to become totally invisible, he could have sought no better sanctuary than this grandiose establishment. After the first greetings of his arrival, he simply became no more than one of the already innumerable black figures. The general goodwill easily included him, but he played no particular role; nor was it clear whether anyone either knew or would have cared to know his history. He was merely the man who had arrived with Theophilus and now inhabited one of the upper bedrooms. Occasionally one of the old gummy grandmothers or aunts or cousins, creaking in a rocking chair, would engage him, but the theme would always be the grand life-career of the son or daughter of some distant relative or other—never himself.

And there began within him a very rapid, very interesting, very encouraging recovery of spirit. Curious, but no sentimental reminiscence of his previous existence ever troubled the silence of his soul. The entire shell of that existence, together with its human-shell companionships, had definitively disintegrated: the man, so to speak, had lost the organs with which to engage it. His brain remembered events, but these spoke as little to his sentiments as had they been of the chronicled biographies of distant kings. Even the memory of his wife—the little bird of a woman, who in her pretty girlhood had infatuated his fancy and in stern womanhood had spurred, sustained, and facilitated his astonishing career—even the memory of that close companion of his full life adventure was too thin to hold the inferno heat of his abruptly revealed and now mightily glowing darkest core. His wife had simply melted into nonexistence. The night womb of Dorothea had received and fostered richly an utterly new life; and now this Africa of a directly living household (the very nadir of what once had been his cosmos), this spontaneously, turbulently metabolic jungle of a sharply suffering, gloriously jubilant world, invited his regerminative sentiments to participate again in the long, slow agony of man.

The first living creature to engage his eye and to fill his heart with an indefinable hope (the sweeter for its nostalgic hopelessness: far stronger than anything experienced in his younger manhood) was that delicious black jewel, Rosalinda. With the most sophisticated understanding of what was taking place within him, he was quietly pleased to feel his heart swell when he would encounter her dancing eye or when he would secretly watch the play of her body beneath a pretty little printed dress. And there were many magical moments when they would encounter each other in the narrow halls or pass on the stairways, or collide abruptly at doors. The girl, ever laughing and without a sign of any interest or suspicion beyond the accident of the moment, would accept playfully his frequently overfatherly politeness, and prettily bound away. Only once, when he was thus holding to both her elbows in a doorway, did she widen her eyes a little and then lift her head to search his features. Suddenly mad with her softness, he should have clutched her to him, but she lightly grinned and shook her finger. "Naughty man!" And she was off. Thereafter, though she never betrayed any recollection of his open moment, he could not but feel a little silly under her eyes. And with the most ambiguous sentiments he began now to watch for, admire, and somehow enjoy the comings and goings, easy love-play, and lively horseplay of young De Vere, Rosalinda's beau.

One evening, about the middle of the fifth week of his residence, as the Great Visitor was descending the split steps of the front stairway, the front door suddenly flew open, and young De Vere came flinging in with a frank call for Rosalinda. Somewhere deep in the house a door slammed, and the seal-sleek girl bounded forth to greet her glad boy with a kiss. The Great Visitor continued his descent of the steps, and with a fatherly bow and smile, proceeded into the large dining room, with its long table set for twelve: the five boys, the two daughters, himself, two of the woman cousins, the mother at the foot of the board, and the genteel brother at the head. He was greeted by the brother's fluttering hands and was bowed to his assigned seat at the right of the butterfly host, directly facing the fiercely scowling, reddish brows of grim Angelina. Before taking his place, he respectfully greeted the mother, who replied sufficiently while passing one of her sons a spoon. Some of the places were vacant, for attendance at the table itself was noisily irregular: the older grandmothers and aunts were upstairs somewhere, patiently sipping tea in a parlor, while most of the other aunts and cousins were functioning in and out of the kitchen. There was a great deal of swapping of crooked forks and chipped platters, spearing of potatoes, pulling in and pushing about of chairs, entrances and exits through every battered door, effervescent chatter and laughter at every turn.

"Hello, De Vere! Hello there, De Vere!" was called in various male tonalities.

"Thirteen!" croaked an old woman cousin. "Discombobulation!" She laughed and rose with her plate and fork. "No place for a sweet old soul like me." The entire company laughed—Angelina, of course, excepted. The crone made off to the kitchen.

"Here, De Vere!" they called. "Okey-dokey now." The gay little couple entered, and the Great Visitor, with scrutinizing eye, watched closely as the young hero lunged into the vacated chair.

"Hello, Mama!" he said.

The woman smiled.

"How's that floozy of yours?" one of the brothers broke abruptly in. "What's she up to now?"

The Great Visitor, shocked a little, sought to evaluate the reaction.

De Vere reached broadly for the meat loaf. "She sure do take the cake," he said. "Sometimes, I don't believe my eyes."

Rosalinda sulked. "You men are horrible," she pouted. She suddenly flashed at De Vere: "What for you stay working for that no-good white-trash she-cat?" The brothers started back, opened their mouths, and roared for joy. Through the noise, the girl pressed her attack on big-eyed De Vere, who was gaily pretending to cringe and squirm. "Chopping her wood and mowing her lawn—them I understand; but this here delivering her breakfast, and now plumbering in her bath…"

De Vere turned from his playful squirming and spoke directly to the brothers across the table. "Know what she done this morning? Goddamn it," he said, "I declare, some day I'll bust a button and give that female more than what she's asking!"

"What she do this morning? Come on, De Vere," insisted the brothers. "What she do?"

Rosalinda set her fork down and turned her head to him, her eyes alert for the worst.

"Well," De Vere said, "you all know the way she is. You all know the way she circumspects and navigates the house in them pink pajamas..."

"Where's her husband?" broke in the remaining gummy cousin.

"He's gone off with the army," one of the brothers briefly explained. "Off to liberate the blacks of New Guinea," he rawly laughed.

Trying to listen, the Visitor, to his deep annoyance, was being distracted by the unctuous solicitude of the little man at his left. "Will you have a bit more meat loaf, sir?"

Already a detail of the story was going lost during the polite reply. Another was going lost while potatoes were offered, again another while beans were proffered. The Visitor sought to catch the tale with his right ear, while matching, with his mechanical smiles, bowings, and scrapings, the elaborate gentility of his host.

"Some of these white women," the host said, "seem to forget our boys is human."

The Visitor weakly smiled.

"I think they like it," the host said, "exhibitioning themselves, where they know nothing will dare happen as natural human consequence."

The Visitor mechanically nodded.

"But I'm afeared a little for De Vere here. He ain't no guaranteed angel."

The Visitor let the story go, and now turned his mind to the host.

"That boy seen the inside of the jailhouse before this."

The Visitor politely lifted his brows in restrained surprise, with a tilt of his head in token of fatherly interest.

"Some of our boys, you know, they runs a little wild," the host continued, "and this De Vere here went with a pretty rough, razor-pulling gang there for a time. One night, they made easy with a private car, and it got wrecked somehow against a house fence."

The Visitor made an effort to receive this information with appropriate surprise. Meanwhile, the story down the table had reached a climax of some kind. The brothers were hallooing, beating the table with their hands, emitting whistles of mock amazement.

Rosalinda exploded. "What do them white trash think we is?"

The Visitor turned his gaze to the young man of the hour, and noted what he had never seen before: namely, a clean scar down the left side of his neck. Something tightened within him, and he experienced a revulsion from the youth. He observed that his sideburns had been permitted to grow down the length of the ear in imitation of the Spanish movie-lover type, and that his clothing was cut after a giddy jitterbug design. The fine nostrils had a cynical flare to them, and this now suggested possible criminal proclivities. De Vere was probably, the Visitor thought, a bad one—not the type at all for Rosalinda. He felt his half-fatherly sentiments assaulted by the young man's lusty presence at the table. Feeling very protective, he turned his measuring eye upon the girl.

In her emotional reaction to De Vere's story about the shamelessness of his white mistress, and in horror before the real dangers that this had opened to her mind, Rosalinda was staring at the tablecloth with a look compounded of terror and impotent rage. Her plump bosom was rising and falling beneath the prettily flowered dress, but otherwise her body was transfixed. Her hands were in her lap. Her delicious pulpy lips were incongruously desirable in this moment of her dread abstraction, and the observer gazed at them overlong. A red flower that she had stuck into her lustrous kinky hair began to burn into his mind. Protective fatherliness all at once dissolved into an unreasonable jealousy of the delights intended for De Vere. No longer willing to enjoy her vicariously with the youth, the man was alone with his ravenous concupiscence. A tide of unmitigated lust began to swim into his brain. His eyes, with a dreadful seriousness, measured the hidden contours of her form. He could almost visualize the vigorous young flesh within the sheath of dress—only a thread in thickness, yet adequate to frustrate his desire. The spinning of his head increased to such a degree that for an irrational moment he was afraid he was about to faint.

His hand reached for a glass, and his eyes, glancing across the table, caught Angelina. He was jolted to discover her staring at him with a savage, appalling steadiness. How long had she been watching?

What had she been able to read from his abstracted features during the moment of his qualm? Mortified, he turned to look down the table, and he saw that the mother too was regarding him. Something in his mind exploded. He was more than glad when the company disbanded. What a ridiculous, paltry life-context for a man of his dimensions to be caught in! What a fly speck of an existence for a personage like him! A high school love triangle! Kids! A repulsive mortification tightened his throat. All he could feel now were the tawdriness of these undistinguished lives and the incongruity of his presence among them. With a suffocating sense of oppression, he strode from the dining room, took his black cape and hat, and broke out into the twilight of the streets.

It is important to note that the man's manner of holding his head had now perceptibly changed. Whereas since the dreadful morning of the great blackening the manner had been without the slightest affectation, his head now was tilted at a self-important angle, a little back, with a sulky seriousness about the mouth and a faraway look of decision in the eyes. The somewhat melodramatic black cape, red lined, which he had always fancied when he was the president, now became the man again. He was no longer the smitten convalescent. Something epochal had happened. He had found himself, had come into himself again. Cane in hand, high hat aloft, he moved with a stride of full-fledged majesty down the center of the miserable lane.

After a block or two, he began to rationalize his expedition as an exploration of the town, a healthy expansion of his horizon beyond the confines of the house, an opening of himself to the community. Rosalinda rapidly melted from his consciousness: she had been but an episode—hardly an episode; only a feature of the environment during his brief sojourn with his servant Theophilus. The historical scope of his world-task now filled his mind again. This moment he was again the man of destiny. Mighty conceptions stirred in his heart, and he was proud of things to come. How far he walked he neither knew nor cared; for he was aware only of a great eagerness to know intimately, thoroughly, the race that he would serve. He narrowed his eyes to study in the gathering dusk the broken outlines of the drab houses. What lives were lived behind those wooden frames?

Not long, and he had gone totally and for all time astray. Every turning, every alley of misery, was so much like the last as to be indistinguishable, and, once passed, irrevocable. Little attentive to the turnings, the great mind had ridden grandly forward, like a knight, and no matter what the direction, always forward. The streets had grown rapidly darker; the infrequent lights, like guides of ambiguous foreboding, and the occasional passing figures, like emissaries of darkness, had beckoned him eternally onward. He felt as though some surreptitious, perhaps even dangerous, promise were animating with its sorcery every shadow in the twilight, every inscrutable house along the way, every lurking shape, every sound. His now excessively animated cogitations were leading him to attribute his uncontrollable, compulsive searching to a most moral, most world-improving, most progressively civilizing super-neighborliness. And so he strode confidently along (but with the grandest manner!), searching the night with a carnivorous eye, like a cruising owl.

He did not realize into what kingdom of unholy magic he had progressed, until a hoarse she-voice hissed at him from a shadow. His senses quickened nervously, but his mind remained magnificently in control. When presently he descried, approaching from another angle, a drab young female making directly his way, he was able to refuse her invitation calmly, firmly, and without betraying the slightest emotion. Curious, however, that after progressing another block, his social project—namely, the exploration of the depths of the depths—seemed to him to demand of his pride a certain abatement. He did not precisely formulate the demand, but when a third time he was accosted—and this time by a young woman of undeniable beauty, simply clothed in a printed wash dress, her dark eyes extraordinarily large and disarming in the glow of the dim street lamp, her flesh tint a warm living sepia, her lips provocatively everted in such a perpetual invitation as dazzled the heart and brain—he paused just long enough to betray his unsettlement. She pressed her hand to his arm, and the touch—the first touch, the first touch since eons and eons of endless, desolate time—the touch unnerved him mightily. "Sir," she said respectfully, "you will be satisfied." Indeed, he wished he were a lesser man, so that he might yield to that strange, impersonally personal all-readiness; but in good time he remembered who he was, and with a certain gentleness, all too reluctantly, yet incontestably withal, he put her from his side and went his way.

His heart, however, was by now ready for a compromise. He could not have borne to turn and quit this forbidden city without so much as a glimpse behind the enigmatic house walls lining his way like sphinxes. When he came, therefore, to an open door with a little lighted sign above it, he paused. "Shadowland," the sign read. A long stairway descended to a basement, and from the invisible depths there came a curious music—not very strong, not very clear—consisting mainly of a series of little tinkling melodies, played monotonously on plucked strings, woodblocks, and little drums.

The hesitation before his decision to enter was hardly more than perfunctory: a momentary pause for the purpose of discovering a formula that would gratify his self-deluding conscience. He glanced, like a boy truant, up and down the dark street—not furtively, however; rather, he surveyed the surface of the far-reaching earth, which he would quit now for a time, as though to assure himself that all was going well enough to survive the interval of his absence. Again he glanced, now with an expression of amused interest, at the lighted sign above the open door: *Shadowland.* "I must go down," said he, aloud, as though reassuring certain invisible witnesses. "I must go down and see."

Whereupon, with slow and excessively circumstantial dignity, he grasped with great left hand his broad lapel, like a statesman offering himself to the approval of the populace. He looked down carefully to assure himself that there was no raised threshold over which to stumble. He stepped into the little lighted doorway, entered a very narrow passage that barely admitted his grand form, and descended, step by step, an extraordinarily long, plain wooden stairway. His descent was slow and firm, while from the still distant and invisible lower room, the sounds of the innocent childlike music rose like upward-moving bubbles through a dense, somewhat fetid atmosphere of smoky light. As the man approached the end of the stairway, where an abrupt turn to the left would throw open a full view of the room, he readjusted his firm grasp of the broad lapel, lifted his head to its world-surveying stance, with half-abstracted, heavy-lidded eyes, and prepared to remove, on entering, his hat.

A gently rollicking sea of playful music smote his senses, and he discovered himself moving into a folk-filled, sulfurous smoke. Clusters of males and females chatted at little drinking tables or stood restlessly about, and there was a continuous shifting from table to table around the fog-hidden cabaret dance floor. There an exuberant, practically naked group of wildly flinging girls could be dimly discerned performing a dance. The Visitor pressed into the atmosphere. The crowd yielded before his unnoted progress and closed behind as he went forward, ungreeted, unregarded, unknown. The fermentation of the childlike music tossed the entire population with its curious power, so that all seemed to be no more than a phantasmagorical precipitation of the bubbling of those sounds. All moved as in a dream, uncertainly, mysteriously, everything luminous and out of all proportion, yet somehow profoundly quieting to the heart.

The Visitor came to the edge of the floor. The wild, nearly nude dancers were a free gift to the senses, as refreshing to the man's thirst as the bubbles of a craggy spring. After the first delirious impact, their pleasantly childlike capers could be taken for granted. Their athletic bodies, their rollicking eyes, and the brief staccato cries from healthy, lavender-lined mouths quickly lost their original fascination. Nevertheless, they remained as a buoyant background—an assurance of the life-abundance of this cavern. Meanwhile, around the walls and at tables, a chattering multitude of amazingly assorted individuals, unattentive to the dancers, gave a heavy life-fringe to the spectacle with their secret-telling, promise-making, joke-breaking, hand-shaking, glass-lifting, smoke-puffing, lip-laughing, and eye-laughing. They were variously garbed: the men in every kind of smoking jacket, business jacket, dungaree, and overall; in forage caps and regimentals, frock coats, tailcoats, tatters, tarbooshes, inexpressibles, jackboots, and canonicals; the women in aprons, bustles, ruffs and denudations, kirtles, mobcaps, pumps and shawls, cottons, sateens, silks and sequins, spangles, bangles, and semiprecious beads.

The portentous Visitor moved among the company first as a foreign body, but then he gradually began to be aware that he was becoming imperceptibly absorbed into the egalitarian, thick commonality. Just as Jonah in the belly of the whale must have been no little alarmed by a slow seepage of digestive juices into the chamber of his mucous adventure, so the present Visitor: a self-protective horripilation began to prickle his skin. Although his eyes were dwelling with envious sympathy on the folk-features—warmly living, wonderfully inviting, gratifying to the heart, and congenial to his blood—nevertheless the hard knot of his immortal individuality resisted the last absorption. His mind, so alert and serviceable, began immediately to play with self-defensive formulae, and a melancholy—a sympathy for his own distinguished, lonely self—began to pervade him.

Alas, the solitude of the Great Man called to lead! Alas, the joys of the simple children of life, but oh, the summons of the dreadful destiny of which their innocence is unaware! The great individual can hear the cry of the world for leadership and feels it incumbent on himself. The born leader is branded, as it were, with the ineradicable sign of a manifest personal destiny, and that destiny is fated to constellate the general destiny of the race. How great, how vast, how wonderful the life agonies of mankind roused from the lethargies of this dreamlike, vegetative, animal-like nature idyll by the genius of a great man! But alas, how melancholy the heart of that history-fashioning personality himself! A Christ in his loneliness, in the solitude of his world-redeeming self-crucifixion!

Such were the meditations of the serviceable mind.

None but the unnoted Visitor gave heed when a new, strong but profoundly painful element—at first scarcely perceptible but gradually increasing—began to make its way into the play of the music. And about that time he saw through the smoke and the weaving nudities of the girls, as though through clouds or through the unsubstantial shapes of the watery deep, a solid figure on polished, gleaming crutches proceeding most laboriously across the dance floor: ponderous, great shouldered, great headed, absolutely bald, a Negro of heroic and serene countenance, his pelvis and the legs attached to it as dead as blocks. The observer was troubled by the features and the proportions of this man, which resembled more than accidentally his own, and by the manner in which the figure had made its appearance to the accompaniment of that strong but painful, intrusive motif in the music. He had come pushing through the general phantasmagoria without directly displacing it, a body of greater density than the others, coming like an iron ball through water; a body of a density comparable to that of the stunned observer. Like a meeting of two iron-suited deep-sea divers amidst the unsuspecting rippling denizens of the ocean floor, these two now came to within a certain distance of each other, and the crippled man, leaning laboriously on his crutches, paused.

"Salute," said he, in a voice even more substantial than his form; and as he spoke, an expanding void cleared around him, as though the sound of his voice were a dispelling wind of continuously increasing power. Furthermore, the childlike music of the place subsided. And the voice went on; and the two confronted themselves, face-to-face, as though alone.

"Listen!" the black apparition said. "Over these hosts I reign supreme. Against Kashalla I marched, and I turned Kashalla into mounds and ruins—destroyed everything within it, leaving not the resting place of a bird. As far as to the sea I smote, and my weapons I washed in the sea. My hand has conquered the four quarters of the world."

The auditor was frozen stiff with horror; for the voice was coming to him from an appalling depth, not so much of space as of time. It sounded—though near to him—from afar. And it was hollow, with a sickening, sweet reek of decay that made the brain slowly reel. "Who are you?" the throat of the auditor whispered, without volition, without effort or sound.

"And there was taken," the other went on, "the household goods of the foe that was in the city; and there was taken three hundred and eighty lords of theirs, eight hundred and seven children of that foe and of the chiefs who were with him, two thousand seven hundred and ninety-six male and female slaves with their children, noncombatants who surrendered because of famine with that foe; besides vessels of costly stone and gold, vases of the work of Kharu, golden rings found in the hands of artificers, silver and many valuable ornaments, furniture, very much clothing of that foe, ivory, ebony, and carob wood wrought with gold.

"Let others render," he suddenly concluded, "grateful account of the temples I have constructed, palaces I have constructed, lands I have benignantly supervised, peoples I have happily housed."

The listening man of destiny was unable to move. Again he tried to speak; but his larynx locked. "Who are you?" his mind said; and this time the apparition replied.

"Like a pestilential wind I have gone out," he said, "through the millenniums, from every capital of destiny. The wilderness I level. I annihilate the native or enslave him to my will. The enemy I break. Behold, I am here."

While this ultimate pronouncement was approaching its terrible close, a numerous company of men and women began to file in slow procession between the speaker and his riveted auditor. These were the people, the denizens, of Shadowland in all their pied-piper variety. And when a few of them had passed, a low humming among them became audible. Where they trod the space expanded, so that gradually the cripple and the Visitor were pressed apart. The procession doubled back. The humming gradually increased in volume. The slow beat of a deep drum broke in. The company began to clap time, and they were presently interweaving in a simple choreography. The area at their disposal continued to increase. The drumbeat doubled, tripled; voices lifted; an old fellow with a wooden leg in tattered soldier cap hallooed, and the group swung into a dance. The great marvel was that though the spectacle appeared to be impromptu, there was an orderliness about it—a kind of planetary orderliness; and though the folk were laughing gaily, swinging, tossing, there was a profound seriousness behind every move. Beneath this tatterdemalion masquerade, harmoniously coordinated spiritual presences were intermoving in a sublime dithyramb: a dance as wonderful as the night-round of the stars. The floor expanded, clearing the smoke; at last the Great Visitor and the cripple were standing at opposite sides of an immense room. The folk, in a gigantic ring, were revolving to the right, arms loosely interlocked, all leaning back together to kick up their feet and now sharply tossing forward with a kick behind.

The ring parted, and from the void beyond it a young woman danced in, naked as a goddess, of the hue of honey, tall and leanly muscled yet with exceptionally massive, shuddering breasts and hips. Very brilliantly, with an almost miraculous ease, she completed a rapid circuit of the floor; then executed a second, swifter and more light-bodied than the first; finally, a third of unbelievable rapidity. Leaping, turning, skipping, running, flashing her great thighs and flinging long, lithely molded arms, she seemed to transcend the effects of gravitation. Then she halted, abruptly wheeled, and, directly facing the Visitor, began approaching him at a quiet walk from across the floor.

Her gleaming ribs, he observed, were rising gently and falling with the breathing of her lungs. Her dark eyes, large and reposeful, gazed at him without blinking. Above her forehead, like an inverted vase, rose an exotic, tall coiffure of flaming hair. The head was very long (of an Egyptian cast), the features regular and fine. Of a sudden, he recognized in her the transmuted Angelina; and he could feel not an invitation but some great ceremonial petition in the approach. Her effulgence filled the room.

She was the image of the life of the world, he thought, and lo, she had turned to *him*! His heart pounded at her coming. She drew, finally, very close to him, so that he could scent her perspiring flesh; and the world paused for the fraction of an instant, while Life—beautiful in the honey hue of her nakedness—and the Great Man stood face-to-face.

"Ah!" he thought, "she has come to me—to me!"

With that, the waiting company uttered a splintering shriek and broke. A din of howling devils shattered the air, and such a stench went up as stopped the nostrils. Outside was heard the tumult of a lynching mob. The company cleared the hive like bees. And the figure before the Great Man was a pus-ridden, broken whore, shaking at him her obscene jelly-bubs. With a choking cough he made to avoid her. But the horrendous voice of the cripple across the floor now came at him with a crescendo and struck him like a bolt:

"Behold! The moon is favorable for Sargon. The moon is favorable for the enterprise of Sargon. Sargon shall rule nine hundred years. And he shall make Akkad a city and shall call its name Akkad. The goddess Ishtar and the god Enlil will favor him. The four quarters of the earth his hand shall conquer. The goddess and the god will fill his hands with fruit."

The Great Man made to move, but his legs were now utterly dead. He leaned on the crutches that but a second before had supported a shape now vanished. He was alone. The brothel had cleared. Only an abandoned radio blared with a voice (how long forgotten!): the meticulously enunciating voice of his onetime vice president—he of the shaven cone of a chin. Somewhere this personage was reading through his bifocal lenses to civilized mankind: "…and we do hereby solemnly bind our minds and hearts," the voice could be heard to say, "to those high principles which, with the triumph of our sacred cause, have now gloriously triumphed for the whole community of man—man without distinction of race, nationality, or creed; those cardinal freedoms, those inalienable rights…" Numb and shattered, the forgotten cripple heavily crutched across the littered floor.

7.

It was a long and laborious operation for the Great Man, now a cripple, to make his way up the staircase to the dark and emptied street, then leftward and along between the houses in the direction of the terrible rout. Ahead could be still heard the moving shouts and a honking of klaxons, but the man was hopelessly outdistanced. By the time he arrived at the edge of the village all had subsided to a desolate silence. He stumped out across the torn fields, lone and black in the moonlight. He approached a blasted tree.

In the midst of the desolation the tree held out its empty noose; at the foot of it, beside a black pool, a woman sat with a corpse across her knee. And when the Great Man arrived, she lifted her eyes at him: he perceived her to be the schoolgirl Rosalinda. Her voice was weary and flat. "We waited," she said. "You came to us. But you never asked the girl what she wanted." The man flinched, as from an unanticipated blow, but with a proud tilt of the head he regarded the horizon, then made heavily to move away. "We are gladdened by no news," the voice droned after him. "Desolate is the womb. For what came to us was this cripple again, whose work, whose mission, whose tangibilation, is branded with the curse of Cain."

The figure made away ponderously. The voice grew dim behind him: "When he tills the ground it shall not yield to him her strength; for the earth opened her mouth to receive from his hand my lover's blood."

The cursed one pressed forward across the mutilated landscape. And he beheld approaching him two long marching columns, which separated from each other in silence to let him pass between. To the right of him paraded a rigid file in military gear, but to the left crawled and staggered miserables in chains: both columns being endless to the horizon. And so there come from before him now, forever, these two columns; and he passes between them, forever. He is ponderous and black in the nadir of our night: slow moving, great shouldered, great headed, absolutely bald—his pelvis and the legs attached to it as dead as blocks.

Jonah Swallowed Up by the Whale (detail; fresco, Italy, c. 1305 A.D.). Giotto di Bondone. Scrovegni Chapel, Padua, Italy. © Alfredo Dagli Orti/Art Resource, NY.

THE BELLY OF THE SHARK

———————●———————

(October 31, 1942–December 31, 1942)

—————————————— *I.*

GEORGE AMBROSE FITZROY, never quite conscious anyhow, was well on the way to New Guinea before it was brought to his attention that there might be something amiss about his understanding of his mission. Sweltering and stinking with hundreds of his generation in the steel hull of a converted luxury liner—fifty men now sardine-packed where formerly one bepowdered dame would lie (cramped, no doubt, with her candy box and bestseller)—this ungainly, cropped-blond youth of lantern jaw and bent rudder of a nose, with prettily smiling snapshots of his wife and girl-baby in a little red-leather billfold, and with a tan pocket Bible presented to him by his "we're just folks" of a mother, shut his incongruously black beady eyes and cringed, on hearing suddenly from the bunk opposite a very cynical, not only deeply sophisticated but immediately sophisticating, sneer. What he had for several days been fearing had now, at last, come to pass. Corporal McGee had uttered a comment upon his existence.

"Listen," McGee said, "for Christ's sake!"

George was a good boy; McGee, obviously, was not.

The two regarded each other measuringly across the narrow crevice between bunks. "Eight days now you've been dripping sweat into that book," McGee said coarsely. "I can't bear it."

George quietly replied, "Corporal, you can go to hell!"

McGee grinned. He had a frank, pug face, with gray, intelligent eyes. The black, starry, pretty lashes gave an incongruously seductive, girlish look to the otherwise thuggish features. His entire character, indeed, was something of a bafflement to the manly yet vague-witted youth before him.

McGee continued, "Are we on a pilgrimage to Jerusalem?"

George Ambrose slowly closed the book and thought whether to commit himself. This was a difficult situation.

"Or on a crusade?" McGee suggested.

In his sweat-sodden bunk George Ambrose wearily rolled over to face the wall. "Aw, go to hell," he said.

There was no more from McGee.

When George woke up, the bunk opposite was empty; but he knew that during the remaining weeks it would not be possible altogether to avoid the vaguely irritating challenger. A man's belief, thought he, was his own private affair—at least, as long as he decently kept it to himself and didn't go thrusting it upon others. What business, then, of McGee's if he should choose to read the Bible that had been given to him by his mother? McGee, as far as he could see, never read anything; he only lay in his bunk or lightly fraternized with the fellows. No one particularly either cared for him or disliked him; no one knew very much about him; he was simply a noncommittal presence, like a stick or something, that was now and then within range of the eye.

Entirely boorish, thought George, that for eight days McGee, hardly two feet away, should have uttered not a word, only now to come out with this impudent violation of even the last shred of privacy left to a private under the present heart-trying circumstances. God knows, one submitted to the circumstances like a man. It was only this prying that one resented. And rightly resented, George Ambrose felt. McGee, somehow, was as foreign and unpleasant to encounter as a fish.

It was two days later, in the bunks again, that McGee forced the conversation. He was lying on his back, stark naked; George Ambrose was wearing untidy trunks.

"How do you reconcile your Christianity with your bullets?" McGee directly asked, hands behind his head, eyes gazing blithely at the bunk two inches above him. His voice was simply matter-of-fact, as a hotel waiter might ask, "How do you take your tea?"

George Ambrose this time felt compelled to reply like a man. "Well, how do you?" he said stiffly.

"I don't," came the blank response.

George Ambrose, having ventured, forced himself now to smile carelessly. "Well, I for one don't find any difficulty," he tolerantly stated. "Besides, it's none of your goddamn business."

"It's very much my business," McGee affirmed hardly.

"How so? Why so?" George Ambrose said.

"Because," said McGee, "it is precisely men of your Bible Christianity that have made this war and impressed me into their service. Now, what do you think of that?" He suddenly grinned his ugly grin and turned his incongruously girlish eyes. "This is a war of Bible-reading Christians," said he, "and now that I'm bunked with one of the breed, I want to be told what it's all about. I feel that you, as an American in the service of your flag, owe it to me to tell me why we're going all this distance to murder people."

The two youths, of equal age, regarded each other strangely; George, with his black, beady eyes, somewhat animal-like in his simplicity, trying to measure into the other. "Aren't you an American?" he asked with a suspicious squint and a note of sudden sternness. He began to feel that he would be getting the upper hand.

"I was born in America," the other evasively answered.

"Then it's as much your war as mine," said George Ambrose, "and it's no more my responsibility than yours."

That seemed to have left the queer antagonist with no way to reply. He watched George Ambrose a while, with an ambiguous, now slightly silly grin, then lay back again and looked again at the bunk very close above. Presently he said thoughtfully, "Yes, but we are responsible after entirely different fashions."

"Why so?" George Ambrose said. He lifted his colorless eyebrows. "How so?" He was deeply interested.

The other delayed to inform him. With languor the other turned away and rested on his side. The thick back, with scattered clumps of coarse black hair, was moist and ugly to see. He let George Ambrose wait. Then he slowly asked, firmly, and without inflection, "What would you have done, do you think, if you had been in a position to be drafted by the Nazis? How would you have felt about fighting for that state instead of this?"

It was an absurd question, such as had never occurred to the simple faculties of George Ambrose, and he had at hand no ready reply. So he answered sharply, off the tip of his tongue, "Why, I'd resist."

"Then you'd be shot."

"Then I'd be shot," George Ambrose stated. Abruptly, he challenged, "What would you do?"

"Just what I'm doing now," came back the blank, uninflected reply.

George Ambrose felt obscurely yet totally insulted: not himself alone, but everything he knew. He leaned a moment on his elbow, staring at the repugnant back and searching for a word; but his mind, now baffled, presently lost its tension, and he fell back into his bunk to stare at the bunk very close above. Never quite conscious anyhow, George Ambrose was unable quite to meditate on the problem or even to locate it; but something somewhere inside him had been fractured.

That night the transport was torpedoed and went down.

_____ 2.

THE SHARK WAS OF NO ORDINARY KIND but of a curiously livid hue, with tufts of black bristles here and there, and distinctly girlish eyes. It came up majestically out of the abyssal waters, swam slowly, with great ease, toward the surface, and moved amidst the swimming and sinking swarms of men. George Ambrose Fitzroy, with a qualm, felt something harsh against his legs, and with a stark terror saw the vast, horrible shape shoot past and gracefully turn. It moved amongst the multitude as though searching; presently putting back again, it headed uncertainly toward the mortally frightened young husband. The fierce dorsal fin broke the surface; like a cutter it made at the youth directly, as though quite sure now. The beast approached and slowly rolled. George Ambrose beheld the tiger teeth, saw the unspeakable jaws, felt the rush of pitiless waters. The harsh gullet had yawned: he was gone.

What more but darkness? Darkness, indeed, as of satin black! No one has yet heard of the shark that could swallow a full-grown man *in toto*, and yet precisely that, to judge by his absence from the surface of the sea, precisely that had this ambiguous, curiously girlish monster done to George Ambrose Fitzroy.

Darkness, satin black: one asks whether any entity, any seed of entity, any pinpoint of a spark of entity, remained to know whether existence or nonexistence existed or existed not. What now of George Ambrose Fitzroy?

Consider the lilies of the field: they know not whether they exist or no; yet neither can they rightly be said to be ignorant of existence. Indeed, do they not struggle mightily for their several existences, and with eager roots beneath the soil? Indeed again, does not the vegetable chaos of the jungle present a pretty battle for soil and light? The plants know not, and yet know well. Similarly the fishes of the sea. What a world of total, spontaneous, unrationalized, unmoralized, unconsciously conscious life, unconsciously conscious battle! The big ones eating the little ones: a mad nightmare of swiftly shifting forms, rapidly consuming and assimilating each other and spawning anew by the million! What matter the momentary, half-conscious shifts of the centers of semiconsciousness from this fish brain to that? The grand flow of living protoplasm from one harsh organism to the other is scarcely punctuated by any pause. Life, eating and eating and eating itself in one continuous, perpetually mobile round!

What, then, of George Ambrose Fitzroy?

Not properly of the sea was he; yet his eyes, when he had cried as a chubby babe, had shed salt water, as of the sea; and the consistency of his blood was as of the sea; and in the sea of his mother's womb he had known gills; and regarded from the standpoint of astronomical or even geological time, it had been only a short breathing spell since his ancestors, platypoid, slimy and cold, had emerged from the mother deep. Herewith he was returned, one might say, to his primordial element, to renew with the lively denizens of that world the lively round of now-you-eat-me.

But hark! A sound, as of a little muffled drum! A throb of time within this living containing space! And now a thick smell, as of a mud-flat! And now a touch, as of an aiding hand! At last, then, the opening of the eyes to darkness, and George Ambrose Fitzroy understood that he was alive within the belly of the shark.

A torpid landscape loomed before him. On a mudflat he was stranded, a tide having long withdrawn. Someone was lifting him to his feet. There was the distant sound of beating military drums. He was terribly tired, terribly limp. It did not surprise him to hear himself addressed in his own tongue.

"Whence have you come?" demanded a harsh, inhuman voice.

"America," he muttered.

"Never heard of it," the voice said. "You'll have to do better than that. Whence have you come?"

"America," he said.

"You're in a very dangerous way, young man," continued the inhuman voice. "Your arrival here on this patrolled coast is inexplicable, I should say. What is inexplicable isn't allowed."

George was unable yet to stand. The man, very strong, was roughly dragging him, having taken him, like a dummy, under the arm. The clammy feet dragged over the slime, then over the coarse grasses of the shore, and presently over soil.

"Stand up," the man said.

George Ambrose dropped in a heap.

Nothing could have been more orderly than the arrival of the little squad, which roughly hoisted him to its shoulders and bore him away like a canoe. He fainted and waked by turns during the long hike along the dark forest road. A town was entered and traversed. Face upward, hour by hour, George Ambrose now was in open country. Above were the starry heavens. He looked for familiar constellations but saw nothing that he knew. He wondered whether dawn ever came to these parts, and as hour after hour went by, he began deeply to fear.

It was a curious circumstance, but, gradually, as his strength returned, the objects of the world began to glow with a strange phosphorescence. And presently, when he began to feel very much himself again, the objects began to show a magnificent brilliance of color and an almost intoxicating vividness of form. The squad bearing him on its shoulders appeared to know immediately when he had come to this state; for, summarily, without so much as a command, as one man they set him down on his feet and clicked along with him in their midst.

It now became possible for George Ambrose to take the measure of his predicament. First, the squad: covertly he regarded them. Eight men, as though cast from a single mold; as tall as himself, but of mathematically regular features; smoothly tanned; dark browed; gray eyed; with black, starry lashes! They were clad in sea-green uniforms and close-fitting steel helmets. They marched with mechanical precision, at a lively clip. But these details were of secondary moment: the important thing about these men (and it extended from them to the farmland round about, with its gently rolling hills, its little wooded areas, and its ripe fields beautifully cultivated and unbroken by any hedges or fences) was the ambient magic which so united all that the apparently individual elements of the circumstance—the eight men, the fields, the dells, the hills—were as but features of a single, wonderful presence. Furthermore, this magic gave to every detail of the circumstance a marvelous, almost brilliant immediacy, so that even the clank of the shining gear of the soldiers carried a soul-stirring enchantment. As he regarded secretly the man just in front and to the left and then realized that the regularity of the ear was something a little beyond the human, George Ambrose felt a curious qualm which itself partook of the delight of the enchantment. George Ambrose marched without the sense of pain; yet he must have marched without boots or socks, and only lightly clad in his untidy trunks. He was unconscious of any surrounding air or of any hardness underfoot but knew only the marvel of the ambient wonder.

Suddenly, however, the element of qualm increased to such a degree as to supersede all else. From the horizon, from all sides, there converged, with a mounting zooming sound, file on file of planes, shark-black, like the spokes of a cosmic wheel. They came to the hub of the sky where they disappeared, as into a maelstrom. The last plane to go let drop a single bomb, which fell with a soul-splitting scream, exploded just to the side of the road, and annihilated the company of eight.

George Ambrose Fitzroy—now alone in untidy trunks and at large in a fantastic countryside which churned a little, here and there —without pausing to study the miracle of his sole survival, made forthwith away along the rubberized ribbon of a highway. And when he saw, off in the fields, what he took to be a farmhouse, he directed his steps courageously toward the little white building nestling cozily under its canopy of tall palms.

There was something strange yet familiar about the stocky, pug-faced, black-haired man who came out the door to greet the arrival. His gray, intelligent eyes, framed by beautiful black lashes, were incongruously glorious in his otherwise repugnant features. Like everything else in this landscape, his presence was breathlessly immediate. "Well, who are you?" he said, in a voice that was deeper than that of the soldier who had questioned George but similarly inhuman and harsh. About these voices there was an unpleasant lack of resonance. They grated; they rasped. They were endlessly hollow. And the man was baffling to behold: he grinned, yet held the visitor at bay. "Who are you?" he repeated sharply.

George Ambrose decided it would be better not to try to explain. "I've just escaped the air raid," he said.

"What raid?" said the man unpleasantly.

"This last one," George Ambrose said. "The sky was black."

"Not here," the man said. He regarded the intruder suspiciously. "That must have been your raid," he said. "We didn't have one here." He fingered his breast pocket and drew forth a pencil and pad. "What did you say your number was?"

George Ambrose was at a loss. "Why," he said, "I haven't any number. I've only just arrived."

"Just arrived?"

George Ambrose tentatively prepared half to nod; but the man, summarily eyeing him, stepped aside and with the butt of the pencil indicated the door of the house. "Step inside," he said, slowly, guardedly. "You're a queer one. Step inside."

George Ambrose stepped inside. The man followed so closely upon his heels that he was fairly pushed into the bleak interior. It was a large, bare room, with a number of butcher tables standing about, only two stiff wooden chairs, and a plain sleeping bunk in one corner. Ambrose and the man took their places in the two chairs and faced each other across one of the tables.

"Now, young man," the man said, "you don't look as though you belong here. You said you had just arrived?"

George Ambrose sought to fathom the repugnant face. The girlish beauty of the eyes only heightened the odiousness of the gross features. The tension that began to build between himself and this man was greater than anything George Ambrose had ever experienced. The antagonism—implicit in the very fact that they were face-to-face—strangely grew, approaching the uttermost, far surpassing in its portentousness the terrors of human conflict, opening out and down into elementary abysses of stark contention.

"Were you not apprehended," said the man, "by the coast patrol?"

George Ambrose failed to reply.

It became known to George Ambrose, as though the significance of the figure before him had by quiet seepage revealed itself to his mind, that this was an example of the farmer class of this people: living alone, without wife, and tending alone the surrounding hundreds of acres with the aid of utterly perfected machines. This man, furthermore, was sheriff of the land he tended. And his territory would be abutted by another, precisely identical, supervised by a sheriff-farmer precisely like himself. And so on, all over the land.

"Where are their women?" George Ambrose thought, with a weight of lust, such as surprised him, behind his rational curiosity. He looked hard into the man's face, to imagine its female.

"You must be examined," said the man, "for classification."

George Ambrose knew now that none but himself and this man occupied not only this butcher house but the entire area of the man's patrol. The soldier in him stirred; he knew that he did not have to submit to this person without a fight.

"I would butcher you myself," said the man, "but jetsam doesn't come within my jurisdiction."

The cause of the instinctive terror stood revealed.

George Ambrose was aghast and nearly voiceless. "Do—you—eat—men?"

"What else then?" the man replied. He fixed the dull youth with his obscene eyes. Suddenly he thuggishly grinned, and then with a cold, bloodless pleasure relaxed to a mood of confident taunting. "You are used to making secondary distinctions, young man. We do not do that here. And we prefer, you will find, the direct approach. Food is life and life is food. Food is food, and we approach it directly. Vegetable matter or animal, we take all indifferently into our gullets and gulp." He made a gesture.

George Ambrose had recovered his poise. He had gained by the man's excursion. He had had time to summon his wits to the now obvious lines of his predicament. He hoped that the man would go on with his boasting. He searched for a way to keep him talking.

"Why, then, do you not butcher me?" he said. "What is the direct sense of this silly business of classification?"

The effect of this question was not wholly good. It recalled the man to his duty. He made to rise. But he grandly paused, leaning with his knuckles on the table. "The living, eating organism," said he, "is the State. What am I but a cell? Every cell, every tissue of cells, has its special, very limited function. My function, and the function of my colleagues, is to derive food from the soil and from our cattle. This is shipped to the metropolis for storage and orderly distribution. But the function of the coast patrol is to gather jetsam to the classification centers, where it is properly stored according to kind." He was about to move away. "I must get in touch," said he, "with the patrol."

But the young man, with a quick motion, sprang to his feet and flung the chair at that offensive head. It struck and splintered, but the head only turned and made fiercely at the assailant. George Ambrose, panic-stricken, sprang like a young lion. The two grappled. The arms of the man were steel. George Ambrose's strength began to fail; but as his energies subsided, the vivid brilliance of his surroundings and the uttermost tensions of his predicament curiously subsided too. Everything was emptied of its terrible magic. All declined again to the earlier, ghostly, phosphorescent glow. Presently even that queer glow was gone; the entire world, including the fierce contest, had simply deliquesced; and it was heart wearying, heart wearying, heart wearying to discover that a judge was now sitting behind a desk, the walls being lined with the innumerable faces of the jury, and the phosphorescent glow was back, but no more than the phosphorescent glow.

"So, you see," the judge was saying, "we are at pains here to determine whether you will better serve as a citizen or as aliment."

All too fast! Everything was moving all too fast. The sense of the development was too obscure to see.

The judge was saying, "One way or another, you are to be incorporated into the State. Now, which branch of the service do you think yourself fitted to join?"

The judge's eyes and all the eyes of all the unnumbered faces of the jury were regarding the discomfort of the youth. They were eyes very beautiful with their delicate, star-like little frames of black lashes; gray, intelligent, girl-like eyes; all exactly alike. And the faces in which they were set could be only hazily perceived, yet they seemed to be identical too: rather square and strong of jaw, with heavy brows, and of a ruthless ugliness. The youth felt that there was no escape for him: the question had to be answered. His impulse was to resist this ferocious induction into a grotesquely unfamiliar and repulsive body politic. He had been tossed ashore in this world-zone; yes! But was he by that accident morally bound to this community? Was he not an entity of an order far above the gross bestialities of this cannibalistic race? Was it not his duty, his duty to his Maker, to bear witness to that God in whose sublime likeness he had been created? Let him be, amongst these people, a humble, premonitory, preliminary sign of that great message of love, truth, and freedom which must one day, in the simple course of time, come to them. Let him be true to that Christian uniform which he unfortunately was now conspicuously without; let him be true to his soldier's oath and to his deepest, Bible-trained humanity.

"I will not serve in your armed forces," said he. "I will make no contribution to your cannibalistic war effort. If you will assign to me, until your war is over, some task befitting human decency, I shall do all within my power to serve, amongst you, the high cause of love and freedom." He was speaking very solemnly; he was speaking with a fine pulpit-vibrato and was delighted with the stately balance of his righteousness and tolerance. "But I cannot so forget," said he, completely carried along now by the momentum of his utterance, "I cannot so forget my inheritance of human decency as to contribute willingly one ounce, one jot, one tittle of my strength—as man, as American, as Christian—to the prosecution of your loathsome war."

The judge leaned a little forward. There was no stir in the portentous room.

"Young man," said the judge, "your statement is not understood. This state is always at war. Life is war, war is life. We experience, indeed, alterations of direct and indirect battle, but never do we permit ourselves to imagine, between battles, that we are not forever at war."

"Who is the enemy?" George Ambrose impetuously interrupted. "For what ideals, for what future, for what cause do you invite me to fight?"

" 'Cause,' 'future,' 'ideals,' " said the judge, "are words of no meaning in this connection. We are not afraid to regard with naked eye the direct fact."

George Ambrose began to feel a little, and curiously, dizzy with the naked beauty of the judge's eye. The judge's fish jaw continued.

"We struggle and gobble for existence, without love or hate for the rest. We shall be gobbled ourselves, in turn, but that, young man, is the sense of the game—and who are you or who am I to resist the game? Nor do we think of ourselves as higher, more noble, more this or more that than our antagonists. We are all of the same ilk, or we should not all be playing the same game, and there would be no game at all if we did not go against each other. And so it's *gobble, gobble, gobble*, young man, from now until the crack of doom. And if you choose not to join in the fun, then, from the standpoint of the game itself, you are already defunct and to be classified as jetsam."

Clang! A bell rang; the walls of the room shifted, and a police squad immediately entered, seized the prisoner, and carried him off. All the members of the squad, of identical height and build, had naked eyes.

It was a metropolis of the most beautiful, mechanical complexity and regularity. Walls of translucent sapphire and emerald rose with their tiers and tiers of windows. Glorious gardens, of geometrical wonder, carpeted with multicolored formlings and waving slowly with every kind of unfamiliar kelp, lay about and reached away into the distances. Little squads of passing denizens, classified strictly according to shape and size, all with those wonderful eyes, all moving on singular missions, could be seen on every hand. There was a wonderful, magical silence. George Ambrose slowly realized that the colors had returned to the world, and with the colors, such a magnetic charm that the horror of his own predicament only heightened the fascination of this crazy world.

They passed a nursery, where a troop of tiny children played leapfrog and splashed in a pool. They passed a great open area, where hundreds of identical mothers sat in rows, nursing identical infants at identical breasts. They passed a hospital, where nurses and doctors could be seen, and patients recovering from gashes and mutilations. They passed a magnificent school, where students frolicked, according to size, on widely stretching greens.

George Ambrose felt appalled that by his righteousness he should have cut himself away from such a miraculously harmonious pattern of existence. Yet he had irrevocably done so. He sought to recall the basis for his denial of this society, but the ideas that had inspired his utterance were now just out of reach of his groping search.

With his squad he approached a curious, very craggy, and strangely wooded hill, which jutted rudely into the regularity of the metropolitan order. His captors swung away to avoid this place and to conduct him around it. Suddenly, from the sky, with terrific screams, descended a bulleting, firing, bombing, havoc-spreading flight of vicious, swift-diving planes, and like a sudden snow there floated down from the sky an innumerable multitude, as far as the eye could see, of parachuting enemy troops. A siren blew. Firing began. Armies from concealed barracks swept forth and engaged the swarming enemy. Ambulances and, horrible to see, brigades of bloody butcher cars, fanned out to gather from the carnage the wildly scattered remains.

Whereupon George Ambrose suddenly remembered what had revolted him from these people so fair of outer aspect. With a violent, desperate, last resort of a resolution, he suddenly broke for it and ran. But the squad must have turned to emergency duties more important than conveying him to a place of butchery; for he found himself free and dashing, everyone too busy even to notice his jackrabbit flight. He headed straight on for the forested, craggy hill he had seen. He approached it with a vast sense of release and relief. The thick growth of the trees, of a dense, rich purple, closed protecting arms about him; the scraggy rocks, of a vivid ochre, opened to him their cavernous retreats; the babble of green brooks and the limpid indigo of springs and ponds soothed and cooled the pounding blood of his veins with the sheer beauty of their sweet presences; and a lovely song of singing girls lightly caressed the tympanums of his ears.

Ah, glorious dream wilderness—retreat from the grim precision of the machine! Ah, soul-intoxicating song—enchantment dissolving the frightful calls of duty! Ah, home and voice of that free creature which is man! Man in freedom! Man the individual! Man perfected in his simple, native joy! Ah, wilderness! Ah, beauty! Ah, paradise!

The forms that descended from the trees were bird-forms with the breasts and heads of girls, sweetly singing weaving harmonies with the gentleness of falling dew. And the figures that emerged dripping from the springs and ponds were fish-forms with the breasts and heads of girls, beckoning deliciously. And there passed a certain deer, which paused to look at the youth with black, beady eyes strangely like his own, then lightly bounded away into the invisibilities of the gentle thickets.

Nothing had to be sought; nothing had even to be asked for: no sooner the thought than the materialization of its answer. George Ambrose experienced in rapid succession the most heart-staying passage of voluptuous forms, all carrying, however, a certain enigmatic oversuggestiveness which his native faculties would never have imagined. When he realized that it was now within his power to conjure up, by merest thought, the sweetest figment of his heart's desire, he was suddenly a little panicky, lest his imagination should somehow fail him and bring forth a Gorgon.

Whereupon, from the opposite shore of the largest of the neighboring ponds, George watched a fleet of outrigger canoes put out, such as used to greet the early mariners when they would arrive at tropical isles. And these came across the waters with a gay, lightsome singing. And as they drew near, he saw that they were filled only with girls, all bedecked with heavily odorous flowers. They made directly for a point of shore not far from the beguiled George Ambrose. He had read and dreamed of such happenings, but never had he supposed that his voyage with the army to the isles of the Pacific might involve him in any such adventure. Here they came, however. They jumped lightly overboard to draw the prows ashore, and then paused only a moment to arrange their pretty flower necklets; then they gathered from their boats great armfuls of coconuts and exotic fruits; and then they turned to carry these his way.

Consider the simple American youth, never quite conscious anyhow, now approached, so to speak, by the garden of life itself: the flowers and fruits in the arms of the girls simply amplifying the statement of their rich bodies. All was softness. All was delicious promise. All breathed an unrevealed expectation, flattering to the manhood of the hero, challenging to his address. As simple and lovely as the self-revelation of flowers was the disclosure of these maidens to his gaze.

Indeed, the disclosure was so full, so frank, so guileless that the youth was hardly startled to see—or rather, he was basically comforted to see—that nothing was to be withheld from him. For these female bodies were not so much clad as decorated in festive exhibition; and it was something for him to realize that he, himself alone, had brought from an unknown distance this superabundant manifestation of an over-readiness to respond to his slightest mood.

In the strangest way, his wife and little daughter at home—as well, even, as the mother who had given him his Bible—were included within the scope of the present event. It was not as though a temptation to domestic unfaithfulness had approached him. On the contrary, mother, wife, and daughter were included in the present visitation, as though they might themselves have been but ambassadors from the soft place of breathings to which he was now about to be deliriously ravished—the isle, no doubt, of some dark queen of queens. He was to learn the secret of secrets; and in prelude to this mystery no secret of the flower bodies now before him remained unexhibited. He acquiesced in their seduction with all his soul.

Without speech, without even a sign, but gently swooning, he was borne to a mighty catamaran and there installed for the magical voyage. Propelled by a hundred gleaming paddles, the lively fleet made away across the waters of the pond, sending out in running wedges the ripples and in heavy airwaves the mingled odors of abundant blossoms. A beautiful, gay yet solemn chant was sung. And on approaching the opposite shore, it appeared that through a certain marshy stretch the canoes could easily penetrate, so that, instead of beaching, the entire company pressed forward through a deeply shaded lotus swamp that converged to an easily running stream. This, in turn, broke down a swift descent, in a dizzily bounding cataract, to a strong, swift channel that debouched into a great coral lagoon. Across the lagoon, at last, the fleet fanned out; then all tightened for the dangerous crossing of the reef. With a prodigious, mad thumping, yet with unbelievable ease, the breakers were passed and the journey was begun out across the open sea.

No one shall say what long, dream-like voyage that must have been. The flowers, the maidens, the songs—all remained fresh and in-exhaustibly wonderful; and the hero, piled high in a marvelous swoon, had no time—for all his leisure—to catch up with the rapid run of meanings. As to what was here transpiring he was in the dark. His former notion that the event involved some challenge to his address had simply dissolved: he was no secret, he was no mystery to this female company of hundreds. He was known through and through, and signified little more than a child piled high in a baby car, wheeled homeward by a vast company of extravagantly generous nurses.

George opened his black, beady eyes to find that all had undergone a subtle transformation. The air was luminous, and the forms—the forms of the bobbing canoes, the maidens, and the heaped fruits and flowers—were of the nature, somehow, of darkness: shining darkness. The girls were dark and beautiful; their lips were full, their noses were flat and marvelously formed, their eyes were pools of darkness, and their tresses, blacker than the black of night and struck with bursting flowers, bid the heart expire in sleep.

Presently an island loomed: small on the horizon at first, it rapidly grew and soon was an overpressing presence. The fleet made for the sweeping shore, was caught from behind by a propelling wave, and with a final swell of exultation glided to the beach.

The hero beheld himself ashore on an isle on which there grew but one all-overcrowding dark and mighty banyan. The secondary roots of this ageless tree came down everywhere, forming a dark, deep forest that pressed to the rim of the shore. The forest floor teemed with flowers. And from the banyan itself, in supernatural abundance, depended every tropical fruit.

The landing company was greeted by a sister swarm which again bore fruits and flowers; and the hero was swept off to a simple couch, where he was unceremoniously relieved of his untidy trunks, bathed, anointed, perfumed, bedecked with flowers, and handled generally in a workman-like, nursely way. Made ready, he was gaily paraded forth for all to admire and cajole with fruits and kisses. They were teasing him to make love here and there, greeting his efforts with applause and flattery, as women greet and assist the first steps of a babe, when suddenly the gales of joy subsided and the company was approached by a small group of stately matrons. From the banyan depths, these moved with solemn pace. They were some sixteen in number, tall and comely, of the hue of very old ivory, their black hair shot through with flowers, their rich necks heavily hung with flowers, their magnificent loins too, but in such a way that the female secrets were exposed. The deep-bosomed women of the Homeric Greeks were not more heroic than these.

Two of the younger girls, at either hand, conducted forward the now terrified youth. Six of the dames advanced to meet him. With a qualm he noted that their eyes were precisely his own: black and strangely beady. It was not at all as though they had come from unvisited banyan depths, but as though they had materialized out of some forbidden area of his own interior that was intimately, secretly known and burning with shame; as though, before the world, his deepest, most inadmissible longing were to have stood, all at once, stripped. Choked with mortification, paralyzed to move, he watched two of the women stoop to his ankles and grasp them strongly. Two pressed against his sides, two secured his arms, and he was heaved, rigid, to the shoulders. As he had been transported by the patrol, so was he now borne away and into the darkness of the grove by the amazing dames. And the grove was silence: silent was the tread of the feet on the floor of flowers; regular the breathing of the stately delegation. After a little, his wrists and elbows were grasped by several hands; his arms were opened out to the sides; and the other women of the company added their shoulders to those already bearing him—so that he now lay as though crucified on a cross compact of matrons deep-bosomed, whose eyes were precisely his own. Therewith, in rich contralto choir, the women began to chant:

> George Ambrose, the young growth,
> George Ambrose, the swelling with sap,
> George Ambrose, the denuded—
> There is no such ardent fellow faring
>   forth from the seaways as George Ambrose.

Ho! The sacred temple!
There shall he sleep.
Hooked on the lure of love;
He overvaulted the fence of death;
He has drunk of unfathomable waters—
Like a young mackerel, superbly, thrillingly leaping,
Darting, at last hauled hither to my hand,
He has risen in this far land.

Ho! The sacred temple!
There shall he sleep.

The moon, the moon sails high,
The moon, overbrimming with dew,
The moon, the desired—
There is no such dew-filled calabash for the
        lips of mother-horizon as this moon.

Ho! The sacred temple!
There shall he sleep.

He turns his face to thee,
Unto the realm of night;
For he is as the sailing moon setting in the netherworld—
It is night.
Death seeks thee in the brilliant darkness
And in the lucid light of day.
Ho! The sacred temple!
There shall he sleep.

They had come to the place of profoundest obscurity; yet here all
was immediately perceptible, as though to the senses of the skin, the
ears, the nose, and even the tongue, rather than of the eyes. The young
man was set gently down on his rigid feet, and the women moved
away. He stood, arms still stiffly outstretched, thoroughly scared, and
facing the black silence of the central trunk of the inexhaustible tree.

Then what he heard—of all things!—what he heard was the muffled voice of his mother, not as last he had heard it, but as it must have
sounded in her young womanhood, when he had been her babe. And
it said, far away, soothingly, "Alas! So sad!" But the form that now appeared to greet him was not his mother's.

A warm wind blew; the tree creaked, and near the roots, where the
black, smooth bark was cracked, he found sitting a grave-eyed woman
with flowing locks and naked bosom. She was neither young nor old.
"Son," she said, with gentle voice, "beautiful fruit of my limbs, mount
now the wonderful tree."

It was like a permission for which he had long been impatient.
No sooner were the words spoken than he was all eagerness to mount
and explore. Like a youngster, and without a second's pause, without even asking himself who this might have been—this grave woman
who had spoken—he placed his bare foot on a bole that swelled from
the trunk, embraced the first of the massive limbs, and cleverly swung
himself into the head. There opened a world around and above: a
paradise of fruits, feathers, and song—the bright, ageless, ever known
yet strangely unknown bird land of the tropical treetops. And in spite
of the thrilling strangeness of the leafy, sun-shot vistas that opened out
and away, endlessly suggestive, this world above the earth and with a
floor of its own was not unfamiliar. The youth wandered easily. He
became more and more delighted with the boundless possibilities as he
mounted and advanced. Chamber beyond chamber of living leafage,
world beyond world, broke out at every hand.

The first creatures he encountered were the birds. These, of every
hue and call, chirruped and sang; hopped, flitted, darted, and circled;
fluttered, cooed and sported in love; pecked with every sort of beak,
and eyes like buttons, at the fruits, the bark, the leaves, the twigs; the
nests were multitudinous and packed with tiny stretching and yawning
gullets; parents prettily fluttered over the broods and skillfully tucked
tidbits into the yeeping throats. It was all love and leafy freedom. It
was all carefree abundance. "At last!" he thought. "At last!"

After a great deal of the bird world, and when he was beginning to
grow a little bored with it, he heard approaching a swarm of twittering,

cackling, squawking, chirruping, chattering, now and then screeching creatures, of a power, nervousness, and multitude very much more grandiose than anything he had yet encountered. He watched to see what might appear. To his full amazement, he saw breaking through the leaves, first one, then five, then twenty-odd, then a host of mincing, twittering, frilled and befeathered human females, garbed in every frippery and frizzle, from millinery creation to tortured shoe. His first realization was that he was unclothed. He made for a screen of foliage and frantically tore at the virginal leaves and twigs to fashion a makeshift covering for the only part of his anatomy that now seemed of any importance. The chirruping swarm drew nigh. Terrified, the desperate youth cried, "Don't come in!"—whereupon a shock of silence froze the approaching van and chilled the multitude. A moment of utter silence; then the chattering suddenly broke again, more voluminous than ever.

With utmost decorum and circumspection the ladies of the vanguard apprised themselves of the predicament, and, after a giddy delay, at last supplied the youth with an intricate garment of flexible vegetable stuff, which he quickly donned. It was a garment totally different from their own—insisting upon the sexual distinction, but in a manner, so to speak, nonsexual. Thus groomed, George Ambrose entered their society and was immediately beset with questions. He was crowded with every manner of anxiety to understand. Faces, faces everywhere, many of them twitching, many with little perversities: a spasmodic wink and a shiver here; there a mechanically recurrent turning of the head and clearing of the throat; there a very violent tightening of the neck cords. They were faces to break the heart with their suggestion of catastrophic breakages overlived; faces to warm the heart with their sleek, old nun–like amplitude; faces to freeze the bloodstream with their statement of fixed beauty: and all rigged out most marvelously according to some notion of style.

The youth was immediately commandeered to a ruthless schedule of activities. First it was lectures on his travels; then it was lectures on the culture of America; then it was lectures on the future of the female; every seven days it was lectures on the habits and prejudices of

Jehovah. And it was always the Good, the True, and the Beautiful that were most earnestly intended; and it was wonderful to note the thrills of pleasure that would punctuate and sometimes stay the general fidgetiness of the vast audiences—their continual readjustment of frocks and ribbons, smoothing down of dresses, and reaching in for shoulder straps; and it was gratifying to feel that one was doing so much good.

The ideals of this lofty community were as numerous as the leaves themselves, all wonderfully suspended in purest air and capable of producing the most enchanting Aeolian harmonies when stirred by a gentle wind. The most noble of these ideals—but thought by many to be *too* ideal—envisioned an ultimate and millennial severing of every connection with that other besoiled and frightful world of the roots, which all knew (of course) to exist somewhere but which it was beyond the pale to talk about and in the worst of taste even to think about. Less utopian was the highly feasible plan—and there were currently many extraordinarily interesting meetings and popular discussions on the subject—of solidly flooring the great head of the tree, so that its denizens should no longer walk in momentary danger of slipping and falling to heaven knows what fate. The completion of this in itself praiseworthy plan, however, might involve a general and deplorable relaxation of manners; for, as had been demonstrated time and again, the delicately mincing step of each and every member of this community, which spoke worlds for the niceness of their breeding, derived primarily from the necessity (the very precondition of existence here) of every minute watching one's step. A single slip, and decency would forbid the remaining community even to think of the whither of one's departure.

As for the economics of this society: with fruits of every kind depending luxuriously from every bough, there was no need for anyone either to labor or to hit his neighbor on the head. All was gentleness and love.

It was after one of his lectures on the habits and prejudices of Jehovah that the flourishing young man—by now fairly convinced that he was, after all, a personage of considerable format—was approached by an excessively nervous and violently impulsive young female, who stood fingering wretchedly the tassels of her handbag until he would have time to deign to turn from his circle of effusive congratulators to herself. When he was ready, she thrust her excessive beak at him, tilted her face, and sparkled her eyes. "Mr. Fitzroy," she gushed, "I *must* see you."

The youth was careful not to appear to wish to step back a little. She had offered him her hand. This he took and cherished.

"I am Phoebe-Belle," she said, "and I thought that what you said about the Father's love for the soul was the most *important* thing I had ever heard. I say, do you think you could *possibly* come to tea with me? I *must*, I simply *must* hear more."

Her features were unbeautiful, but there was about her such a compelling, though peculiar, personal emphasis that she almost succeeded in bringing, as it were, the entire weight of the cosmos into stunning focus in herself. It was as though the Maker had abruptly popped her forth and declared in cynical triumph, "'Twas this I intended, all the time!"

The cozy tea was served on a pretty little sun branch open to the cumulus sky. Phoebe-Belle poured exquisitely and served delicate little berries.

"What I so want to hear," she said, "is your interpretation of the mission of the Son. What was the secret of his Tree of Agony?"

The youth, without the first conception of her meaning, sat baffled, suddenly afraid lest his adventure be here at the breaking point.

"We think of love," she said, "as the great power. For love is stronger than death. Love is stronger than reason. Love is the glory of the spirit. Love is the purifying ray that converts the appetites of the flesh—" But at the word "flesh," she coughed. Immoderately flushed, she took a desperate gulp of tea. She cleared her lips with the napkin, set the cup down, lifted her startling beak, and strained forward with suddenly effusive solicitude. "Would you like another little berry?" she said.

The youth replied that perhaps he would, then grinned.

"The sweetest are those farthest out," she said. "I couldn't reach them alone."

He turned to measure with anxious eye.

"You are so tall," she flattered, "you will hardly even have to reach. But do be careful; be very careful..."

He was reaching carefully. A difficult moment, and he just plucked a pretty little clump.

They settled cozily again. More tea was poured. Phoebe-Belle presently was saying, "You see, we all know your inspiring history." She fluttered her eyes. "You represent to us the heart of love. It was your heart, your wonderful heart, that brought you to us safely from the cities of those unspeakable..." She shut her eyes. She covered her eyes with her manicure, then reached, desperately again, for her cup. One sip, and again she lifted her brows. "Just another little berry, perhaps?" She brightly teased, tilting her head with pitiful winningness. Urged, he hesitated; but she cooed with such urgency and was making of it all something of such intimately personal consequence that he could not but acquiesce. The prize, this time, was hardly a degree beyond the first. There was just the possibility that Phoebe-Belle herself might have to assist him. He was carefully stretching, inching out, and the berries were still no more than the least teetering degree beyond, when her hand, her immaculately manicured, nervous hand immaculately touched...

A foot slipped; he toppled, plunged, struck crazily the branches, plunged, struck water and sank, limp, into a tepid mire.

Slime, the silence of the undifferentiated, no-stir, primordial ooze—fragments vaguely float. Eyes at the ends of stalks peer out from habitats of mud: the zone of disintegrations, the zone of the ravenous crocodile, the zone of the sucking roots. And from crannies of the root labyrinth, crabs dart to seize and quickly scuttle back. Now a flatfish, now an eel sleepily ripples out of and into again the torpidity, thickly fluent. A dim phosphorescence lingers. All sleeps; all is alive; with slow, tepid combustion all consumes. Fragments, reminiscent, wearily dissimilate: the squid waves sucking arms; living parachutes swim throbbing by.

Amidst the hydroids, the polyps, the flatworms, the sea walnuts, the strands of rotting kelp, the shreds of fish disintegration, George

Ambrose heavily rolled. When he had struck, all had started back, and for a long while he was alone. Presently, then, the strange fringes and silent tentacles began everywhere again to flower forth; the first swirl of the leaf and stick fragments having settled, the crab now scurried again; an eel flowed by; a jellyfish throbbed its way; the ink of the octopus having cleared a little, the crocodile made to stir.

George Ambrose felt himself enwrapped, as though by the living roots of the tree. They must be searching, sucking everywhere. What ravenous circulation from these reeking, plasmic depths must go to support the teeming, blooming, giddy abundance of the overreaching head! Something nuzzled at his side. There was a quick stir: a young shark swam by. He perceived the horrible crocodile now approaching from the roots. He beheld something strong and black swimming with a queasy motion; but, as he watched it, it acquired rapidly the form of a swimming, naked hag: her dugs hanging like fins, her eyes blazing a red-yellow, her bony teeth conspicuous in the jaws, her ravenous, lean body tufted with clumps of coarse white bristle. Her voice, when it came—not directly from her spiny lips, but circumfluently pressing through every pore of his already putrefying skin—sang in his body like a sweet gleam of silver: "Ah," she said, "my sweetheart, you have come!" She reached a crone's hand and took one of the hairs of his head, which she then drew to herself and began to wind. The hair came continuously, like twine out of a box. She settled to the bottom, squatted at his side, and wound the hair on a crooked spindle-finger. Softly, sweetly, tenderly, she was speaking. "The fallen fruits and leaves," she gently said, "the wonderful sunken ships; all—sweetheart—all: they come at last. How delicious of you at last," she said. And her voice was as gratifying as the silent sigh of sea kelp waving in abyssal seas. "Back once more to the night," she sighed, "the black night of the crone! How many times? My delicate berry of the tree, open your delicate flesh to me." The fingers continued to wind. "The night," said the voice, "is tepid. The night sea is tepid and congenial; congenial the return; congenial the sweetness of the deep and the night of love." She leaned to his side and whispered, "Ah!" With the

long running of the hair that she wound, relentless, on her finger, his
interior unraveled and ran out.

HIS MIND HAD COLLAPSED when George Ambrose Fitzroy, never
quite conscious anyhow, was hauled from the tropical sea, stifled in
kelp. Prone on the wildly tossing deck of a sturdy little boat, his tongue
and nostrils freed from slime, he was steadily and loyally worked on
for the better part of two hours before he became conscious, dimly,
of a fierce wind mechanically rushing out of and into his two aching
lungs. A pair of powerful human hands was pressing and releasing the
stagnant diaphragm in a steady, tireless rhythm. When his eyelids fluttered, there was a stir of feet around him. The slow, regular pressing
and releasing continued.

Watching, meanwhile, from a huddled blanket in the scuppers
were the eyes of Corporal McGee, gazing from a pug face now haggard
with exhaustion, more ugly and inhuman than ever. Everywhere on
the soaking, sickeningly heaving deck were similarly bundled hulks,
some squatting, some lying flat, a few—like George Ambrose—with
an oil-smeared, strong-armed youth in dungarees squatting astride the
upper legs and faithfully pressing, releasing, pressing, releasing. There
was no breeze, only a broad groundswell that kept the chunky boat
bobbing like a cork; loose objects were rolling and slamming about
the cluttered deck. Figures moving among the rescued young men
administered to their requirements. And a queer silence overhung the
scene. The boat chugged in ranging circles, still searching, in the first
gray light of dawn.

By the time George Ambrose found himself in condition to turn
his head to the side and look around, the sun was blazing high. He
was now lying on his back. The hard deck, now parched under the
merciless red eye of the heavens, rolled with a quieter motion. Sea-
birds gliding on reposeful, powerful wings hung in irregular forma-
tions overhead, side-slipping, turning their heads, braying, winging a

little, or plunging abruptly at the sea after some bit of waste. George Ambrose had been watching them. He had been greatly enjoying the return of the air to his lungs, the gentle rocking of the vessel, the vast blue reaches of the cloudless heavens. The white birds had been the first things to greet his consciousness, and he had regarded them with a clear sense of fellowship. They had come to his little boat from unknown guano-plastered, wave-beaten rocklets in the reaches of the sea; had come winging from all points of the compass. And they would hang here for a period, only to wing away. Never had he beheld precisely these individuals before, never would he behold them again; furthermore, they were unaware either of him or of his fellowship. They were as impersonal in their presence as the black, sleazy smoke streaming from the saucy stack. His eye shifted to the smoke, and for that too he felt fellowship: the smoke particles, pouring to evanesce into the blue heavens, had never existed before this living moment, and they would immediately be scattered into invisibility; but during that moment of their passing they gratified his senses, and he loved both them and the air into which they disappeared.

Through the smoke George Ambrose could stare into the merciless sun. It was like a fierce eye exchanging with him a look of secret understanding. He took the message to himself. That was the eye from which the life of the world proceeded: George Ambrose remembered his school geography—about the energy proceeding from the fires of the sun. That was the red gaze that held the world alive. He let his head turn to the side to embrace in his view the boat and its population. What he caught was the glazy eye of McGee. The corporal had slumped a little; his blanket was flapping over the right half of his face, so that one eye only was staring mercilessly; it never blinked. George Ambrose regarded it with conscience undisturbed. Presently he knew the eye was dead. Without a skip of the pulse, he let his gaze dwell in quiet fellowship on the unchanging, ugly countenance before returning his regard, for another spell, to the soaring gulls.

The Buddha, touching the earth upon achieving enlightenment (carved schist, India, c. late ninth–early tenth century A.D.). Courtesy of the Los Angeles County Museum of Art.

THE LORD OF LOVE

———————•———————

(February 24, 1945–April 30, 1945)

THE CARETAKER OF THE LITTLE BUDDHIST TEMPLE on Abraham Lincoln Street was slow to realize that the large bodhisattva image in the vestibule had disappeared from its bronze lotus seat. It was difficult to imagine why or how the burglar—if it were a question of theft—could have removed only the image, for the image and the lotus had been cast of a single piece; and difficult, furthermore, to imagine how anyone could have transported the loot away, for no truck had stopped this morning at the curb.

It was the Sunday of the Japanese attack on the naval base at Pearl Harbor: a beautiful, clear morning. The battle had been at such a distance that little rumor of the event had penetrated to the hibiscus hedges, kiawe trees, and tall coconut palms of Abraham Lincoln Street. Yamato-san, quietly at work about the heavily shaded lawn with his wooden rake and basket, had been unaware of everything until the tiny Japanese house girl from across the street came running, fluttering like a butterfly, and excitedly told him. Yamato-san dropped the rake and flew aimlessly about the yard; the house girl fluttered home. But after that minute or two of panic, the wonderful plant-world quietness of the hedges and trees along the peaceful little street again prevailed, and sturdy Yamato-san returned to his rake and basket. These he gathered hastily into the shed, which he firmly padlocked; then he hurried to the temple and pulled the door behind him. To keep himself from thinking, he directly applied all his energy to the hundred and one odd jobs that always remained to be done within the building. It was then, while repairing one of the mats in the vestibule, that he came to realize that the image had disappeared.

Particularly treasured by the members of the community, the image had been presented to the temple many years before by a certain half-fabulous Dr. Tokashi Okumura, who had discovered it during his travels in India and had transported it back to Abraham Lincoln Street as a token of the fundamental unity not only of the Orient but of all mankind. A beautiful and fascinating image, it had sat on a great bronze lotus in a relaxed, playfully regal posture, girlishly holding another lotus in its delicate left hand, its right arm languidly resting on one knee. The fine head had been wistfully tilted, half-regarding with serene eyes the matted area of the vestibule, half-brooding inward, while the sensuous, sweet lips remained fixed in a gentle, strangely noncommunicative smile. Dr. Tokashi Okumura had provided that the motto "God is Love" should be displayed beneath the image in English (in Japanese the connotation would have been shockingly indelicate); and what Yamato-san beheld when he scrambled to his feet was only this motto, the vacated lotus seat, and the other lotus stem that the graceful bodhisattva had once held in his delicate left hand, which was now simply placed across the lotus base like a long pipe stem across an ashtray. The bronze tiara that had embellished the fine head of the bodhisattva was later discovered within the main chamber of the temple, where it had been carefully set on the floor, against the wall, just to the left of one of the doors.

Yamato-san hurried to the telephone to communicate with the priest at his home, but the telephone-central curtly informed him that the military emergency had made civilian calls, for the present, impossible. Cut off, he looked desperately around the pretty little matchbox of a temple. Silence alone replied. Wringing his helpless hands and breathing sharply in through his teeth, he hurried back again to the vestibule; but when he this time beheld the empty place, his nerve abruptly failed, and he went down, sturdy little man that he was, like a sack. His knees struck the clean wooden floor, and he fell on his face across the mended mat.

_____ *2.*

THE STENOGRAPHER'S TYPEWRITER occupying Lilian Copeland's ten mechanical fingers was becoming a hardening wall of pressure that threatened to flatten her, and the rest of her body reacted against it with soft agony, as the phlegmy voice of her employer dictated through the reek of a chewed cigar.

Lilian was a vivid and challengingly neurotic blonde beauty of about twenty-five. As she sat straight-backed in the efficient typist chair—elbows in, arms lightly poised, fingers hammering rapidly along—something about the way her irrepressible bosom protruded into the work suggested that, though she might be expert at this clever performance, her person had been shaped for some totally different occupation. When she flung herself abruptly out of the chair to fetch a folder from the files, she strode with a strangely bounding movement, her great hips obviously set a little high. She was very tall, very beautiful, yet peculiarly proportioned. Her golden hair, caught neatly into a snood and hanging to the level of her shoulders, swung jerkily as she tossed herself about. It flattened against her white neck as she lowered her head to peer, nearsighted, into the files, her deft talons, brilliantly manicured in red, flashing through the classified papers. When she had found what she wanted, she gave the metal drawer a brief slam and came lurching back to her chair.

"What was the number of that order?" The shattered voice of her employer, Morton Warren, rattled like a phonograph record played with a worn-out needle. "I'm getting fed up with that bunch of goddamn jerks." He gave his cigar a flick, looked at the end of it, stuck the butt into his face, and leaned complacently back in the swivel. A beefy, golf-tanned, short but huge-shouldered bruiser, he had been a guard on a celebrated Yale eleven some thirty years earlier. He had served in the last war as a captain in the field artillery before return- ing to marry his roommate's sister, and then, after a brief try at Wall Street, had moved with his wife to her family's holdings in Honolulu. There he had rapidly steamrollered his way to a position of weight in one of the offices of "The Big Five." For twenty years now, he had been quite a big shot in the islands—with two very popular, run-of- the-mill daughters, now of college age, and a chunky, pig-eyed, chip- off-the-old-block son, just leaving for a prep school in the East, who was expected to be a worthy successor to the old man. His wife—a leathery, whiskey-seasoned "good sport" of about forty-eight—had kept her girlish figure, and could still knock off a pretty handsome round of golf. Her tennis game lately had deteriorated, but she was still a great one on the fairway—a frequent winner of the handicaps—and still a charmer with that cute little way she'd always had of wrinkling the sides of her nose when she smiled. She and her massive corker of a husband were a welcome couple at every lawn and cocktail party: you would find them standing, shifting from foot to foot, in the endless waiting line of guests at every fashionable wedding. True, her Mor- ton was no *kama'aina* (which is to say, he had not been *born* in the islands), but he had taken to the "Paradise of the Pacific" like a duck to water: he was the real McCoy, and everyone had gone for him from the start. "Morty" had fitted into island life well, like Miss Copeland, his present stenographer, into her form-revealing crepe de chine. He was a real guy, a great mixer, and a shrewd head.

Straining her eyes, her nose close to the folder, Lilian read aloud the information he required in a voice slightly quavering and harsh, while her right hand fingered the amber beads of her necklace. Her employer, leaning back, listlessly regarded the large white thigh that had suddenly become exposed when she had flopped into the chair. The girl concluded the reading, lifted herself a little from the seat and swiftly ran her hand underneath to place the dress, then cast a quiz- zical look at her employer, tilting her head and waiting to hear what he should say. He was studying again the ash of the cigar. "Well," he decided, "we'll shoot along with the letter." She flipped the folder shut, dropped it neatly to the floor, and adjusted herself to the back of the chair. When the letter began to come, her fingers flew. Miss Copeland was again in expert and controlled operation. Her gratified employer, again taking the cigar into his teeth, continued to dictate in measured phrases through the smoke and his heavily rattling phlegm, letting his abstracted, dull gaze repose, meanwhile, upon the soft, irrepressible, slightly stirring hillocks that indignantly confronted the hard machine.

———————————•———————————

FOR YEARS, Lilian had been aware of the waves of masculine lust that filled the atmosphere wherever she walked or sat. She was such a striking figure of a woman that even as a youngster, striding along King or Fort Street, she had been endlessly accompanied by an appreciative accolade of tomcat calls and whistles from the sailors, soldiers, and marines, truckers, butcher boys, and drugstore heroes of every race and age that graced the thoroughfares of the crowded port. Among her classmates in the Punahou School there had been hardly a youth—whether Portuguese, part Hawaiian, or white, Japanese, Chinese, or Filipino—who had not at one time or another, in one way or another, crudely or discreetly, indicated to her the desire of his callow heart. In a world of preponderantly dark-haired beauty, she had been a conspicuous aberration, gangling and very blonde. She had even thought herself a freak until the male population had begun to respond to her; then she had realized she was something pretty special. From among her assorted suitors she had ultimately chosen for herself a handsome Chinese boy named Philip Wang, who was a considerable phenomenon on the football field and a great favorite of his class. During their senior year on the idyllic campus, Wang and Lilian were the wonder and delight of their little world.

It was on a remote beach during an all-day senior picnic and swimming party that the event occurred which Lilian had ever since regarded as the great crisis of her coming-of-age. A caravan of ukulele-playing, flower-bedecked, brashly singing boys and girls had rolled in a file of assorted cars out of the city, past Waikiki and Diamond Head. Wang was driving his giddy coffee-colored jalopy, Lilian was in the seat beside him, and some half dozen others were stacked around their necks, in the rumble, and outside on the fenders. There was a hilarious shouting to passersby, who waved pleasantly in return. The day was glorious—as always on the islands—with cumulus white clouds in a blue sky capping the sharp, volcanic, olive-colored ridges and floating in slowly dissolving little fleets out over the sea. A combination of tropical garden odors, sea tang, Polynesian memories, and modern, up-to-the-minute concrete gave to the atmosphere the peculiar, invigorating quality of a cocktail. The young company, of one age but of every race and miscegenation—sleek-necked part Hawaiian, heavy-cheeked Mongolian, pinch-faced and sharp-eyed Western—assorted, compounded, and blithely garbed, played and sang, with ginger leis round their necks and hibiscus blossoms in their hair.

Most of the details of the adventure had faded, but Lilian still could recall with a great nostalgia their moment of arrival at the beach, their peeling off outer coverings and breaking forth in bathing suits to scamper and scatter about the sands and dunes, and the general helter-skelter of swimming, dashing of water, acrobatic displays, hauling and tugging, laughing, and screaming that had embellished the better part of the day. Deviled eggs, mangoes, figs, and no end of waxed paper were passed from hand to hand; sandwiches riddled with sand were masticated, washed down with swigs from pop bottles. A softball game was arranged, followed by a number of swimming contests and a universal tug-of-war. It was by then late afternoon. Finally, while some went in for another dip, others began to pack their things and themselves back into cars. One by one, the vehicles pulled away, two or three at a time. Some of the youngsters lingered; a few had disappeared among the dunes. The sun had begun to descend. There would be a moon.

Wang and Lilian, who had gone strolling hand in hand down the beach along the line of the breakers, were now trotting a little, splashing up to their knees sometimes or cleverly curveting around the foamy tongues of the sea. Wang was a tall, clean-chested youth, clad in a scanty pair of trunks, loose-jointed, easily running, pleasantly laughing, and with a soft Hawaiian voice and Chinese eyes. Looking back now through the years, Lilian could only wonder at the innocence of the boy and girl: she could recall her pride in Wang's athletic body, and in her own—both tanned and gleaming in the sun. Her bathing suit was a prettily flowered affair, her golden hair was flowing, and her white cap was in her hand. Wang said, "Let's swim-it round the head!" "Okay," she said. Gathering up her hair, she replaced the cap, fixing the strap beneath her chin.

They broke into the sea and swam. It was an easy half mile around the volcanic rocks to the little beach with its fringe of coco palms beyond. When they arrived, they sprawled on their backs upon the warm sands, with their arms behind their heads.

"Nice," said Wang.

"Wonderful," she said.

They were silent a long time, and happy.

Presently Wang reached his hand to her, and they lay there holding hands. When he spoke he used the tough-guy, "Portugee" accent affected by the young men of the islands. "We gonna graduate soon," he said. "This high school stuff's gonna end."

"Let's not think about it," said Lilian.

"Why not?" insisted Wang.

"Oh, let's not spoil our day," the girl said.

Wang released her hand and turned to her, propping his head, his elbow in the sand. He regarded her a moment, then began to speak very seriously, slowly and correctly, discarding the "Portugee." "Something tells me, Lilian," he said, "this will be our last time together."

She turned her head to study his eyes. "Don't talk like that," she said. "Don't be silly." She was displeased.

"Will you marry me?" he asked her. He was looking at her quietly. The girl was suddenly afraid. "Will you marry me?" he repeated.

Something important broke inside and the girl felt she was about to cry. Her eyes, large, with their immense nearsighted pupils, gazed at him; but then they blurred and his features disappeared from her behind a veil of mist. She quickly covered her face with her hands, and there came from her throat a groan of agony disproportionate, one would have thought, to her age. "Oh, Wang," she said. (She preferred his Chinese to his Christian name.) "Dear Wang!" She sobbed. The youth regarded her. Presently she felt his gentle hand reach over to her neck; she kept her face covered and continued to sob into her palms.

After an endless interval, she heard again his voice. "My fadha talk to me d'other day," he said, again using the dialect. "My fadha-muddha," Wang said, "they come from China; my fadha wanna know. See what I mean? He wanna know. 'She gonna *marry* you?' he say to me. See what I mean? I never worry, never worry, juss like you. But then I seen it. Right away I seen it, and it bust up the whole thing. Goddamn it, Lilian—" The boy abruptly broke off and rolled away from her. Uncovering her face to look at him, she discovered him on his stomach with his face buried in his arms. Now her boy was sobbing too.

The girl sat up. A light breeze was blowing. She brushed the sand from her hands musingly, and sweeping the hair from her eyes, pushed it back and slowly gathered it at the nape of her neck, then fixed it with the rubber strap she had clumsily shaken from her white cap. She moved over to Wang and began to brush the sand lightly from his beautiful back. His shoulders were broad, his hips narrow, and the long slope of his muscles pleased her eye. His skin was smooth and flawless. He was a beautiful, wonderful boy.

"My dear, dear Wang," she said, with a tender, motherly voice, "it isn't what you think. I'm never going to marry anyone. Never anyone—*never*, Wang—never anyone at all. Besides, we're much too young. We've college yet—both of us. It's much too soon. For *me* it's too soon." Wang rolled his head, but gave no reply.

Having brushed all the sand from his back, Lilian began abstractedly to scratch doodles with her fingernail on his shoulder. "You don't know," she said, "how repulsive it is to have all those ninnies calling at me in the street. You never heard some of the things they say. But you…" She paused, on the brink of declaring something, but then thought better and sat mute for a moment. Suddenly, with a fierce intensity, she exploded: "I *hate* it!" She withdrew her hand, folded her arms around her knees, and gazed red-eyed, angrily, at the horizon. There were the makings of a sunset in the sky. The girl reached back and impatiently pulled the confining strap from her hair, so that it blew out and around her in the breeze. She got up and walked pensively away, down to the breakers, watching her long brown toes dig into the beach. Gathering in her hair again, she put on the cap and plunged into the waves. A good way out, she turned, and Wang was sitting up. She waved to him. He replied, but she could not see whether he was smiling. She beckoned. He got laboriously up. Rubbing the sand from his strong arms, kicking and limbering his fine legs, trotting and jogging like a boxer, he took his good time getting down to the sea. Then he backed away a little, started a short rapid run, sharply plunged like a lance into a breaker, shot through, and came out plowing with a masterful crawl. Lilian straightened in the water, got slowly under way, gathered speed, and with her long lead gave him a good race back to the towels in the waiting car.

THAT HAD BEEN A LONG, VERY LONG, TIME AGO: nine rotten years! And she simply hated to think about what those nine years had done to her, the way her life had disintegrated since that pearl of a moment. She had wished to interpret her relationship to Wang as harmlessly, as self-righteously, as she could; but even at the time she'd had some inkling of the import of the adventure. And now she knew that something within her had understood, for two years after that day on the beach, during her sophomore year at Vassar, when she'd heard the news of Wang's marriage to another *hauli*, another white girl, her entire soul had turned over, and she'd had to face the ugly fact that she was a coward and a cheat.

Lilian Copeland was a coward because that day on the beach she had been afraid not only to think of marriage to Philip Wang but even to admit that fact, because doing so would have meant that she was a cheat. She was a cheat because, in her heart of hearts, she had known from the start that she would never dare to marry Wang.

(There were many mixed marriages on the islands, but none in the upper economic brackets. Though sociability in high school was accepted, even encouraged, as a sign and proof of democracy, after graduation one's Asiatic schoolmates inevitably found themselves no longer invited to the exclusive tennis courts, clubs, and homes— except for the most gala affairs. Unostentatiously but surely, they were pressed back into their place. What had happened to Wang had happened many a time before.)

Lilian Copeland was a double-cheat because knowing this—and, indeed, precisely because of knowing this—she had chosen Wang to be her boy. Lilian Copeland—deeper even than her heart of hearts— was afraid, totally afraid, of life, of the ugly demon that forever lurked and leered after her from every window, every barroom, every lane; yet she could not wish to forgo the prestige that came of adventuring it with conspicuous success. And besides, she was curious. Curious, but afraid.

El Morocco, the Stork Club, Café Society, and the other chic dens of New York became witness during a couple of seasons to the handsome tête-à-têtes of a stunning tall and vivid blonde with various young and middle-aged gentlemen of the world: all pleased as punch to be seen with such a miracle; each flattered by her neurotic gales of response to his aphoristic witticisms into imagining himself to be the undiscovered marvel of the century.

The greatest such case had been that of a weird young husband, Howard Jones—a gratifyingly tall, dark, and handsome scion of a fine old Philadelphia family, who was living with his scrawny but interesting manic-depressive wife in a studio apartment in Greenwich Village; both were undergoing psychoanalysis and practicing their arts. Howard was a writer—he had actually written a book review for the *Herald Tribune*—and his plucky wife, Patricia, a painter of delicate pastels.

Patricia's younger brother—a frail and sensitive-looking, very intellectual, well-dressed senior at Princeton—had brought Lilian, late one evening, to a shindig at "The Studio." She had entered the smoky bedlam like a vision from beyond the grave: tall, beautiful, her great hips set a little high perhaps, but her black gown (astonishingly simple) artfully composed to compensate. The V-neck was cut so low between the breasts (" 'Thy two breasts,' " her cultivated males would always ultimately quote to her, " 'thy two breasts are like two young roes that are twins, which feed among the lilies' ") that the human eye could be expected to forget itself there in dream. And when, upon recovering his senses, the abstracted one would lift his eyes, he would find her challengingly and appreciatively smiling into his soul. The red mouth was a cruel, bleeding slash cut across her pale, slightly agonized features; the vast, nearsighted eyes never quite made contact with the world; the sudden toss and turn of the nervous head, with a spasm of pain at the corner of her lips, was a fascinating revelation of shocking spiritual torment; the slow lifting of her arm and careless outward flick of the wrist was a gesture to split the mind.

And so this was the apparition that entered the apartment of Howard and Patricia Jones about eleven forty-five one fine evening. Curious to say, most of the company—scattered about on the windowsills and chairs and on the rug before the fireplace or standing in little groups, holding glasses and nibbling tidbits between important sentences—hardly turned to note her coming, and when they spied it, simply returned again to their affairs. But Howard, the host—tall, dark, and handsome, as she immediately perceived—set down his glass, quickly brushed some crumbs from his mouth, and with the slight stoop at the neck which he had developed to take care of the six-foot-six of his unutterable length, gulping down whatever he had bitten and smiling with soiled teeth and dark, eager eyes, came quickly to relieve her of her wrap, be introduced, and take her hostfully by the arm.

But more than hostfully: his right hand was like a vise, and it grasped her at the elbow, so that her left arm was helpless as he hauled her through a brief series of perfunctory and bored introductions on the way to the large table with the drinks. Her escort had quit her and could be seen shaking hands in all directions, stooping and laughing to his acquaintances on the floor, back-slapping and pumping vigorously with those about the walls. Lilian, with a little catch of panic, felt herself in the iron grip of an overpowering, obscurely driven, immediately unpalatable monster, his nose a bit too long, his breath a bit too close to her, and his complexion a bit too gray. Without releasing her elbow, the man dumped whiskey into a tall glass, dropped in ice, added a little water, put the drink into her free hand, and said, "Why have I never seen you before? Where have you been?"

Though her left arm was numb, the glass in her right hand gave her back something of her sense of poise. She rattled the ice and smiled, like a sphinx, directly into his eyes.

Stooping, he brought his face very close. "You are maddening my blood," he told her. He looked as though she really were, and before she could credit what was happening, his great left paw had slipped between a shoulder strap and her skin, and was in complete possession of her right breast. "'Thy two breasts,'" he hoarsely breathed, "'are like two young roes that are twins.'"

She thought she would smash the glass against his face; however, instantly something else, much smarter, occurred to her. She had discovered a smart rebuff in her educated brain.

"'Stay me with flagons,'" she replied calmly and icily, retaining the impenetrable smile, "'comfort me with apples: for I am sick of love.'"

The lout released roughly the numbed elbow, but with his other prodigious paw gave her right strap a vicious tug. It snapped, and the one breast was hanging bare. He struck it with a disdainful jolt and wheeled away.

The girl, utterly stunned, believed for a moment that she was about to faint. She hoped she could play her sophisticated role out to the end. The madman had left her. She was alone, leaning against the table.

Gripping the heavy table behind her, Lilian slowly, deliberately peered into the glass and rattled the ice a little, then lifted it slowly to her lips, holding it in such a way that her arm protected her. Then she cast a carefully steadied look about the room.

Few, apparently, had seen; but among the observing eyes had been those of the brute's wife and Lilian's escort, the youth from Princeton. Before another moment, there was the sound of a resounding slap at an opposite, murky corner of the room, a cry, a rush of excitement, and the thump of a heavy fall. "Pick a feller your own size," somebody shouted; and the whole company arose to move into that corner. Lilian, now left entirely to herself, with quivering hands set down her glass, caught up the strap, and slipped away to seek a dressing table—badly shaken but rather proud of herself. And in her pride, she returned presently to rejoin the now disordered party, to accept the abject apologies of her hostess, and to queen it amidst the adulation of a great number of fawning males. More had beheld than she had supposed, and she became not a mere Bohemian incident but the epoch of the season.

Poor idiotic Howard increased his visits to the analyst. Patricia took harder to drink and conceived the pesky notion that her husband should see as much as possible of the blonde—"to get her finally either into or out of his system." The Princeton youth became a slave magnificent. And the whole city opened like a broken bundle. Lilian leaned her sharp elbows on every tabletop in the town, folded her hands beneath her chin, and gazed with lacquered perfection—very beautiful, blonde, and tall—through her magnificent nearsighted eyes into whatsoever face it happened to be.

———————●———————

No WONDER SHE HAD FLUNKED OUT OF VASSAR in the middle of her junior year. Then news arrived that her father, on his way to fetch her home, had been killed in the wreck of a transcontinental airliner. She was on the brink of a nervous breakdown. It was the Joneses, curiously enough, who pulled her together and assisted her on her way. But the marvel of it all (and this is known by God, Howard and Patricia Jones, and no one else in the whole wide world): she was still a virgin.

The morning of her return, the perfumes of *Hawai'i nei*—beloved Hawaii—wafting over the soft blue waters of the sea greeted her nostrils the moment she opened her eyes. She leaped out of the berth, glimpsed through the porthole the wonderful island miraculously there upon the waves (the steamer was passing, at that moment, the great, crouching-lion form of Diamond Head), and then dashed into her clothes. She hastened to the dining room, where a few latelings like herself were quickly tossing off their orange juice and buttering bits of toast. The white-jacketed waiters, rushing about and standing peacefully, were beaming smiles; all the scattered breakfasters were beaming and offering each other blithe Good Mornings; Lilian, smiling within her heart and bounding in her chair, was impatient to gulp the blistering coffee—happy, happy—delighted to be coming home.

The first person she spied as she craned over the ship's rail—squinting with her nearsighted eyes through borrowed binoculars, searching the wildly waving, beaming, white-clothed and beflowered crowd, while the Royal Hawaiian Band played "Aloha" and four portly native women, wearing big lauhala hats, sang in a way to break your heart—was her poor, harried-looking mother, waving, holding a handkerchief to the corner of her eye, and making believe to smile. That sent a pang through all the layers of the excitement. Lilian forced the sorrow down into a little void inside her, where it disappeared, and continued to try to make the most of this unreal, ephemeral moment. Rapidly she searched the crowd on the pier but could not discover Wang. Then she took another good look at her mother—the woman's searching face had not yet discovered her—and returned the binoculars, with a shattering smile of frank enjoyment, to the tall and interesting foreign-looking gentleman who had let her use them.

There were already many leis on the steamer passengers: they had arrived with the welcoming committee, newspapermen, and privileged friends who had come out from shore on the harbor tug and swarmed aboard. A lively young group discovered Lilian, flung soft, fresh leis round her neck (white and yellow ginger blossoms, pink carnation, yellow and pink plumeria, purple and white mauna loa, tuberoses, pikake, royal orange–colored ilima, and mokihana), kissed her, jumped hilariously up and down, shook her arms, laughed, and hugged her.

"The Great American Girl!" That was Wang's greeting as he came pressing through her little circle of friends to drape a handful of leis around her already heavily laden neck. It was good, soothing to her heart, to see the crowd, the dear old crowd again. She was caught with them into the old life again; she rushed with them about the deck; two of the young men helped with her bags. Like a May Queen returning to her people, she came bounding down the gangplank, at last, and into her mother's arms.

Sorrow marked the sallow, perspiring, sadly hairy chin of Mrs. Copeland, as she embraced her golden girl, messing the front of her dress with the pollen of the leis. Sorrow grew upon her as the gay festival of the landing gradually transformed itself into a problem of luggage and transportation. Sorrow had her entirely by the time she and her daughter were installed, now lonely, lonely forevermore, in the fatherless, empty house.

"We have sold the house," the mother told her.

The child broke into a tantrum. But when she learned there was no money, she was sobered. And when it was revealed to her that she would now have to earn a living, she was appalled. When it was decided she should go to business school—she wept.

Six dreary years! The idyllic island had become her jail. Every detail of the life had been simply killed with repetition. She had read every friend through and through to the marrow: and they were dull; god, they were dull!

About a year after she returned to the island, the Wangs invited her to their daughter's second birthday party, and she arrived with the air of the woman of the world. Philip greeted her at the door. "The Great American Girl!" he said, and he smiled. Lilian felt irritated (What did he mean, dammit? Here, twice now he had said that!), but she responded with a gale of friendly laughter and banter and came attractively into the room. The only other unmarried person in the place was the tall, handsome foreign-looking gentleman who had loaned her his binoculars on the steamer, over a year before. He recognized her glance; she replied to his smile with a quickening eye. Gallantly, he approached, clicked his heels, and bowed to kiss her hand: it was the first time her hand had ever been greeted in this way (it made her tickle inside and feel silly), but she accepted the courtesy with the mien of a countess-dowager. She took the man's arm a little too quickly when he arose—to make the point, perhaps, that she and he were from another world. However, since the Wangs had invited him expressly for her, she need not have manifested so much emphasis. The gentleman (she would have to learn his name somehow) compensated for the forwardness by patting the girl's hand affectionately, as though they had known each other for ages.

"Such a pleasure," he said, "to see you again." His accent was on the German side; his back was excessively straight. His gray eyes were keen; his features, severe: a man of mystery (she could feel) and intrigue—perhaps a spy? She was thrilled.

After a minute or two of pretenses around the baby (prettily rigged out with pink flounces, in her pen) and an exchange of insincerities with the happy mother (Philip had married a very plain girl, after all; Lilian remembered her from school: simply a pale, straw-colored blonde, well built in a sturdy way, but with no characteristics whatsoever), Lilian dallied a little with the companions of her remote past (all married now and dowdy, the girls blowing up like balloons every year and then suddenly going flat when they had given the world their burden: god, how Lilian loathed, simply loathed, this eternal menagerie of squalling brats!), and then returning, at last, to her gallant catch, she faced him squarely, with a cup of tea.

"You have been enjoying our beautiful islands?" she said.

"Very much," he said. "They are sublime."

"And you have visited the big island, Hawaii? Have you seen Maui and Molokai?"

"All of them," he replied. "They are sublime."

She studied the handsome, deeply sunburned features, with an air of slightly suspicious interrogation.

"I am a geologist," the man explained with a smile. "My special subject is volcanoes." She thought she detected a hidden trace of banter in his tone. A sudden question broke into her brain.

"Do you think there will be another war—in Europe?" she asked. She was shocked at her boldness the moment she had said it.

The gentleman stirred his cup with a spoon, tilted his head, and looked into the tea. "I am a geologist," he insisted, but with obvious discomfort. "Such things I cannot say."

She now was sure. Satisfied, she wished to undo the confusion. "The islands," she said, "I mean in those geological ages, you know, when they were erupting up out of the ocean: they must have been sublime!"

"Sublime!" he said, looking up at her, shaking his head and shutting his eyes for a little moment of affected rapture. "Simply sublime!"

("My god!" she thought to herself, "this is ghastly, we're a bore!")

Her interlocutor set the spoon down in his saucer, slowly and gracefully took a sip of tea, set the cup down, and slipped his tea napkin from between the saucer and his hand to give his lips a gentle tap. Lilian felt so vaguely excited and frustrated that she began to bounce a little, glancing helplessly about the room, drawing back the corners of her red mouth in a heartless smile, taking up and setting down her cup.

"You are a stenographer?" the man asked her.

She was recalled to her senses. "Yes!" she blurted excessively. She steadied herself down. "I work for Castle & Cook."

"I see," he said respectfully. "And you like your—vocation?"

"Uh-huh!" she muttered. "It's all—right; I...guess!" She bit at a cake and uselessly laughed.

"You are shaped for better things," he told her. She watched his eyes to see what he meant by that, but they betrayed no sign. "You have seen more of life than our friends." He made a brief motion toward the company. She felt a rush of gratitude. He smiled. She smiled into his eyes. He made a gesture toward a window seat; they moved to it and sat down.

"What do you read?" he asked with sudden interest.

She told him. They talked—they *conversed*, long, about books and learning. He was a pedagogue—she could feel it: a professor, perhaps, from Heidelberg. The spy thought gradually melted from her mind, and she became absorbed in his world of vivid, vital, vigorous ideas and astounding intuitions. "Hawaii," said he, "could become the sublime bed of the sacred marriage of Orient and Occident! I have the bad feeling, however, that it will take something of a violent jolt to bring the upper classes here to their senses. They are too complacent, too little humble before the contribution of the Asiatic majority to the civilization, not only of these islands but of the world." He nodded toward Philip Wang and his wife. "There should be more," he said earnestly, "of that sort of thing." Lilian felt her elation dissolve within her. "I just love that little couple," he said. He smiled at them with benevolence. "They have stepped one hundred years into the future." Then he turned to her, apparently quite unaware of what he was doing. "Don't you simply love them?" he said. "And the little Queen of the Sandwich Isles there in the pen!" He laughed and rose, then suddenly turned and clicked his heels. "Well," he said. He bowed to kiss her hand—the second time in her career—but ah, how different this time from the first! She forced a smile. He wheeled and paraded to his host and hostess, bowed, clicked, kissed, bowed, clicked, and was gone.

THAT MEETING HAD WORKED INTO HER MIND. She never had learned the man's name. There was a rumor, shortly after England declared war on Germany in 1939, that a mysterious figure named Von Sydow had been caught departing from the islands with a lot of meticulous maps of Hawaii and Molokai; but whether the culprit had been her man, or the maps perhaps honestly geological, she never knew. The Sunday the Japanese bombs exploded in the ships and waters of Pearl Harbor, the image of the marriage flashed for a moment in Lilian's mind—but she put it quickly out of her head, as at once disloyal and obscene. Next day, in the office, the image was back in her head again, but it was fumigated away by the sober reek of her employer's cigar.

Lilian and Morton Warren had long ago arrived at their mutual understanding. Their relationship was a difficult one to define. In a polygamous society it would have been regularized as that of man and wife: she the younger, second wife. The cheated wife of his dull middle age, the older, was the proud bearer of his children and ruled the home; the younger, the mere beast of burden of his daily grind—skinning and tanning the hides, so to say, of her master's dollar-hunting.

He had attempted an amorous advance, of course, at an earlier period of their career together—some ten days, in fact, after she had first come to work for him. It had been a ridiculous episode—too ridiculous, too mortifying to remember. Both were certainly ashamed of it and had buried it, buried it deep. Yet it had drawn the decisive line in their lives. It had established on a solid footing everything that had been built during the seasons since. It supplied the geological substratum to the utilitarian lawn that had been grown and trimmed: a substratum shaped in prehistoric periods of higher volcanic heat—unbelievable times of unbelievable eruption.

Miss Lilian Copeland—the tall, blonde, impeccably dignified secretary—had stopped in an unwary moment to retrieve a large sheaf of papers that had scattered over the floor beside her employer's stained mahogany desk. The adult male—a massive, short but extraordinarily broad-shouldered captain of industry (for some days he had been watching her)—suddenly, in an access of spontaneity, had thrown civilization to the winds and with a bold, broad thug of a hand had delivered, coarsely, an insolent swat to the magnitudinous and but thinly protected seat—which then he unceremoniously clutched and powerfully gathered to his lap. The young woman, less terrified than startled, totally mortified and indignant, kicked vigorously against what she took to be the assaulter's shins (they were the legs of his swivel chair), while the male, with asthmatic guffaws, clutched delightedly at the wildly flinging, long and handsome limbs. She tried to batter his face: he laughed at her with a raucous glee. She grabbed instinctively for the hair of his head, but the pate was bald. Inevitably, then, a thick hand of his having trapped one of the knees, the man began his lewd advance up the inside of her left thigh. She uttered a shriek. He withdrew the hand to gag her mouth. She savagely bit, kicked again, and with a hysterical sudden ferocity brought her brilliant manicure in a successful, vicious, four-pointed cat-raking down his cheek. Morton Warren catapulted her away from him with such force that she flounced onto an oriental rug five feet away. Clutching a handkerchief to his bleeding visage, he gave a rush to the office door, which he summarily locked. Immediately someone tried it from the other side. "Everything's okay," he called. "Never mind! Never mind!" Then he turned in wrath to the young woman on the floor.

"Get up!" he commanded.

She was putting on one of her shoes.

"For god's sake," he commanded again, "pull down your clothes. What do you think I am?"

With as much dignity as possible the young woman gathered herself to her feet. She walked deliberately to his desk, picked up the phone, gave quickly the number of his home, and quietly watched him.

The man came at her and snatched the instrument away, giving her at the same time another shove, so that her heel caught and she again tumbled. While she was recovering, Morton Warren retracted the call and set down the phone. Lilian was presently on her feet again, back to the upright posture of the human animal.

"I am going to report this affair to your wife," she said. She looked at him sharply. He did not reply.

In the office there was now an atmosphere of rumpled domesticity. The woman bent brazenly to adjust her hosiery, as careless of his regard as though he had been her spouse. The man picked a dead cigar up from the ashtray and looked at it with peevish sullenness. Then he fumbled in his pockets, finally discovering the matchbook on the floor among the scattered papers that had been the proximate cause of his fall from grace. With an asthmatic wheeze, the portly, ex-all-American guard laboriously stooped, took up the matches (leaving the papers where they were), and applied a flame to his expensive weed. Smoke puffed, puffed, puffed again. He shook out the match, set it thoughtfully down, and painfully resettled himself into his chair. "Miss Copeland," he said at last, with an attempt at the office manner *ante quo*, as though nothing whatsoever had taken place, "will you please clean up these papers?"

The girl had collected her handbag from a drawer and was preparing to go to the ladies' room to rearrange her hair. She went. When she returned, the rebuffed employer was sitting where she had left him, thoughtfully applying a handkerchief to his cheek and staring into the ashes of his cigar. She gathered up the papers—beginning from precisely the position that she had assumed when she had begun the work before. This time the operation proceeded without event to its normal end.

Lilian later phoned Morton Warren's wife. The two women arrived with ease at a perfect understanding. From that day the man behaved with irreproachable propriety. His eyes lusted still, but he never again attempted the unthinkable. Meanwhile, among his male companions he enjoyed a great deal of self-flattering banter touching on the this-and-that of his "beeootiful" blonde; touching on his enviable social tact in keeping happy both a young wife and such an office companion; and then touching on his deducible virility: "What a man! What a man!"

"The Great American Guy!" Lilian named him to herself. But the satisfaction she derived from this devaluation of his case little compensated, in the end, for the sterility of her own. She knew that though he never touched her again, his eyes were always lusting—not violently, but wearily, helplessly. His was but a variant of that same gaze which had been measuring, optically ravishing her ever since she had come into her own; and she was bored, continuously bored with it…

…though not left unexcited: a low-powered charge of active sexuality infected her and her entire world wherever she moved, never strong enough to carry her out of her state of barrenness. She began to think of it as a fatal, irreparable current leakage, and terribly to fear it. Yet there was nothing she could do. She was herself so infected with the element that with a fatal, horrible compulsion, she continuously primped, beautified, painted, and gave emphasis to the very traits of the anatomy that were her curse.

The years of daily intercourse with the employer—boring, unintermittent—had the quality of a tedious, impotent love prelude, which, though it never had broken past the first barrier, nevertheless went on. Or again: it *had*, it *had* broken past the barrier, and the fruit of the continuous, low-powered play were these yards and yards of business letters, all imprinted with the linked initials of their sire and dam: "MW:lc." The stenographer's typewriter, that is to say, had usurped the function of her womb. The sterile womb had become, as it were, externalized, horribly desanctified, and mechanically submitted to the unremitting use of her employer, her lord.

———————————●———————————

THE EXCITING MORNING after the catastrophe of Pearl Harbor, Lilian was more aware than ever that she had drained her life into the obscene, soul-mortifying machine. Though years had passed, she could not get out of her head the humiliating conversation at the Wangs'. The fruitfulness of her body, the fruitfulness also of her soul, she had forfeited. She had not managed to utilize—rather, she had desecrated—the sublime marriage bed of Hawaii, the marriage bed of the world. She had frittered away the wedding night of her life in pre-adolescent play, and with only this Great Guy here as her ridiculous parody of a fructifier. And this pretentious office—air-conditioned, up to the minute, mahogany and bronze—had been her sole, her only bower of ecstasy. And these cliché-riddled "business English" letters had been her firstborn and her last. Soft agony was her unique reply.

And so it was that she stepped forth, this day of days, into the still feverishly quivering city; under her left arm, a smart green purse tucked against the quivering prominence of her bosom; her handsome, long legs striding with their slightly bounding step; her broad shoulders back; and her fine, sensuous head proudly held, with its vividly yellow hair caught neatly in a snood. This was the first day she could remember that no leering Romeo cooed or whistled or assaulted her ear with a filthy gush of monosyllabic Anglo-Saxon. The energies of the USA had been diverted—in a big, big way.

An army truck loaded with Japanese civilians suspected of being spies, driven by a Japanese lad in a military uniform and supervised by a huge Hawaiian guard carrying a tommy gun at the ready, rolled around the corner of Bishop Street and pulled up with a jolt at the curb. Lilian slowed in her walk and then loitered for a moment with the crowd. "Move along!" the gruff Hawaiian commanded, with a great wave of his left arm. He began to climb down from the truck but discovered that he could not manage it with one hand. Without a moment's thought, he handed the tommy gun to one of the prisoners to hold, grabbed the side of the truck, and let himself down to the pavement. Then he rearranged his uniform, reached up for his weapon, waddled around to the tailboard, let it down, and commanded his company of lithe little charges, some solemn, some grinning, to jump down and file into the building. The observers winked and smiled; one waved to one of the prisoners, who nodded confidently, with a pleasant flash of teeth; and the crowd dispersed.

Some of the buildings were guarded by Hawaiian-Japanese soldiers, who stood at their posts with terrific seriousness. There were rumors of enemy parachuters in the hills. There was an unwonted liveliness in the normally torpid streets. Most noticeable was the utter absence of the prettily flowered Japanese kimonos that formerly had been a prominent feature of the street life of Honolulu: the Japanese women were wearing Western clothes. The Chinese, on the other hand, were wearing proudly their traditional black pajamas.

Lilian made her way through the agitated crowds to the drugstore at which she had been taking lunch the past four years. "Hi-yah, Lily, old kid!" the pimply smart aleck behind the counter called loudly. "How's the girl?" He took a malted out from under the machine and with a flourish of acrobatics poured it into a tall glass; glass and metal container he set together before the young Filipina girl who had placed the order. With a soiled wet rag he then efficiently cleared a space at the counter for the blonde. "Same old ambrosia?" he asked with excessive pleasure. She smiled, nodded, and took her place on the high stool. "Ham-and-cheese, wheat on!" he shouted to his colleague, another frisky acrobat down the other end of the line. Lilian glanced into the wall mirror behind the malted-milk machines. She became lost in herself, tilted her head a little, and tucked back an invisible wisp of hair.

While the dispenser was adroitly mixing a Coke for her, Lilian let her eyes ramble leftward along the mirror, studying the reflections of the people sucking straws and looping their mouths around uncontrollable sandwiches. Then she began to peruse the people to the right. When the soda acrobat noisily set the Coke down, he made a play for a great big smile; but the girl's attention had become riveted on something in the mirror. The clerk turned, and with one lifted eyebrow craned melodramatically to follow her gaze. When he grasped the situation, he rolled his eyes romantically, shrugged, and with a wink to one or another of his friends returned to the vaudeville act of squirting chocolate into a glass. Even when he came, some three minutes later, with the ham-and-cheese, his blonde was still absorbed.

The face in the mirror was dark, not of Mongolian cast, not of Polynesian either. The features were sensitive and regular: the eyebrows fine and gently arched; the nose flared at the nostrils, sensuously; and the lips, though not full or everted, were so emphatic, so perfectly bowed—but with a long and graceful bend to the bow, which for Lilian was quite new—that the spirit immediately flew to them. Yet she felt that to kiss them would be to kiss a mouth as cool, impersonal, and unresponsive as a mouth of bronze—which only heightened the agony, the wall-battering, cage-battering, wildly crying agony.

Lilian, as she regarded the mouth, ached with a hunger of the soul. To have been born to behold yet not to know such lips, to see yet not to experience them, was more than she could support. And the hands, which were created to have caressed her, moving gently, possessing, taking claim of her—ah! she actually could feel them; ah! but alas!—alas! them too she could now behold. Sensitive, lissome, dark, beautiful as an apparition from the wilderness, the youth was sitting at the counter some three persons away from her, not unconscious, perhaps, of her regard, yet not the least attentive either. She had not yet glimpsed his eyes, for he was sipping through a straw a glass of fruit juice, and the lids were looking down. They were voluptuously fringed with lashes, black, luxuriant, regularly set. And they would be larger eyes, she judged, than any she had ever beheld. She waited, knowing that they would have to show themselves.

The youth's right fingers took the straw from his lips, and looking down with a gentle, curiously affectionate smile, as though he loved the glass too when he drank from it, he stirred the ice peacefully for a moment and sipped again. She had never *seen* anything so intimate— provocative! She experienced a quiet reeling of the senses. The youth, smiling still and with a slightly tilted head, lifted his eyes as he set the glass down. His eyes were as dark as two forest pools in the night; the whites, like flashes in the dark. And they were wide eyes—very wide indeed—curiously yet beautifully formed. They passed quickly over the ravished reflection of her mirrored face, as he placed a tip down on the counter, took his check, and made to rise. His eyes had swept lightly over the glass, that sweet smile upon his lips, greeting the reflection of her own with no more than a feather touch in their swift passing, yet she felt—She felt? She knew!—that they had perceived her. And that feather touch! It had been as though the hand of a lover had passed, for the first time, along her body. She had caught her breath, deliquesced into nonexistence: space and time collapsed. She broke clear, for a moment, into the fire reaches of eternity. But the moment closed. She recovered herself, still sitting at the counter. And she was looking, still, into the mirror. The youth was gone.

Lilian was so shaken she could scarcely extricate herself from the tall stool and break away from the counter. She was quivering, ghastly pale. She had a feeling she was going to be ill. Both the soda clerk and the dull woman behind the cashier cage at the door noted her case. They looked quizzically at each other across the width of the store and made a sign. The clerk rang up a check, placed it on the shelf beneath the glass bowl that held the tips, then began, with a look of boredom, to clear the untouched ambrosia away. The cashier made a notation, picked up again her nail file, straightened her movie magazine before her, and returned to masticating wearily her cud of gum.

———————◆———————

THE STREETS OUTSIDE WERE HOT. Lilian nervously fingered the green handbag, searching the active crowds, her poor nearsighted eyes squinting anxiously, totally heedless now of her effects upon the world. She suddenly spied a nimble form just disappearing into a bus. Her heart exploded: It was he! It was he! She waved frantically; the vehicle pulled away. Distracted, Lilian bounded to the curb and began running hideously along the gutter—stumbling on her high heels, quivering like jelly, her hands trying to retain hairpins, handbag, necklace, bosoms, stockings, and sundry streamers. When she came to the bus stop, she drew shakily to a halt, peering to see whether she could identify the departed vehicle among the blurring forms that swam before her vision.

Opening her purse, she drew forth a tiny lace-bordered handkerchief, with which to mop her overheated neck. Tears welling from her eyes had begun to spread her mascara. Her snood had been jogged out of place, and her hair was coming free. And some hidden structural element of her costume had been felt to give way, so that she did not know what mortification might next befall her.

A pleasant womanly voice called from close beside her. "What's the matter, Lilian?" A Ford sedan had pulled to the curb. Mrs. Wang was craning out the window from the wheel.

Startled to her senses, Lilian vigorously lurched her brassiere into place and gave a quick, futile pat to her hair. Bending to reply, trying to work a smile into the fearful spasm of her features, she gave greeting to the plain Jane in the car, eyes noting immediately that the woman was well on her way to a second baby.

The woman sweetly asked, "Can I help you?"

"The bus," said Lilian, "I missed it."

The woman pushed open the car door. Lilian ducked to enter, flounced into the seat, and settled, dabbing the handkerchief to her forehead. Then Lilian blew her nose and wiped beneath her eyes. Reaching across, her hostess slammed the door, and with a little jolt the car began carefully to roll. Mrs. Wang studiously shifted gears.

"Where are we going?" she asked pleasantly.

"The bus," said Lilian, "there is somebody on the bus."

The woman glanced at her with quickly measuring eyes. Mrs. Wang—Mary, her name was—had a plain round face with a healthy touch of tan, and washy blue eyes. Her body was soft and shapeless; her wash dress, printed with a faded blue tracery, hung to it without style. She drove very carefully, risking nothing. The gray bus was just visible, several blocks ahead; but whether they could ever overtake it in the city traffic was a wide-open question. Lilian chewed her lower lip, straining forward in the seat, violently fingering her green handbag.

When they had paused for their second red light, Mary ventured, "Do I know the person?"

Lilian, who had just torn a cigarette from her bag, shook her head in thunderous silence. Before shutting her bag, she took out her mirror, gave it a glance, and froze at the sight before her. Tucking the cigarette hurriedly back into its container, she began with all her soul to study the problem of the shattered features.

Her companion, undaunted, continued mildly. "I doubt whether I can catch that bus," she said. "Perhaps I could drive you to his...or is it a he?" With friendly archness Mary turned.

Lilian was working desperately at her face.

Receiving no reply, Mary shrugged, gave her attention again to the road, and drove carefully in what was now obviously a losing race.

"My god!" blurted Lilian at last. "Can't you step on this damn thing?" She moved forward and backward in the seat, like a youngster working a sled.

Mary only pressed her undistinguished lips together and bent a little forward over the wheel. Lilian had put away her vanity case and begun to tear efficiently at her garters. "Have you got a safety pin?" she demanded curtly.

Mary deliberately drew the car to the curb. "Lilian Copeland," she said with a firm and unemotional voice. "Who the hell—just who the hell do you think you are?" She shut off the motor, turned toward Lilian, and, leaning back, put her left arm on the wheel. Her elbow struck the horn. It hooted, she jumped, and Lilian started with an exorbitant look of fright. Mary again settled back, this time more carefully, as Lilian suddenly broke into a flood of tears. Mary let her cry.

"Oh god!" wept Lilian. She looked up madly at her companion. "I couldn't help...I must be going out of my mind!" Her makeup was again streaking. Mary studied her without comment. Lilian covered her face with her arms, sobbed, groaned, and tried to look away.

"Why don't you get married and give up your running around?" Mary asked. "Are you afraid you couldn't settle down to just *one*—Lilian, dear?"

Lilian, now weeping into her hands, shook her head.

"Philip has told me about his talk with you on the beach, that day of the picnic." (God! the voice—persistent, solicitous: it was a skewer rasping ruthlessly through her nerves!) "Philip says," the voice went on, "he thinks you're an idealist: too fine, too high-spirited for these islands, made for some bigger, richer world, like, for instance, Paris. Philip worships you still, in a way. But it's a way, Lilian, that doesn't matter a damn."

In amazement, Lilian turned. What she discovered was a calm, surprisingly hard unfriendliness in the washy eyes. They regarded her with a cruel repugnance. Lilian was so confounded, so out of countenance, she could neither hold to the woman's beastly gaze nor continue to look away. Blindly she fumbled to burst through the door, but instead of releasing the latch, she only turned the handle that raised the window. Thus trapped for a moment, she lashed back with her mind at the oppressor. With an air of measured thought, obviously in proud possession of the fruit within her womb, Mary continued, "Idealism, Lilian? I wonder. Where did you get it from, and where has it brought you?" Mary abruptly relaxed into a display of old school-chum solicitude, reaching to pat Lilian devotedly on the arm. "My dear," she said, "don't you really think there might be...you know, perhaps...some psychological answer of some kind? I never think of it as idealism anymore, you know...I mean, I believe the modern psychologists now call it something else."

"*Philip's* worship," Lilian was saying, incongruously replying to an earlier point, "yes, I can understand. It wouldn't matter a damn." Suddenly the door flew open, and she burst to her release. Her purse fell as she stumbled to the street. She stooped to pick it up and stalked away.

Mary reached to shut the door, then started the motor, carefully put the car in gear, and released the brake. The car jolted and began to crawl. "Bitch," she muttered, as she straightened her cautious vehicle into the road.

Lilian, meanwhile, was searching to find out where she was.

Mrs. Wang had deposited her on the corner of Abraham Lincoln Street, hardly three blocks from the rooms she shared with her mother. The young woman began to walk on her stilted heels like a giraffe, leaning anxiously at the hips, neck stretched a little forward; her earlier bearing gone. She passed the Japanese Buddhist temple, quiet now under the cool shadows of its kiawe trees, an exotic, pretty oriental structure, neatly carpentered in wood. The peaceful silence, the architecture too, helped to compose her mind, as she minced her way along the rich hibiscus hedges, under the shadows of the palms. No return to the office! No return, anymore, to anything! Her life had cracked and smashed, at last; let it go, let it go.

———————●———————

RETURNING TIRED FROM THE MARKETS, Lilian's mother discovered her daughter prostrate on the couch. "Why, Lilian!" she said. "Are you ill?" A black kitten with three white paws, sleeping on the girl's stomach, opened its eyes, stretching out its little legs, got to its feet, humped its back, and yawned.

The poor woman hastily put down her bundles and came anxiously to the weeping girl, who turned to her a face of agony. The animal hopped to the floor and, becoming engaged with a green fly, whirled off into a distant corner of the room. Mrs. Copeland placed her palm against her daughter's forehead, then felt her cheek. Lilian suffered the solicitude. When her mother left without another word to fetch a thermometer, she swung her feet around to the floor, pushed her hair back, found her handkerchief, and began to wipe her eyes and nose.

Mrs. Copeland returned, shaking the thermometer. "Open your mouth."

"Oh, *Mother*!" Lilian protested, but obeyed.

"Lift up your tongue," the woman ordered, inserting the instrument between her daughter's teeth. "Have you got it?" Lilian nodded. "Good. Now be still."

Mrs. Copeland glanced at her watch, then went over to her bundles, gathered them up, and marched efficiently to the kitchen. The kitten, spinning after the tip of its tail, came flying into the middle of the room. Lilian leaned forward and tapped the matting on the floor with her fingernails. The kitten, heeding the sound, instantly paused, crouched, stalked the fingers like a lioness, and pounced. Lilian caught it by the scruff and gathered it into her arms.

She was sitting, cradling the little animal, scratching its neck and rubbing her cheeks luxuriously against its fur, when her mother returned and plucked away the thermometer in her fingers. Tilting her head and swaying to catch the light, Mrs. Copeland said measuredly, "You don't seem to have any fever." Her anxiety apparently allayed, she regarded the girl critically. "Tell me, Lilian…have you had another of your quarrels with Paul?"

Lilian stood up impatiently, dumping the kitten to the floor. "How could I have quarreled with Paul?" she snapped. "We haven't seen each other in two weeks. Besides, it's midafternoon." She proceeded with indignation to a hanging mirror, and after a look, began to search for her purse.

The kitten now was rubbing its side against Mrs. Copeland's ankles. The woman stooped and gathered it into her arms with a series of gestures exactly duplicating those of her daughter only moments before. She rubbed the soft black fur against her cheek, briefly, with a distant look in her eyes, and then carefully set the animal down.

"I wish you'd pull yourself together, Lilian," she said. "You can't go on like this forever. There must be something wrong with your notions about what a young man ought to be. Paul was a perfectly splendid fellow. So was Dick. So was John Wilton. So was that Evans boy. So was Charlie Fitzpatrick's son. What in heaven's name do you *do* to them? What do you *expect* of them?"

Lilian, having recovered her purse and now working in front of the mirror, began to whine, "Oh, Mother!" But then she broke abruptly into a sharper protest: "Let's not start *that* lousy row again."

"Well, you're not going to be attractive to them forever," Mrs. Copeland said, studying her daughter's back from across the room.

"You'll be thirty in three more years." The kitten leaped against Lilian's skirt, clung a second, turned its head, then dropped to the floor. The girl bent to examine her clothes, smoothed them out, and returned to her makeup. "In a way," her mother persisted, "I can understand how you feel. I was late marrying, myself. But I must say, my dear, you're carrying this thing too far!"

"But *you* found *Father*," Lilian retorted with sharp petulance.

"Your father," Mrs. Copeland said sternly, "was very much like Paul when he was young."

Lilian wheeled indignantly. "Mother! How can you say such a thing?"

Mrs. Copeland held her ground. "Your father," she repeated, "was once very, very much like Paul."

Lilian stamped, and threw up her hands—one with the compact, the other with the handkerchief. She returned hopelessly to the mirror. "Paul is an unimaginative bore," she moaned. "He's no better than the rest of these pineapple heads. Pineapples, sugarcane, dollars and cents, golf, whiskey, and radio programs! God, do you want me to live the rest of my life with *that*?"

"Well, that's what *I* lived my life with," her mother snapped. "Until, that is, your father flew to rescue his dear daughter from the fine, intellectual society she had discovered in the East!"

"You did not," Lilian flashed in return, again wheeling and stepping away from the glass. "Daddy was not like that at all."

"He was!"

"He was not!"

"He was!"

"He was not!"

Mrs. Copeland was beginning to lose control of herself. "You never knew him as *I* did," she expostulated with a suddenly heightened voice. She had begun to tremble. Perspiration was breaking on her unappetizing, hairy chin. "You were his pet, his toy, his doll. You didn't have to *sleep* with him, as I did!"

Lilian exploded in amazement. "Mother!"

The two women stood staring at each other, shocked at what had popped between them. The older, after a mortal moment, tore her hat from her head and abruptly hurtled out of the room.

The younger moved reflectively to the couch and slowly sat down, and the kitten was presently again in her lap. There was silence in the place for a considerable time. Then water could be heard running in the kitchen, and then the clack of the lid of a teapot.

Lilian set the kitten down, gave it a pat, and arose. She walked to the mirror and adjusted her beautiful golden hair in its snood. She was looking very well now. All her poise had returned. Moving calmly, she gathered her things and tucked them carefully into her purse. She kicked off her shoes and went to a closet, from which she drew a sturdy pair with low heels. Then she looked at her dress and decided to change her clothes. Presently she was ready, in a light, pleated skirt and a colorfully flowered silken shirt. It was a pretty shirt, of Japanese silk, cut like a man's. She left it open at the throat. This was her rig for hiking. She transferred her things to another handbag, and then went to the door through which her mother had disappeared.

"Mother, darling," she called with a sweetened voice. "I won't be home for dinner."

She paused to receive the answer, but none came. The water was still running. Mrs. Copeland appeared from the kitchen, drying her hands.

"I won't be home for dinner," Lilian repeated.

Her mother lifted her brows. "Back to the office?" she asked with resignation.

"No," said Lilian, "I have to look for some…something I lost."

Mrs. Copeland scrutinized her daughter with a look of annoyed puzzlement. "Something you lost?" she queried incredulously. "What do you mean?"

Lilian tucked her new purse under an arm decisively and made to turn away. "Something very important," she said, "I have to find." She moved to the door. "I may be late."

"Lilian, you *can't* be late," Mrs. Copeland said, beginning to follow her. "Now, don't do anything foolish. There's the blackout: you can't play fast and loose with martial law."

The girl, having already flung open the door into the hall, turned on the threshold with a trace of tenderness. "Mummy, don't worry," she said consolingly, shutting her eyes, tilting her head, waiting to be kissed. The woman gave her a peck on the cheek so as not to destroy her lipstick. Lilian scampered down the stairs, then bounded away.

Mrs. Copeland closed the door. The kitten was again against her ankles. She picked it up and immediately set it back down, then walked to the couch and rested back in it with her hand across her eyes. Presently she had her tea, and after that, a lonely dinner on a slightly dilapidated card table; she sat up reading into the night, growing nervous after curfew and the blackout. At last, she dozed off to sleep, still sitting in her chair. Her beautiful daughter, that night, simply failed to return.

———————•———————

LILIAN'S QUEST BROUGHT HER FIRST TO WAIKIKI. That had been the destination of the bus, and she thought that perhaps her quarry might be resting on the sand. What she found, however, was an unprecedented spectacle: no languid sunbathers sprawling on the narrow beach before the big luxury hotels, no swimmers in the broad ocean, no surf riders or brilliant surf canoes—only two coast guard vans unloading gigantic spools of barbed wire, and scattered crews in dungarees strewing the vicious stuff along the shore. Lilian sensed an atmosphere of tension and hurry that frightened her. Sentinels, looking as though they really meant it, were roughly turning away stray loiterers.

Disoriented, not knowing where to go, Lilian presently found herself standing waiting for another bus. She had searched, without success, the lush lobbies of the three big hotels. She now felt hopeless, helpless, realizing that this odd quest for an unknown youth who had blasted her soul from her was to be the search, henceforth, of her life. On and on and on it would have to go—until she quietly went mad.

A bus drew up nearly empty, and she entered it, riding the short distance to the end of the line at Kaimuki. She got out and wandered up to a little hot-dog stand. Though she had not eaten a crumb since early morning and it was now well into the afternoon, she felt no pang of hunger. Abstractedly she gazed at the display of candy bars, smelling the fat smoke from the greasy griddle. A little old scrawny Chinaman standing beside her was carefully smearing mustard onto the two sides of a split roll, while cackling pleasantly about something in the news, talking to the waddling, black-featured barrel of a Portuguese woman who was drawing a cup of coffee for him, nodding somberly and interjecting brief remarks.

The woman ultimately set the coffee on the counter, stood back, and wiped her hands on a dirty apron and the perspiration from her mustache with the length of her arm. She turned to Lilian and, lifting her thick black eyebrows, inquired, "Miss?" She was chewing something.

Lilian, preoccupied with her own interior, was measuring the possibilities of future hunger. This would be the last food place for many a mile. After an overlong hesitation, she pointed to a chocolate bar. The woman opened the back of the glass showcase and reached in with a great air of seriousness. "Two," Lilian said. "No, three!"

The woman gathered up three, slipped them into a little paper bag, and handed this to Lilian over the glass showcase. Then, while wearily holding her heavy hand out for the coin, turned to resume her talk with the Chinaman, who was now attempting to fit one thick end of his savory purchase into his wizened face. Lilian handed her half a dollar. Still talking to the Chinaman, the woman moved to the cash register, rang up the sale, fingered the change, slammed the cash drawer closed, and then, while her free hand was snatching some salted peanuts which she tossed into her mouth, returned to drop the coins into Lilian's palm. The woman was wiping her hands again on her apron and moving with crowded mouth back to the Chinaman, when Lilian turned, tucked the chocolate into her purse, and stepped away.

What to do? Where to go?

Lilian thought of returning home, but the recollection of the conversation with her mother held her away. She considered traveling back to town, but a lone girl searching the streets at dusk…and the curfew…no indeed! She wished she might hike out to the little beach where she and Wang—long, long ago—had had their fateful conversation. But that was a very distant place, and there was no public transportation beyond the present point. Besides, the beaches were all heavily watched.

Lilian's feet took her away from the hot-dog stand and the bus line. With her bounding stride she passed through a drab little Hawaiian-Portuguese settlement like a fresh breeze. Kids were playing in the road, tiny children carrying still tinier ones on their backs. A few waved, a few pointed; Lilian greeted all with her smile, and soon she was out the other side.

She had never before visited this section of the island, the Palolo Valley. The hills, cutting back to the high mountains, were arid and rather bleak, but she found a pleasant little brook supporting a rich, dark growth of tropical jungle trees and vines. The stream charmed her. As a child she had frequently explored such waterways, stumbling through the rich growth to the head of the valley. They had always enchanted her, their dark, romantic fastnesses suggesting fantasies of the remote Polynesian past. She thought today that it would perhaps do her poor soul good to seek a moment's solitude and return-to-earth in the lonely, narrow little jungle of this inviting brooklet. Perhaps she would manage to collect her mind. She required peace. She required solitude. She required a simple, direct contact with the untroubled quietude of the elemental dark.

Lilian was very soon well on her way into the mysterious retreat. The lure of the waters, the thought of the remote, unknown head of the valley, carried her forward. She was alone, excited, even happy in this craggy, tangled, gradually darkening, thoroughly wonderful, increasingly fascinating wild retreat. Here was her dear childhood again. Here was the original wholeness she had lost: fresh life, young knowledge of abundance, no inkling of loss or defeat. And here, at last (not in the lewd streets of the cities), her glorious beauty was clean, her life was clean, her sex. Like a growing, lovely flower, a supple shoot, a burgeoning tree, Lilian knew that this, this lovely mountain-womb, was her home; the world to which her radiant body belonged was this living world of the bursting flowers and the trees.

Lilian climbed through the heavy vegetation of a precipice, clinging to various branches, finding crannies for her feet in the rocks. Strange birds were calling that she had never heard before. And she was aware of the deep silence behind the birdcalls: the universal, cosmic silence. It was the silence of the abundance of the soul. She began to feel that she was approaching spiritual harmony again. She began to know that there was reason for her to hope. She began to believe that if she could only fix this quality in her heart, she would understand where to seek her love and how to lure him. She came to the brow of the precipice, tired, hot, a little torn, but exhilarated. During the ascent, she had dropped her bag. It lay at the bottom of the cliff; she would retrieve it on the way home. Meanwhile, she would ascend the stream just a little farther, to return before dark.

Lilian peered through the treetops to the sky. There still was light. There would be plenty of time. The mosquitoes had not yet begun to fly. She would not be afraid of the forest in the early twilight.

Removing her shoes, she knotted them together and slung them around her neck. Then she drew her stockings off and, rolling each into a little ball, tucked them into the shoes. She dipped a toe into the water, then, kilting up her skirt, stepped carefully, gingerly, from her rock. She found her footing, and like a bird—like a beautiful white and golden long-shanked, miraculous, lonely wading bird—made her meticulous way up the stream.

When she arrived at a second precipice, higher than the first, Lilian knew that her adventurous ascent had met its end. A gentle, silver fall of water tumbled down to a shallow pool. She waded to the center, bent, splashed her face and freshened her arms; then, standing erect, she began to unhook the side of her skirt as she waded casually ashore. She found a cozy little place between the roots of a mighty tree, sat down, and prepared to remove, at ease, her clothes. She set her shoes down side by side, then pulled her shirttails out and began to undo her shirt buttons from the top. But scarcely had she come to the third when she realized that she was experiencing a queer premonition of somebody watching. She was going chill with dread. The fingers of her hands automatically, but furtively, reclosed the buttons of the half-opened shirt.

Twilight, she now perceived, had descended. The forest, formerly so wonderful, had suddenly become for her a dark haunt of questionable fears. Wild animals? There were none, so far as she knew, in these valleys. Nor were the old demons of the Polynesian days to be apprehended anymore. There had been rumors during the past twenty-four hours, however, of enemy parachuters lurking in these hills. Scattered shots had been heard, here and there over the island, the night before. Lilian was afraid to breathe. The mosquitoes had begun to hum. A light wind was stirring high among the trees.

Absolutely certain of a presence, Lilian groped for her shoes, straining every sensory nerve to search the noncommittal, peacefully standing trees, the hanging screens of green. She drew on and hastily hitched her stockings, donned and tied the shoes, and then, with her back against the tree, began carefully to rise. No question of returning home: another fifteen minutes and she would be unable to see. All she wanted was to be ready to shift her position quickly. When everything was black she would slip as quietly as possible to another shelter.

She was terribly afraid.

She felt now that she was the hunted—here, as in the city streets, only here with a vengeance. What if the covertly watching eyes should prove to be those of the hunted enemy: the hunted, himself now hunting? What violence might she then anticipate? No beauty anymore: her lovely wilderness was the place of primordial dread, the house of fear, of stalking. She had a momentary vision of a travel movie she once had seen of the game lands of Africa, teeming with antelope, wild ox, and gazelle: a billion eyes, watchful; ears, alert for the resounding lion roar; velvet muzzles nuzzling to crop, to drink, nervous ever, waiting for the blow of annihilation, the ripping gash of fangs. Her woman-body—the fruit, the beautiful blossom, the vivid form that was her joy and pride: Born to be here broken? Here to be left to rot? She would be dead, reeking like the abandoned carcass of a dog.

In the brush! A stir! Lilian turned, alert, to watch. But it was nothing. Nothing? Her eyes remained there long.

When she returned to her former position she was instantly startled to perceive quietly standing, only a few paces away from her, the figure of a man—a young man: the beautiful young man whom she had glimpsed that afternoon. Lilian beheld, in spite of the darkness, the details of his appearance. Indeed, the area just around him seemed to her eyes to be somehow a little luminous. Everything else in the wood was growing darker, yet this presence—this perfectly amazing, heart-shattering, soul-delighting apparition—was becoming momentarily more distinct to her view.

Head tilted, sweetly smiling, he was regarding her with serene eyes—or perhaps not quite regarding her; rather, it seemed his eyes might be brooding inward. They were wide eyes, beautifully formed. And the youth was clothed in a shirt, very like her own, of Japanese flowered silk. His doe-colored slacks were spotless and creased perfectly, as though he had stepped directly from a tailor. Beautiful, a bit dapper, very dark-complexioned, fascinating—there he stood. And he was decked with a single lei of white ginger blossoms. The blossoms were absolutely fresh. The lips—those wonderful lips again—were as impersonal still as bronze. The lips, the eyes: the eyes, she noted, never blinked. But whether it was her own presence or some mysterious, general, less-specific presence that the lips and the eyes were enjoying, she was at a loss to know.

"Is it not a little late," he said, "to be out scouting in the woods?"

Lilian experienced the crash of a suddenly severed stress, an inbreak of exhilarating joy. Though gentle, his voice was deeply resonant with a tone that profoundly resounded, breaking walls into her inner distances: a voice with the thunderous echoing beyond echoing of the roaring of a great lion! And as a gazelle can only yield and relax to the lion fang (with an ecstasy of sweet pain shuddering back to the original mother-dark), so Lilian at this moment yielded to the voice.

"What is it," he asked, "that you have come so far to find?"

The eyes remained unblinking, still half-brooding inward, but now she knew that it was she who was regarded, penetratingly: more destructively than she had ever been regarded before. She could feel that she was defenseless before those eyes, defenseless to the heart, defenseless to the marrow of her bones. Whatever had happened to her body on the streets of Honolulu was here surpassed: but to a degree! What was written on those eyes was not lust, not lewd desire, but satisfaction, full enjoyment. The youth was tasting, already tasting her, and with gratified delight. The young woman quivered. He was looking, watching, waiting for her reply.

Lilian's fluttering mind began searching nervously for its resources. "Uh!…I don't exactly know," she stammered. "I mean…" She hoped she could pull herself together. She looked away, first to the right, then to the left. But her eyes had to go back to him again. There was no longer any sense of danger. Wonder was the feeling that was besetting her: soul-pacifying wonder, mixed incongruously with a soul-ravishing desire. Lilian drove her mind to the task of reestablishing herself in her poise. She was attempting to force an attitude of playful, coquettish challenge. "How about yourself?" she managed to bring out. She tilted her head—as he had—and smiled. "Isn't this costume just a bit unusual for a forest ranger?"

The beautiful youth continuously regarded her with the look of one intimately enjoying the taste of a delicious mango. "I am not a forest ranger," he quietly replied, "but a divinity."

This unreasonable pronouncement surprised the girl but at the same time eased her mind. Somehow, its obvious absurdity precisely matched the incredible ambiguity of the entire experience. Something within her was believing (for there is always a level of human consciousness prepared to credit dream), yet her mind had no term to cling to. The word "divinity" exactly fitted her feeling of "the well known yet obviously impossible."

"Are you a real divinity?" she asked. "I mean, in *person*?"

The youth responded with good humor and a pleasant flash of his miraculous teeth. "That is a very subtle and technical question." He opened his hands, like a showgirl exhibiting herself. "What you are now seeing," he said, "is an understatement. My present form is an accommodation to your limited powers of understanding."

The magical eyes—dark, mysterious, beautiful—what were they? What metaphysical light ignited them?

Lilian succeeded in assuming an attitude of archness. "You find me limited?" she asked coyly.

The young man easily countered. "What were you afraid of just a moment ago?"

A little jolted, Lilian was stirred to a serious plea of self-defense. "How could I know that you weren't some kind of enemy?"

"What enemy?" the youth demanded in reply.

"Why, the Japanese," said Lilian. "Haven't you heard yet of the war? And you a god!"

The apparition, taking a step in her direction, plucked a twig from a nearby tree. It blossomed in his hand. "You are born," he said, "you are beautiful; you will dissolve. Blossoms flower and dissolve—everywhere. They are beautiful. So also the worlds." The petals scattered from his hand; a dead twig remained, which he tossed aside. "The heavenly galaxies—multitudinous, innumerable—burst and go; and you are as beautiful as they. For what is brevity, what is long endurance, in the reaches of the endlessness of time where all dissolves? And what is dissolution, since all is forever returning, ever anew?" Reaching, he plucked a twig; it blossomed in his hand. "This moment—now," he said, "with you!" The blossom broke, and again he tossed away a twig. "Are you the blossom," he asked of her, "or the life that burns it?"

Enchanted by this wonderful game, Lilian hazarded a guess. "Well," she said, "I suppose I must be the blossom."

"No," he said. "You are the life. You will never die."

And with that he advanced toward her. She immediately realized that she too was decked with garlands, all the blossoms absolutely fresh. Furthermore, her eyes, gazing into his, no longer blinked. There was an atmosphere, moist and luminous: a glorious collyrium that bathed not only her eyes but her heart. She felt curiously elated. "Oh my, oh my!" she said. "This is exciting! I'm beginning to feel very close to you. A little giddy. Do you mind?" Her voice was not as before but richer, smoother, sweet as honey. She felt quite equal to her man.

"Let me ask you," she said securely, "Why have you been haunting me? Why are you running about, accommodating yourself—is that the word?—accommodating yourself to my limited understanding?"

"I'm out on a little tour," the divinity replied.

"Then you are exploring?" she inquired.

He nodded.

"Exploring me?"

He nodded again.

"But why precisely me?" she asked. "And at this hour! Here! I should think," she went on, now very pleased with herself, "that you would prefer some beautiful, wonderful goddess."

"I have learned," he told her calmly, "that you are the Great American Girl."

She was alarmed.

"Furthermore," he continued, "this is the hour of the marriage of East and West."

Her interest, she found, had abruptly waned. She desired to run away.

"Hawaii," the youth persisted, "Hawaii, the world, is to be the marriage bed. I felt you needed me."

Lilian felt that this was an impingement on her privacy. Where had he learned these phrases? She decided to brush him off. "Somewhere I've heard all that before," she said curtly. She turned away and began to walk. The young man strolled beside her. She noticed that the ground they trod was no longer rough with rocks and roots, but glowed with a subdued luminosity; and its configurations, its contours, were not ragged but cleanly defined. The pool and the little, trickling fall were liquid, cool, purling fire of silver and blue. The precipice above was variously multihued, and the vegetation—abundant, overhanging, thick as ever—was dark, though distinctly visible. It was as though the idyllic pool which she had visited by the light of day now had reappeared to her in a dream, transformed yet recognizably the same, mysteriously eloquent of herself, and luminous with the fascinating secret energies of her own dream-creating, deeper consciousness.

She felt the youth, at her left shoulder and a step behind, as a presence supremely important to her yet for some reason terribly unwelcome at this time. She wished that he would relinquish her yet knew that if he did she would immediately dissolve into her own emptiness. She heard him speak.

"You need me," he said.

"Oh, I do, I do," her heart replied.

"Why is it that you need me?"

"Oh, my life!" she sighed. "The emptiness! You wouldn't understand..." Suddenly angry, Lilian turned on him and flared. "That's a horrid thing to say!"

The amazing youth regarded her as quietly as ever. The queerly unchanging, warmly alive yet annoyingly immobile regard, forever looking as though he were tasting her, intimately tasting and enjoying, rankled now into her womanly flesh, and she began to resent it with her whole being. "That oriental stuff," she said hotly, "just doesn't go in the West."

The youth casually plucked another twig. Nothing bloomed on it. He stuck it over his right ear, like a flower. "Hawaii is not the West," he said. "The world is not the West. Life is not the West." He smiled. She had to blink. The garlands around her neck had disappeared. "Life is Orient *and* Occident: the two in one."

They were standing on a rock, jutting over the phosphorescent pool. Lilian sat down. The youth moved a little away.

"That was a sermon," Lilian said, taunting.

"Not at all," he said. "That was the answer to your earlier question. That is why I am haunting you. That is why the bombs fell yesterday morning on Pearl Harbor."

"I don't see any connection," Lilian retorted.

"Think it over," he said.

She scrutinized him sharply. "You are Japanese?"

"No," he said. "Not exactly. Not in this particular form of accommodation."

"But you can excuse the Japanese for what they've done?"

"I can neither excuse nor accuse. I love."

"You love the enemy?"

"I love life."

"Life, though, you say is emptiness. You love the emptiness?"

"I *am* the emptiness," he said.

A bird sang. The glow of the surrounding forest increased. The purling of the waters became a sound of music. And from a high tree descended a brilliantly red, very large, broad-winged bird, long-necked, with yellow slashes on its wing feathers and tail, lifting a vivid yellow crest. The phenomenon fluttered to the little pool. No human eye, certainly, had ever seen such a thing before. It settled in the middle of the shallow basin, stilting on its long green legs; then it waded, craned, quickly darted its bill, and came up with a superb, wriggling, trout-like, flashing fish. It beat again its vigorous wings and with a long, harsh cry drew its legs dripping from the pool and made away.

Whereupon, as though every cell of the surrounding trees had become a little lighted room and every molecule of the earth a shining jewel, the entire forest became alight and gleaming in a blaze of innumerable, individual combustions. Lilian was astounded then to perceive, seated in each cell center, a duplication of the youth who a moment before had been standing before her. And everywhere was that perplexing smile. Delicate, graceful, seated in a relaxed, unstudied posture, with his right knee flexed to his chest and supporting a languidly reposing arm, the young man—now myriadfold—surrounded her. The illusion remained for but a fraction of an instant, flashed, and immediately burned out. Then the tropical forests were plunged into their natural darkness; the rock on which Lilian sat and all the rugged ground, the precipice, the trickling fall, the quiet pool were as though no miracle had come to pass.

Thoroughly dazed, pulse throbbing to the pounding of her excited heart, the girl sat exhausted, staring at the dark. Her dazzling companion had disappeared. So had her mind: all thought had been blasted away. She simply sat and slowly turned her head from side to side, not even trying to see. She began to realize that she was hungry. Mosquitoes were biting viciously, and there was no defense against them. She was very tired. She would have to invent some kind of protection from the insects and then arrange herself for sleep. She gave a slap to her left calf, brushed the length of her arms, and was wearily on her hands and knees in the act of getting to her feet, when out of the pitch black she heard, with a shock, that voice again. This time she nearly fainted from fright.

"An eyeless multitude of many millions of blind folk, not knowing the way, would never arrive at the city they wished to reach." She could not see the speaker in the utter dark. He seemed only a short distance away, perhaps sitting on another jutting rock. "But if there should be among that multitude of blind folk," he went on, "a single woman or man with eyes, then undoubtedly all would attain their destination."

Lilian, no longer strong enough to care, only tired, terribly unstrung, ready to be irritable, and desirous of sleep, let herself sit back on the rock, leaning heavily on her left hand, and with her right palm wearily pressed her forehead.

"Please leave me alone," she said. "You have frightened me enough."

The youth did not reply.

Lilian brushed her arms. "Divinities are out of date. I'm not impressed." She slapped another mosquito on her calf. "You're beautiful," she said with a tone of boredom, "and your tricks are pretty cute; but enough's enough!"

A number of seconds lapsed before the youth spoke again. When Lilian heard his voice this time, it had lost its supernatural, profoundly echoing quality. Harder, tighter, though pleasant still, it was now easier to locate in space. It proceeded from a point about ten yards down the stream, where she began to apprehend the presence of a tangible form.

"Divinities," the voice was saying, "are not entirely out of date."

The remark reminded the girl of her college days—the all-night sophomoric arguments. She replied with undisguised superiority, "Of course they are. Now go away."

But the youth persisted. "Millions in the Orient still believe."

Lilian cut back at him. "Don't be tiresome. Illiterates don't count."

There was a moment of pause, during which the girl congratulated herself. The youth's next attempt came from another angle.

"Do you ever go to church?"

"Oh, blaa!" said Lilian. "Of course I do. It's a fine old Christian custom."

"You are a Christian?"

"One could put it that way, I suppose," she said.

The invisible interlocutor asked, with an inflection of teasing amusement, "Well, then, suppose I were to tell you that I am a form of the Holy Ghost—what would you say?"

Lilian retorted with educated ease. "I would advise you to pay another visit to your psychoanalyst."

She heard a pleasant, ringing laugh.

"The Holy Ghost," she went on, delighted with her skill, "does his mashing in feathers, not tennis flannels."

The pleasant laughing simply ceased.

Lilian felt she had made a blunder. She was embarrassed and again annoyed.

"Did you not behold a bird?" the voice interrogated, with a baffling return to its earlier seriousness. The queer cogency of the absurd question jarred the girl with a little shock of fright. Then again the voice changed, and now she detected in it a distinctly threatening quality. What she felt (and this was the most terrifying fact) was no longer the slightest overtone of the earlier lion resonances but an undeniable affinity with the coarse lecheries familiar to her from the city streets. "Since you deny me as your god," the brutal voice was saying, "I shall be forced to come to you as a man."

Lilian bristled. "What! What do you mean?"

The voice threatened lewdly. "Three guesses."

She prepared to move.

"Do you not desire me?" the presence insisted.

The girl was afraid he had begun to approach. "Don't!" she cried. "Don't! Don't!" Then she lost her head. Uttering a shriek, she darted from the rock, stumbled, fell, and, striking a nasty jag of sharp rock, badly gashed her cheek. She heard again the pleasant, ringing laugh.

"Silly girl!" the voice was saying, "you will be seeking me again in another hundred years."

The instant of her swooning, she beheld, as in a vision, a great niche of light, golden in the dark. And within it there was sitting a variety of Buddha, holding a blossom extended in its left hand. The flower bloomed as she beheld it, and broke. Then the head of the exotic figure shattered, like the blossom, but another head immediately sprouted from the neck, bearing not a single face but three: one staring full upon her, terrifically, with blazing eyes unblinking; the two others facing away, one to either side. Before she could grasp what was happening, a second cluster of three faces sprouted above the first, and then a third above the second—a veritable pagoda, now, of heads; never had she seen such a horripilating sight! And oh, the eyes! The eyes!! The figure broke forth, suddenly, a mill of beating arms; and then a culminating head, with but a single face, exploded from the top. This last was the face of the beautiful youth whom she had loved.

Absorbed into the vision, her consciousness vanished into the void, and she was quenched.

3.

YAMATO-SAN, NEXT MORNING, early, entering the temple, set to work about the altar. A special ceremony in observance of the miraculous disappearance of the treasured bodhisattva had been scheduled for that afternoon. Committees of parishioners had held a great series of extraordinary meetings during the intervening forty-odd hours, and it had been decided that at the earliest opportunity, public and formal recognition should be accorded to the disturbingly indeterminate phenomenon. The bronze lotus stem, formerly held in the bodhisattva's left hand, had been permitted to remain, as Yamato-san had found it, lying like a long pipe stem across the heavier lotus bowl of the pedestal. And the tiara, placed by the miracle on the floor, against the wall just to the left of one of the doors, no one had yet presumed to touch.

Yamato-san puttered about the altar with a dust rag, performing the little tasks of the conscientious janitor, while his good wife, Yuriko-san—a chunky little old woman in a plain, neat work kimono, scuffing across the floor mats and chattering continuously to her spouse—made straight the remainder of the room. The two moved quickly through their tasks, each knowing precisely where the other would be every moment of the time.

When she had finished her fixing and dusting, Yuriko-san turned to the very special work for which she was particularly appreciated by the members of the congregation: her sensitive and always succinctly appropriate arrangement of flowers. A sheaf of selected twigs and sprays gathered by her husband were lying, wrapped in a newspaper, on one of the little lacquer tables against the wall. Pausing in her chatter, she opened the paper and studied the material. Yamato-san, having finished at the altar, came strolling over to her side. They studied the material together with occasional brief remarks; then suddenly her light flow of chatter resumed, and her husband turned away.

Lifting and studying the sprays one by one, his wife began her pretty task, while heavy-shouldered little Yamato-san, hiking at his belt, moved to the vestibule. He passed through the door. Almost immediately his wife heard a thud, as though something had fallen to the floor. She turned and called, but there was no reply. She called again. Setting the flowers down and calling anxiously, she shuffled across the mats. A sprig that had caught to her kimono jerked from the table a few sprays that trailed and detached themselves as she proceeded. She arrived at the vestibule, crossed the threshold, and saw her husband, lying facedown, breathing heavily.

A bodhisattva was sitting on the lotus. The flower stem in his left hand he was presenting delicately, almost girlishly. The tiara was on his head again, as though nothing had come to pass. And his bronze lips were fixed, as ever, in a gentle, strangely noncommunicative smile.

Member of the Hamat'sa (Cannibal) society of the Kwakwaka'wakw tribe (photograph, Canada, 1913 A.D.). Edward Curtis. Courtesy of the United States Library of Congress.

VORACIOUS

———————●———————

(July 11, 1945–August 6, 1945 & October 11–12, 1946)

I.

MR. AND MRS. HOPPER had been so proud of their son that it was no wonder they were deeply afflicted when he died. But their neighbors in the little Alaskan community where they lived were beginning to feel that the grief of the Hoppers was now moving to excess, and that if the bereaved couple would not, like all good folk, finally rest their sorrows in the Lord, something unholy would come of it. The Reverend Phineas Adams had even seen fit to make mention in his Sunday sermon of a sin which he aptly termed "the revolt against the manifest will of God"; and though he permitted himself no mention of names, everyone from the first pew to the last understood that as the representative among them of their Maker and Judge, the conscientious pastor had felt compelled to attempt to counterbalance the bad example of their respected elder.

Mr. and Mrs. Hopper approached the clergyman at the conclusion of the service. It was a generally gratifying and edifying moment when the great, rangy citizen, clasping his valuable ten-gallon hat in his vast left hand, deliberately turned his ponderous steps in the direction of the man of God and, stretching out his arm, solemnly shook hands.

"Phineas! Brother!" the great neighbor said, brows bristling. "That was a mighty fine talk."

He did not release the other's hand but shook it long, very firmly, then continued to hold it, giving it a shake from time to time. "Mrs. Hopper and I have taken a might of consolation from your words."

The Reverend Adams was a frank, astonishingly simple personality, direct and tactful, with not only a grasp of the part his community expected him to play but a power to enliven and transcend it; no one except Hopper could have thrown him into the position, which he now had to try to overcome, of playing his clerical role without one ounce of naturalness. For Hopper's storybook Americanism allowed no deviation from certain standard formulae of conduct that it somehow flung out, as if by magic, upon all those around. Hopper had been said to look like Abraham Lincoln, and though the smallness of his features would have disappointed anyone trying to find a duplication of the fabulous Republican, he nevertheless systematically enacted the stately part. It is very doubtful that even his wife had ever beheld (before this shocking blow of the death of their son) any thoroughly compelling symptom of a living man beneath his hackneyed role.

Orating, therefore, rather than conversing, Mr. Hopper held the clergyman's eye, and he was "Courageous, Afflicted Man" democratically exchanging words with the accredited representative of God. "The boy" said he, with a gaze of challenge, "was a genuine hero."

"He was indeed," the clergyman replied. "No higher honors have ever been awarded to a young flier."

"Yes," said the father, "and he had returned to take up his place at his father's side."

"The Lord giveth," said Phineas Adams stoutly.

"Yes," said the father again. The arm holding the conspicuous hat lifted, and the back of the sleeve absorbed a manly tear from the corner of the eye. "Now I know." He pressed anew the pastor's hand.

It had been a very impressive thing to see. The members of the congregation would have remembered it with piety to their dying days, had later event and conduct only confirmed it.

Mrs. Hopper was moved, at that moment, to advance her two hands and take her husband by the arm that was constraining the pastor. She was a tall, well-groomed woman, stately in her sorrow. She had always faithfully supported with tender understanding the solemn enactments of her not-quite-convincing spouse, bringing to his side a warmth of human bearing that gave a quality of depth to his trite presence. Her patient seconding of his tedious act seemed somehow to bespeak life's approval of the manly character that must underlie it—hidden from the common view. And so she distilled among his auditors a trust and sympathy comparable to her own—which, however, only redounded to the man's further conviction in his impossible role.

"Martin, dear," the woman reminded him, "Arnold was no longer very strong."

The beetling father did not relax his stare or permit the eyes of Phineas Adams to move an inch. "The boy," he said, "had been wounded. Half his intestines were gone."

"Yes," responded the clergyman, with a tone of honest and respectful realization, "we know." And it was he who now gave another tightening of the grasp and offered a glance exchange of courageous understanding. Mr. Hopper broke away. And the field was left to those others of the little frontier congregation who had been standing respectfully in rapt appreciation and now moved in to congratulate the shepherd of their souls.

But there was actually little ground for optimism: the case of the Hoppers had by no means been resolved. Douglas Hyde, the bookkeeper at the mine, continued to observe the disquieting signs of his manager's preoccupation. Every morning Martin Hopper would arrive on the dot of nine—as he had been arriving for the past twenty-five years—hang his characteristic hat on its peg, and then move with his well-known, eloquent silence to his rough-hewn worktable. Once there, instead of beginning to go through the papers piled before him with his customary slow but steady hand—controlling with exact efficiency every aspect of the operation of Raven Lode, one of the richest strikes of the great Northwest-Magnesium Corporation—he would now let his deep-gazing eyes become fixed to an unoccupied table just across the room from him, which he had prepared for, but which had never been occupied by, his son; and then an unconscionable time would elapse before his mind would be brought back to its affairs. That was all—that was all that ever happened; yet it was enough to begin to endanger the operations of the plant. Labor difficulties, un-adjusted at the instant of their inception, began to increase both in frequency and in seriousness, and the community grew to sense in them a threat to the general peace. For Raven Lode, employing some four hundred lusty miners of every race, nationality, and social prove-nience, would be more than the little town of Indian Hat could cope with if its affairs got out of hand.

One afternoon, Douglas Hyde suddenly left his desk, flicked his black felt hat from its peg beside the vivid ten-gallon affair of his "Chief," and on the pretense of an important errand, hurried out of the long wooden building, down the flight of rough wooden steps that zigzagged from the administration offices, to arrive, at last, at the rug-ged outskirts of the wooden town. Indian Hat was nestled in a great crease at the foot of a high-lifting mountain that rose sheer from the waters of its fiord to a sublime, gleaming brow of permanent ice. The walks of the town were of wood; the buildings also were all of wood. There was a dirt road, about six miles long, running around the bend of the hill to "the Nest," a cluster of relatively pretentious shingle resi-dences overlooking the water approaches; but otherwise there was no highway for the driving of a car. In the town, indeed, there were but seven cars, all possessed by the residents of the Nest. The other vehicles were the heavy trucks and vans of the lode. In the town of Indian Hat everybody walked.

Since the death of their son three-quarters of a year ago, in the middle of the winter, the Hoppers had remained in their place in town. Douglas Hyde therefore required only a brief brisk walk to arrive at their unpainted picket gate. A lean, excessively rigid, tight-lipped young man of about thirty, he mounted the steps to the porch, turned the old-fashioned bell handle in the center of the door, and

impatiently waited, glancing anxiously back over his shoulder to see
whether he was being observed.

A square-set Indian woman, of a distinctly coppery complexion
but a cast of features reminiscent of the Chinese, opened the door a
very little and stood inhospitably in the way. "May I s-s-see M-Mrs.
Hopper?" the young man demanded, with a bad stutter but an air of
businesslike dispatch. Perhaps recognizing him, though giving no sign,
the woman released the doorknob, stood back, and let him hurry in.
While he went familiarly to the living room, full of insignificant bric-
a-brac, worn stuffed furniture, and faded pseudo-oriental rugs, the servant, without hurry, shut the door and trundled up the wooden stairs.
Presently, the quicker step of Mrs. Hopper could be heard descending. Mr. Hyde had not yet placed his hat down when she came into
the room with a friendly smile but an inquiring tilt of the head. She
was a little taller than him and, dressed in her simple black, a woman
of noble and impressive bearing. Taking his hand, she expressed her
pleasure, bade him disembarrass himself of the hat, and showed him
to a chair. He was very obviously ill at ease.

She paused to let him deliver his heart of its secret, but when he
only fidgeted and fumbled, finding it impossible to break past the first
consonant, she lifted her brows. "Is it about Martin?" she asked.

He nodded and began very diligently to work on another syllable,
when the woman lifted her hand to check him. She nodded signifi-
cantly toward the door, where the Indian woman was arriving with
a tray of drinks. Mrs. Hopper directed her to place the bottles and
glasses on the table beside the guest; and when the two were alone
again—Mr. Hyde politely pouring Scotch into a jigger and his hostess
wishing only a touch—the tension cleared, and it became possible for
a conversation to construct itself between them.

"You should take him away," said the young man. "It's this
p-place—the mine, the town. God knows, we are all shut in here with
whatever we…w-w-whatever we…m—"

"Yes," said the woman abstractedly. She had set her drink aside
and was manipulating the wedding ring on her finger, sitting nervously forward in the heavy Morris chair, her elbows resting on the

wooden arms. "But Douglas, dear Douglas," she went on, "how can we do that? This place, his work, that mine—these have literally *saved* him. You don't know…"

"The c-corporation could assign him to another post."

"You don't understand."

She arose, went to the window, and then, turning abruptly, began to pace the floor, losing herself in a strangely compulsive soliloquy. "You know what it would mean to him to return to the States," she declared. "He was unable to face the thing when he was young. What would he do against it now?"

The tête-à-tête began to have the quality of a soul meeting, queerly formal and full of pretenses, not in the least erotic, yet profoundly instigated and of old standing. Douglas Hyde had provoked and witnessed such soliloquies before. Clearing his throat percussively, the young and very tense visitor lifted his hand to speak, expelling air through his tightened nostrils with a curious, characteristic snort. But the woman stampeded on.

"Martin Hopper was a broken man, a youth disillusioned about himself the moment he stepped out of engineering school and the first blows struck him. I loved him then, I love him now. And I have built him back into a man…this place and I have done it. Here he found himself, like a *real* American. Our great pioneers, Douglas Hyde, were men like Martin: men broken in the sordid cities, who took flight to the wilderness and there carved themselves a world."

Whether she believed what she was saying would have been difficult to judge. She was a magnificent woman, dark and regular featured, with a rich voice now filled with passion. But she seemed only to be rehearsing a speech that had been delivered with just these gestures and inflections many times before.

"Martin Hopper," the young man stated firmly, "is not a man at all. He is the m-m-m-makeshift of a man."

One would have thought that this should have jolted the woman like a blow; but again, it must all have been thrashed out between the two before. These were the opening gambits to a point that would presently be made.

"He had one great truth in him, Douglas," she continued, "and that was his love for his boy. Everything else was constructed, one might say, from the movies. It was all out of storybooks and his great ideas about who and what he was. But that love was real. It was the life of his existence, and it has sustained us to the brink of our old age. But that is gone now, Douglas, that is gone—" The woman abruptly broke into tears. "That is shattered too. What...what...?"

The two had apparently come at last to the unpredicted, and the youth sprang to his feet in concern.

"Oh, my dear Douglas," she wept, "I am living with him in his loss—even fostering his sorrow—because that too, that too, is honest—the only honest thing in our two lives..."

The upright, high-strung young man took the older, larger woman in his arms, like a birch supporting a leaning oak. Awkwardly he patted her elbow, and then attempted to reason forth his point. "But Mrs. Hopper," he said stiltedly, "Martin is beginning to lose his grip. Th-th-things are getting dangerous."

"I don't care!" she wept. "I don't care!"

"But we have to care," the bookkeeper stated stoutly. "This town's a powder keg, while Mr. Hopper thinks of nothing but himself and his personal loss." Then, suddenly realizing what he had said, he stopped, and faltered to apologize: "You don't understand."

"Oh, yes, I do! I do!" answered the wife desperately. "I know very well!"

There was a sharp clack outside at the picket gate. "My god!" Mrs. Hopper gasped. She pressed Hyde away and tried to dry her eyes. There came the thumping of great footsteps up to the porch. The excited young man turned for his hat, and then began to bow with his back rigid, trying to look as though he were concluding a business visit. When her husband's great dark figure loomed in the doorway, his eyes glowering from their rugged sockets with eagle-righteousness, Mrs. Hopper was tucking her handkerchief into her bosom, pressing her hair back from her blotchy cheeks, and preparing to confront him. The suddenly agile young bookkeeper made a rapid series of absurd remarks about "important considerations" and being "so pleased" and their soon "reassessing the matter," then hurriedly broke away.

Hopper disregarded the stuttering exit. Slowly lifting both hands to the broad lapels of his black coat and clasping them there, the Western fetish-hat still on his head, he placed himself in an inexorable giant-stance and contemptuously surveyed his confused wife from crown to toe. She endured the arrogance and, when he was through, courageously met his eyes. He nodded ponderously, decisively, melodramatically; and then breaking his stance, he tore the hat from his head, flung it onto a chair, pushed his hands into his trouser pockets, and began to pace the floor.

"Martin!" Mrs. Hopper said. "Don't be a fool!"

The man stopped in his tracks. "A fool!" he blasted. He turned to her. "You call me a fool?"

Compromised, the woman approached him. "Martin! Dear!"

"Don't!" he cautioned, holding out his hand as if in horror and backing away. He brushed against a rickety cabinet of bric-a-brac hanging on the wall. Something fell. He ignored it. He stepped forward, and the entire cabinet descended with a crash. He instinctively turned to see. Mrs. Hopper went to the clutter on the floor, got to her knees, and began placing broken bits of porcelain and glass in the palm of her left hand. "Martin," she said, speaking rapidly, but without lifting her eyes to him, "Douglas tells me things are beginning to go badly at the plant."

The man, for a moment disconcerted, did not reply.

She hurried on. "Perhaps you should have a little rest, a little change."

He broke into an affected, thundering laugh. "Fine reasoning, that! Just like a woman," he derided. "Things are beginning to go bad, so I should take a rest. Ha!" He stormed across the room. She continued to gather fragments with her back to him. He bellowed from the opposite corner, "Those goddamned sons of bitches!"

"Which sons of bitches, Martin?" she quietly inquired.

"Which? Haven't I told you a thousand times?"

She reached up and deposited a handful of the fragments into an ashtray on a nearby table. Then suddenly abandoning the project, she struggled to her feet, declaring, "I must call Anna to bring a dustpan and broom," and moved to the door. Her irate husband was left alone.

Dinner that evening, served by the Chinese-looking but coppery woman servant, was consumed in a lowering atmosphere of imminent catastrophe. What thoughts—contending thoughts—must have played behind the two incommunicative countenances it would have been impossible to gauge. The man sat stiffly, tore at his bread hatefully, masticated everything on his plate, and washed it down with ravenous gulps of coffee. Once he covered his eyes with his hand, while his wife covertly observed him with a measuring eye. Mrs. Hopper, on the contrary, ate practically nothing, only breaking things on her plate a little with her fork. The man perceived this but had nothing to say. Their eyes met only once during the meal and quickly sprang apart.

It was in the thick of this atmosphere of unresolved misunderstanding that the event took place which stunned and baffled the whole community, and which, if it is at all to be comprehended, must be taken as the inevitable cosmic consequence (somehow) of the distracted couple's overdriven grief. The terrific, completely irrational tension in the household may have operated to precipitate precisely at this moment the event toward which the powers of the two tortured lives had been for nine almost unbearable months irretrievably moving. How, indeed, explain it? The members of the little church later declared that an unholy miracle had come to pass, as a moral consequence of Martin Hopper's unabated "revolt against the Will of God."

In any case, the fact remains that after a dinner of weird silence, the couple returned to the living room, where Mrs. Hopper moved to get out the cribbage board. "Never mind," commanded her husband. "Not tonight." She settled in a rocking chair and became engaged in a sewing enterprise, while the man seemed to be more or less at a loss as to his role. He could only sit staring at a recently blank spot on the wall. After a very long period of this, he got up and stepped toward the door as though in a state of trance. Mrs. Hopper watched him depart. She heard his feet going heavily up the stairs, and presently, a door being opened in the upper hall. Then again a period of silence fell, after which her husband's voice, tight and sharp with fear, called out, "Elizabeth! Elizabeth! Come!"

Mrs. Hopper hurriedly set aside the sewing, and with a look of utter dread, got up and made her way through the door. She quickly mounted the stairs. Down the hall she perceived her husband's back, in the doorway to the room that had been Arnold's, their son's—the room in which the youth had died nine months ago. The father's back was immovable. Mrs. Hopper hastened down the hall and when she reached him placed her hand on his great shoulder blade, peering past his shoulder into the room. On the bed lay sleeping, as it had in death, the body of their boy.

_____ 2.

ANNA, THE SERVING WOMAN, gave the dreadful word of the event to her husband when he returned home late that night from a meeting of the Cannibal Society. In spite of decades of missionary labor—first Russian Orthodox, then American Protestant—the aborigines of this remote fishing community had kept their traditional social customs, rites, and superstitions pretty much alive. They still outnumbered the whites, nearly two to one. Their totem poles, standing along the waterfront just to the left of the docks of the salmon cannery like the masts of a gathered fleet, constituted a striking characteristic of the view from the fiord of Indian Hat and supplied a counterstatement to the machinery of the Raven Lode that was visibly cutting into the face of the supporting mountain. These obstinately sprouting poles represented the powers of a dark, image-ridden, timeless past. Through them loomed visible the ancestral, protective presences that nourished and sustained in this place the mysteriously motivated, very secretive race of land-rooted primary Americans. They seemed to challenge confidently the busily chugging engines at the opposite extremity of the town—as primordial darkness challenges the light world that has evolved out of it and must return to it again.

"Cannibal John" Baranof, Anna's spouse, was one of the principal figures of the flourishing Indian community. Supposedly a remote descendant, on his father's side, of the first great Russian governor of Alaska (Aleksandr Andreyevich Baranov, 1747–1819), he was nevertheless practically entirely aboriginal. And his besetting hatred was for "this white-ant race of usurpers," as he termed them: the "Americans so-called" who had swarmed across his people's continent from Europe; had swept and rooted out of the native soil every seed and sprout of indigenous life; had flung their successful machines across the plains, through the mighty mountains; and now had reached even to this formerly idyllic fastness of Indian Hat, here to rip the salmon from the mother sea with immense seines and to blast into the body of the father mountain with dynamite. "The old Russians," John Baranof would always say, sitting among his cronies on the wharf or on some sawed-off barrel top before the grotesquely painted wooden meeting house of the powerful Cannibal Society, "the old Russians were a better people: they respected us; they married us; they had dignity; they did not violate the land."

Furthermore, they were of Asia: that was the principal point for these Indians, though they never formulated it that way. The Siberian races and themselves, separated only by the Aleutian chain of stepping-stones, were of one deep spiritual past; and the later Russians, mingling with them, still were of Asia. Aleksandr Baranof, the old governor, had arrived in Alaska from the same direction as all the rest of John's remote progenitors. But the "white-ant Americans"—digging, blasting, pushing their noses into every cranny of existence—had come against both the Indians and the Russians. And from the "opposite side."

Or so, at least, insisted Cannibal John. This grizzly old hero of the native resistance—a stocky and square, very sturdy man of about sixty-five—physically resembled a certain type of Japanese. He had a short-cropped, black mustache—as had many of the old natives of his Northwest coast—and a complexion weathered to a deep and permanent tan. Clothed in Western garments but wearing over his shoulders, defiantly, like a shawl, a magnificent old Chilkat blanket, he came pushing into his home this evening, deposited a load of ceremonial implements, together with his shawl, in a heavy, curiously carved and painted casket placed conspicuously in a corner of his otherwise Grand Rapids living room, and then strolled casually into the cluttered kitchen where he and his wife ate, slept, and lived.

Anna, a little taller than him and much heavier, was working over the stove and did not turn to greet him when he arrived. He grunted something and went without hesitation to an unpainted kitchen chair beside the oilcloth-covered table under the darkened window. A naked electric bulb glared from the tilted ceiling, and a warm, comfortable odor of baking bread filled the fly-infested air.

A very long and, so to speak, basic silence ensued after the husband had settled in his chair. Anna continued her operations at the stove. No word of the meeting of the Cannibal Society, no greeting, no questions about the day. A quality of long-seasoned understanding pervaded the atmosphere, with each flourishing in the other's presence just as quietly and naturally as the moon and the sun.

Anna communicated, at last, the dreadful news of the day. "Arnold Hopper is back," she said in their native dialect.

"You see him?" the man asked.

"No."

She removed three loaves of bread from the oven, critically regarded each, and consigned the ballooning lot to a shelf. A tough-looking tomcat emerged, stretching, from an invisible corner; passed, leaning, across her heavy shins; and sauntered out the kitchen door. John pushed his black braided hair away from the shirt pocket over his heart, drew forth a little pouch of store tobacco, and began to build himself a cigarette. The long silence descended again, and the two continued at peace in the kitchen until it was time for bed.

A week later Cannibal John arrived at the Hopper house, ostensibly to present a fresh salmon to the kitchen, but actually to catch a glimpse of the mysterious youth who was said to have returned. The entire town was talking: folks in the Indian community, the white community, mining barracks, cannery offices—everyone. It was rumored that the young man was exceedingly delicate, had consumed not a morsel of nourishment since his return, shone with a dim yet clearly perceptible glow, and moved about in his parents' house without the least show of either interest or boredom. But no one had had an opportunity to see the youth—no one, that is, except his parents and Anna; and soon, Anna had told Cannibal John, the Reverend Phineas Adams, who would be present that night for the family dinner. Cannibal John managed to keep Anna talking while she prepared dinner, in hopes that he too might be added to that number.

Martin Hopper was sitting in one of the threadbare chairs in the living room when the doorbell clanged, announcing the arrival of the guests. He got up, went before a fogging wall mirror to adjust his large black tie, stood back glaring through his eyebrows at the reflection of his glaring eyes behind their eyebrows, lifted a rugged hand to his lank black hair, and gave his jacket a hitch at the neck. When the footsteps of the servant became audible in the hall, he turned and, clasping one of his broad lapels with characteristic solemnity, began to pace the ample length of the room.

He looked up fiercely as the friendly pastor entered the room, said, "Good evening, Martin," and advanced to clasp the tall man's massive right hand with both of his.

The host boomed, "Good evening, Phineas."

"Mrs. Adams is so sorry she couldn't come," declared the minister, with a polite grimace of regret. A head shorter than the host, he looked up at him with a certain flare of challenge.

"Mrs. Hopper will be disappoint..." the other ponderously began, breaking off as the woman's footsteps could be heard coming down the stairs. The two simultaneously turned to greet her entrance. She came in with her hand held out and welcomed their guest with honest pleasure.

The clergyman immediately warmed. He reminded her of the upcoming choir rehearsal—she remembered—and offered his wife's rue at being unable to come. Mrs. Hopper expressed her regrets and remarked upon the energetic woman's continuous services to the community. Chairs were located, and the three were just sitting down when the dinner chime was sounded. Mrs. Hopper's features betrayed a momentary exasperation; but since it was an axiom in the community that native servants could never be trained, the three arose without comment from the cushions they had scarcely touched, and after a brief square dance of exchanged compliments at the door, processed in proper order into the dining room.

The table was set for five; consequently, when only three were seated, the minister hesitated with a look of inquiry before tilting his head forward and reciting grace. The trio emerged from the prayer as from under water, smiled graciously at each other, and felt for their spoons. The meal began.

When due attention had been paid to the first spoonfuls of tomato bisque, Mrs. Hopper tilted her head to the clergyman at her left, and with an indicative nod at the empty chair and cooling soup dish directly across from him, said with motherly concern, "Arnold frightens us; he never eats. He has not taken a single morsel since his return."

The frank, somewhat boyish face of the guest grew a little pale. He lifted his brows and visibly controlled the expression on his countenance. Martin Hopper cleared his throat and without lifting his head continued methodically to dip up the soup. The guest, then setting his spoon down, studied the chair across from him, glanced anxiously at his host, and returned his attention to the unhappy woman.

"Is the boy not well?" he asked.

"He seems well," replied the woman, "but very strange."

"Very strange," repeated the father, "very, very strange." He did not look up from his work.

The Reverend Phineas Adams sat back in his chair and pressed the soup plate a little away.

The woman explained. "Arnold seems to have forgotten who we are. He is very kind, very sweet to us—many of his earlier, rather difficult traits have disappeared—but..." She paused, as if in search of a way to formulate the problem.

During the ensuing silence her husband finished his soup, set the spoon down, and wiped his lips. "Phineas," he said, leaning forward—there was an air of stern decision in his manner—"this young man is *not* our son."

"Oh, Martin! How dare you!" cried the woman.

He glared. There was a rattle at the kitchen door, and she controlled herself. The three subsided to an excruciating silence while the impassive servant very slowly gathered dish after dish, returning with each to the kitchen, then came out with the plates for the next course, and placed the roast before the glowering thunder-flinger at the head of the table. Obviously, the dinner had already been totally destroyed; it would have been impossible, however, to fail to go through with the whole empty shell of a performance. Anna carried in the vegetables. Martin carved with skill and dignity. Phineas Adams made the proper gestures and comments when asked would he have this and how much of that.

It was when the guest was beginning to ladle gravy onto his mashed potatoes from the boat held at his elbow by the servant that a step was heard above, on the stairway, and a light but firm descent. The minister, in an access of nerves, knocked the ladle against the side of the service and sent a great splash to the cloth, some of the gravy going to the floor, and a bit to his left trouser leg, just missing the napkin on his knee. The servant and hostess were impetuous to help, and he to fill the air with his apologies. Martin, who had already begun to eat the food before him, disregarded the whole affair. He turned for a moment to meet the possible entrance of the personage descending the stair, but when the steps turned away, in the direction of the living room, he resumed his forking of the food into his jaws, leaning over the plate and making no effort to cope with the predicament of his embarrassed guest.

When all had calmed, the servant having left the room and the semblance of a dinner party having been restored, Martin had gone pretty well through his meal. He pressed a last bit of roast to his fork and plastered over it a tasty compost of mashed potatoes mixed with gravy and studded with peas; but when he had this morsel halfway to the goal, he paused, regarded the fork a moment, then set it down. His mouth was still full. He chewed, poured in some coffee, then set the cup down, wiped his lips, and leaned very thoughtfully toward his guest.

"I repeat," said he, in a subdued yet magnitudinous voice, "the young man now in the living room is *not* our son."

His wife widened her eyes; he glared her down.

"You were with us, Phineas," he said, "when we opened the grave."

The woman shut her eyes.

Phineas set down his knife and drew a handkerchief from his pocket. Refusing to meet the other's gaze, he only stared with a look of incipient nausea at his plate, all the while patting his beaded lip and temples.

"The body was still there," the host asserted, "was it not?"

The minister had to nod.

"Is this some demon," Martin Hopper suddenly demanded, with an inflection of angry challenge, "that you have sent to punish us?"

The minister stared aghast. "I?"

"Martin!" his wife cried. "Don't be a fool!"

"A fool?" he retorted. He sprang to his feet, pushing back the chair. "This is the second time, my dear woman, that you have used that term—"

"Sit—down!" she commanded firmly. She stared at him. He jutted his chin. But the Jehovah wrath was forced to fade; and the man sat down.

The woman turned sensibly to her guest. "Mr. Hopper can hardly stand it," she explained. "The talk you gave that Sunday..."

"Phineas," interrupted the host, but now with a look of fear, "can you not explain?"

The clergyman turned from the woman to the man, met his eyes, then lowered his own to study the handkerchief as he folded it. He leaned forward thoughtfully, tucked the handkerchief into the back pocket of his trousers, and then took up his napkin to his brow.

At that moment, there was a sound at the door, and a young man came into the room. Dressed neatly in a suit of dark blue serge, he was slim, rather short, and very beautiful. His features were almost too regular and fine for a male, with his eyebrows gently arched and the parting down the center of his slightly wavy hair giving to his presence a character of absolute equilibrium and repose.

"Good evening, Mr. Adams," he greeted, coming around the table to shake hands. The minister hastily arose. "Very nice to see you again." During the gracious greeting, the two stared into each other's eyes, the youth calmly, the clergyman with an air of professional inquiry.

"Won't you sit down, Arnold dear," the mother said, as though speaking to a delicate invalid, "and join us for a bit of dessert and coffee?"

The youth smiled and without a sign of unkindness replied, "Thank you, no. I was just crossing through to visit with Anna for a while."

The father and mother exchanged a glance. The minister controlled surprise. When the youth had passed from the place, Martin Hopper flung his napkin on the table, rose to his feet with a savage curse, and stormed from the room. Elizabeth Hopper, meanwhile, had broken into tears.

Phineas Adams considered his plate. After a time, he reached and took the woman's hand. "There, there," he comforted. "There, there." But he had no word of hope or consolation for such an occasion.

Mrs. Hopper eventually pulled herself together and declared they would take their coffee and dessert in the next room.

"Oh, nothing for me," he said.

"Please, Phineas," she said, "we must."

He studied her eyes; she met his regard; they forced a smile.

"Very well," he consented.

She clapped her hands, and Anna appeared at the door. "We'll have our coffee and dessert in the living room," Mrs. Hopper said. The servant turned and departed, the door swinging-to again at her heels. Mrs. Hopper and her guest removed themselves to the room across the way, where Martin was standing, staring at a blank space on the cluttered wall.

Within the kitchen, Arnold sat at ease on a table, kicking his heels back and forth and suffering with good humor the long and serious scrutiny of Cannibal John. Anna went to the percolator and poured the coffee into a silver pot that she set on a tray.

"But you do not shine," said the Indian.

The youth smiled. "That was only the first few days."

Anna opened the icebox, took out the cream, poured a little pitcher full, returned the bottle to the icebox, and slammed the door. She arranged the cups and sugar on the tray.

"Have you started to eat?" her husband asked.

The youth shook his head.

"Would you like to?"

Arnold shifted his position and leaned a little forward. "Why, of course...of course I'd like to eat."

"I can help you," said Cannibal John.

Anna, lifting the tray on the palm of her left hand, balanced it with her right, backed against the swinging door, entered the dining room, made her way carefully around the abandoned table, and approached the company across the hall. Mrs. Hopper was clearing the end of a long table, making ready for the tray. When Anna arrived she assisted her and began to give instructions for the preparation of the arrangements for dessert.

The two gentlemen were earnestly talking by a window, the clergyman pressing an attack: "You've got to take a liberal attitude, Martin. We just can't expect to dictate to our children. This is a period of transition—trial and error. The older order is giving way to the new."

Martin Hopper, leaning like a gallows over the perky face scolding up at him, was wagging his stubborn head. The first moment the other paused, he retorted, "God dammit, Phineas! You're as bad as one of them sons-of-bitches agitators." Behind his molasses drawl was a compacted pressure of fury. "I never thought to hear the likes from a man of God."

Phineas backed away, Hopper remaining close upon him. Then the pastor halted and began to advance, and Hopper backed away. As Anna left the room, Mrs. Hopper called to them, "Dessert will be along in a minute. Would you care for your coffee now?" The serving woman pushed her way into the kitchen and discovered Arnold and her husband on their feet. When she entered, both turned to her.

John Baranof rubbed his left forearm with satisfaction. "The young man is coming," he said.

She proceeded to the sideboard and put down the tray. "Where to?" she asked, opening the cupboard for some plates.

"The medicine lodge," he answered. He turned to the young man and winked.

Anna went to the window for a large pie that she had set to cool. "Why you going there?" she asked her husband.

"To learn to eat," he said.

She placed the pie on the tray, and then turned to confront him squarely. "You wouldn't do that," she said, looking directly into his eyes.

"Of course I would," he responded. "Why not?"

The young Arnold sat up on the table again, wagged his legs, and watched.

The woman said to her husband, "That would be bad."

He shook his head. "Not bad," he said. "Good."

The two held each other's gaze.

Then the woman turned, gathered her tray, and, as she backed against the door, paused to study the young man. He met her eyes and smiled.

"You will go?" she asked.

He nodded.

She shook her head regretfully, backed out the door, and stepped away.

John took the young man by the arm. "Let us go. Now is the time," he said. "You got a coat?"

The youth sprang lightly from the table. "I shan't require a coat."

"How do you know?" the man protested. "You never been out of the house."

The youth patted him on the back. "Come on, grandfather," he said. "We must be off."

Without further ado, arm in arm, they went out by the kitchen door into the lingering twilight. John was a bit the taller, very much the sturdier, and he walked with a heavy tread. They took a shortcut through a series of backyards, so as not to expose themselves to the front windows, and when they reached one of the wooden sidewalks, turned downhill toward the waterfront.

"Tell me more about this Cannibal Society," said Arnold. "Do you eat men?"

"Not men," answered his guide and companion, "spirits."

Arnold lifted his delicate brows.

John laughed. "Don't be afraid," he said.

When the pair reached the salmon cannery, they swung to the right and headed into the Indian section. The first sign was a slight increase in the number of dogs. Unpainted wooden buildings along their left backed onto piers that reached across littered flats to the languid ripples of an ebbing tide. Rowboats and motorboats at the ends of long tethers lay on the mud amidst debris. John saluted by name some of the people resting on the wooden stoops or now and then crossing the darkening street. Here and there the sound of a radio emanated from a lighted window, but on the whole, there was little noise. The atmosphere was that of a village already settled in for the night.

When they came to the last of the houses backing onto the piers, John tightened his grip on Arnold's arm, led him to the door, and knocked. They waited hardly a moment before the door swung open to a little lighted room, with a store counter along the back of it and a show of groceries set about on disorderly shelves. A handsome girl with a round, dark face set like a flower on a stalk-like neck smiled prettily at John as she shut the door, then glanced at his companion and became lost in the contemplation of his eyes.

"Father in, Mary?" John asked.

She did not hear. Arnold suffered her stare for a moment, then turned, without rudeness, and cast his eyes about the shelves. John advanced to the counter, leaned over, and called to someone through an open door. He turned again to observe the youngsters. The boy had gone to the grocer's weighing scale on the counter and was examining the brass tray. The girl was absorbed in him, without consciousness or shame. She was very slim, dressed in black sateen. Her high heels made her a little taller than Arnold. John Baranof watched her sweet flower-face in its rapt absorption, and his heavy features smiled with fatherly understanding.

A big fat man came through the door and stood behind the counter. His hair, like John's, was in braids. He knocked with his knuckles, John turned, and after a brief, guttural conversation, the fat man waddled out the door again. John went over to the Indian girl, took her arm, and patted her cheek.

"Arnold," he called to the youth, "this is Mary, my niece."

Arnold turned from the grocer's scale, smiled, bowed politely, and approached. The two young people shook hands. John left them to invent a conversation when the fat man came out to the counter again, slapped a handful of meat down, ripped a length of paper, wrapped the parcel, and handed it over to him. The two Indians gave Arnold a long, measuring look and exchanged a knowing wink. Then John's grip was again on Arnold's arm, the girl backed a little from the swing of the door, farewells were exchanged, the door was closed, and the two adventurers were back on the street.

They made their way toward the great lodge of the Cannibal Society, situated a little way into the woods, just beyond the Indian graveyard, where the fresh-painted heraldic figures on several new totem poles loomed like mythological monsters. It was nearly dark, but John required no light; he knew the way. A gentle drizzle began to fall. They followed a footpath halfway around the cemetery enclosure and then up a considerable stream into the woods. By day the cries of calling ravens filled this spacious grove; but now there was only the sound of moisture dropping from the trees and the ripple of the stream.

The lodge, standing in precisely this position since the remotest times, was constructed of immense planks pegged, lashed, and nailed to a frame of prodigious beams. The facade was grotesquely painted with a strangely stylized portrait of the Cannibal Demon, who was the patron and guardian of the place. A towering totem pole stood slightly to the side. The entrance was a low door.

Bending over, John and Arnold entered. They were alone within.

"Come over here," John said. "We have to make a little fire."

Locating a cache of firewood stacked beneath one of the benches

along the wall, John built a small fire on the dirt floor. The smoke
rose toward the lofty, invisible ceiling, as the flickering flames tried
in vain to illuminate the gloom. The lodge was simply enormous: its
nether regions could not be seen but only sensed as a vast area of utter
stillness.

"Here," John said, handing the package to Arnold. "You unwrap
the meat while I go get a spit."

The man stood up and walked off, leaving the youth alone.
Arnold undid the package, smelled the meat, and set it down. Then he
sat, waiting, gazing into the flames and refreshing them from time to
time with little sticks of wood. The wait dragged on. Arnold lifted his
head to search into the darkness, heard a clattering sound behind him,
and turned. He beheld, just coming into the range of the firelight,
flickering through the shadows, a curious bird-like form on human
legs. The head was very large and vividly painted, the body of decorated cloth or hide. The wings were like arms; one of them carried a
little drum, the other an iron spit.

"Well," Arnold said, "I thought you would never come."

The birdman sat down with some difficulty and, handing Arnold
the spit, told him he should thread it into the meat and set it to broil.
Arnold did as he was bid. The other began to tinker with the drum.

"What kind of meat is this?" Arnold asked.

"Whale."

They remained in silence. The meat began to sizzle.

"You will find it hard," said the birdman, "but you must swallow
the first mouthful. After that, you will find it hard to stop." Holding
the drum to the flame to tighten the head, he added, "Don't mind the
little song that I will sing. It's just an ancient custom."

Arnold turned the spit, and after a while, his companion pro-
nounced the morsel done. The birdman took the meat on his knee;
then he reached under his bird mask and fingered around in his hair
until he located a little scab on his scalp, which he carefully lifted off
with his nail and placed on one corner of the steak. "Eat this corner
first," he said, handing the meat to Arnold. "Don't be afraid."

The delicate youth took this corner into his mouth and bit it off.

The old man began to beat the drum and sing. Arnold chewed hard for a considerable time, but at last shook his head and deposited the chunk into his hand. John stopped. The youth smiled at him. "I just can't," he said, staring at the half-masticated chunk of whale meat.

The birdman leaned forward and studied Arnold, studied him a long time. Even in the dim firelight it was apparent that something had begun to happen to his features: they were beginning to lose their regularity.

John sat back and began to remove from his head the great wooden bird mask. "Don't worry, my dear grandson," he said. "I think it will be all right. I think we can take you back to your house now."

 *3.*

ARNOLD AWOKE IN THE MIDDLE OF THE NIGHT with an unbearable gnawing in the pit of his stomach. He remained awake—tossing miserably from side to side, stomach to side, side to back—the sheets gradually bunching into ropes. Finally he understood that it would be impossible to go back to sleep because the demands of his immense hunger had to be satisfied. He unsnarled himself, got up, and, glancing in the mirror over his washstand, noticed that his features had queerly altered. Their fineness and symmetry were gone: one whole side of his face had dropped, so that his left eyeball hung low at the outer corner of the socket, and his mouth was pulled awry. He then discovered he could not focus both his eyes at once, but had to shift from one to the other, turning his head from side to side like a bird. As he studied his lopsided countenance—peering now with this eye, now that—he found the visage, on the whole, rather humorous: comical and melancholy, at once. He smiled; the face in the mirror smiled, the mouth drawing askew in a concupiscent leer. He laughed; the crooked mouth sprang open, and the odd physiognomy laughed and laughed. This was certainly the funniest miracle of new companionship in the whole wide world.

Arnold was thoroughly, honestly, delighted; for while his former state of equilibrium had not in the least irked him, Anna's curious work in the kitchen had suggested to him something interesting about the nature of living flesh to which his cool balance had not exactly corresponded. And while his perfect poise had never been troubled by the least suspicion of its own deficiency, now that it had been dissolved, and he himself transmuted into this leering image of ravenous need, he was filled with a strong and wonderful joy: time broke out in a vista before him, and he knew—he perceived—that a world of amazing developments lay ahead of him, lay ahead of that fellow in the glass. And he laughed: the crooked little fellow in the mirror—hungry, comical, and melancholy—laughed, delighted with this sudden precipitation of a destiny.

As he dressed, pulling on a pair of flannels and an open shirt, he reviewed briefly the event with John, and in his agitated mind he tried to imagine what miracle of silly magic might have brought to pass the circumstance of his present, life-eager metamorphosis. The warm juice had gone down his gullet; perhaps the dirty seab too. He had felt at the time neither revulsion nor delight; but now he knew that in that moment he had taken into his system the infection of the world. And what he had there tasted slightly, his hunger now demanded he ravage to the full—if full there could ever be, for his own flesh was already being consumed by the ferocious starvation fires within: his ribs now corrugated his chest, his belly was cavernous, his eyes glazed, his teeth aflare. Arnold sat on his bed and stooped hurriedly to tie his shoes. Then he arose, dashed out his door and along the dark hall, trotted lightly down the stairs, expertly flitted through the darkened dining room, negotiated the swinging door, stepped into the kitchen, and turned on the light. Then he opened the refrigerator, took out the remains of the roast, rummaged about in a drawer until he found a carving knife, drew up a chair, and settled rapidly to work.

For the first two hours, taste was less important to him than bulk. He inhaled the roast, sucking every scrap of meat from the bone. This gave him a sense of having gotten under way. Then he again opened the icebox door and removed two bottles of milk, a bowl of cold mashed potatoes, some peas, the raw salmon that John had delivered, the leavings of a roast duck, a bowl of soup stock, two bananas, a cup of bacon fat, half a pound of butter, and three-quarters of a bottle of cream. These victuals kept him busy until the first light of dawn. He went next to the breadbox, where he found the remains of the pie, two loaves of bread, and a number of rolls. After swallowing these baked goods, he started to feel appeased and began to take notice of the varieties of taste. By the time his mother appeared, he had cleaned the cupboards and was experimenting on the bins of cornmeal, coffee beans, and flour.

The woman stood appalled. Arnold regarded her and smiled—the new, leering smile of his oddly disordered physiognomy. "My child!" she exclaimed. "Have you been taken ill?"

Mrs. Hopper hurried to him. He felt her warm hand pressing to his forehead. He had never before taken note of such a sensation, of another touching him, and for a moment he was overcome with poignant solitude; but then, strangely enthralled by the crisp-laundry aroma of a delighting presence, he reached and gathered her hand into his own, ran his palm up her smooth arm, drew her head down to his lips, and kissed her. Startled, she recoiled; but Arnold continued in mounting eagerness, pressing closer, clasping her mouth to his, until she broke away, exclaiming, "Arnold! Are you mad?"

The sea of queerness that enveloped his head, flooding his senses, left him unable to grasp what had taken place or to formulate a response. He was alone. The woman had disappeared. He stood still and soon began to be filled with a considerable sense of pleasure and of lively expectancy. With a laugh, he turned again to the flour bin. Suddenly the door crashed opened, and the towering figure of his irate father appeared. The man advanced, thundering, "You confounded devil!" He seized him by the neck, gave him a bash across the eyes, and flung him to the floor.

Arnold rolled against the kitchen table. Mrs. Hopper, who had reappeared, was crying, "Don't! Don't! You'll kill him! Our own son!" Lying in a heap, quite stunned, the son felt a storm of wrath mounting, banging at his mind. His mother was trying to press her angry husband out of the kitchen, when the back door of the house opened, and Anna, the serving woman, stepped in. Just then Arnold, furious and blind as a mad cat, sprung up, made a quick dash, and leaped at the head and chest of the man who had struck him. The entire family—father, mother, son—toppled to the kitchen floor.

Anna must have understood that there was some relationship between this scene and the thing that her husband had done the previous evening, for with celerity altogether alien to her, she turned quickly, dashed down the steps, and hurried across the yard toward the back of the house next door. The morning was a chill, dreary envelopment of gray cloud and drizzle, such as is common in northern latitudes. Rain had fallen throughout the night and would probably continue for the next few weeks—giving place, at last, to the snows that would soon descend upon Indian Hat, isolate the town on its fiord beneath the mountains, compress the inhabitants in upon each other, and send the bears to rocky dens. Yet already the perceptible aspect of the town was of an indrawn, somewhat secretive, way of life. Many of the house windows were lighted, but there was little traffic on the wooden streets: only a passing of stray figures along wet walks and a steady filing of men up the zigzag wooden steps back of the town to the entrances of the mine. A few stragglers of the fishing fleet were wagging their masts languidly at the docks, and beside the cannery wharf, a great purse seiner with its broad, empty deck, rolled on the tide. Somebody was boldly rowing a little peapod of a boat from the piers of the Indian section into the open fiord.

Anna, with her alarm of havoc, stumbled hastily through this scene of arctic peace, first disrupting the quiet of the family next door. Arriving at their kitchen window, she beat on the glass until an eager, blonde girl of about twenty turned with her dish towel, spied the frantic Indian face, and flung up the pane. Anna cried out, "The men! Arnold Hopper crazy! Get the men!"

Whether or not the girl quite caught the import, she quickly turned, and Anna quit the window to scuffle through the rain toward the stoop across the way. Everywhere squawking gulls were dropping like sandbags into the water and beating out again like ducks, winging occasionally over the hills or hopping like robins around the garbage

cans in the backyards. Very soon the neighboring houses began emitting their inhabitants. Telephones rang in the remoter parts of town.
Front, back, and side entrances of the Hopper home were assailed, a
rush of strenuous arms broke in, and an end was made of the hideous
spectacle on the floor: old Hopper on his back, black in the face, gasp-
ing; his son like a mad animal at his throat; and his wife, clothes torn,
hair streaming, face and arms bloody with bites, desperately trying
to wrestle the youth away. No one had ever seen or heard of such a
fracas. The women stood in horror and received the shattered mother
into their ample arms. The men, gaunt for the most part, vigorous and
sinewy, were divided into two galvanized groups: one overmastering
the son, the other working feverishly to restore breath to the wheezing
father.

The astonishing sequel was that as soon as Arnold's grip on Martin
Hopper's neck was broken, and he was carried to a distance, the curious little youth, head tilting like a bird's from side to side, simply sat
and observed with inoffensive curiosity the company of rugged citizens hemming him in. Across his nose was a cut where the first terrific
blow had caught him and his shirt was torn from one shoulder, but
otherwise he was fit; moreover, the feeling of hunger had again begun
to gnaw. As he watched the milling confusion in the kitchen, people
gradually became aware that the storm had passed. The majority, finding themselves superfluous, straggled away to their respective occupa-
tions, for most of the men had time clocks to punch somewhere. The
women—a capable, sturdy group of many ages, not unused to sudden
catastrophes and unexpected calls—had transported Mrs. Hopper to
her room. Talk would go on for days to come—as it was even now
being rehearsed to the latecomers, still arriving at the door, looking
anxiously in, and lingering to be told. The event itself was over. The
stories, however, were already so numerous and conflicting that nobody could be certain of what had really come to pass.

Anna, after alarming the first few neighbors, had pressed on down
the street and back to her home in the Indian quarters. Martin, after
some twenty minutes of rescue operations performed by skilled though
rugged hands on the dining room floor, was on his feet, dignified and

tall, declaring to all within earshot that he would have to be hurrying soon to his office at the mine. The neighbors—husky men, not malicious yet long familiar with the sudden way of the fist—were quick to comprehend: he was doing everything within his power to play down the scandal.

At Martin Hopper's arm was the stuttering bookkeeper, Douglas Hyde, who had arrived late from his distant boardinghouse, but not too late to assist his employer to his feet. For the first five minutes after his resurrection, Mr. Hopper had disregarded his faithful servant; but now he turned to him with the air of a general about to bestow a mighty trust upon a rigid and attentive adjutant. "Douglas," he said, his voice still rather shaky but his manner well in hand, "I want you to take charge here while I hike up to the lode."

The young man started to reply but became snarled in a stutter—eyes blinking helplessly, neck and back very stiff—while two others in the surrounding company broke in with protests and advice.

"Hadn't you better just take a rest?" counseled a massive, mountain-seasoned yet professional-looking bald man of about fifty, with gray, quiet eyes and three fingers missing from his right hand. He took Martin kindly by the elbow, while an agitated, sallow, cadaverous face craned forward and asked brusquely, with a German accent, if Martin meant to abandon his home and wife to that phenomenon in the neighboring room. Martin replied that he'd been told the boy was subdued.

"Yes, sir, he is," declared a flat-nosed, wiry-headed little man with a red goatee. "I never seen a more milder, tamer looking sparrow since the day they put the diapers back on Pa."

That got a laugh, which released the vocables from the honest lips of Douglas Hyde. "M-M-Mr. Hopper," he stammered, "I think the boy should be locked f-fast in a room."

Towering Mr. Hopper slowly came about to face him. "Douglas, you're dead right, there; dead right." He thrust an indicative finger at his young adjutant's chest. "See him up to his own room and bolt the door."

The faithful bookkeeper started to say something else, and the rough company hung suspended while he battled to bring it forth. "M-Mr. Hopper, I m-m-must s-s-s-say I think you're correct about the n-n-need for you today at the office."

The great man nodded, his brows beetling and a regard of dark seriousness clouding his somewhat unconvincing face. After a moment's consideration, he left the dining room, surrounded by his convoy of friends.

When he paused in the front hall to remove his ten-gallon hat from the antlers mounted beside a large cupid and acanthus–framed mirror, Janet Strobe—blonde, agile, and alert, the nubile girl from the house next door—came tripping prettily, with the grace of an athlete, down the stairs. The great leader, towering over his company, turned. "Mrs. Hopper doing okay?" he asked.

The girl stopped on one of the lower steps and held picturesquely to the banister, obviously aware that a group of males was appraising her trim physique yet more obviously confident that none would discover anything undesirable. She was clearly competent to face, satisfy, and treat with asexual ease the brotherhood of men.

"No, Mr. Hopper," she replied brightly, "your wife is ill."

The great American seemed a little annoyed. "But she is in good hands," he suggested quickly.

Something humorous flashed in the girl's eyes, but she replied without a trace of a smile, "Oh, yes, Mr. Hopper!" Taking another step down the stairs, she added indifferently, "I don't think you have to worry."

The great husband reached for his hat. He corrected the dent at the top. "Well, Janet," he resumed, not lifting his eyes, "you take good care of the little woman till I come home." She had reached the floor and the men were respectfully making way, but the rigid Douglas Hyde had begun to move in her direction. Janet paused while Martin completed his commission. He was now looking at her with a melancholy seriousness. "Lizzy's the most precious thing in the world," he said. "She's a might of comfort to a man." He began to turn, and to lift the hat. "I know I can trust you," he said, "with her care."

"J-Janet," said Douglas impulsively, "is she really ill?"

The hall had begun to clear. One of the company—an elderly but sturdy, barrel-shaped fellow with a square, gray beard—suddenly discovered that he had left his coat. He turned and searched the walls and chairs of the hall with keen blue glance, then went heavily pushing, against the current of the company, to the living room door.

"Mrs. Hopper," Janet said to the anxious young man before her, "has suffered a terrible shock."

"But what happened? What the d-devil happened?"

The pretty girl shook her head. She looked around. The last backs were going out the door. They were almost alone. "If you ask me," she whispered soberly, with an attractive wrinkling of her brow, "I'd say old Hopper must have pushed some of his authoritarian stuff too far."

"W-What do you mean?" challenged the young bookkeeper, stiffening to the defense of the great American employer.

"Oh, Doug," Janet replied with overt disgust, "for heaven's sake! You know as well as I do what an impossible old blowhole he is. Arnold has always hated his guts."

Douglas, beginning to protest, became caught in a rigid spasm of clearing his throat, blinking, and snorting through his tightened nostrils. Janet silenced him with an exasperated frown, as the grizzled, barrel-shaped codger searching for his coat passed by them on his way into the dining room. When he was gone, Douglas started again with a great show of indignation: "I'd be damn p-p-p-proud," he said, "of a f-father like Martin Hopper."

The girl tossed her head with disdain. "That's just your trouble, Douglas Hyde."

"What do you mean?" he bristled angrily.

"You know he's a phony," she answered coldly. "You've told me so yourself. And yet, in a pinch, you defend him."

The two stared at each other—blonde against dark—in absolute opposition.

After a moment, the girl swung free, turned, and started toward the kitchen. Just then, from within, the voice of the old man searching for his coat croaked with a loud crack of agitation, "Hey there, you honeymooners. The bird has flown the coop. Ain't no critter in this goddamn kitchen but a skinny cockroach."

Douglas stood in confusion. With a frightened little cry, Janet ran to see.

4.

ARNOLD, THE VORACIOUS BIRD, had remained harmlessly on his chair, the hunger increasing in his stomach, while the milling multitude gradually thinned to an assortment of a dozen or so men—some in business suits, some in dungarees. Many of the original rescuers had departed to their jobs; others had joined the group congregated in the dining room. Those now remaining in the kitchen were late arrivals, curious to know and discuss what had come to pass, not at all aware that they were supposed to be policing the son and heir of the home they had entered.

Sam Wallach, the proprietor of the local drugstore, put his thumb into the pocket of his vest, drew out the watch at the end of the heavy gold chain circumscribing his belly, enlarged his black eyes in alarm, and shouted that it was nearly nine o'clock. The company started; several cursed and dashed away. Wallach came appraisingly over to Arnold, who stood up and tilted his right eye at him. The two were of equal height; the elder, plump; the younger, lean.

"Let me take a look at you, lad," said the druggist. "I don't think I've seen you since you got back from the wars. Didn't I read somewhere an article, you were killed?"

The youth laughed familiarly, all his features going awry in different directions. He perceived that the man was studying him with a look of great curiosity, but what he wanted was to get out of this place and settle down to another heavy meal. He pulled his shirt over his shoulder, but the buttons were gone. He opened his belt and tucked the shirt into his pants.

"You were flying in the Pacific," said Wallach.

"Yes," Arnold said indifferently, spying an overcoat on the kitchen table and moving to pick it up. "The Pacific." Grasping the neck, he lifted the garment into the air and drew it on. It came to his ankles but left him free enough to walk. "You going downtown?" he asked.

"Yes," said Wallach.

"Well, let's go then." Arnold made a sign, calling "So long!" to the tarriers in the room. He held the door for the druggist, followed him down the kitchen steps into the drizzle, and conducted him by the backyard route—the way he had gone with Cannibal John—explaining, "Shortcut." And the two went down the hill to town.

The streets of the town were alive at this hour with grimy, roistering fellows out from the night shift at the mine. Every alternate shop along the street was a billiard hall, patronized by an astonishing number of natty little Filipinos. Not a few big fellows were rolling drunk. A number of whores were at strategic posts and strolling their beats.

They passed a greasy restaurant called The Grill. Arnold's companion, wanting breakfast, said, "I'm stopping here for a bite to eat."

"I'll come in too," said Arnold. "I'm starved."

They went to a booth. A weary, drab waitress with a pimpled pear-shaped countenance—her cheeks were blotchy and her face round, but the crown of her head pressed in and small, topped by a finicky coiffeur of black curls and loopings—came over and cheerlessly applied a sour-smelling rag to the maroon-veneered, unappetizing table.

Wallach ordered a glass of orange juice, ham and eggs, a stack of flapjacks, a cup of coffee, and a couple of hard rolls. Arnold declared that he would have the same. When the waitress had shoved the green pencil into her locks and trudged away, Wallach rubbed a stubby hand over his thinning, moist-looking hair. "Say, Arnold," he began, knitting his brows around his dark eyes and peering at the youth with a gaze of earnest inquiry, "what does your father say about this situation up at the lode?"

Arnold neither knew nor cared what the man was talking about; he was impatient for the food. The hunger pains throughout his intestines were almost unendurable. He followed the slow exit of the waitress with glazing eyes.

Wallach cleared his throat and began again, more loudly. "Is it true, do you think, this night-shift crowd may not go back tonight?"

Arnold continued to follow the path of the waitress, who shoved through the swinging door into the kitchen. Through a small porthole, he could spy something of the white-apron world within. He was oblivious to everything else.

Just off Arnold's shoulder, however, a churlish, heavy-featured fellow at the lunch counter swung around on his stool. Examining Wallach belligerently through merciless, narrow eyes, he muttered a series of threatening obscenities. Interlarding these with information, he finally spit out that the portly druggist could bet various parts of his person that the workers were out of that son of a bitch of a mine for good.

Visibly quailing, Wallach fingered first the watch chain, then the edge of his cuff, while assuring the heavy features before him that he had only the highest regard for the obviously just cause of the workers. The man, swearing unwholesomely, leaned heavily back against the counter and let go another stunning series of obscene inventions.

Working behind the counter, a second waitress—apparently the younger sister of the first, but neater and more appetizing in appearance and with a flash of life in her eye—gave her contentious customer on the stool a sharp poke on the shoulder blade. "Hey you, jerk," she warned, "don't talk like that—there's ladies present."

Relinquishing Wallach reluctantly, the big fellow, coarse shirt open at the neck and a black forest of crinkly hair crowding up his chest, rotated slowly back around to face the girl. Wallach watched while he became involved with her in a loutish exchange. She pertly slapped his cheek when he tried to chuck her bumptious little bosom, and the scattering of men along the counter laughed. "Atta gal, Petroushka!" called a husky Swede. "One milkshake," piped a grinning youngster, leaning manfully over a bowl of Quaker oats. He looked right and left for approval, but nobody seemed to care.

The drab one returned with a tin tray and slapped silver onto the table in a rough arrangement. She set down two glasses of orange juice, two sets of rolls, two pats of butter, and two plates of ham and eggs. "Draw two!" she called wearily to the counter as she turned away.

Wallach leaned toward his companion, who had gone directly to the ham and eggs. "This town," he whispered, with a cautious glance to the side, "is a powder keg. God help us all if your father fails to negotiate that new contract this afternoon!"

Arnold went on to the rolls. When their waitress came back with the coffee, he looked up. "I want ten more of these," he said.

"Ten more of what?" she asked with boredom.

"Ham and eggs."

The dull girl knitted her nose. Wallach set his orange juice down, leaned back with open eyes, and carried a paper napkin to his chin. The girl looked with uncertainty from one to the other. "You kidding?" she whined.

"Why, no," he replied, demolishing his last roll. "Hurry up. I'm starved."

She hesitated. He finished the roll, and then tilted an eye at Wallach. "Mind if I eat your rolls?" he asked. "She can bring us more." He turned to the waitress. "Bring us lots of rolls."

Watching the food disappear, she rubbed the back of her neck in perplexity, emitting a fetid odor from her armpit, glanced at the spellbound Sam Wallach, and moved away.

Arnold had consumed his companion's ham and eggs by the time she returned to set down the flapjacks. Then, when the additional ham and eggs began to appear, Arnold asked for a few more plates of flapjacks.

The portly and genial druggist had ceased eating some time before and was simply watching with growing astonishment the performance of his unsociable tablemate. After a time, he began to study, rather than marvel at, the ravenous young man. Wallach was not devious: an open-faced gent, he made no attempt to conceal his curiosity and discomfort, until Arnold asked the waitress on one of her trips to the table for something really filling and substantial, at which point Wallach finally found his tongue. He leaned forward with a measuring eye. "Arnold," he asked, "is this something that happened in the war?"

Swallowing a mouthful of cakes, the youth shook his head. "No," he said, "just today." He turned to the girl for a suggestion. "Well, what is there?" She just stood there with a look of blank compliance. Wallach proposed a steak. "Bring me a dozen," Arnold told the girl.

"My god!" she exclaimed. "What the hell is this?" Stepping away in a daze, she paused halfway along the counter, leaned over the plate-cluttered barrier, and said to her sister, "Get a load of the pip-squeak in the booth."

The sister came along her side of the counter, gazed, and then stood staring over the head of the belligerent loudmouth, who looked up at her from his empty plate. "Well, sister," he leered, "what's the news?"

She disregarded him and began to stack the dirty dishes, all the while watching the gluttonous display in the booth, where Wallach sat like a poker player lost behind a wall of chips. The bellicose boor at the counter swung around to see what she was studying. When Wallach saw him turn, he inserted his thumb into his vest pocket and again drew out his watch. "Oh my, Arnold," he said, starting. "It's ten o'clock. I've got to go." He craned around, looking for the waitress, as his antagonist resumed his vigorous cannonade of foul abuse.

Arnold, pushing away an empty plate and reaching for a full one, was just beginning to relax, ingest less greedily, and enjoy the tastes of his bountiful repast. Feeling it was now feasible for him to pay attention to his companion, he lifted his eyes and beheld an expression of anxiety on Wallach's countenance. Arnold cocked his left eye at the brute spitting epithets from the stool. "Well," he challenged, "what's eating *you?*"

The fellow turned on Arnold. "Watch it, wise guy!" he threatened nastily.

Petroushka gave him a sharp poke on the shoulder. "Come on," she put in, "knock it off, Misha. Pick on somebody your own size."

"Oh yeah?" the lout challenged, turning back.

"Come on," she again entreated. "Don't be a jerk."

"Oh yeah? Who's a fuckin' jerk?"

She slapped him. "Don't talk like that to a lady," she commanded. "Didn't I tell you not to talk like that to a lady?"

Misha lurched across the counter, but somebody pulled him back into his place. "All right," he scoffed. "Go to hell." He trundled back around, rested his elbows on the counter, and keenly watched his two enemies in the booth. When Petroushka's drab sister returned with three steaks, each garnished with hash brown potatoes and a heap of peas, Wallach nervously asked her for the bill.

"You payin' for both?" she asked.

The druggist glanced at Arnold and caught his eye. "Why, yes, of course." He laughed awkwardly. "That's the least I can do for a wounded friend just back from the wars."

The unpleasant observer at the counter made a thick-faced grimace of disgust. "That little so-and-so, a goddamned soldier!" he taunted coarsely.

"Listen, you!" came a call from down the line. "Say another word about the fucking army, and I'll shove this fucking counter up your ass."

Misha threw the man a lowering look, but seeing his size, subsided into silence.

The waitress was adding up the check. "Two orange juice, two cups of coffee, six plates of rolls, twelve ham and eggs, nine flapjacks, twelve steaks—the rest are coming…" She paused to scratch her scalp with the pencil. "Now, let's see…" She lifted her elbow and thoughtfully scratched her armpit. "That's twenty, ten…"

The crude observer turned back toward Petroushka with a look of wonder; the heavy jaw of the girl behind the counter dropped. Several others along the counter had begun to grasp the situation, as had the people in neighboring booths. Arnold, finishing his last stack of flapjacks and starting on the steaks, was unaware of what was building up.

"Pick up your steaks!" came a coarse cry from the kitchen. The waitress interrupted her calculations to fetch the order. She returned with three more steak dinners, which Arnold set to devouring with a fresh fervor. Suddenly, a gaudy whore with blonde hair, black along the parting, lifted her fat arms and cried, "For Christ's sake, where does he put it?"

A husky Swede sitting at the counter laughed. "If he ever starts to shit," he said, "by Yeesus, we all gotta leave town."

"Pick up your steaks!" came a second call from the kitchen. This time the waitress tarried to complete the check, so Petroushka went to fetch the order. When she arrived at the table with another installment of steak dinners, Arnold noticed that she gave off a tang of musk. He lifted an eye. She sent him a wink. "Hello there, cutie pie," she said, setting the plates on the table in a sprightly manner.

The whore came up and, pressing Petroushka to one side, placed her fat behind on the arm of Arnold's bench. Somebody whistled offensively. From the corner of her hard mouth the whore rapped back, "Shut up there, pin prick!" The counter company laughed, while her tormenter—a handsome Brit with a self-consciously cropped mustache—wriggled sheepishly, trying to smile as though the quick barb had not struck home.

But Arnold had begun to sense an annoying conflict within himself: Petroushka and the whore had started that dizzy queerness again, yet he was still very hungry and had to continue at his work. Furthermore, the crowding of curious observers was becoming distinctly unwelcome: they represented an increasing threat to the continuity of his operations. He drew a little to his corner of the booth and applied himself with renewed dedication to his task: he sought to blow from his quivering nostrils the musk and body smells of Petroushka and the whore, filling his lungs instead with the aromas of his steak. Like a monk, he strictly discriminated between the nonessential and the essential, the passing distractions of the world and the enduring cry of his unique inner being. Like a hero, he steeled himself to one vital task. And since his heart was pure, and he was strong with the strength of ten, the instruments of his passion—fork and blade—continued to convey chunks of broiled meat, heaps of potato, and precarious consignments of peas between the rapid sequence of uncomely platters and his ravenous, crooked face. The work that had previously been a spontaneous, self-innocent manifestation of his voraciousness had become his consciously realized vocation: the One Task, the all-consuming, life-feeding action on which the continuity of his being depended.

For if fires burn universally in the body and texture of the world— the plant cells, the animal cells oxidizing, breaking everything around them into the liquid flame of their present protoplasm; the sun, the stars, burning, burning—the voraciousness of those fires was vividly personified in gobbling Arnold. And if the rough populace was crowding and staring, it was partly because he was a kind of revelation. They themselves could stoke more lazily their relatively low-burning furnaces and then go on to the affairs of the billiard parlor, their anxieties of family life, and the employments of civilization; but in Arnold, raw and feverish, the first principle of existence had broken to an all-consuming, all-else-eliminating primary statement; the normally concealed secret of the body was here unveiled.

The first to receive the full impact of this epiphany now mysteriously manifest in a humble grill was the blonde and aromatic whore. She reached a soft baby hand to caress the cheek of the shy youth who had retreated to his steak, but the moment she touched him her hand drew back. "My god, he's hot!" she said with a look of fright.

"Let me," said Petroushka. She leaned across the table and felt his forehead. "Wow!" she cried, and she shook her hand.

She tried again. It was fun.

Arnold looked at her with annoyance and roughly pushed her away, but when he returned to his platter, the whore repeated the experiment, resting her hand upon his brow and turning to Wallach with a look of motherly concern. "Why, the poor kid's sick," she said. "He's got a fever."

When the coarse refrain—"Pick up your steaks!"—again came from the kitchen, the weary waitress ripped her check from the pad, set it down by Wallach, and turned to fetch the final lot. Arnold broke free from the whore. "Better order me a dozen more," he called to the waitress.

"Yeesus Christus!" bellowed the Swede, and the whole place broke into a roar; some went running into the street to summon friends; the gruff gorilla on the counter stool pushed himself up and came over to the table to stare.

Petroushka leaned to Wallach. "Who is the kid?" she whispered. "What's his name?"

The hosting druggist, who was studying the bill, leaned backward and to the side, and reached his hand into his trouser pocket. "Martin Hopper's son," he answered, "just back from the war."

"Martin Hopper's son?" exclaimed the whore. "Why, he's dead!" Arnold felt the flesh of the woman's arm going clammy around his neck.

The tough fellow at the end of the table, however, began to jut his jaw. His eyes narrowed evilly. Preparing a fist, he muttered with menace, "Martin Hopper's bastard son of a bitch!"

And with that, he suddenly sent a jab to Arnold's head, knocking the youth against the mothering whore, who flared at the pugilist with indignation, while Petroushka whirled on the lout, commanding, "Pick a jerk your own goddamn size," and cracking him on the cheek. He reached a mauler's hand to her face and shoved her backward over the corner of the table. Arnold felt her fall with a shriek against his chest; the big blonde beside him was shrieking too; and then Petroushka was caught between the whore and the edge of the table, kicking wildly and screaming that she was hurt. The mauler took another sharp slug at Arnold, who was kicking to break free. Wallach stumbled to his feet, grabbed at Misha's hair, and received a blow that sent him crumbling to the bench.

By now, everybody in The Grill was seething, shouting, slugging, and pressing in on the contenders from all sides. The boards of the booth began to creak under the pressure of converging bodies. Something snapped in Arnold's head, and he lunged at Misha. The table broke from the wall, dropping Petroushka to the floor among the plates. Arnold, quaking with a chaos of blind flashes, all the weight of his emotions focused now on the work of clearing the field for himself, caught Misha by the head and carried him down on top of the table— Petroushka underneath—collapsing the partitions with a crash.

Misha, with his prodigiously powerful body, was a raging, lashing animal, hammering with both fists at Arnold's head and neck. Then suddenly he was rolling and shrieking amidst the debris, when Arnold, feeling he was easily the master, gouged out one of his eyeballs. Misha brought up his knee, and Arnold, hurt, sank his teeth into the beast's neck. Someone behind began to tug at Arnold's shoulders, but then another body slugged in and a second fight developed above the first. Arnold kept his teeth in Misha's neck. Petroushka, beneath the table, was still. A shot was fired. A man, slugging right and left, ploughed ferociously through the chaos, heading for the door. Arnold felt the burly body in his clutches soften and succumb: he was swallowing its hot blood. And somewhere nearby, a quiet crying could be heard.

When the troopers arrived at The Grill, it was a shambles. The Greek proprietor was standing by the kitchen door in his bloody apron, waving his arms, fat tears rolling from his eyes. Rain poured down, and the muddy street outside the scene of horrible murder was crowded with bystanders, every billiard parlor and barbershop in town having emitted its swarm of burly inhabitants. Rumors were running to the effect that Martin Hopper had just shot a man, that Hopper himself had been shot, that a flag had been desecrated, that a dead man had come to life, that somebody had caught fire, that a whore had had a miscarriage, that the floor of The Grill had broken through into hell, and that Sam Wallach had committed suicide. Presently, however, the dominant opinion was that Martin Hopper's soldier-son had murdered a worker. The dangerous throng retreated back into the billiard parlors and barbershops, breaking throughout the rest of the day into scattered arguments and fights. The town of Indian Hat was primed to explode.

But curiously, after Arnold had been dragged from the clutter of bodies and debris, transported in a van to the jail, and tossed along with a number of others into a large but already crowded cell, he suddenly realized to his amazement that the overcoat, which was still clinging to his back, now fit him exactly.

——————————————————5.

THE PUGNACIOUS MISHA WAS DEAD. Petroushka and Sam Wallach were in the hospital and would die. The whore would live. A considerable company had been treated for abrasions, contusions,

broken bones, internal injuries, hysteria, knife wounds, and shock. A
still larger group stewed in the jail.

The town of Indian Hat was in a poor position to cope with the
situation. Raven Lode had financed the construction of the large and
absolutely modern jail, which was already more than filled from the
extraordinary number of arrests that had had to be made during recent weeks. Raven Lode required and always enjoyed strong govern-
ment protection, and the town's allotment of territorial troopers had
been increased earlier in the year. The troopers had been furnished
with the most up-to-date equipment for the quelling of riots, mutiny,
and strikes; and yet if the lawmen broke, it would be frightful for the
town. Raven Lode was these days in considerable trouble, and the entire community, consequently, was as taut as the head of a drum.

Arnold was standing in the midst of an angry cluster of fellow
prisoners in a large holding cell used for riot emergencies. Several of
the prisoners were threatening to do him violence; others were pressing his annoyers back. A sharp command was heard from the prison
guard standing at the gate with a Thompson submachine gun. The
men continued to grumble but began to move around.

What troubled Arnold, however, was not the men but the hunger. It was perfectly clear to him that pretty soon he would have to
eat. He paced the area, like a solitary in a forest: profoundly indrawn,
hands behind his back, head down, eyes fixed with meditation. But
Arnold's meditation was not precisely one of thought; it was, rather,
a total concentration of his faculties on the experience of rat-gnawing
accumulating in his belly—an experience so vivid, as though actual
rodent teeth were breaking through the stomach walls and consuming,
to his momentarily increasing pain, the entire interior of his emaciated
physique.

Arnold was of more than average height now, lean as a rail, gaunt
cheeked, with the look in his eyes of one about to scream with hunger.
The coat, somewhat torn, hung from his shoulders to midcalf, and,
comically, his trouser legs were now so short that they left his lower
shanks bare. His shoes so cramped him that at one point in his mad

pacing he stopped, tore them from his swelling feet, and flung them to the floor.

Nobody approached him anymore. Indeed, beginning to be apparent among the herding men was a quickness to make way for this human animal, pacing their common cage in his growing frenzy. Through the crowd a channel would open before the pacing apparition, then close behind him; and any man who chanced to be brushed by the passing form would instinctively start, with a sudden look of alarm. Not that any should have feared him: these were competent huskies, each confident that he could cope pretty well with anyone who might come his way. But from Arnold's wild features emanated a horrifying look of death—death walking, death ravenous to consume; and it was this emanation that kept the life-protective ones away.

The crowd in the big cell had been aimlessly swarming thus for some time, when a loud, metallic, staccato voice cracked from beyond the bars: "Mr. Arnold Hopper! Mr. Arnold Hopper! Report, at once, to the gate!"

Arnold, on the side of the cell opposite the gate, caught the name. He stopped and gazed; a way cleared for him, as by magic. But when he started his pace toward the exit, a low, dangerous muttering began among the herd of his crowding cellmates. By the time he was halfway across the floor, the grumbling had mounted to something of a din. That Arnold Hopper, the known murderer, should be the one among them to be singled out and summoned to the exit aroused immediately a rapidly defined suspicion. The name of Hopper was synonymous in Indian Hat with Raven Lode and private law: no one doubted that well-known, invisible wires had been pulled, and the scion of privilege had been abstracted from his doom.

Arnold was three-quarters across the cell when somebody shouted, "There he goes: crown prince of the lode!" A howl went up. A giant miner broke from the group, stepped into Arnold's path, and stood like a bear athwart the approach. Arnold's fist cracked out; the man went down without a sound. And the mysterious demon of starvation strode without a moment of hesitation from the cage, the gates slamming behind him. The miner had ceased to breathe. Indignation from the storming multitude inside the coop was mounting; the guards stepped back a little from the bars, holding their tommy guns at the ready.

Arnold, with a prison guard at his elbow, was led directly to the front office, where the Reverend Mr. Phineas Adams was standing nervously in a raincoat. A handsome, intelligent-looking, dark-haired young woman at his side peered searchingly at Arnold when he came in; but after only a glance at her, Arnold turned to the clergyman, who had half-extended his hand and stopped, his smile of greeting freezing in astonishment.

"Mr. Arnold Hopper?" asked the officer at the desk—a seasoned sergeant in the uniform of a trooper, his large hat hanging on the wall behind him.

"Yes."

The man leaned forward. "You are released." He reached out his hand. "It's an honor to know you, Mr. Hopper. We are very sorry for this mistake."

The Reverend Adams, who had reassembled his mind, protested uncertainly, "But this is not the Arnold Hopper we came to see."

"Not Hopper?" queried the officer. He withdrew his hand and sat back with stern regard. He glared at the cadaverous scarecrow in the crumpled coat.

Arnold actually smiled, surmounting for an instant the volcano of hunger. He turned to the remembered clergyman, "Mr. Adams, I have changed since we shook hands last night at the dinner table and I left the company to pass along into the kitchen."

Adams studied him, beginning to show fear.

"Well," broke in the officer, "is this your man or is it not?"

Adams hesitated, fingering his hat. The girl stepped forward. "Yes," she stated, "this is Arnold Hopper."

The officer studied her eyes. Then he relaxed and laughed. With a knowing wink to the clergyman, he said, "I guess your daughter ought to know."

The Reverend Phineas Adams looked entirely uncomfortable. Arnold Hopper turned again to the desk. "Sir, may I go?" he asked.

The officer tilted his head and rubbed his nose. His eyes were steely gray beneath brows that pushed together at the root of his nose. He had a deep dimple in the cleft of his chin, a large wart at the side of his mouth, and a distinctly undistinguished, top-sergeant look— tough, unbeatable, hard to please. He continued to scrutinize the scarecrow. "Have you got some identification?" he asked. "Just, you know, for the record?"

Arnold tried to think. This delay was becoming unbearable. He hurried his brain, and then drew attention to the "A. H." initials on his silver belt buckle. Baring his belly, he pointed to a great scar. "This is where they took out half my guts."

The girl was now looking at him proudly, though her father still had his qualms. The officer watched this human constellation for a moment, and then, leaning forward again, reached out his hand. "Okay, son," he said. "But you better stay out of sight for the next few days." He gave Arnold the look that signifies "a gentlemanly under-standing," but when he felt the fire-grip of Arnold's hand, it changed to a look of shock. And without so much as a nod or a thank-you to either the pastor or the girl, Arnold, the fantastic oddity, tilting a little forward in his eagerness to be gone, passed out the door and down the steps into the rain.

Arnold knew where he was going. During his hours of confine-ment, while suffering the gnawing torture in his belly, he'd had a presentiment of the precise haven to which he should proceed the mo-ment he was free, to obtain the food needed to appease his inner rat. The town was turbulent. Arrests were taking place on every block. A small dark fellow standing on the sidewalk pointed at Arnold striding barefoot down the middle of the muddy street. Suddenly other by-standers, talking excitedly, were staring, pointing, gesturing. A crowd started to gather, augmented with a rush of clients from a neighbor-ing pool hall, but immediately dispersed when an armored car cruised slowly down the street, paused in front of the dangerous cluster, and leveled its guns.

Arnold came to the cannery wharf, wheeled right, and proceeded along the walk he had followed with Cannibal John. The number of dogs in the street had increased, and on most of the wooden porches corpulent Indian mothers sat gossiping in rocking chairs or herding kids. Presently Arnold realized that someone had been at his heels for some time. He turned and saw Phineas Adams's daughter following him with hasty, sometimes trotting, steps. She was a fresh, dark-eyed, prettily serious young woman in her early twenties, with the look of one devoted rather to art, books, and ideas than to the marriage enterprise. Wearing a hunter-green skirt and wooly sweater beneath her transparent oilskin and sporting a white and red neckerchief, she was a pretty vision—the only thing not gray or mud colored in the town. Arnold paused to let her come beside him and then proceeded on his way.

"Well," she panted, out of breath. "You're a fine one!" She had to keep trotting to stay at his side. "Five years, and not so much as a hello!"

Arnold was not at all aware of why he had paused to let her join him. Thinking only about his now unbearable need for food, he kept striding through the rain, tilting forward, without reply.

"Arnold!" she entreated. He did not respond. "Arnold! Speak to me!" she insisted. "Are you angry? Are you ill?"

He continued along. She trotted, panted, and followed quickly.

"Are you afraid I will try to hold you?" she asked. "Arnold, it was beautiful. I don't think of it like that," she pleaded.

Plodding on through the mud and the rain, his pace never relented. They were now approaching the end of Indian town. On their left, only a few wooden structures remained, each backing onto a rickety pier. "You're ill, Arnold," said the girl. "That's why I'm with you: because you're a little mad."

Ignoring her, Arnold turned, mounted the steps of the last house, and gave a rap at the door. While they waited, he regarded the upturned face of his companion. She was a little shorter than his present stature and tended to stand a bit too close to him. Her manner of staring up into whichever eye he cocked at her had a little too much soul pressure behind it for comfort.

The door opened. "Come right in!" said a man—not the proprietor, but one of the several older, generally stocky fellows (members of the Cannibal Society) who were standing about talking busily. Arnold and his shadow entered the store. The men's talk hushed when they realized who had broken into their midst, and apprehensive glances were exchanged. The enormous, blubbery proprietor hurried around the end of the counter and approached the pair, but before he could say a word, Arnold roughly demanded something to eat. The man appeared to be anticipating nothing less; and seeming even a bit relieved, he lifted his massive head, drew out the accordion ripple of his chins, and shouted over his shoulder, "Mary!" followed by something Arnold was unable to understand. Moving aside, the man gestured graciously toward the door behind the counter. "Will you just step around into the kitchen?"

Brushing past him without reply, Arnold walked around the counter and through the private door—still trailing the disquieted young woman in hunter green. He strode through a small dining room nearly filled by a large circular table and chairs of cheap mahogany, the walls papered with a brash floral design and pictures—Niagara Falls, a girl with a rose, the *Mona Lisa*, General Custer's Last Stand—taken from the newspaper Sunday sections. Arnold continued through another doorway into a cozy kitchen, where he was greeted by Mary, the Indian girl—now somewhat shorter than him. She had an efficient and determined look about her and was wiping her hands on a decorated apron that covered her from neck to knee. Surprisingly, old Anna was in the room, industriously setting full platters on a kitchen table. Janet Strobe was also there: blonde and trim, pertly attired in a yellow checked dress, she was walking back and forth, arguing with old Anna.

When Arnold entered, Janet stopped pacing, abandoned her argument, and simply stood, rooted, studying him; then, noticing the young woman behind him, she gave a start, and stared at her with frank incredulity. The Indian girl conducted Arnold to a ready chair, while Anna, scrutinizing him silently, continued to set out the plates. The two white girls stood quietly, measuring each other for several moments; and then, with the indications of a readiness to smile, slowly approached each other, like two figures in a dream.

"You're Betty Adams, aren't you?" suggested the girl in yellow.

The other narrowed her eyes, tilting her head in questioning scrutiny. "Why—Janet—Strobe!" Betty exclaimed. "My dear!" The two embraced. "When I left," she declared, "you were a little girl."

Janet smiled. "I've often imagined you in your New York studio..." She broke off. "When did you arrive?"

"This morning's boat." Betty hesitated. "I had to find out," she finally blurted, "about Arnold."

Side by side, Betty and Janet turned their eyes to Arnold. He leaned crazily into his fodder, elbows winging out, tearing savagely with his teeth. The Indians, young Mary and old Anna, were busily and silently plying plates from icebox to stove, stove to table, table to sink, with the look of ministrants carrying food offerings to a greedy demon. The two—brunette and blonde, hunter green and chrome yellow—stared a moment, then the older, Betty Adams, leaned toward the younger, and without averting her eyes whispered, "What does it mean? This queer talk that Arnold was dead?"

"No one can understand it," Janet replied softly from the corner of her large, slightly over-made-up lips, her brown eyes remaining fixed on the incredible transaction at the table.

Betty whispered again, "But what does it *mean*?"

Shrugging, Janet murmured, "I don't get it."

They gazed for some time in silence.

Betty resumed, "He's looking simply terrible. Whatever happened to the left side of his face?"

"Some shock of some kind, I suppose."

"The war?"

Again Janet shrugged. "Perhaps."

Betty Adams's eyes filled. "Oh Janet..." She shook her head and looked away. "I could just die." She began to weep. Janet reached over helplessly and patted her arm.

The unfathomable Arnold had not said a word. His coat was still humping on his back. The two Indians seemed to have been prepared to meet this curious emergency: Mary had hardly uttered a sound; Anna had simply advanced into action.

When Betty Adams had pulled herself together, she dabbed at her eyes, gave a little blow with her nose, and, wiping it, courageously changed the subject. Without looking at her neighbor, she asked, "What brings you down to Indian town, Janet dear?" She turned her head away and dried her eyes.

Janet's expression changed. "Well," she began, nervously tucking her yellow bobbed hair back behind her right ear, "Mrs. Hopper had a terrible shock this morning, and I came to see if I could bring back Anna, her maid." She nodded toward the serving woman. "That's Anna, there."

"Who's the girl?" continued Betty.

Janet whispered. "I don't know. They call her Mary. She's the daughter of the owner of the store."

Betty Adams wrinkled her brow, giving her nose a final tap and putting her handkerchief away. "It's a queer sort of store."

Janet moved even closer. "I don't think it's really a store. Those old guys outside... it's some kind of secret headquarters for something. Funny atmosphere!" The two looked around uneasily. They moved a little out of the way of the door into the room.

Arnold, by this time, had made his way through numerous nameless dishes: meats of various kinds, boiled and broiled; potatoes; heaps of heavy vegetables. He was still very far from appeased and hardly conscious of the surroundings. He had known that this would be the place where his singular problem would be understood. Indeed, now he had found that this return of his had been actually anticipated. What he did not realize was that he was in the process of being trapped.

Most of the older folk of the Indian section had been apprehensive about this visit ever since Anna had come stumbling home in terror earlier in the day. The old Indian women (those, at least, who still believed in the old-fashioned mysteries) had labored most of the morning preparing and storing victuals for the monster. And now the demon was going through them, like fire through stacks of straw.

The big man came into the room, beckoned his daughter, and took her outside into the store. Presently, the two began carrying in baskets and large parcels, which they set about the walls. Betty and

Janet at first stood aside, but then Betty caught the Indian girl by the arm. "Can't we help?" she gravely inquired. "Mary, isn't it? Your name?" she added.

The girl set down a wash basket full of assorted groceries, stood back, and wiped the lank, black hair from her eyes. She was a little taller than them, less plump, with Asiatic cheekbones, a delicately tilting head, and a more awkward way of balancing in her high heels. Willowy, with a secret vigor, she was akin to a wild creature yet reposeful in her self-confidence. She did not smile. "Well," Mary hesitated, "but this is nearly all." Her voice had a curious, reedy quality. "Perhaps, the next lot, you can help." She looked at a bruised place on her hand and worked her fingers. Her voluminous father, wheezing, came hulking in with a heavy box and set it by the door. Glancing in the direction of the girls, he went out again and did not reappear.

When Mary moved to go back to her service of the table, Betty again took her arm. "Couldn't we help with that, Mary?"

The girl seemed uncertain. She glanced at Anna, who was shifting pots around on the stove. Betty stepped a little nearer to her and was now standing a bit too close. She spoke very softly. "What does it mean?" She confronted the girl with deep anxiety. "It's so very strange!"

Mary stepped back a little. She seemed anxious to leave.

"Tell us! Please, Mary!" put in Janet. "We are his friends."

Mary contemplated their eyes for several moments: brown eyes— their eyes were brown; hers were satin black. Finally she spoke. "Old John Baranof did something terrible last night. The men are going to see if they can fix it."

"What men?" asked Betty.

"The Cannibal Society."

Betty and Janet exchanged a look of horror. "What will they do?" asked Janet with concern.

"I don't really know," the girl replied. "They have a system for doing away with dangerous spirits. We're trying to keep him eating here until they're ready. They're all over at the big lodge right now."

"Will they hurt him?"

"I really don't know. It's hard to say." Mary moved away.

The two white girls stood in great distress. They studied Arnold a while, moved a little closer to each other, and took each other's hands. Looking like conspirators, they began to whisper again, trying very hard not to move their lips.

Whispered Betty Adams, "We must try to save him."

Janet slightly nodded. "How?"

"I don't know."

Mary glanced at them from the stove, and they froze like rabbits, squeezing each other's hands. Mary returned to her task, and they waited to make certain that she was not suspicious.

"Let's try to bring him the word," said the younger girl.

Betty nodded, and shut her eyes for silence. Presently the two moved to join the Indian women with the work of the kitchen. They were not repulsed. After a time they all were in full swing. Nobody said a word. The day wore on.

Two and a half hours passed before Arnold sat back, beginning to feel a little more at ease. Twilight was descending, the lights were on, and with the hunger that had raged in his interior being appeased, he began to take some note of his surroundings.

The strong older woman left the stove and set herself to rest in a chair across from him: Anna. She was familiar and pleasant to his heart. He noted her massiveness, her sturdy frame. He studied the formation of her head: the Chinese cast of her features, the black hair caught back very simply at the nape of her massive, fleshy neck. He recalled her warning before this madness had begun.

Arnold started to watch the handsomely moving figures. The Indian girl in the pretty apron he remembered also; he had talked with her, in his former state, the night before. The dark-haired girl who had caught up with him in the street and the other in the gay dress of yellow—these two seemed very close to him, like friends from some forgotten past. The blonde one's young body had a way of joggling as it walked that began to make his head swim. Her every step seemed an advertisement of her entire anatomy. And whenever he glanced at the one in hunter green, he was touched by the mysterious comfort of her eyes.

For a while, Arnold held to his earlier routine, concentrating on the potatoes and meat; but as it became apparent that he need have no worry about the food supply and that the present company seemed devoted to satiating rather than hindering his primary desire, the anguish of his life-agony finally began to be appeased. His eyes became fascinated with the nuances of the curvaceous females serving him, while his heart allowed itself to contemplate more and more the increasing probability of his further enjoyment of their voluptuous forms.

It was Mary who unwittingly provoked his initial assault. Betty and Janet were conferring in a corner, perfecting plans for their projected rescue, when Mary, having just placed a great platter of meat before the diner, leaned across him to gather a stack of empty plates. As her delicate dark arm flashed before his eyes, her knee pressed against his thigh, and he reached to touch her coppery skin. Feeling the surprising heat of the unexpected hand, she drew back impulsively, and he seized her by the wrist, equally impulsively. She struggled, with a stifled cry of fright, and he simply pulled her closer. Her ankle buckled, she collapsed against his chest, and he began feverishly kissing whatever his mouth could reach: the front of her apron, apron strap, her delicate collarbone…

Anna clambered to her feet, with the most determined look she'd worn that day. Reaching across the table to intercede, she immediately found that she was in a bad position, and came around to tug Arnold away. By now he had pushed Mary's head onto the table, right into the great meat dish she had just set before him, and with the dreamiest look of silly bliss, he was slowly brushing his hot lips back and forth across the cool skin of her exposed neck. He felt Anna pulling at his shoulder, then at his hair; Mary, meanwhile, was trying to kick, slap, and wriggle free. For an instant, Betty and Janet stood in amazement; then they rushed to either side of Arnold, where they wrangled with his arms.

Arnold felt that this roughhouse was very different from the recent episode at The Grill. The curious softness of these limbs pulling at him, these bodies crowding in on him: it was something he had been wanting for a long time, even though he couldn't recall ever having thought about this queer requirement; but now that the demand was being satisfied, he was enjoying the tussle immensely. The girl in the dish was becoming fatigued; his lips had just discovered her mouth, and she was trying to disengage it. Arnold adroitly followed the quick turnings of her head; then, when her lips escaped him, he gave a sharp, playful bite and caught her cheek. The girl shrieked. He'd broken the skin, and warm blood began to pour. Arnold had a taste of the blood. He tasted again. Then a new idea began to occur to him.

It was during this love skirmish that a remote explosion could be heard—a dull thud only, yet it shook the frame of the house. After that, a second thud smote the air, and nearby, a tinkling of glass resounded as a loose pane shattered to the floor. None of these occurrences interrupted Arnold's vigorous operations on the girl. Anna's tugs were becoming desperate. Betty leaned forward quickly and whispered into his left ear, "Come, Arnold! Take me!"

He turned from his slightly bleeding prey and encountered the eyes that had so touched him moments ago. The beautiful young woman in hunter green was smiling sweetly and reaching a devoted hand to caress his cheek. Anna and Janet, suddenly aware of the new development, stopped tugging, but still held fast; the helpless, appetizing object with her face in the platter lay still, watching with patient eyes the precarious progress of her gentle rescue.

Leaning closer to Arnold, Betty slipped her hands inside his open shirt and pressed the cool flesh of her bare arms to his burning body. Arnold quailed, all his senses overwhelmed. Shutting his eyes, he let his head fall to her bosom. Mary lay very still; Anna and Janet almost stopped breathing; and this situation precariously endured—it did not move on to its logical next stage but only hung with everything in uncertain balance: Arnold, breathing quietly in his bliss, retaining a grip on the prostrate gazelle before him; Betty softly stroking his emaciated sides.

Then Anna got the idea of trying to soothe the fire demon down. With a quiet wink of assurance to Janet, she began to massage Arnold's neck soporifically. Janet was unskilled in such matters, and finding herself clinging to his right arm with nothing to do, she began to stroke the inside of his forearm with her fingertips, idly; and he, feeling the lively tickle, opened his eyes, saw Janet, and from his pillow on Betty's lovely breast, he smiled at her; and she, now nervous about the outcome, leaned toward him and whispered, "Arnold. Go with Betty, Arnold. She loves you."

No doubt Janet hoped to further the project of Mary's escape, but the effect of her breath on Arnold's cheek only aroused his interest in her. He reached up, encircled her neck, and drawing her head against his burning cheek, caught a little glimpse inside her dress. Wishing to see more, he released his grip on Mary and peacefully tore open the front of the yellow dress, exposing Janet's pink undergarments. The shocked girl tried to pull away. Anna gave Arnold a quick jerk backward, Mary sprang from him, and he was suddenly unbalanced. The chair tipped back, and the moment he sought to save himself, Janet too was released. Sprawling on the floor, the romantic hero needed a moment to regain his feet, and during that moment, his four birds scattered, each to a different wall. He gazed around stupidly, cocking his eye from one to the other; then he opened his crooked mouth and laughed. "Okay," he granted—the first word he had uttered since entering the room. He gave a surprisingly good-natured shrug, settled his coat back on his shoulders, and set up the chair.

The muffled sound of gunfire could be heard in the remote distance: something was occurring in the town. A brief glance at the window would have revealed the glow of flames in the night sky: the mining operations and main street of Indian Hat were ablaze, and tongues of fire were beginning to lick their way into the Indian quarter. The uncontrollable conflagration had begun shortly after Arnold Hopper's release from jail. When the gate of the big cell had next opened to admit a new capture of rioters, those already incarcerated made a concerted break, overpowering two of the guards. Many of the men were shot in the desperate scramble, but before authorities could contain the situation, unsavory elements of disorder had escaped, scattered, and infected the already touchy tinder throughout the town with their virulent indignation: irresponsible, semi-barbarous drunken maniacs were pouring from every hidden cranny and running amok. Before long, every street was a scene of scattered battle, and fires were crackling everywhere. Two explosions sounded at the lode—the second of them annihilating every stick of wood and bit of human tissue in the administration offices, Martin Hopper himself going up like a rocket on the Fourth of July. Armored vehicles, overpowered, were turned against the police. Soon billiard halls became battlegrounds; brothels, fortresses of flame; and the town's inhabitants, white and red alike, were refugees streaming into the hills.

But nothing of the outside world impinged on the company in the room, as tensely concentrated as it was on its own risky affair. Mary and Janet, backing against their respective walls, were considerably disheveled: the former was bleeding from a constellation of tooth cuts in her cheek, and her hair and neck were soiled disgustingly; the other girl, wide-eyed with agitation, was like a cupboard with the front panel let down.

Arnold's eyes dwelled on the appetizing exposure. Janet scowled, angrily lifting the torn panel back into place and holding it with her right forearm, while Arnold decided that he would feign disinterest for a while in order not to frighten his pretty birds away. Trying to appear entirely harmless, he lifted his gaze to Janet's brown eyes and smiled; but his smile, unfortunately for his plan, was a crooked leer. Not at all reassured, Janet glanced uneasily at Betty, who, with her head, made a quick motion toward the door. Mary too, like a hunted thing, was watching the carnivorous foe. And Anna, studying him stolidly, was apparently revolving some project in her mind.

Arnold let his leering view survey them all, and then, without a word, he returned very calmly to the table. Eating would bring them to him again: when the food began to disappear, they would know danger was growing. He set himself to the great platter that Mary had delivered and discovered it now garnished with several strands of her hair, which he wrapped, with a flourish, around a piece of juicy meat. Taking this morsel into his mouth, he savored it, feigning particular relish, making smacking sounds with his lips and tongue. Beholding this horrifying gesture, the terrified and quaking gazelle, having lost one of her shoes, kicked off the other, and holding handkerchief to cheek, darted from the room. Janet immediately followed. And so the two real delicacies of Arnold's projected feast eluded him before he could gather his wits.

He gaped for a moment, and then sprang from his chair; but before he could start for the door, Anna had placed herself in front of him. He met her fearless, old-mother eyes.

"Clear the way, Grandmother!" he demanded.

"You sit down," she commanded. This old soul was dear to him. He'd sat in the kitchen and talked with her, those curious days before the transformation. "You leave those girls alone."

He smiled and patted her cheek.

She brushed off his hand, flinging at him a look of scorn. "You should be ashamed of yourself."

Arnold caught her wrist. She resisted, but it was futile against him. He pressed her gently to one side. "Grandmother," he demurred, "I liked the taste."

"You evil thing. You are destroying us."

He tried to smile—but again produced only that leer.

"You are eating the world to death."

"I haven't begun."

Anna squared herself. "You will have to be killed."

"I cannot be killed." He grinned.

"The men will have to kill you."

Arnold was touched by her stand. "I am here to stay."

"Well, then," the old woman stated, "you will have to be changed."

There was a certain quality of threat in her pronouncements that seemed dangerously self-assured given the irresistible power of the young man before her. Arnold at last was moved. "Changed?" he queried soberly. The idea touched him with a strange presentiment.

"You have already been changed once," she declared. "It can be done."

Betty, meanwhile, had been half-consciously advancing toward the table with an expression of intense curiosity, drawn by a conversation that could not have been readily understood by anyone unacquainted with the mysterious character of Arnold's recent history.

"Grandmother, you are interesting," Arnold was saying, "but I am now going to those two upstairs."

The woman replied. "You are mean, or you would leave them alone."

"Old Mother," he said, tweaking her nose, "they will be good to eat." She smacked her tongue at him contemptuously. Then he said to her, half-seriously, "Perhaps this will change me." She frowned at him, and they looked at each other a moment, as though grappling with an inexpressible query.

Betty had reached the table and accidentally bumped against it. Arnold turned, and she caught his eye, holding his gaze without aversion. The young man experienced in the woman's gentle willingness none of the wild terror that had been so stimulating in the others, but rather a soft call that it would have been unnatural to disdain. Anna observed their silent conjunction for a moment, then returned to the stove and sink without relaxing her attention.

"Arnold," Betty said, "you haven't spoken a single word to me."

Arnold stood with the knuckles of his right hand resting lightly on the table, regarding Betty with what at first was only quiet curiosity. It was more than strange to be addressed in a tone of such intimate want by a woman one had never previously known, a woman beautiful in the warmth of her eyes and in the vigor and poise of her body: her eyes were dark, her body presented a promise of softness, her white neckerchief prettily framed her head, and her green costume accentuated her splendid shoulders and hips. As she pressed closer, he noted the delicate and cleanly delineated formation of the slightly aqueous inner corners of her eyes, the regularity and long curve of the lustrous lashes flowing from the outer margin of the lower lid (there being between this black margin and the opalescent eyeball an exquisitely beveled rim of flesh), and he began to desire the pitch-darkness of the two pupils opening up at him and summoning him down into the night of the soul.

Her moist lips were parted, disclosing teeth a little too large; as he gazed, they invited him to feel how smooth and cool they were. The young woman moved close to him, so close that the tip of her left breast made gentle contact with the side of his arm—and his ready senses were once again assailed. He began to feel choked with a mad desire to rip open this blood and warmth–permeated vessel and extinguish himself within, but he simultaneously felt an impulse to be gentle, to swoon at the tangibility of her pellucid skin.

"Arnold," she whispered, "I want you just once again."

It now seemed to him too that this would not be the first time. He enfolded her in his arms.

"I love you, Arnold."

She gave him her lips, enduring the burn of his terrific fever without any struggle of surprise or resistance. Arnold had known that the moisture of her mouth would be dear to him, and the form of her body welcome to his frame. He pressed her close to him, while Anna turned from the sink and, wiping her hands on a kitchen towel, became alert for whatever danger might develop from this new exchange.

"Sweetheart," Betty purred, "Let's go out back onto the pier."

He had begun to lift her up onto the table and did not respond.

"Arnold, sweet," she cooed, "we cannot do it here. This house is dangerous."

By now, Arnold had sat Betty on the table, pulled open her blouse and sweater at the throat, and with increasing fervor was kissing the skin of her neck. Her neckerchief remained intact.

Anna started toward them. "You will hurt the girl," she scolded. A powerful woman, she attempted to cumber Arnold's arms, yet he was not greatly troubled. When Anna grabbed him, he simply gave Betty's gaping clothes a quick tear and peeled them back, exposing her nearly naked breasts. Then he brought his own chest against hers and had just begun to press her back, when the door burst open. Arnold, looking up, discovered the virtuous bookkeeper Douglas Hyde, holding himself ramrod straight, flanked by two heavy guards' holding submachine guns.

"You g-goddamn b-beast!" Douglas said angrily, glaring fiercely at Arnold with the eyes of an American eagle.

Arnold released the girl, albeit slowly.

"D-do you know what you have d-done?"

Arnold prepared himself for an encounter. The men with the tommy guns were securely braced, their eyes continually shifting from Arnold to Douglas, watching for their command. Douglas stepped forward firmly. "Arnold," he said, with a note of reasonableness, "you are insane."

Arnold's odd body, terribly tall, visibly growing by the minute, stooped in his direction. "Who are you?" he asked.

"I have c-come," said Douglas, "in the name of your f-father, the father you have k-k-killed."

"Come to do what?" asked Arnold seriously.

Douglas moved forward, one step more. "I have c-come to take you in charge," he said, "in the n-name of the law."

"What law? Whose law?"

"There's only one law," retorted Douglas. "Now come!"

Arnold blinked, then smiled. He threw back his head and laughed; held his sides and laughed, seemingly endlessly: a terrible, hair-raising laugh that sent a frightened Betty darting into the arms of Anna.

"Listen…" Douglas said something, but his voice was inaudible.

Arnold stopped laughing, his eyes wet and sparkling with hideous delight. He leaned a little forward. "You poor chap," he said, towering over his young challenger like a giant over some Jack of the Beanstalk. "What do you know about the law?"

The bookkeeper was discomfited. "I n-n-n-know…" he tried to say something about what he knew, but the stutter overwhelmed him, and he was unable to proceed.

While Douglas struggled to break this barrier, the square, stocky figure of Cannibal John Baranof pushed through the door just behind him. Douglas and the guards were so absorbed in their encounter with Arnold, however, that they took no note. The head of the monster had nearly reached the ceiling, and he needed to stoop in order to fit in the room. His coat was like a jacket; his trousers like a pair of shorts. His flat belly was bare; the great gash of the half-healed war wound like a cruel flame.

John Baranof walked quickly along the walls to the corner where
Betty and Anna were clasping each other. He began talking earnestly
to his wife. Arnold turned to him. "John," he said with a mad, hideous
smile. "Look what's here!" And he gave a nod toward the trio at the door.

"I n-know," Douglas at last spat out, "what we d-do with murderers. Men!" he snapped. The guards tensed themselves.

Arnold turned calmly back to his annoyer. "But Cannibal John
has come to take me too," he said without excitement, and as though
to tease, added, "What do you think we ought to do?"

Douglas briefly glanced at the old Indian, who had turned from
his wife and was watching the confrontation.

"John has come to take me too," Arnold repeated.

Douglas retorted indignantly, "He has no authority."

"Authority?" Arnold echoed mockingly.

"Seize him, men!" Douglas commanded. The two men took a step
forward, but Arnold made a threatening gesture, and they fell back a
little, their guns at the ready. It was clear that if the terrifying figure
were to be taken, it would have to be with his consent.

"What *authority*," Arnold taunted, "do you think you represent?"

Douglas blinked a moment; he glanced at the Indians, then at his
guards; and finally, biting his lips very nervously, he looked Arnold
squarely in the eye. "You're a white man," he said. "Don't make believe you don't understand what this is all about."

Douglas stared at Arnold, who shook his head and turned his gaze
to Cannibal John Baranof, who had detached himself from his wife
and begun to cross the floor. Arnold perceived the look in John's eye,
and with a malicious smile, he turned back to Douglas. Baranof came
close to Douglas and said, "Son of a bitch."

Douglas disregarded him, but Baranof would not be denied. "You
son of a bitch," he insisted, and he snatched at the bookkeeper's arm.

Cries could be heard in the street. The flames of the burning town
were no longer a mere glow through the window but a visible fury,
eating down the cannery piers and dropping fiery beams into the sea.
Arnold turned to watch the spectacle, leaving the two to fight it out.
But at that moment Betty and Anna moved apart—the Indian woman

going to her husband, and the white girl to her lover, so that Arnold had barely withdrawn from the argument, when he felt a little tug at his sleeve.

"Arnold, sweetheart!" Betty pleaded softly. "Let us run!"

"You son of a bitch," Baranof said again to Douglas. "What makes you think *you* know what's going on? All you bastards can ever do is make things worse."

"Arnold, dear, we can break for it!" Betty declared. "We can leave by the pier."

Her fantastic lover lowered his ear to her, but his eyes remained fixed to the window. "We must hurry," she urged.

In a low voice, Baranof began to reason hard and seriously with Douglas.

"Why do you wait, Arnold?" Betty asked.

He detached his gaze from the window and turned to her. He said in a low, somewhat desperate voice, "I'm getting hungry again."

"Oh my god!" she gasped.

"I've got to eat," he said.

"God, god," she repeated helplessly. "Arnold," she said in desperation, "Arnold, I love you." His gaze returned to the window.

Suddenly the voice of Douglas Hyde shouting furiously at Cannibal John Baranof filled the room. "But *you* are the cause of this whole thing!"

Baranof quietly pressed his argument. "Young man," he insisted, "believe me. Please! You don't know what you are doing. You cannot control him."

Douglas cast a significant look at the two tommy guns.

"You cannot kill him," the old Indian stated. "You just don't know what we've got here."

"Come, Arnold!" Betty was entreating. "Arnold, I'm not afraid. It will be all right. Anything you want."

Baranof took Douglas by the arm. "Come," he said. "Let me have him. You can come too, if you want. We are ready at the lodge; we can do something; we understand these things."

"You're a bunch of stinking mutineers," Douglas replied icily. "You want him for your stinking Indian mutiny."

Baranof hardened, dropped the man's arm, and backed away.

Douglas made a quick sign to his two gunners. They turned their weapons in the direction of the old man. His wife rushed up with a little cry and threw herself between. Cannibal John took her arm, forced her aside, and began berating his enemy. "You rotten hypocrite," he shouted. There was a crash at the window as a pane shattered from the outside heat. "What can *you* do to cure him?" he demanded. "You and your rotten shooting tribe!" He had lost his head. "You're the curse of the earth! You're the curse of the earth! Look! Look here! You and your goddamn guns! I spit! I spit!" And Cannibal John Baranof spat. "I spit at your goddamn guns."

"Men!" Douglas commanded. "Seize him!"

John Baranof slugged the first man to reach him. The other fired. John fell, and his wife on top of him, like a sack. Betty screamed.

Something flashed in Arnold, and he turned on his adversary. "You devil," he snapped.

Douglas challenged, facing him squarely. "Men!" he commanded. "In the name of the law!"

"Why, you perfect dunce," said Arnold, suddenly calm again. "You haven't grasped the problem."

Betty was standing, hand to her mouth, wildly staring.

Douglas proceeded: "Fire!"

The tommy guns resounded—the noise in the little kitchen was terrific—and continued without let. Arnold could feel the bullets passing through his body—but not with pain. Bullets were ricocheting off the walls. Several struck Betty, and she collapsed without a cry. Arnold had the feeling that he was growing tremendously, but his stature was actually not increasing. He simply stood there, the bullets passing through, something crazy happening inside. The men kept their guns flaring at him. Douglas began to look afraid.

Abruptly, something gave way many miles (it seemed) inside Arnold, and the hunger that he had known since early morning was suddenly gone. Instead, he experienced perfect ease and disconnection

—like some profound, concussive break had happened deep inside. The feeling proceeded mightily, quickly, expanding through every cell of his frame, every atom of his earthly coil. And with a sudden shock his whole physique flashed. The detonation shook and cracked the house. The house dissolved.

The roar of the world's greatest explosion spread: it shook and cracked the very flames of the burning town of Indian Hat; consumed them; ripped out to all points of the compass at a speed 200,000 times the speed of light; shook and cracked the planet, hot as a blast; consumed it; and might have been seen in the cosmic reaches (if there had been anyone to see) as a pinpoint flash in the endless night.

PART III

LAST PARADISE

c. 1943

An Offering before Captain Cook in the Sandwich Islands (engraving, England, between 1770 and 1800 A.D.). John Webber. Courtesy of the United States Library of Congress.

THE PERSONALITY OF TOM WALLER was disturbingly familiar to me from the moment I met him, two weeks ago, when I arrived with Major Fineman, the adjutant investigating Waller's plantation manor. We had hardly clambered from our jeep when the front door of the great white Georgian home was opened from within by a really old native servant, and almost immediately, an oddly crane-like figure appeared, bowing and scraping, wringing his hands and seeming to sweep out along the walk toward us. The door behind him remained open.

"So glad to see you!" The man repeated his cracked cry three times as he hurried to greet us. "So glad to see you! So glad, so glad!"

I came around the jeep and stood like a soldier, while Major Fineman, tugging down the front of his khaki jacket, addressed himself to the meeting. "Mr. Waller?" he queried.

"Yes, yes, oh, yes!" the man replied, extending his hand.

The major accepted the handshake coldly.

"Won't you come in. Won't you come in." Waller urged.

The major cast a disparaging eye over the facade of the magnificent home, as I studied our would-be host, for I was struck with a sense of having known the man before.

"The place is yours. Won't you please…?"

Major Fineman turned away and with a knowing air, as if assessing the entire property, surveyed the gently rolling, meticulously tended lawns, studded with gardens and the astonishing forms of great banyan trees, mangoes, golden shower trees, palms, and numerous other growths of the sumptuous tropics. The perfumes of the trees and gardens, and of the bizarre flowers nodding about the open entrance, were heavy in the slightly stirring, very sultry air.

The major's survey returned to the building. He tugged his jacket down over the front of his corpulence once again and then paraded firmly forward toward the yawning front door. He was slightly shorter, much heavier, and more powerfully built than our host, Mr. Waller, who loped along beside him.

I came behind, greatly puzzled, trying to recall where I could have met Mr. Waller. Somewhere, I was very sure, I had known him well. His every nod and gesture, the cracked inflections of his voice, his unctuous hanging, his curious way of seeming to sweep along while continually bobbing and bowing—they were as familiar as could be. And yet his name was new, unfamiliar. Furthermore, before the army had transported me to this remote tropical isle, I had never been west of Chicago. My traveling as a student had been to Europe; and after returning to the States to settle to the grim task of making my way as a music critic, I had had neither money nor time to venture beyond the reaches of the subways of New York.

Major Fineman strode before me into the tidy foyer, where he nearly lost his footing when he stepped onto a hooked rug and it shot from under his right leg and slid along the polished floor. Our host, with a sharp cry, caught his guest's arm but was immediately forced to withdraw his support with profuse apologies when the officer glared at him with the indignation of a man who had been touched.

Yanking down the front of his khaki jacket, the major asked peremptorily, "How many rooms do you have?"

Mr. Waller broke into a vast flutter, like a giant butterfly. He was a surprisingly large man, particularly across his shoulders, and his arms dangled when they moved, his hands like buckets hanging from a yoke. "We have fifteen up there," he said, making a great sweep with his right hand to indicate the upper stories. "Fifteen up there," he repeated. "Fifteen. Down here, down here…well now, let's see, let's see, let's see. Do you mean…?"

Host and officer proceeded slowly into the spacious living room, while I tarried, examining everything with the minutest care in an effort to discover some explanation for my tantalizing presentiment of recognition. The old servant had remained by the front door, which he now quietly closed. He was pure Polynesian, with snow-white, closely cropped hair; large, round, staring eyes—a little moist, as though with tears; and broad but slightly stooped shoulders. He moved silently to straighten the rumpled rug.

The building was a beautiful enlargement of a New England Georgian mansion, adapted to suit the requirements of the tropics. Homes of this type, I would later learn, are common in Anglo-Saxon settlements throughout the Pacific, and for the managers of plantations, pretty much the rule. There was a great fireplace in the living room—though the world would have to undergo another glacial age for a fire in this particular spot to be endurable. The furnishings were largely Chippendale, with a battered and bepatched antique set here and there conspicuously. The windows were a bit small, as though to keep out the cold; and yet the wonderful amplitude of all the rooms, the great breath of air coming in from the vast, perfectly screened veranda, the wealth of cut flowers on every shelf and table, and the perfume from their blossoms wafting throughout let it be felt that something had happened to the New England conscience under the influence of the tropical sun.

Having delayed to study the details of the interior, I arrived on the veranda to find Mr. Waller apologizing for the absence of his wife, who was attending choir practice at the church. "You see," he explained, "we feel that the Lytton-Meredith plantation is an outpost of Christian democracy. We have workers here of every race and creed."

I had seen the workers' shacks on our approach to the manager's great estate. They were in good repair, for the most part, neat and trim. Dense fields of sugarcane, silvery green, spread around them in all directions, for miles and miles.

"Sergeant Currie," Major Fineman said, as I crossed the threshold from the living room, "how many men do you think I could bed on this veranda?"

Quickly I measured the area: an immense porch running the length of the house and overlooking from a great height a wildly beautiful, ruggedly indented coast of lava, where tremendous breakers were crashing and leaping skyward, shimmering white against the sapphire of the sky and sea, all along the foot of the ranging cliffs. "With a little crowding," I calculated, "I should think a hundred."

Mr. Waller winced but retained his persistent smile. He blinked at the major, like a man awaiting sentence. The major scanned to right and to left, glanced at the Pacific, glanced back at the living room, straightened his khaki jacket, then turned to his host. After loudly clearing his throat, he said in a husky voice, "Tell you what I'll do." Stepping a little closer to Mr. Waller and beginning to tap him on the chest—not the least like a major—he concluded, "You got a prettier place here than what's his name, the other side of the island."

"Mackenzie?" Mr. Waller suggested. The major nodded. "Mr. James Mackenzie," Waller hurried on, "of Pacific Sugar."

"Yeah," the major said. Again he cleared his throat. "That's it."

"Yes, yes. Yes indeed. Our old friends, the Mackenzies."

"Mackenzie's got a first-class place, you understand. But your place here is prettier. Understand?"

"Well, I wouldn't say—" began the humble host.

"Listen," the major interrupted. "I know, see? I been around." He laughed roughly and gave a yank at the sleeve of his khaki. "I ain't been wearing *this* thing all my life."

Mr. Waller, uncertain how to reply, tightened his painful smile and wrung his hands. The major broke off the conversation, as the old servant appeared, moving with an unsteady gait. He was carrying a tray arrayed with glasses, an ice bucket, a pitcher of water, and a crystal decanter that he set on a low serving table. The host, welcoming this reprieve, picked up the decanter, turned to his guest, and, lifting his brows even more than before, inquired, "Will you have some Scotch, Major? We have some of the genuine stuff."

"You got bourbon?"

"Yes."

"Well, I'll have bourbon. I like bourbon."

Mr. Waller bowed, set down the decanter, whispered something to the servant, who quickly disappeared, and then began dropping ice into a glass. "Do you prefer plain water," he asked, "or soda?"

"You got Coke?" replied the major, who had begun to plunder a humidor of cigars on an adjacent table.

"Why, yes, why, yes," the host said. "Why, yes, I think we have." He set down the glass and straightened up his back. Noting the work at the humidor, he exclaimed, "Oh, do! Oh, do! Do help yourself, Major. Do make yourself at home. Please do!"

The servant came back and was again sent away, this time for Coca-Cola.

The host turned his regard to me. "How about you, Sergeant?" he asked. I was watching him carefully to see if he betrayed any sign of recognition. He laughed nervously. "Are you allowed to drink in the presence of your C.O.?"

He turned to the major, who had bitten the end off a cigar and was trying to spit it out. "This is a democratic army, Mr. Waller," my C.O. said, returning his laughter while removing the cigar tip with his fingers.

Waller laughed again. We all were supposed to laugh.

"Well, then, Sergeant," said our host, "will you have Scotch or bourbon?"

"Scotch, if you please. And water," I added.

"Ice?"

"Yes, please."

He prepared my glass. The Coke arrived, and he mixed the major's drink. Then he fixed his own libation. There was not a moment when the man seemed to have the slightest notion of ever having seen or known me before.

The major sat down in a creaking wicker chair, and I settled myself on a settee, somewhat apart. I looked at the view and listened to the dialogue.

"Now, let me tell you," said the major, "what I want you to do." He put down his glass, flicked the ash from his purloined cigar, and took a puff. Mr. Waller, all eyes and ears, was nodding, watching, nodding, and listening.

The major examined the nose of the cigar. "We got a lot of boys in bad shape—pilots, navigators, bombardiers," he elaborated. "Understand? These boys need a rest. They need a lot of rest. Understand?"

Waller stopped wringing his hands.

"We also got a lot of wounded beginning to come in now from the west…" the major broke off reflectively. Our host began to pluck unsystematically at his closely cropped mustache.

"But that's another proposition," the major resumed. "That's the one I think I'll assign to what's his name—Mackenzie?"

"Yes, Mackenzie. James Mackenzie," Waller volunteered. "Mackenzie."

Major Fineman exchanged his cigar for his tumbler, rattled the ice, took a long and conclusive drink, and then set down the glass.

"What I want you and Mrs. Waller to do," he said finally, "is give these boys—these flyers, you understand?—give them a taste of home. You got a first-class place here, and they're tired. Tired out."

Waller sat silently. I again looked at the view, and then examined the furnishings.

"We'll send you thirty or so at a time. They'll like it," the major assured him. "Plenty of whisky, lots of rest. Do them a world of good. You got a first-class place here, Mr. Waller."

The major stood up, and I did as well. Mr. Waller, who was alert to be of service, sprang to his feet.

Major Fineman gave a tug at the front of his khaki. "First class," he repeated as he started out of the room. I followed. Then the major stopped, turned, and pointing a finger at our host, insisted, "Believe me, Mr. Waller, I know. I been around."

_____ *2.*

THAT WAS THE BEGINNING OF MY PROBLEM of recall. The image of the plantation manager remained with me throughout the following two weeks. I even dreamed of him—in a vague way: he seemed to be bowing, handing me something, in a heavily furnished, smoky room—but the glimpse was not very clear and only added to the annoyance of my mind.

Everyone has had this kind of experience, but the conundrum is not often quite so baffling: I was certain I had once known the man well, yet our worlds were as remote as could be imagined—spiritually as well as geographically. In New York, in Germany, and in Paris, I had had wonderfully little to do with people of business and affairs.

To make solving my puzzle the more difficult, our post was a good forty miles from the Lytton-Meredith plantation, and no one in our local stores could tell me much about people and things so far away.

Oh, yes, of course, they all knew Mr. Waller.

"Allee same, numba one big stuff, Messa Walla," I learned, for example, from Tom Ping at the Cross Roads Cafe. My barber, Mr. Kamura, readily confirmed how long the man had been manager: "Ten year, ten year…Yeah. Dass righ'," When I asked about *Mrs.* Waller, he added, "Missi Warra? She rong time-uh. She toooooo muchee rong time-uh stop."

I deduced from all this that she was the daughter of a local island family and had been living here a long time, but that *he* had arrived at a comparatively recent date.

And what sort of man was he to work for?

I got the answer to that one from a young Filipino I tapped in the pool parlor: "Boy, he tough!" That was the sum of that. Apparently, Mr. Waller's unctuousness would disappear when he was dealing with men beneath him.

Illumination came to me, as I was determined it should, during my second visit to the mansion. I was again transporting Major

Fineman, who wished to buzz over to see how things were going—and to grab another handful of those cigars.

We arrived as before, but this time we found the lawns populated with a quiet scattering of young men: some were strolling, some resting beneath the great trees. A baseball game was in progress. From within came the strains of a moderately competent boogie-woogie piano.

The major clambered from the jeep. I settled back, preparing to await his return. Then he surprised me. "Come on, Sergeant," he barked gruffly. "You might as well enjoy this." I thanked him properly, disembarked, and came around the jeep.

As I followed his heavyset form along the walk, I observed that some of the flowerbeds had been trampled. The front door was open, and when we entered the foyer, I noticed that both hooked rug and polish had departed.

The major strode into the room with the fireplace, and the several young men lounging about sprang to their feet.

"Sit down, boys," commanded the major, gazing around. The place looked "lived in," I must say—the antiques had been put away, the arrays of freshly cut flowers were gone—but the walls and furniture were still intact, and on the whole, the home had not yet been destroyed.

The major approached a dark-browed young man, who again snapped to his feet and saluted. "Relax, Lieutenant! Relax," the major ordered.

The young man dropped the salute, but looked exceedingly uncomfortable.

"*That's* it, *that's* it," the major reassured him. "Now tell me, Lieutenant…" he paused to jerk down the front of his jacket, "How is everything? Okay?"

The young man succeeded in relaxing. "Everything is just fine, Major," he replied pleasantly, with something of a southern drawl. He had a way of shutting his eyes and tilting his head when talking.

Major Fineman stepped a little closer. "First-class establishment!" he declared.

The lieutenant opened his eyes and quietly regarded the major, who lifted his brows and in a coarse whisper demanded, "Ain't it?"

The young officer nodded and began to speak.

The major interrupted, "You telling me!" He went on, "They treating the boys okay?"

"Sure are!" the lieutenant said.

"You telling me!" the major proclaimed. "These folks are high class, Lieutenant. Understand?"

The lieutenant, who was gazing over the major's shoulder, saw Mrs. Waller appear in the doorway and caught the major's arm. "Here's Mrs. Waller now," he said.

Major Fineman turned. A young woman, dark and with black sparkling eyes, was briskly crossing the room, a Siamese cat clutched under one arm and under the other, a beaming two-year-old, whom she was scolding. "Bad Bobby! Bad, bad boy!" Oblivious to the scattering of soldiers, she darted past us. Bobby, who was waving something, let it fly. It broke against a table leg and gave up its contents: an old watch. One of the young men lunged to recover it, and Mrs. Waller, greatly cumbered, turned back. She was wearing a red and yellow flowered wash dress, protected by a green kitchen apron trimmed with a white frill—a picture of young wifely efficiency and vivacity.

Major Fineman, his heavy features fixed in a half-incredulous smile, was obviously enchanted. The young woman, stooping to receive the shattered watch, caught his eye. That moment, the cat slipped from her.

"Damn!" she exclaimed. "Excuse me, Major," she quickly added, with a frank laugh, before attending to the thanking of the youth who was at her feet. Baby Bobby, beaming from her shoulder and waving his right arm, started to wave his left too, and it struck her face. "Stop it, Bobby. Stop!" she commanded, shifting him to her hip. "Never mind about Tabby," she told the soldier, who now had started for the cat.

"Mrs. Waller," the major began inopportunely, advancing and offering his hand, "my name is Fineman—" He corrected himself: "I'm Major Fineman."

The young woman, straightening to a standing posture, nodded at the baby in her right arm and laughed again. Twisting herself toward the major, she managed to give him her little finger. "I'd guessed that's who you were," she said. "You've caught us at a psychological moment. Bobby has just bitten his sister, wet his pants, choked one of our kittens to death, and broken out in a rash. If you'll excuse me..." She started away—Bobby gurgling, waving both his arms, and beaming back at the major—and then she paused, calling over her shoulder, "I'll be right back!" Bobby made a gleeful noise. "Ha!" his mother said as she took him away. "Ha, ha! You're a fine one! You're a fine one, you are!" And she left the room.

The young men in the room were watching the major and exchanging winks. He turned to the young officer at his side. "I didn't realize they had little children," he said.

"Three," the lieutenant replied, tilting his head and shutting his eyes. He opened the eyes and regarded the major. "One's about a year older than this; the other's younger—an infant."

"Well," the major said, looking harassed, "I'll be damned." Then he asked sharply, "Where do they keep them?"

"The kitchen end of the house. They've a garden there, and they live in the rooms just above."

The major, ill at ease, jerked down his jacket.

I, meanwhile, having studied the young woman closely, was pretty sure that I had never seen her before. She was not a creature one would have forgotten. Nor could I make any connection between this sparkling, vivacious little wife, and the psalm-singing image that her husband's apology for her absence two weeks ago had brought to my mind. She seemed considerably younger than Mr. Waller, and, to me at any rate, a much more attractive human being.

While I was brooding upon her, she returned, without the apron. Her hair had been tidied. She wore no lipstick but had red polish on her nails. Approaching the major with a frank air of greeting, she held out her hand, and he stood stoutly to receive it.

"My husband has told me all about you, Major," she said. "Too bad he isn't here; he would have loved to see you. Can you stay for dinner? He'll be here for dinner."

The major demurred.

"Well, you'll have a drink anyhow. He may be back before you're through. Bourbon and Coke?" she said.

The major broadly smiled.

"You see!" she said, with a charming tilt of her head. "I know all about you."

Major Fineman squirmed with pleasure. He was still groping for words when she turned her attention to me. "Sergeant Currie?" she asked, extending her hand. Her grasp was firm and boyish. "You see?" she said, looking back at the major. "You're right at home here; you're an old friend."

I was beginning to understand something of Waller's obvious success in the world. While the young woman was flattering us, the old servant, whom I recognized, appeared with a tray laden with several bottles and a number of glasses. He set it down and retreated. As Mrs. Waller prepared the concoction for the major, I noticed her observing me from the corner of her eye.

"You know," she said to me, at last, as she handed Major Fineman his glass, "you remind me of a boy I used to know in New York."

I was amazed and greatly gratified. I was sure that I was about to learn the answer to my riddle; but more than that—there was something very pleasing about the recognition of such an attractive woman.

"His name," she said, "was Jack Coe."

My heart collapsed.

"Jack Coe!" exclaimed the major. "Why, I know him! Know him well. His father's in the hotel business."

I felt the peculiar discomfort that comes of being compared with someone you have never seen.

"My god," said the major complacently, "what a world! Ain't it the truth?" And he turned to the young officer for corroboration.

"Would you *believe* it, Lieutenant?" he said with satisfaction.

I, meanwhile, recovered myself, and pressed my advantage, for the kill. "Mrs. Waller," I said, "you have been in New York?"

Her attention returned to me from the major, and she nodded. "I went to school and college in the East." When she started to prepare my drink, I offered to pour my own, but she held me off while she measured out two brimming jiggers.

"Is that where you met your husband?" I demanded. It was over-bold of me, but I had to know.

She added some water. "No," she answered, abstractedly, measuring. She tilted the glass at me. "That okay?"

"That's beautiful," I told her.

She gave the glass a brisk stir.

I returned to my theme: "But your husband *did* live in New York, at one time."

"Yes. But that was long before *my* time."

"Was he born in the East?"

She nodded.

"What did he do there? What was his work?"

She regarded me with a quizzical wrinkle in the corner of her eye—as though it had just begun to dawn on her that my cross-questioning was pretty direct and fast. She laughed.

"Well, he tells me," she answered easily, passing me the glass, "that he had a simply horrible job—in his university club—on Forty-seventh Street. Why do you ask?" she added, with another of her rollicking laughs. "Do you think you know him? Don't tell me you're as old as that!"

She then invited the young men in the room to help themselves.

3.

THE CLUB—I REMEMBERED IT WELL, for it once had been one of my favorite haunts—was an old, substantial, white marble–faced building, just off Vanderbilt Avenue. The interior had been designed to suggest the civilization of London. Its heavily wainscoted, vast lounges were always populated with a sufficient scattering of oldish denizens, while the more active, younger tribe that continually passed through the revolving front door proceeded vigorously to the squash courts, solariums, locker rooms, and Turkish baths. During my student years, the club library had been my New York headquarters. And after my return from Europe, when I settled myself in the city and fell pretty much out of the sphere of my university interests, I continued to use the club as a convenient midtown lunching place, and its swimming pool as an occasional midwinter resort.

When Mrs. Waller mentioned the club, my memory was jogged. For a moment I tried to think of some person I'd met there who could possibly have been the original of the man in whose fabulous home I now was standing. Then I recalled my dream: a heavily furnished, smoky room; a figure bowing, handing me something....Gradually the figment became a specific young man—pale and seedy, with a black, cropped mustache, painfully solicitous to be of service—handing me a book: the librarian who, in my first years at the club, had been my silent companion for many peaceful hours.

I had totally forgotten him—together with a multitude of people, circumstances, feelings, and ambitions that had been very real to me in that now deeply distant time. For the blithe world of the late twenties has been so definitively dissolved by the disasters that have since crowded upon us, one can hardly credit as real what then was common fact: the optimism of a civilization that had fought its Last Great War and would go on to cultivate the arts of peace. Those days, it was the right, not the duty, of a citizen to vote. Europe teemed every summer with visiting Americans; New York showered its ticker tape down on visiting Channel swimmers; Freud, Picasso, and the Lindbergh flight were in the news; and Wall Street was the destination of choice for almost everyone.

As for me: I was then still a student—my father's business had not yet collapsed—and I foresaw for myself many long and happy years of unmolested study in the great universities of Europe; the Boulevard Montparnasse, the Munich Hofbräuhaus, the Arno, and the Strand were equally known to me; and if today was fair, tomorrow would be fairer. Briefly (to reverse the celebrated dictum of Caesar's poet): "Let *others* rule mankind and make the world obey, disposing peace and war their own majestic way." The world, with all its wonderful cities, was mine to enjoy and to love.

But now that I'd come to think about the club, I remembered the pitiful librarian, whose full name, by the way, I never did learn: we used to call him Tom.

After I'd become a familiar figure to him, he began to greet me when I entered his book-lined lair with a hungry look: he was eager to talk; and whenever I was the only reader in the room, he would inevitably discover something to do in the neighborhood of my deep chair. On such occasions we would exchange a few brief civilities, and now and then these would develop into conversations.

"You are reading Summer, I see! *Folkways*!"

"Yes," I would answer.

"He's the one—isn't he?—who invented the term 'mores'?"

"Well, 'mores,'" I would reply pedantically, "is a Latin word."

"Yes, of course. I know, I know."

"Summer introduces it as a sociological term."

"Yes, I know, I know."

Apparently Tom was brooding in his silent den—day after day, month after month—brooding deeply and resentfully, while members consulted him about which detective stories they should read and asked his opinion of the various books currently on the bestseller list. I started to regard him as a symbol, a sorrowful representative of all the misplaced, ineffectual spirits of our massive, terribly impersonal civilization. Tom so got into my mind that presently I began to welcome, rather than resent, his conversational intrusions.

One day, as Tom was rearranging a set of the Loeb Classics, he turned to me. "Mr. Currie,"—though I was some six years his junior, he had to address me with the respect of a servant—"have you read O'Brien's *White Shadows in the South Seas*?"

"I read it when it came out—about ten years ago."

"Well, his descriptions of Tahiti," he offered carefully, as though beginning a confession, "they made an awful dent on me."

"Pretty lush!" I agreed, with a great air of sophistication.

"And I got to thinking," he pressed on, "I got to thinking, what a

ridiculous, dry grind I'm living here, when I might be—just as well—
be enjoying a wonderful, natural life like that."

I began to feel immensely superior.

"You know," he continued eagerly, "that book started me on a
regular binge of South Sea island stuff: Melville, Stevenson, Captain
Cook, Jack London. And then with all this new material that's been
coming out...it got me to wondering what it would cost to make the
trip. You've traveled. How much do you think it would cost?"

I looked up at him with some surprise. Facing me was a man
whose expression suggested that he was actually on the point of daring
to do something pretty wild. "Well, let's see," I said, trying to calcu-
late, "the round-trip to San Francisco—"

"Round-trip?" he interrupted. "I want to *stay!*"

"You want to stay?"

"Why, of course. That's the whole idea."

I squinted at him incredulously. "Don't be a fool. You can't get
away from yourself as easily as all that. Besides," I added with a gesture of disgust, "those islands aren't the way they look in the picture
books."

"Oh, I know, I know all that." He looked around to see if anyone
had come into the library, then drew a little closer and suddenly lowered his voice. "But you know what?" He looked ridiculous: behind
horn-rimmed spectacles his unhappy brown eyes were opened so wide
that white showed all around; his inflamed lids appeared sore. "I've
discovered a valley that hasn't yet been touched," he whispered.

"Discovered a valley!" I burst out laughing. "Why, you haven't
left this library."

The young man retained his seriousness. "I told you," he said,
shaking his head with a bit of annoyance, "that I was reading."

"Well, then, the guy who wrote the book was there, and the place
is done for. One white man is enough," I insisted. "The mission of the
white man is the mission of death."

He looked a little disturbed.

"And besides," I added, "you are a white man yourself."

I laughed; but since he retained his sober, thoughtful countenance,

I returned to his original question: "Okay. Let's see…one way to San Francisco, and then passage to…hold on. How are you going to get there if there isn't any traffic with the world?"

"It's like this," he explained, suddenly all eagerness again. "You see, this place—Last Paradise, I call it—it's a remote and unfrequented valley on a certain island."

"Which island?"

"Never mind which island. I'm not telling anyone." He smiled. "I know all the little islands in the South Seas are being ruined, but this aloof valley is on one of the larger islands, and it's useless. There's no road to it, the port is many miles away, and the people living there are—"

"Lots of beautiful big girls?" I teased.

He smiled and flushed. "Well, I don't know about that."

"Lots of beautiful, big breadfruit trees? Plenty of coconuts?"

He laughed.

"Well, you'll be the ruin of the place," I joked. "Poor beautiful girls! Poor beautiful garden land!"

"How much?"

"You could probably get there," I guessed, "for a couple of hundred dollars: train to San Francisco, then a freighter to…wherever you like."

He brightened. "You *think* so?"

"Of course. I *know* so."

"Why, my god, I've *got* two hundred dollars—in the bank."

"Then you're off! The world is yours."

"Do you mean to say," he mused, "that it's as easy as that to get away from this goddamn civilization of ours?"

"No," I replied, with an air of great wisdom, "it's not."

He slowly turned and moved away. That was an afternoon, if I remember correctly, sometime in the middle of winter. Early the following summer, as I recall, I left New York for Paris; and when I returned after several years abroad, the faces everywhere had changed. I forgot en masse the more casual of my earlier acquaintances. And in the library at the club, I discovered, instead of the wide and sad eyes of Tom, the keen grey orbs of an officious, unwholesome little toad of a book arranger, who had been nicknamed by the members Dr. Gus.

4.

IT IS REMARKABLE how completely forgotten episodes, when touched with a word, open to the memory—at first vaguely, like the recollection of a dream, but then with increasing clarity and certitude, until at last all is again present, and one wonders how such scenes could have ever been forgotten. My early years at the club had been erased and written over by later events, and the club itself, by the anxieties and activities of war. I believe that if Mrs. Waller had never said anything about her husband's "horrible job" at a club on Forty-seventh Street, I would have never, in a hundred years, made the connection between Tom the librarian, whose features had reappeared from the darkness, and Tom Waller, the oddly crane-like lord of the manor, who had first stirred my thoughts when he appeared at the front door, wringing his hands, and then, bowing and scraping, swept out to greet us.

Needless to say, my curiosity was now greatly aroused, and my interest was more alive than ever; but it was impossible to satisfy either while sharing cocktails and brief verbal exchanges with a company of comparative strangers. Later, however, I made it my business to hunt out and piece together everything I could discover about Tom Waller's arrival on the island and his subsequent career. He himself willingly disclosed much of the story; his wife told me what she could; and Hina, the comely, dark-eyed, dusky heroine of the greater portion of his adventure, confided even more.

But how shall I begin?

The whole island, and particularly Waller's portion of it, has been transformed to such a degree since the fateful moment of his inconspicuous arrival that it is almost impossible to reconstruct the earlier character of the place. They tell me that in those days—hardly fifteen years ago—there was not a blade of sugarcane on this side of the ridge, but rather a desert, a wild and barren landscape of naked hills, with a single, wonderfully verdant, remote valley that opened to a rocky coast: my young librarian's "Last Paradise," where the tropical idyll of the Noble Savage lingered on into the twentieth century, as in a timeless dream. But even the other side of the island, I am told, then supported only a single little town, which in the 1840s and '50s had been a port of call for American whalers.

The ships were met, all the old voyagers have written, by gay and brightly laughing natives in little flotillas of canoes and by droves of swimming girls. The lively welcoming committee would come swarming aboard at every quarter, up the anchor chains and bobstays, wreathing their slender forms about the ropes. "All of them," Melville wrote of one South Sea island arrival, "at length succeeded in getting up the ship's sides, where they clung dripping with the brine, and glowing from the bath, their jet-black tresses streaming over their shoulders, and half enveloping their otherwise naked forms. There they hung, sparkling with savage vivacity, laughing gaily with one another, and chattering away with infinite glee." It was the dream moment of all the huskies aboard, and they returned the vision with a contribution of rats and disease.

The miserable history has been often told. When the whaling fleets disappeared, the navies—French and British, American and Russian—still pulled into port every now and then. The towns were brothels by the time the missionaries arrived. And then, at last, came the planters, who, finding that the natives were unwilling laborers, imported from the overcrowded coasts of Asia swarms of coolies—Chinese, Japanese, Filipino—thus sowing the seeds of a pretty complicated future. Plantation towns sprang up, and each day the morning whistle blew; smoke lifted from the refineries; wharfs were run out into the sea.

Tom Waller, it seems, arrived on an old freighter that had taken over twenty days to come from San Francisco. There were no water nymphs to greet the vessel; but he was not surprised, for he had not expected that there should be. He was standing forward, at the very bow, leaning on the rail, his face against the cooling trade wind, his widely staring brown eyes surveying with excited attention the long sweep of shoreline and the dramatic background of the precipitous ridge that, as he knew, divided the isle in two.

"Thank god for that ridge," he said to himself, aloud. That was his one prayer as the vessel was maneuvered to its pier. He observed with admiration the white of the clouds hanging upon the peaks, the blue sky, the blue waters, the dark green of the island, the perfume of flowers coming out from the shore, and his spirit was filled with a cleanliness of joy that was for him tantamount to a rebirth. It had all been so easy—purchasing his tickets, crossing the continent on the train, booking passage on the freighter, and then the quiet enjoyment of the sea. It had all been so easy that he could not but wonder why he had not released himself from his bondage long before.

Tom was dressed in a blue shirt and dungarees. The duffel bag at his feet contained two extra pairs of shoes, some shirts and trousers, and the books which, after long reflection, he had decided were the ones to take with him to his tropical isle: James Joyce's *Ulysses*, Homer's *Iliad* and *Odyssey*, and Henry Clarke Warren's *Buddhism in Translation*. He had had the wit to provide himself with an extra pair of glasses. And he had still some fifty dollars in his pocket—enough for a lifetime of the kind he now proposed to lead.

When the ship was finally warped into its slip and Tom heard the gangplank rattling into place, it was for him a marvelous, miraculous moment. Derricks had already begun to lift cargo out of the hold and swing it ashore. The crew were shouting back and forth. No one in the world cared whether he was aboard or ashore. He shouldered his bag and made his way to the gangplank, where a pockmarked young Chinaman, wearing portions of some sort of uniform, examined his landing papers carelessly and let him pass.

The first thing that caught the young adventurer's attention as he stepped from the rough wharf to the unpaved single street of the little town was a luxurious Packard station wagon standing untended before the office of the wharf. He paused to regard it with an unfriendly stare; but in a moment a brisk young woman wearing expensive riding breeches came swinging out of the office door, calling back jokingly to someone within. She gave him no more than a glance—which never-theless stopped his heart—before slamming her way into the waiting car, stepping on the starter, and with an easy purr speeding down the street and disappearing from view. This was the youth's first vision of the girl who would one day be his wife; and though it is perhaps too facile to say that he was already in love with her, it is certainly true that from that moment on she was a permanent element in his mind.

He provided himself with some canned supplies and a few scraps of information, and then against all advice boldly started on his way. The difficult hike up the steep ridge that divided the isle in two and then down the other side, the trek across a barren desert area, and the more grueling traverse of a second, smaller but hotter, ridge brought Tom to his rich valley destination, but took three entire days and left him nearly dead.

Traveling the dirt roads through the fields back of the town was easy. His subsequent ascent of the heavily wooded ridge required the greater part of the first day. At the top he found himself in a thick mist of cloud, which made it impossible for him to survey more than a few feet of the surrounding woodland, thoroughly saturated his already sweaty clothing, and brought a bad chill upon him the moment the sun went down. Throughout the night he shivered miserably, and ev-ery bone in his body was aching before the sun rose again—or rather, before the cocoon of cloud enveloping him became luminous enough for him to see. When he struggled to his feet, he realized that he had lost his glasses, which gave him a fright; and for a moment, his physi-cal pains were forgotten while he felt about the leafy ground. He felt something crack beneath his left knee—and there were the glasses, snapped at the nose and with a shattered lens.

Tom's trembling fingers could hardly open the duffel bag, and it took him almost ten minutes to discover where he had stowed his extra glasses. After he found them and put them on, he carefully stowed the unbroken lens away in their box. Whereupon he was suddenly afraid that he had lost his can opener; but it was on the ground under his left foot. He pulled himself together, adjusted the glasses to his eyes, and after a hideous breakfast of canned tomatoes and sardines, made to move again, dragging the bag and still shivering so violently that his teeth were chattering. Suddenly the bag tore on a jagged edge of rock, several objects fell out, and Tom found that he had begun to cry. He stuffed the objects back into the bag and tried to lift the thing; but today it was too heavy for him, and he set it down, still crying, and began to drag it hopelessly behind him, letting it catch and rip again and again, spilling out what it would, while he made his way, heartlessly, down the slope through the completely silent woodland.

When he broke at last from the head of cloud he found himself a few yards from the edge of the woodland. Before him laid an immense sweep of absolutely treeless, rocky cactus waste, descending miles and miles to the distant sea. As the hot sun began to warm his bones, he was overcome by an irresistible requirement for sleep; without another thought, he flung the tattered remains of his bag against the foot of a tree and fell down to the ground.

Tom woke to find the sun overhead. During his slumber, he had recovered his mental, if not his physical, vigor. He sat up and took account of his state of affairs: he was stiff, but his chill was gone; his clothes were dry; his exposed skin had begun to burn; and with the bottom of his bag having been ripped apart, all his belongings were gone. That was a huge blow. He decided to retrace his steps and retrieve whatever scattered property he could find.

By the time he was ready to resume his advance, the sun had begun to descend the heavens again. He fashioned his recovered possessions into a kind of laundry bundle, which he fastened to the end of a long stick. With this contrivance over his left shoulder, he gathered heart, made his mind ready for the long transit, and with a great deal more courage than common sense, set himself in motion once again.

The crossing was some forty miles; and it was just as well that he had started late in the afternoon, for a full day's trek beneath the blaze of the tropical sun would have slain him. Fortunately, he had found his powerful flashlight, which enabled him to continue traveling throughout the night. By the following noon, he was at the foot of a second, fairly steep, dry ridge, and he began his final, painful ascent. His feet were by now so sore that he could hardly bear to set them on the ground, and when he slipped and was jolted to the earth, he would lie there weeping, sometimes for a full minute, before finding the courage to try his luck again.

Waller declared that it must have taken him a full three hours to make that ascent of barely more than a mile. When he got to the top, he realized that somewhere along the way he had abandoned his staff and bundle and was without a thing—save the ragged clothing on his back and the paper money he had placed in his trouser pocket. But his spirit revived, and he knew his life had been saved, when he gazed out and saw spread before him a wondrous valley, green and glorious: his Last Paradise.

This remarkable phenomenon of a valley was a deep cut in the lava, like the gap left by a slice of pie, with countless springs bubbling from the precipitous cliffs on both sides. At its head was a tumbling stream; its floor, verdant with abundant vegetation, was like a garden; and where it abutted the sea, rolling breakers crashed hard against tumbled rocks, projecting geyser-like sprays high into the air, where they gleamed in the sun. As the victorious voyager sat blissfully on the high ridge, his eyes drinking in the dramatic beauty of the landscape and pounding sea far below him, like a world beneath its god, he was greeted by the heavy smell of blossoms, oozing fruit, and fertile land.

Waller told me that he could not recall how he felt or what he thought as he made his way down the difficult slope. All he remembers is that he was no longer very much worried about his feet, for his was a plunge more into joy than disaster, and as he slipped and tumbled, every yard he fell was a yard deeper into paradise. And so he came, battering himself through the candlenut trees, the tangled vines, and the heavy bushes of guava, pausing now and then to bite some succulent fruit that he thought he recognized—sometimes delighted by the taste, sometimes shocked. About halfway down the drop, he arrived at a wondrous cascade that fell perhaps two hundred feet down the side of the wall into a large and beautiful pool, where a small group was bathing. As he gazed down, his foot slipped. He tried to catch himself, but the rock that he grabbed came loose, and he began to slide. A shower of debris shot out from beneath him and peppered into the pool. Looking up and spying him, the bathers cried out in alarm. He tried to coast on his seat, but the ground dropped away, and he fell, struck something, was thrown, and plunged....

The next thing he remembers is that he was lying on his back with a frightful pain in his left arm and shoulder, while several hands were massaging his chest and sides, neck and arms. When he tried to focus his eyes—now minus their glasses—he discerned three dusky faces, young and female, peering down at him. Having watched his eyes flutter and open, they had begun to chatter excitedly in some language that he was unable to understand. The massaging stopped, and his head was lifted to a soft and apparently bare bosom. The young man swooned. When he recovered, he was again on the ground, and the girls were laughing.

It was too bad that Waller had lost his glasses, for he never really beheld anything of the valley. All he could ever see were the people and things just around him; the rest was no more than a voluptuous haze. But he lived luxuriously with the marvelous family whose children had found him. The father, Mr. Kanaka, was a vigorous and expert fisherman, who soon taught him how to fling a net into the surf, spear an eel, and maneuver an outrigger canoe. The man wore, in old-fashioned style, a loincloth and a bark-cloth cape; so presently, Tom too was wearing a loincloth. And marvelous to relate: it was some three weeks after his torn dungarees had been ripped into lengths and converted into a rag doll for Hina, the third of the three sisters, that the young man thought of the fifty dollars that had been left in a pocket; but the pocket was gone.

 5.

IT IS POINTLESS to describe the uneventful life of the simple people of the valley. They were no longer the bold pagan warriors of old. A little Christian church perched upon a bleak promontory, looking out to sea; and though it had been abandoned some fifteen years ago, after an epidemic of influenza had all but wiped out the congregation, it stood nevertheless as an assurance that no heathen images or obscene rites would ever again assault the sensibilities of the Christian visitor. Remnants of earlier times could still be found throughout the valley: overgrown stone walls and enclosures, two deserted temple platforms of heaped-up lava stone—one at the head of the valley, not far from the cascade; the other, like the church, upon a promontory by the sea—and in the shade of enormous mango trees, signs of house sites and earlier habitations. But there were no chieftains anymore, no mysteries of the taboo, no festivals, great gatherings or dances, no gods. What had once been a populous, ceremonially ordered world was now a rank land of gloriously teeming vegetation, peopled and cultivated, here and there, by a few listless families. For Tom, however, all of this was heaven, and he blissfully settled into family life and learned to speak the language.

The first break in his reverie occurred several months into his residence. He was hoeing the taro garden one morning, when one of the family's naked youngsters ran past hollering that horsemen were filing through the groves of the valley. Tom, immediately resentful, stopped hoeing and turned to see what would happen in the compound. Almost at once the family matriarch in her red-flowered calico Mother Hubbard came ponderously out of one of the grass houses. She said something to the boy, and he darted into the door behind her. He immediately reappeared, fastening a pair of overalls, and then scampered up the path toward the cascade to carry the warning to his sisters.

Before Tom could grasp what was happening, a horse whinnied, and he beheld a company breaking from the forest, hardly fifty yards away. They were riding languidly, in a file that finally numbered seven, with a heavily set Japanese in the lead. One of the women pointed, calling back to the man behind her; he leaned forward and then looked toward Tom, who realized that he was the object of interest. The procession of riders filed past the garden fence en route to the cascade, and Tom, observing them through the haze of his nearsighted vision, was shocked to realize that the young woman was the one he had seen at the wharf when he landed. As the equestrians were passing, the man riding behind her—a grey-haired gentleman in his late fifties, with a golfer's tan—abruptly reeled his horse from the path, reversed course, and came down to the fence.

"Nick around?" he asked, his voice deep and resonant.

Tom felt ridiculous—nearly naked, messily bearded, leaning on a hoe—but he tried to behave as though his mind had not been disordered. "Nick?" he asked, approaching the man. "Who's Nick?"

"Well, I call him Nick," the gentleman replied, smiling easily. "I mean the old man. Your boss?"

Tom had a curious sense of remembering the man who was speaking to him. He was greatly confused. "Nick?" he asked again. He rubbed his forehead and looked around distractedly, trying to solve too many things at once.

The horse whinnied, pawed the ground, and shook his head, flecking Tom with foam. The rider, handling the animal masterfully, began to turn him away; but then he swung the horse back around and said confidently, "My name is Butterfield, J. P. Butterfield."

"Butterfield"—the name echoed in Tom's mind. "Butterfield": he knew that name. Squinting hard at the man, he started to feel the atmosphere of the club. Then a light went on: Mr. Butterfield! Mr. Butterfield? "Oh, Mr. Butterfield!" he exclaimed. "I *thought* I recognized you."

The gentleman looked surprised. He had obviously expected recognition, but of a different kind.

"Don't you remember *me*?" asked Tom. "I'm Tom. From the club." The gentleman on the horse was the one who now looked confused. "From the club," Tom repeated. "In New York: the university club! The librarian…?"

"Well, for the love of god," the man said, his eyes opening wider. The horse, anxious to move on, danced sideways and needed to be controlled again. The man guided the beast through a complicated figure that brought them back to the fence. "Tom?" Butterfield queried disbelievingly. Leaning to examine the transplant, "Good god!" he exclaimed. "I wouldn't know you in a million years. What brings you here?"

That was the great scene, as Tom Waller remembers it. Both he

and Mr. Butterfield have recounted it a hundred times: Waller declares that it was the supreme moment of his life—the turning point;
Butterfield maintains that it was the greatest meeting in the history of
the island. At the time, however, neither understood what had taken
place.

Butterfield declared that he and his daughter Eleanor, together
with the Mackenzie family, had come for a holiday. His family had
a hunting lodge some two miles down the valley—though there was
nothing on the island to hunt except rats and owls. "Do drop around,
Tom, for a call!" he offered, starting to ride off. Almost immediately,
he drew back the reins, paused, and turned back. "You know," he
stated, "I *own* this valley—this whole side of the island, in fact." He
shook his head and began to laugh. "But it isn't worth a damn." Then
he spurred his horse, and the excited animal galloped away.

Tom watched the buttocks of the departing steed and the straight
back of the powerful rider, which soon disappeared from his nearsighted gaze. He made a few heartless swipes with the hoe but quickly
realized that he was sick and could no longer work in the garden. He
heard the voices of the girls and children returning from the cascade,
and rather than face them before he had recovered his poise, he set the
hoe against the fence and moved away.

Before he had gone a hundred yards, Hina, who was about four-
teen, came skipping up behind him and called, "Tommy?"

He turned and smiled. She was a dark bird, very pretty in her
calico, with a blood-red hibiscus in her ebony tresses and enormous,
active eyes.

"I think I will walk with you," she declared in her native dialect,
speaking very distinctly so that he should understand. "You are my
husband, you know, and I am afraid that rich foreigner, Miss Butterfield, has turned your head."

Tom was startled. His heart gave a great lurch and began to beat
rapidly. (He declares, jokingly, that it has continued to beat that way,
to the present day.) He scrutinized the girl to discover how she could
have read in him an emotion of which he himself was not yet aware.
Hina, returning his glance with a challenging smile, reached and

grasped his hand; and the two walked silently—she, gaily and trium-
phantly—along the path.

Her two older sisters had not paid much attention to the grotesque
young man who had tumbled into the family circle, for they were going with boys of their own: the eldest, with Charlie Ping, a Chinese lad
whose father ran a tiny general store at the foot of the valley; the other,
with a dark and surly native youth, who resented everything that had
happened on the island since its discovery by Vancouver. Hina, however, who was too young to be regarded romantically by the young
Corydons of this Arcadia, made believe that Tom was a demigod who
had descended from the sky on a rainbow; one night, when she had
grown up, he would carry her away.

"Tommy," she said solemnly, "you are still thinking of that bad
foreigner."

The bearded deity beside her threw off his abstraction and
squeezed her strong little hand. "No, Hina," he declared gallantly, "I
am thinking of you."

She shook a finger at him. "That is a naughty fib." He started to
protest, but she silenced him and continued. "You have to make me
a promise, Tommy. And if you promise, I will show you a special
secret."

"A secret!" he exclaimed, falling into the spirit of the game.

She nodded sagely. "A special, wonderful secret. The most wonderful secret in the valley."

Tom, curious, confessed that he would love to know. The girl
stopped on the path. Her big eyes studied him seriously. Hina was
indeed a girl, but soon to be a woman. Waller now declares that he
realized then that this episode was not insignificant.

"You have to make a promise, Tommy."

"What do I have to promise?"

"That you are my husband."

Tom took her other hand. He recalled the long-brooded impulse
that had brought him eight thousand miles to this last wilderness; he
felt powerfully its weight in his heart, and that moment he dedicated

himself to the continuation of his project—to the end: this darling girl was what he had found.

"Do you promise?" she demanded.

Her eyes, like the eyes of a wild deer, reflected the beauty of this remote, wild, and peaceful valley; and now, when the words of the horseman had left him shattered and the lure of the man's daughter was vibrating in his blood, at this critical juncture, her eyes were speaking to him more deeply than she herself could know.

The Butterfields were precisely the "goddamn civilization" Tom had traveled such a great way to leave, and yet their passing had seriously tarnished his hope and undermined his confidence. He had seen himself from their perspective, and now everything within him belonging to that other world (which, of course, was a great deal) rose up and asserted itself against his present way of life.

Not only was he aware of the paltriness of his paradise—no more than a penny, so to speak, in Butterfield's purse—he was also moved in the profoundest reaches of his being by the sophisticated beauty of the vivid daughter of that world's civilization. The cut and name of Eleanor had driven themselves into the dark substratum of his consciousness, and so his simple break for freedom had now aligned against it the absolutely ineradicable power of incipient love.

Gathering his thoughts against these forces, Tom held the hands of the wild and wonderful girl Hina and gazed very seriously into her eyes.

With her to help him, he perhaps could win.

Tom stood silently for so long Hina lost her smile. But at last, when he'd found his answer, he gave her hands the squeeze they wanted, and he brightened.

She showed her teeth and laughed. "Promise?" she repeated, and she cocked her head.

Tom nodded, as one does to a child.

"Then you must give me a kiss," she said, moving in to be embraced. She lifted her lips and kept her eyes open. He hesitated. She made a kissing sound. He took her in his arms and kissed her. Tom, the truant librarian, a preternaturally callow lover in spite of his fifteen years' seniority and his unkempt beard, greatly underestimated what his feelings would be when he took her to his naked chest, and when she pushed him away, he thought it was lucky she had stopped him and did not offer to proceed. Hina caught his hand. "So now," she said, "I am going to show you the greatest secret."

She started brilliantly up the heavily wooded side of the valley, somewhat in the direction of the cascade, and Tom found that he was hard pressed to keep at her side. She began to chatter like a bird. "Oh, I am so excited!" she said. The underbrush was thick; the trees above, simply enormous. They were alone, shut out from every view, and Tom's curiosity increased as they pressed upward over the rugged and sometimes treacherous terrain. They came to a footpath running along the mountainside between two parallel walls of lava rock. They entered. The trees along this way were all prodigious candlenuts and mangoes. They passed ancient stone walls. "This walk," the girl explained, "was where they drove their pigs; that's why they had the walls—to keep them in. Nobody lives up here anymore." But every now and then they would pass an ancient house site, along with other signs that the neighborhood had once been thickly inhabited.

Tom began to hear the sound of the cascade. He was afraid that they would become visible to the riders who had gone there to rest and refresh themselves; but all at once his guide skipped over the stone wall to their left. He followed, and they started up the hill. Hina suddenly stopped, turned, fixed her eyes on Tom, and childishly shook her finger.

"Now, remember," she warned, "you have promised."

"Yes, I have."

"And you will never, never forget?"

He shook his head. "Never."

She widened her eyes. "Because *this*," she said, "is not *my* secret only. This is the secret of the valley."

Tom felt a presentiment of awe. There was a sudden flutter in the bushes beside them, and he turned to see a small black bird teetering on a swinging twig. It cocked its yellow eye at him and kept twitching its head; then it emitted a brief trill of song. "Daddy says," Hina continued, "that nobody knows about this anymore." She took his hand. They went around a great jut of lava rock and pushed behind a heavy thicket of guava. Tom felt that the ground beneath him had formerly been pressed beneath many passing feet—perhaps for centuries. Hina pushed aside a clump of brush, revealing a deep cavity in the ground, hushed him, and beckoned. He approached with a sense of mystery. The smell that greeted him as he leaned in was acrid, and he felt his head begin to spin, as though he were about to faint.

He recoiled. "What is it?"

"A burial cave."

He was now certain he was forefeeling the presence of the ancient dead.

"We are going down," she said, "going in."

Tom did not want to proceed, but when Hina lowered herself into the hole with a serious expression on her countenance, he was ashamed not to follow. Once inside, she helped him down into the dark. The cave was chilly, and his heart began to pound. He felt presences everywhere in the silence. Hina caught his hand and slowly began to conduct him away from the light of the entrance and into the pitch-blackness. Tom felt as though they were moving into the bowels of the mountain. He was utterly silent. The girl seemed to know what she was doing. Tom lifted his free arm and swung it; his fingers brushed the rough, clammy side of the vault.

"Where are you taking me?"

She did not reply. They continued, on and on, against a wall of black that continually yielded. After a period that Tom could only feel was timeless, he thought he perceived before them the dimmest glow of light. "There it is," Hina whispered. Increasing her pace, she drew him toward a narrow slit through which light was indeed shining. She bid him peek. He put his eyes to the cranny—and what he saw was the desert countryside on the other side of the protecting ridge.

"We're in a lava tube," she said. "Isn't it wonderful?"

Tom realized that they had walked, actually, right through the mountain.

"The old people used to use it for a lookout—and as a burial cave."

Tom was still peering, almost incredulously, through the crack.

"And so now," said Hina, snuggling against his side, "you must never leave me." Tom was uncertain whether she knew what she had done; but he felt (so he tells me, even to this day) that she had somehow committed him not to herself alone but to her people and that land, though he never understood how she had committed him, until the moment came when he betrayed her trust.

 *6.*

WALLER SWEARS THAT THE VALUE OF HIS DISCOVERY of the lava tube never once occurred to him during the following two years of his idyllic residence in the valley. I argue with him, however, that he must have formulated the whole brilliant stroke in his unconscious, and furthermore, that he must have known it would be the means of his conquest of Eleanor. He declares that he had put Miss Butterfield out of his mind, but I insist that her image had simply shifted from his mind to his heart, and that she—and his premonition of the life he would win with her—had moved and determined his every step, and every "misstep" too, from the day he quit the valley a miserable pauper to the moment three months later when he sat behind his desk, a millionaire.

Waller's great career began with a nasty cut which he sustained while out fishing on the reef with his foster family. The expedition, occasioned by an extraordinary run of small fish that the father had noted earlier in the day, was a gay and picturesque group event. The husbands of the two older daughters were helping to carry the long net into the waters and circle it round for the great catch. Charlie Ping, the good-humored Chinese lad who had married the eldest girl, kept making comical mistakes, pretending that he knew nothing of this complicated native art. Lasa, the husband of the middle sister, on the other hand, was sober about the whole operation, as though he were celebrating some religious ritual. He was a superb specimen of carved mahogany, with the mighty shoulders and pectoral muscles of a swimmer. His face, with its great flat nose, was a solemn mask. And when he lifted his head to regard with silent disapproval the fantastical gyrations of wiry Charlie, in his eyes was the disdain of the ages for the impieties of present humankind. Their wives were sitting on the rocks, the eldest nursing her infant, the second obviously pregnant. Their voluminous mother was sitting cross-legged on the shore, preparing things to eat. And the younger fry were scampering, chasing each other about and wrestling, getting hurt, and splashing into the sea.

Hina came wading out onto the reef to lend a hand with the net. Two years had passed since the plighted troth of the lava tube; Tom was fabulously happy; he and Hina had explored the valley's every marvel; and the family had accepted him willingly as her prospective husband. He had observed with delight her beautiful flowering toward womanhood. She was now sixteen, and to his thinking as magnificent a creature as he should ever see. The sun gleamed from the dark satin of her shoulders as she hauled and manipulated the net. She kept her eyes upon him, and he, in his turn, never tired of watching her. If the golden age of innocence was ever known to man, it was in the work and play of those beautiful people: this was the youth's perennial feeling and belief.

But his foot slipped into a cleft in the reef, and he cut his calf and thigh on the treacherous coral. Such accidents were not infrequent when reef-fishing, and neither Tom nor anyone else gave the momentary incident much thought. He continued in his position at the net, though with less agility than formerly, and the day went on as planned. The catch was multitudinous, and soon the women and children were at work cleaning and preparing the fish—some for a great meal, some to be salted and dried.

When the family returned home in the evening, everyone was well fed and happy, but tired, and took immediately to their beds, so Tom did not realize until the next morning that the gashes on his leg were going to be troublesome. They were painfully inflamed, his leg was stiff and full of soreness, and in spite of all the home remedies that were applied to the wounds, they failed to close and heal.

Now *that* is the detail which makes me speak, in this case, of the force and fatefulness of the unconscious: such cuts Tom had sustained before, and they had healed; but in this instance, his body was in revolt against getting well and continuing to live the life that he had found and seemed to be enjoying. That phase of his strange destiny had been completed. The valley and its folk had taught him what he had been ripe to learn, but it was not in his heart to remain there in primitive enjoyment the rest of his days, fathering a passel of offspring and fishing the reef with Hina, Lasa, and Charlie. Latent within him was thought of the Butterfields' world and its judgment, as well as the ineradicable (though suppressed and consciously forgotten) allure of the figure and manner of that girl. I believe Tom unconsciously knew that his destiny was now ripe for its second stage, and that his body had seized upon the trivial incident of the coral cuts as the first accidental opportunity to create a new situation. When the cuts refused to heal, it became clear to everyone, even himself, that he needed to make a trip across the ridge and pay a visit to a doctor in the town.

Charlie Ping, who undertook bimonthly expeditions across the ridge to fetch the merchandise for his father's general store, offered to take him. Charlie had been making these trips ever since he was twelve, and he accomplished them with ease: departing just before dawn with a little caravan of burros, he would follow what was by now a well-worn trail, arrive in the town about an hour after sundown, put up for the night with one of his uncles, leave the empty baskets, load his animals with the full ones, and be back in his father's compound the second day. He had been planning to make his next trip a week hence, but when it became apparent that his prospective brother-in-law was in some danger, he proposed to advance the time for his journey, and after an argument, Tom was persuaded to accept. Charlie supplied a pair of trousers and a shirt, as well as a couple of dollars to pay the doctor. An extra pony was saddled, and, in the dark, Tom mounted with considerable pain. Hina was present at his stirrup. But when he stooped to kiss her, he was troubled to discover that her face was wet with tears.

"Do not worry, sweetheart," he consoled. "I shall return soon."

She kissed him long, tears streaming from her closed eyes, and then, breaking off, turned away, covered her face with her hands, shook her head, and sobbed. Tom, attempting to comfort her, brought his pony around. "This isn't serious, Hina," he assured her. "I'll be back in a couple of days." But she only stood there, crying into her hands, until he finally had to leave. "Goodbye, my Tommy," she sobbed as she heard him move away.

Charlie Ping was a cheerful companion, and the two, with their caravan of burros linked by halters trailing along behind, completed the transit without untoward event. Tom marveled at being able to traverse so easily the very terrain that had been such an ordeal for him three years before. He cast his eyes about to see whether he could recognize any landmarks, but he had been in such a daze during his earlier crossing that his mind had retained only a general impression of the landscape. Besides, they were following a trail that was far removed from the direction he had followed. Tom suddenly remembered the three books he had lost, and he marveled that he had neither missed nor even thought of them during his three years in the valley.

"Someday," said Charlie, interrupting his reverie, "all this land is going to be sugar."

Tom expressed surprise. They were talking in the native language, for Charlie could speak no English, and Tom, no Chinese.

"Yes, sir!" stated Charlie. "Mr. Butterfield owns it all, you know."

Tom felt his heart lift at the name. "So I hear. But why—"

"Well," Charlie went on, "about five years ago he hired an engineer to devise an irrigation plan, but he didn't pursue the project because it would have soaked up too much money."

"Then why do you say—?"

"Because I think engineering will improve—get better—and someone will find an easier way." He laughed, and made a slow, sweeping gesture with his left arm. "So much land cannot remain this way forever."

They rode on in silent meditation of this theme.

Night had fallen, and it was already dark when they pulled into town, but Tom's leg was throbbing with pain, and Charlie insisted that they proceed directly to the doctor's home. When they arrived,

Charlie helped Tom dismount, half-carried him up the front, rang the bell—which clanged, just the other side of the door, like a fire alarm—and supported him while they waited. The veranda light switched on, the door opened, and a very small Italian gentleman, neatly dressed—even dapper, in his tailored pongee—stood before them, his prominent, mud-colored eyes glaring angrily. "Why do you bother me at this time?" he demanded. "Why do you not come at my office hours?"

Charlie could not understand. Tom replied that they had just arrived from the other side of the island.

At this moment, there was a cry in the street. Someone was cursing Charlie's herd of burros, which were wandering all over the road. Charlie whispered to Tom that he had to leave but would be back in about an hour; and before the doctor could realize what had happened, Tom was leaning on his shoulder, and Charlie was out on the road, in the dark, hollering Chinese at someone and disentangling his burros.

The doctor's office was as neat as a pin, and as the little Italian moved about it with the air of a dandy, Tom could not but wonder what might have brought such a man to such a place. He seemed to regard Tom (who was not only an intruder but a pretty filthy spectacle) as an object of disgust, but his attention to the wounded leg was reassuring.

After examining the limb, the doctor immediately became its guardian and patron, and he reprimanded Tom for having neglected it: "You should have brought this to me two days ago."

Tom did not reply. He watched the man pick up clean instruments and angrily toss the used ones into a tray.

"Where are you staying?" the doctor asked.

Tom replied that he was planning to stay with a Chinese shopkeeper in town, a Mr. Ping.

"Ping!" the doctor scoffed, staring up with his popping eyes. "Why, you can't stay in a place like that! How can Ping take care of you? Two of his kids have whooping cough this minute, and Mrs. Ping has just given birth again. They have no place for you."

Tom did not know what to say.

"Don't you know anyone *else* in town?" demanded the doctor.

"Well, I used to know…" Tom hesitated. "But no, that would be impossible."

"What would be impossible?" snapped the doctor. "Who'd you used to know?"

"Mr. Butterfield."

"Butterfield!" exclaimed the little man. "J. P. Butterfield?" Tom nodded. "Why, my lord! Why didn't you say?"

He picked up the telephone. Tom tried to protest but was waved away. "Hello, hello! That you, Nitobe? Give me J. P."

Tom felt that everything was flying out of hand, but there was nothing just now that he could do.

"Hello! J. P.? This is Bigongiarno. Listen. I got a young fellow here from over the hill. Says you know him." The doctor looked at the card Tom had filled out. "Thomas Waller," he read.

There was a pause for listening.

"Waller," the doctor repeated. "W-A-L-L-E-R." The doctor slowly lifted his eyes to Tom with a look of questioning uncertainty.

"Mention *Nick*," Tom suggested, not wishing to be thought a fraud.

"He says to mention Nick," the doctor stated.

There was another pause. Then Tom could hear something buzz, like a voice, in the receiver. With a look of pain, the doctor moved the instrument a short distance from his ear.

"Yes," he said. "That's the one." And then he explained what he had on his hands. "Do you think you can give him a bed, with the servants?"

He listened.

"Can you send Nitobe?"

Another pause for listening.

"Right away?"

The doctor thanked the telephone, set it down, and turned to his patient with instructions and commands. A short while later, Tom found himself in a prodigious kitchen, drinking soup and being waited on with excessive attention by every Japanese servant in the vast Butterfield home.

—————————————— 7.

THE BUTTERFIELDS' SEASHORE ESTATE—with its lounges and cocktail verandas, its swimming pool, tennis courts, fragrant gardens and arbors, pagodas, stables, and immense garage—was this summer entertaining Eleanor's college roommate, Mary Coe, and her brother Jack. The two were used to splendid things, and so they knew how to move with "savoir faire," as they called it, through the impressive rooms and about the magnificent grounds. They were a great pair, excellent sports and favorites of their generation. Though Mary's semiblonde complexion was rather commonplace, and she was a bit fat, her principal problem was a short nose that drew her upper lip into an apparently disdainful sneer; yet she resolved everything by holding her head high, to establish poise, and letting her long and truly beautiful lashes play as conspicuously as possible—which gave her an air of dignity that harmonized satisfactorily with her expensive grooming. Her brother, however, was continually annoying her with a set of nicknames that pointed attention to her flaws. He had played on the polo team at Harvard; had a firm, compact physique—though a little short; had a flair for throwing a scarf around his neck; and was already getting places in his father's New York office. Jack had met Eleanor at his sister's Barnard junior prom.

"Ellie," the young man queried, as the family sat overlooking the rolling waves, sipping their rickeys and old-fashioneds, following an afternoon swim in the pool, "who would that odd number be that I've seen sitting out by the boathouse these days with his leg in a sling?"

Eleanor regarded him with puzzlement. She turned to her father, who said nothing. "By the boathouse? News to me!" Then, suddenly, "Is he young?" she asked, pretending to be alert and eager and flashing to go.

Jack looked disgusted. "Ellie, you're a card," he said, tossing off

his drink impatiently, and then rattling the ice and peering with displeasure into the glass. Eleanor had refused his proposal of marriage
just two days before.

The girl clapped her hands on her bare knees, straightened her
spine, and twinkled her black eyes at everyone. "If he's young," she
challenged, winking at Mary, "he's mine." She pretended to pant. "I
want him."

Mrs. Butterfield, who for some years now had been trying both
to subdue and to understand her rampageous daughter, made a sign
of mortified annoyance. Sitting upright in her red-cushioned lounge
chair, she was a comely, stately woman, with her daughter's eyes and
hair but a more vigorous jaw and more heavily proportioned physique.
She was wearing a white tennis dress with the dramatic addition of
a brilliant red and yellow cape that she had found years ago, somewhere on the Riviera. "Eleanor!" she reprimanded. Then she relaxed
and turned her eyes to Jack with a sheepish, sympathetic smile, as if to
say, "We understand, don't we? I've done what I could; from here on
it will be up to you."

Mr. Butterfield set his glass down, stood, and began stamping his
feet to get the blood back into his legs. He adjusted his light-blue scarf
and straightened the lapel of his white flannel blazer. "Eleanor," he
said, going over to kiss her, "I'm going to investigate." He winked.
Then he turned to his wife, more seriously. "It must be the young fellow that Bigongiarno phoned about. I forgot all about him."

"What young fellow?" Mrs. Butterfield demanded.

"Oh, nobody particular," he replied carelessly. "Some young fellow from over the hill, with a damaged leg and no place to sleep. I had
Nitobe give him the room up over the boathouse."

Mrs. Butterfield was exasperated. "John," she said, "you make me
tired—taking in every lame duck on the island. How do you know
what kind of villain he may be? Why, we all may be murdered in our
beds!"

He stooped and patted her hand. "There, there," he reassured, planting a kiss on her forehead. "This one isn't dangerous. His father went to college with me. I knew him in New York."

His daughter brightened. "Is he the one we saw over in the valley a couple years ago?"

Her father nodded.

Eleanor clapped her hands on her knees again, bounced a little in her chair, and blinked at Mary as though ravished. "Oh, *he's* romantic!" She pretended enthusiastically to be gone on him.

Mary managed a sickly laugh.

"He used to be the librarian at the club. His name is Tom. I was thinking about him only the other day." Mr. Butterfield shook his head. "It's the damnedest thing. I can't imagine what got him out to this part of the world. His mother was left a widow, I seem to recall, and then *she* died when he was still in college. We gave him a job at the club—and last *I* remember, he was doing pretty well." He started to move away, then stopped. "Tom had a knack of always knowing what it was you would like to read," he recollected, "and the older members used to like him for it."

Mrs. Butterfield, who had lost interest and withdrawn from the conversation, was groping under her seat for her tennis racket. She stood up to go. "Well, all I know," she stated haughtily, "is that I don't like to see strangers walking in and out of our *bed*rooms." She struck the racket against her thigh, challenging her husband with her magnificent eyes.

He smiled with admiration. "Evangeline," he said compassionately, "it isn't costing us a thing, and you never can tell when we may collect a dividend." He put his great arm across her shoulders, and the couple strolled away.

Tom was surprised and flattered to see his fine host come ambling toward the boat landing. His leg had begun to mend, but he could not yet walk on it. Unable to communicate with Charlie before his return with a loaded caravan to the valley, he'd had three days to brood. The Butterfield household had easily accepted him, and his physical needs were well tended: Japanese servant girls brought him clean clothes, another shaved him, and all gave care to the healing of his leg—for a day or so he had self-consciously protested, but at last he relaxed and let it happen. Yet he had been unable to find anyone the least bit interested in his problems of communication, finance, and ultimate departure. When he saw his host arrive he felt, for a moment, like the kid who had been caught with the jam.

Tom made to rise; but it was obvious that he should not attempt such a thing. Mr. Butterfield waved him down. Tom was a little uneasy when he faced the man; for during his convalescence, his recollection of Charlie talking about the irrigation of the land on the other side of the island had combined with memories of the cascade and the lava tube to form as pretty a plan of hydraulic engineering as the mind of an amateur could wish to conceive, a radical solution to a certain engineering problem that he knew this man would give a fortune to know: a great funnel to catch the water of the cascade and conduct it some two hundred yards to the first opening of the lava tube was all that would be needed to bring an immense quantity of water into the desert; and once there, the usual type of plantation channels and conduits could distribute it over the entire plain. Tom's head had buzzed when the image broke in it. But he was loyal and swore that he would renounce it, with everything it signified, for the sake of Hina—and his promise.

"Welcome, son," Mr. Butterfield said as he approached. "Have they been treating you properly?" He shook Tom's hand.

Tom was copious in his thanks.

The man cocked an eye at him. "I think I'd recognize you now," he said, "without the whiskers. But don't I remember glasses?"

Tom nodded. "Busted," he explained. "But I didn't need them over in the valley." He failed to realize that the tense he had used was the past.

Butterfield drew up a camp chair and sat down. "What the devil brought you out to the island, Tom?" he asked, with a show of sensible interest. And Tom was forced to recite his tale.

The rest is quickly told.

Eleanor paid him a visit the following afternoon. "I've come to see the animal," she said frankly as she arrived.

Tom made a conspicuous effort to rise.

"You don't have to kill yourself," she said, settling quickly on the wharf at his feet. She clasped her hands around her knees, leaned back, and scrutinized him boldly.

Tom felt his heart surge, quiver a moment, and disintegrate.

"You sure made a dent on Butch," she told him.

"Butch?" he repeated stupidly.

"Butch," she offered in explanation, "is my dear, cute papa."

Tom was a little shocked.

The girl leaned forward and sparkled her eyes at him. "Isn't my papa a darling?"

Tom had to hesitate.

"No," she said, "of course. You were too much impressed to see. Well, let me tell you: He's a dear." She suddenly got up and seemed about to go.

Tom tried to think of something to say—fast—that would detain her. He had not realized what a deep joy it would be to talk to a girl of his own race again, and in English. The words, silly as they were, meant more than could those of any newly acquired language. And furthermore, the presence of this particular girl, who had lodged in his heart three years ago, seemed inevitable, and he knew that her absence would be more than he could bear. As Tom regarded her, he was certain that he was watching the woman who was going to be his wife.

"I don't understand," he blurted, "why you are so kind!"

"Oh, for heaven's sake," she said, tossing her head. "Why, Butch would do as much for a horse."

Tom felt rebuffed.

"Besides," she added, "I think he thinks you're an investment."

Tom thought of the water project and began to resist what was happening.

"Butch says you must know a great deal about that valley over there," she told him flatly. "He says he believes you're going to be a

valuable friend." She gave him a vivid laugh, and with a parting flourish of her hand left him to his wounds.

From that day to this she has had him—as they both declare to
everyone, most willingly—with a ring in his nose, though for my part,
I must confess I cannot comprehend why a woman of her freshness
and beauty would want such an odd one at all. Perhaps there was
something romantic and wonderful about him right after his adventure, but the years since have turned him back into what he was at
the club—but on a bigger, richer scale and without the yearning for
rebirth. I know absolutely nothing of their romance, but I suspect that
it developed as the plans took shape for the valley project.

Love is blind, they say. Waller tells me that in that moment he
never had any sense of betraying Hina and the trust she had placed in
him. The advantages of the project to his Kanaka friends (as he now
called them) in their cutoff valley were finally so obvious that he found
it difficult to imagine how he could ever have hesitated. The fact that
as a little girl Hina had entertained romantic notions about her favorite woodland nooks was charming, of course, but in the light of history
and adult reasoning, unimportant. As for the violation of an ancient
pagan burial place: why, even Christian cemeteries were being ripped
up every day by the wheels of progress! Tom finally realized that if *he*
did not do it, somebody else would; and he reasoned (quite logically, I
believe) that the people of the valley would fare much better under *his*
protection than under that of some unsympathetic, purely materialis-
tic character. Besides, Butterfield made it clear that he was planning
to develop that desert in the near future, willy-nilly, and that saving
several hundred thousand dollars would incline him very favorably to
the young man who made it possible.

Suffice it to say that some three weeks after Tom's leg was well
enough for him to attend his first Butterfield cocktail party, the wheels
of progress began to break a major highway across the ridge. Digging
machines of various types were scattered over the desert area, chugging, creaking, and swinging their scoops and shovels, while a brisk

company of young surveyors began plotting a clean line through the guava brush up at the head of the valley.

 *8.*

IT REQUIRED SEVERAL WEEKS of fervent detective work and long conversations with all the parties involved to piece together the history: a curious tale of seeming coincidences, and yet of inevitability. Waller himself brought me to the lava tube and showed me with pride how the cascade had been channeled into it. One of the great advantages of the natural conduit, he declared, was that it did not deface the really remarkable beauties of the valley. A great pipeline would have been unsightly, but this means of conveyance was completely invisible. And the vast development of what had formerly been a desert was truly a boon to the whole community. Plantation towns now flourished where before there had been only cactus.

This, however, was not to be the end of the story, for the cocktail conversation that first sent me on the trail of the past also proved to be a critical juncture for the future—and through another coincidental recognition, like the ones that had already distinguished Waller's relationship to Butterfield and my own to Waller. The coincidence this time was through no less a personage than my commanding officer, Major Fineman, who, it will be remembered, had loudly exclaimed at the mention of the name of Jack Coe just before I hit on my great clue of the club. When I had paused in my conversation with Waller's lovely wife to try to follow in my mind some of the recollections that it had wakened, the major had vigorously stepped into the interrupted dialogue, so that by the time I had identified the present Mr. Waller with the half-forgotten young Tom of the New York club library, the next epoch in the history of the island was already well under way.

"Jack Coe!" Major Fineman had said, "Why, I know him! Know him well. His father's in the hotel business."

A moment later Tom Waller came swooping in through the door, moving as always with an odd suggestion of subservience, bowing and scraping, crane-like, coming swiftly toward us, holding out his hand.

"Why, Major Fineman!" he said with a painful smile. "So glad, so glad, so glad." He shook the major's hand, then he turned to me. "And the sergeant, Sergeant Currie!"

It was clear that the major was simply bursting with some big idea to break to Mr. Waller; but I was bound I would get my word in first. I held the man's hand. "Tom Waller," I said with a new voice—and I looked at him very steadily, "you don't remember me."

He was brought up short, and his eyes through their distorting glasses scrutinized my face. Mrs. Waller too became attentive, and the major suddenly regarded me with a new respect. Waller slowly shook his head. "No, I can't say that I do."

"Currie?" I said, suggestively. "*White Shadows in the South Seas?* Mr. Currie who was reading Sumner's *Folkways* in the club library."

The look on the man's face was something I shall never forget. And I cannot say whether it was shock and displeasure or only surprise that flickered across his mobile features: he is such a curious—to me, unreadable—personality that I can never tell where he stands. His wife became uneasy, as though an awkward discovery had been made— something from the days before her time, of which she was ignorant. But in the fraction of an instant Waller's strange look vanished, the awkward moment passed, and he seized my elbow, shook my arm violently, and started heavily clapping me on the back. He was acting out a truly hearty joy.

At last he turned to his wife. "Eleanor, my dear, this is the man who gave me the nerve to pack up and go."

His brilliant young wife was living up to the occasion, though unaware of what it all was about. She lighted up attractively. "Go where?" she asked with interest.

Waller and I gazed at each other with the curiously measuring, slightly humorous regard of two people who have not seen each other for many years. Fineman was completely in a fog.

"Tom," I said at last, "so this is the garden land you found!" I was not yet aware, of course, of the history. And turning to Mrs. Waller, I smiled. "And this," said I, "is your dusky, dark-eyed maid."

The faux pas was immense. I was aware something had happened but could not know what or why. The buoyant major, however, stepped into the breach.

"And Mr. Waller," he said, "you know, I too have something to say to you."

The man looked as though he had had enough for one day, but the major would not let him retreat. "I understand," he proclaimed, grasping Waller's lapel, "that you know Mr. Coe—Mr. Jack Coe, of New York."

Waller drew his eyebrows together thoughtfully. "Coe?" he queried. He turned to his wife, then suddenly brightened and laughed. "Oh, Coe!" he exclaimed. "Of course, of course! Of course!"

"Well," said the major, "I have a big idea for you. A colossal proposition." He still had his host by the lapel. "Listen, listen," he said as he turned him around and conducted him to the veranda. Mrs. Waller gave me a questioning look, but I shrugged and shook my head: I didn't know.

The old native servant returned about this time, moving with an unsteady gait and carrying a large tray of cocktail snacks that he set down on a low table. Mrs. Waller thanked him, and he stepped back, awaiting further orders. She shook her head, and he withdrew.

Waller and the major remained on the veranda for some time, talking earnestly, and it was evident that the host was now as interested as the guest. When the two of them returned into the living room they were arm in arm.

"My dear," Waller said to his wife, "this is really good." He grasped her elbow. "You remember Coe?"

She laughed and made a washing gesture with her hands. "Never forget him!" she said brightly. "Never forget him!" She looked at me and winked and laughed again, though I had no notion of what the joke was.

"Well," said Waller, trying to keep the track, "our friend, Major Fineman here, believes that he would be interested in opening—"

The major brusquely interrupted. "I *know* he would," he declared. "You folks don't realize...why, the Coes are the biggest hotel people in the country. This here would be peanuts."

Mrs. Waller was alertly turning her head from one to the other, trying to catch the thread.

"Peanuts! Understand?" repeated Fineman. He held out the palm of his left hand and began tapping it vigorously with the index finger of his right. "You know how much champagne alone I shipped their chain of hotels the year before the war?"

"Major Fineman," Mr. Waller explained quietly to his wife, "is in the wholesale liquor business."

"Oh!" Mrs. Waller said, turning with a display of admiration to the major, who immediately dropped his argument, beamed at her with great satisfaction, and bowed. "Well, well!" she said.

"Fineman, Pingitori, and O'Hara," he informed her, producing, as if by magic, a card, which he placed in her hand. "At your service."

Waller resumed his explanation. "Major Fineman believes—"

"I don't just believe," insisted the major. "I *know.*"

Waller corrected himself. "The major *assures* me, dear, that Coe would be interested in opening a deluxe resort, right down below here in the valley."

The vivid young housewife widened her eyes. "Oh, boy!" she enthused appreciatively. "Oh, boy, oh, boy!" She gave us all a brilliant wink. "I guess that would brighten up our little corner, all right, all right."

Waller grinned. "You like the plan?" he asked.

"Well, I should say I do," she answered. "It's been seventeen centuries since I last saw a dance floor, and believe me, gentlemen, that's a long, long time!"

Her husband turned and called for the old native servant, who was presently standing by. "Nick," he said, "bring the major, here, a box of those cigars, please."

The major lifted his brows. "Ah!" he declared with admiration.

The old Polynesian turned to go, but Mrs. Waller detained him.

"And Nick," she added, "while you're out there, will you tell Hina to give the children their supper? I won't be up for a couple of hours."

At the time, of course, I knew nothing of the background of those two names; I had not yet learned of the idyll of the valley years.

"Tom," I said, when he had relaxed a bit from his attentions to the major, "do you recall our last conversation at the club?"

He lifted his brows in such a way that for the first time I really recognized the old expression that I remembered from the past. He vaguely shook his head. The big eyes behind their glasses looked alarmed—but, then, they always looked alarmed. I had a feeling for a moment that he was an exceedingly repulsive man, and for some reason I wanted to tell him something that would hurt. "You thought you would get away," I said, "and I told you that you wouldn't get away. And so now here it is, the whole thing. You've brought it here yourself."

He scowled. "What whole thing?" he asked defensively. "What whole thing? What are you talking about?"

I laughed, to break the tension and gaily clapped his arm. "Why, 'this goddamn civilization,'" I answered. "That's what you used to call it."

He peered at me, very much surprised. "You don't mean to suggest that this reminds you of New York?"

I nodded confidently. "Indeed, I do. I think it's wonderful." And again I laughed.

Waller shook his head. "Mr. Currie," he told me coldly, "I don't get you." And he turned away to speak with Nick, who had returned with the major's cigars.

APPENDIX

STRICTLY PLATONIC

*The Romance of a Bookworm
Who Lost His Goat and Found Himself Famous*

1931

The varsity hero (photograph, United States, c. 1920 A.D.). Courtesy of Cushing
Memorial Library and Archives, Texas A&M University.

ACROSS THE CAMPUS from the Gothic gym was the Georgian, red-brick Philosophy Building, where Old Dittman spent his office hours filling an oblong book-lined room with a stinking brand of tobacco smoke. By a window he sat with his long thin legs crossed; a saxophone pipe curled down against his silky graying beard.

Jim Weston sat in a hamstrung chair, watching him, a big-shouldered young fellow, threadbare in his dark suit, his shoes down at the heels.

Old Dittman said: "So I can't advise you, Weston, to be too stubborn about this thing."

Old Dittman frowned. "I like your ideals—and—well—your spunk; but, just the same, Weston, your attitude seems to *me* to be altogether injudicious."

Jim opened his broad hands. "But why is it injudicious?"

The old smoky man smacked and rumbled. "Because Weston, these fellows have the power and will to break you." He pointed with the moist stem of his pipe, rounding his eyes.

"This football crowd's been closing around our throats here like a garrote. You ought to know, Weston—you played for them yourself once. They're fanatics. They've a stadium now worth more than any three buildings on the campus. They've a coach—my Lord, they pay him more than any ten professors! They've the alumni, the students, the trustees on their side; so they're the masters, that's all." Dittman settled back. "And we? You and I? The mere professors?" He answered himself rhetorically: "We're the hired bits of camouflage stuck around to give an athletic club the complexion of a college."

Jim said: "But, sir!" He rubbed his neck. "We can't just let these fellows wipe their feet on—on scholarship—on everything Wilton College used to stand for! Now *can* we? Why *have* these eligibility rules if we're not to flunk a football man when he flunks?"

Dittman was impatient. "Those rules are part of the camouflage. Those rules don't mean a thing when a man like Cobb comes into question. Do you realize who he is?"

"Yes," Jim answered, "I realize. All-American half-back two seasons in a row."

Dittman nodded, looking grim. "Tickets for this game are going at fifty dollars apiece because it's Larry Cobb's last game. And now your flunk makes him ineligible. Weston, they'll kill you! *Kid* these playboys, can't you? No use just being stubborn."

"But I'm *not* just being stubborn." Jim argued sincerely. "We can't hand Wilton over to that gang, sir. Now *can* we? Not for Cobb or anyone else!"

Dittman eyed Jim. "Not even for Bob Stanbury?"

Jim flushed.

Now the Wilton College chapel bells pealed out from their chaste white belfry, summoning two thousand respectful students from the dormitories, libraries, and fraternity houses to the great religious exercise of the week—the football rally in the stadium back of the gym!

Old Dittman said sympathetically: "Son!" And he rubbed his hands. "You used to talk about Stanbury's daughter as though you wanted to marry her. Do you still?"

Jim settled back. Mopping his jaw with a cheap handkerchief, he nodded, looking away. "But it's such an impossible mess—I mean since the business smashed and dad died!" He twisted a wry smile. "And Margaret isn't the kind to be able to struggle along on a few hundred a year, so we're keeping it a kind of—well, a kind of Platonic arrangement till I can earn something." He looked up. "Her father saw how it was. He offered me a job once—insurance. I couldn't go it at all."

"My Lord!" exploded Dittman. "You passed up a job like *that*! With *Stan*bury! And yesterday you told Cobb you were handing in a flunk for him. Well, Stanbury's the big brother who found Cobb on a high-school team and put him on the pay roll. Stanbury's one of the big trustees, you know."

"I know," Jim answered flatly.

"Well, and he's sort of a hero too—professional alumnus, you might say. Always around the coaches—keeping up the old fraternity noises. Your fraternity, by the way—am I right?"

"Right," said Jim, disquieted.

"With the whole crows on his side he can probably fire you."

"I've a contract."

"They can get around a contract. They can frame you—get you to spill the beans yourself."

"Oh, they can't do that."

Dittman was grim. "The wheels are moving, Weston. This morning Stanbury phoned me, raging like a bull; declared he's stopping at absolutely nothing to get Cobb into this game."

Jim could see that things were black. From the stadium came zooming the rhythms of a zip-boom-bah where cheerleaders flung megaphones and swung in concerted action.

"Well"—Jim clenched his fists on his knees—"I'm not afraid of losing a job, sir."

Old Dittman asked: "How long since you graduated? Three years is it, Weston?"

Jim answered with a stiff voice: "Three years ago last June, sir."

Dittman polished his nose. "So till we gave you this instructor's job you lived on nothing for three years."

"Oh, it wasn't quite as bad as that." Jim frowned at the nails of his thumbs. "Dad left me a couple of thousand."

Dittman considered his pipe. "He died the month after you

graduated. But you kept right on here, working like a dog for your Ph.D."

"Well—"

"Like a dog, Weston; I *know*. Without that bull physique of yours you'd probably have gone under. You eat work—you lose yourself completely in your work." He cleared his throat. "Weston, the faculty have decided—absolutely decided—to offer you—offer you for next year the Liddel Traveling Fellowship. Paris—Munich—Berlin! You'll work with the biggest men in your field. You'll come back thoroughly fitted out."

"Lord!" Jim said. "Gosh!"

"Three thousand dollars," Dittman continued. "On that, you and your—your wife could live two years abroad *at least*. But if you let these fellows *fire* you"—he lifted his fist and thundered—"you'll lose that fellowship flat!"

He faced Jim, pipe in his fist. "Weston! It's outrageous to throw away a chance like this because some—some thick-headed chump doesn't happen to know a mess of facts he'll never want to know *any*how!"

Jim made a helpless gesture. "But, sir," he said, "it's the *principle* of the thing!"

Dittman exploded. "Principles be *damned*, Weston. Will Cobb know an ounce more? Will this football club reform, do you think? You're like a dumb heathen throwing your life into the fat jaws of an idol, that's what you are, Weston, for all your pious noise about ideals."

Fists shoved into his pockets, Dittman stamped off to the bookshelves. There he stood, grumping and breathing up at the books.

At eleven, his heart thumping in his ears, Jim entered the Alpha Beta Mu house and an enchanted realm of collegiate love and intrigue.

About a punch bowl in the hall were a number of pious football votaries.

Jim was startled to discover among them Stanbury himself—resplendent in a shirt front—with that firm set to his massive head, that touch of gray above his ears, that Episcopal look in his eyes.

When Stanbury saw Jim, he set the glass down, plucked the sleeve of a neighbor, turned about, and was gone.

Something was up.

Jim hunted for Margaret. He spied her, at last, beaming over a shoulder, trying to catch his eye. She was dancing away, a perfectly splendid creature, tall, lithe, with athletic shoulders broader than her hips. She was all in black, and her chestnut hair was caught into a knot at the back of her neck.

He pushed out and touched her partner's arm. "May I cut in?"

But, holy cat! It was Larry Cobb! *Football* season, and Larry Cobb at a dance!

Cobb was a magnificent blond with fine straight eyebrows, straight nose, and square jaw. Though he was only six foot one, he seemed to tower over everyone. And he could slap your back and josh you with just enough condescension.

Margaret detached Cobb and let herself into Jim's arms. Then:

"Thank you *so* much, Larry," she said. And with Jim she danced away.

They saw the fellow storming off to the punch bowl.

On a settee upstairs they recovered breath and poise. Jim was excited, with the marvelous girl and her perfume so close to him.

"You're sweet!" he said.

She kissed his ear Platonically.

Presently they could talk.

She said: "Jim, dear, don't you think that—well—that if you tried again a *little* bit you could make a go of insurance?"

"Has something happened, Peg?"

She bit her lips. Then she was suddenly in his arms. "Oh, Jim, it's Dad! You know how he's been ever since you gave up insurance. 'Why can't I open my eyes?' he asks. 'Shall I spend my whole life waiting around for a bookworm to get rich?' Oh, Jim, you know the way he talks."

Jim squeezed her hand.

"Jim," she continued softly, "do you think I could marry anyone else—anyone but you?"

Jim felt his throat tighten. He tried to kiss her eyes.

"Jim, can't we get away? Run away to Europe or something? Live in a little flat somewhere alone?"

She was in his arms.

But they were snapped out of the clouds when a sudden voice cracked out. Stanbury's voice: "Jim Weston!"

Stanbury moved across to him.

"Jim," he said, "will you come upstairs? I'd like to have a talk."

And there was Cobb, like a stuffed policeman, tremendous in the door.

Margaret looked frightened. She had evidently sensed the threat. She gripped Jim by the hand.

Jim set his teeth. Giving his Peggy's hand a squeeze, he followed them out.

Upstairs, in a stuffy room, Jim sat in a broken Morris chair and Stanbury shut the door. Cobb stayed below. Jim had a job on his hands, and he knew it. By a table gashed with initials he sat. The room was a tumble of neckties, sweatshirts, and oilskins, four double-decker iron beds, and photographs of dizzy-looking girls.

"Now what's the big idea, Jim? You trying to go high-hat on us?"

The question had the quality of a threat. Jim tried to restrain himself.

"I don't know what you mean," he said.

Stanbury doubled his fist, then abruptly broke into a smile.

"Jim! Remember old times? Eh, Jim boy?" He was dragging up a chair. He settled astride, leaning over the back, and being pals. "You used to be a good egg, Jim. What's got into you? Gone cuckoo, Jim?"

Jim began to feel his gorge rise.

Stanbury clapped his shoulder, produced a cigarette case, and offered a smoke. Jim refused. Stanbury took one for himself and tapped the cigarette on the top of the case, advising: "Now, Jim," he said, "you got to realize it's for the glory of old Wilton, boy. What's a couple of damn' fool questions? Think of old Larry out there on that field—smashing into that line—eh, Jim? Headlines! Think of the advertising!" Stanbury was in earnest. "Jim," he said, "you got to realize

Cobb's done more for old Wilton than all the old profs in the place. He *has*! Looka here now, Jim! Sit down."

Jim had to walk.

"All right—stand up, then. But listen." Stanbury flourished his cigarette and gripped the back of his chair. "Larry's a national hero, Jim boy. Headlines, all the newsreels, *millions* of unseen radio fans, Jim, all over the country.

"Why, he's bigger almost than Lindy—or even Rudy Vallee! Jim, they're *crazy* about him—all over the country."

Jim couldn't hold himself. "All right," he said, "but what of it?"

"Well, Lord, Jim—can't you see?"

"No."

"Looka here, then, now. Sit down."

Jim shrugged, kicked a gin bottle, and sat down.

"Now, Jim, see here. Suppose you flunk Larry—just suppose, say. Well, and all over the country it goes—millions of unseen radio fans, Jim—headlines all over the place." Stanbury squinted, leaning back, and he drew a line in the air with his cigarette. " 'Faculty Rules Old Larry Cobb Ineligible!' Can you see it, Jim? See what it'd do to Wilton?"

"What'd it do to Wilton?" Jim said.

Stanbury acted amazed. "Why, it'd give us a fine black eye!" he roared. "Looka here now. We'll just take—take a young chap thinking of coming here to school. Suppose he's a triple-threat man—we'll just take that for instance. Be a dandy first-rate asset. Just the kind of boy we want. He sees how a faculty ruling broke old Larry here at Wilton. So what does he do?"

"Go on!" Jim urged. "What does he do?"

"Well, he doesn't *come*, that's what." Stanbury leaned at him, excited. "He goes off some place where a guy can play *without* a faculty ruling."

"Where's that?" Jim demanded.

Stanbury growled at the cigarette. "I'm not saying anything, Jim, but—but that's where this fellow goes." Stanbury stood up. "And we lose a healthy lot like that, too—all because this faculty here's so high-hat about questions." He began pleading. "How can you ask a coach to build up a team if he hasn't *men*? And how can you *get* any men, Jim, if your blasted failing goes and frightens them all away? A bunch of bookworms, that's what you'll get. And you can't go building a football team out of bookworms. Understand?"

"Well, I'm sorry," Jim said decisively, "but you'll have to do without Cobb."

Stanbury squinted uncertainly; then he grinned. "Say now, Jim, listen," with expansive friendliness. "Couldn't you take old Larry's paper and look at it some new way so's maybe it'd make sense?"

Jim was boiling. "I've marked it, and that's that."

Stanbury blinked; then suddenly grinned again. He spoke in a high-pitched wheedling voice: "How'll it look, d'you think, in the headlines? 'Cobb Flunked; Prof in Love with His Girl!' Fine stuff! Pretty family group, eh?"

"Mr. Stanbury," Jim said, "you—you can't frighten me."

Then it burst. Stanbury went livid. "I'm not trying to frighten you. I'm trying to save your job, that's what—and your head from a damn good beating!" He lifted a big fist. "Margaret's my daughter—and, by gad, I'm not going to have *her* ruined—her and Wilton as well. See? I'm fighting for them both. See? And I know how far I can go, Weston. I *know*. Get that? I *know*. One week from today, Weston, and if Cobb receives that flunk—well, I know what I can do. Get that? I *know*. See? Get that?"

In Pikeny Hall next morning Jim sat before a multitude arranged in mounting rows, blinking down at him. A door opened and Cobb stalked in—aggressively late; sat in the front row.

A stamping thundered, and Jim knew something was up. A voice rang out from the back of the room: "Mr. Weston!"

"Yes, Mr. Myles," said Jim.

"I wonder, Mr. Weston," the fellow cleared his throat, "would you explain Platonic love?"

Nobody laughed. The eyes were watching.

"Mr. Myles," Jim tilted his head, "in Plato's *Symposium* you'll be able to study that matter out for yourself."

Mr. Myles insisted: "But I've *read* Plato's *Symposium.* I can't just make it out! Couldn't you give us just a hint, sir? I've the *Symposium* right here."

The book came down conspicuously and elaborately from hand to hand. Cobb received it last. He brought it with a serious bow and set it on the desk.

The thing was organized. Jim felt Stanbury behind it.

He reached for the book. He turned the pages, and the room was very still. Then he read, with his throat thumping, the banquet speech of Socrates:

"He who aspires to love rightly ought from his earliest youth to seek an intercourse with beautiful forms, and first to make a single form the object of his love, and therein to generate intellectual excellences."

The room waited—like a panther.

"He ought then to consider that beauty, in whatever form it resides, is the brother of that beauty which subsists in another form. And if he ought to pursue that which is beautiful in form, it would be absurd to imagine that beauty is not one and the same thing in all forms.... He would consider the beauty which is in souls more excellent than that which is in form."

"Mr. Weston," Cobb called out, "and is *that* Platonic love?"

Jim warily eyed him.

Cobb didn't attempt to move. He sat with his eyes fixed. He said slowly: "That what you and Peggy were trying to pull on us last night?"

Jim swallowed his gorge. They wanted to get his goat—have him explode—have him disgrace himself!

The roar very steadily died down, and the hall was again in a hush.

Cobb spoke again: "Do you like the way she kisses, Mr. Weston? So do I."

Jim, with his blood buzzing, arose. Cobb arose. Jim toppled the desk back. With a crack they flung at each other.

There was more to the thing than bashing in. Everybody was popeyed. Nobody yelled. Nobody could stand up. They sat ranged, panting, with their fists working, teeth clenched. Jim went suddenly over the desk. Cobb flung at his ears. Every wallop resounded.

Jim lay with Cobb on his chest. But his legs were free. Jim moved them. If he could last a bit! He tightened—tightened up everything—his guts and all his tendons. Then he waited. Then he was set. Up swung his legs with his knees out wide. They swung, and caught Cobb in a body scissors, locked him, twisted, and squeezed. Cobb groaned. Jim's legs were iron bands, under which Cobb's ribs cracked one by one—until darkness filled Jim's eyes.

Jim was used to the sheets by now, and to the prodigious size of his head. The world made little noises, far away, of Margaret moving. She was something pleasant in blue. She sometimes sat by his head, or poured a liquid on to the bandages. Now she came and smiled down at him mildly.

"Well," she said, "two more have come!"

"What day is it?" he asked. "Wednesday?"

Margaret nodded.

"All this mess in less than a day and a half!"

"But it *isn't* a mess, dear."

"It is. It's a damned disgusting mess."

With a noise, the door flung open, and Stanbury came bursting in, immense in the little white room. He wore a splendid light-gray golf suit. He flourished a bunch of envelopes. He roared: "Three more endorsements! Three endorsements and a movie contract! Wow!" He flung them aloft. They scattered down. "Whoopee!"

"Shhh, Daddy!" Margaret warned him. "Please!"

But the man was a balloon. "Old son of a gun!" he bellowed. "Mitt me! Put it there! Say! Never saw such a popular win in all my life. Old prof! Old bookworm, you! And you know what I says to Old Dittman? 'Ditt,' I says, 'old sorehead,' I says, 'you won't go blowing *now* about scholars can't get rich, eh?' How's that, Jim? Pretty good, eh?"

Jim swallowed and felt like hell.

Stanbury pranced about the room. "But I don't know where you'd 'a' been, old horse, if we hadn't suppressed the news about that flunk."

Jim tried to sit up. "Suppressed the flunk! Larry's to play?"

Stanbury swung around at his daughter. "*Listen* to him! Get that,

Peg?" He gurgled like a Jabberwocky. "Say there, old champ, you! Larry's out for this season, boy, with a case of broken bones!"

Jim was excited—up on his elbows. "Then what's the big idea?" he demanded. "Who was it suppressed that flunk?"

Stanbury roared: "Nobody suppressed your flunk, man! Hell! Who cares about a flunk? What we suppressed was the news of the flunk."

Jim settled back, a little bewildered.

Stanbury mopped his booming jaw. "Cobb's out of that game because of Jim Weston—'Old-Time Football Hero'—up and knocked him out. Great stuff, eh? Battle about a girl. Wow!' The Goliath suddenly sobered. "Say, and you know, Jim—the old registrar! Been *flooded* with applications! Every football man in the country! Zip-bing he-man faculty! Even the bookworms at old Wilton have a pair of socking fists, eh? Say, and they've published all your old football records—millions of unseen radio fans, Jim, all over the country…"

Stanbury ranted. Jim lay still. Margaret tried to urge her father from the room.

"And, Jim boy, the faculty's out to give you a special honorary degree. Howzat? Any degree you want. Say, boy, believe me—millions…"

Margaret got him out. She shut the door. She gathered the envelopes and stacked them on a table against the wall. She came and sat down.

Jim frowned at the ceiling.

"I suppose," said Jim, "the sensible thing would be to accept these offers!"

The girl withheld a smile.

"They come to over a million, Jim—enough to set a family up for life," the girl offered quietly.

Jim turned to smile at her eyes. "Still, we *could* get along on that fellowship! Be cute, kind of, don't you think?"

She leaned and gently kissed his nose.

Jim said: "The millions of unseen radio fans—would they accept, do you think?"

"I think they would. They'd figure they owed it to their children."

"And to their wives."

"Yes."

Jim bit his lower lip.

"So it's really the only sensible thing to do!"

She nodded, smiling.

Jim burrowed into the sheets. "Good! Shall we burn them all in a bunch, then?"

Margaret wrinkled her nose. "Oh, no! Let's not!" She patted his paw. It was fine how she understood things. "It'd be so much more delicious one by one!" she said.

A JOSEPH CAMPBELL BIBLIOGRAPHY

———————————•———————————

Following are the major books authored and edited by Joseph Campbell. Each entry gives bibliographic data concerning the first edition or, if applicable, the original date of publication along with the bibliographic data for the edition published by New World Library as part of the Collected Works of Joseph Campbell. For information concerning all other editions, please refer to the mediagraphy on the Joseph Campbell Foundation Web site (www.jcf.org).

Author

Where the Two Came to Their Father: A Navaho War Ceremonial Given by Jeff King. Bollingen Series I. With Maud Oakes and Jeff King. Richmond, VA: Old Dominion Foundation, 1943.

A Skeleton Key to Finnegans Wake. With Henry Morton Robinson. 1944. Reprint, Novato, CA: New World Library, 2005.*

The Hero with a Thousand Faces. Bollingen Series xvii. 1949. Reprint, Novato, CA: New World Library, 2008.*

The Masks of God, 4 vols. New York: Viking Press, 1959–1968. Vol. 1, *Primitive Mythology,* 1959. Vol. 2, *Oriental Mythology,* 1962. Vol. 3, *Occidental Mythology,* 1964. Vol. 4, *Creative Mythology,* 1968.

The Flight of the Wild Gander: Explorations in the Mythological Dimension. 1969. Reprint, Novato, CA: New World Library, 2002.*

Myths to Live By. 1972. Ebook edition, San Anselmo, CA: Joseph Campbell Foundation, 2011.

The Mythic Image. Bollingen Series c. Princeton: Princeton University Press, 1974.

The Inner Reaches of Outer Space: Metaphor as Myth and as Religion. 1986. Reprint, Novato, CA: New World Library, 2002.*

The Historical Atlas of World Mythology:

Vol. 1, *The Way of the Animal Powers.* New York: Alfred van der Marck Editions, 1983. Reprint in 2 pts. Part 1, *Mythologies of the Primitive Hunters and Gatherers.* New York: Alfred van der Marck Editions, 1988. Part 2, *Mythologies of the Great Hunt.* New York: Alfred van der Marck Editions, 1988.

Vol. 2, *The Way of the Seeded Earth,* 3 pts. Part 1, *The Sacrifice.* New York: Alfred van der Marck Editions, 1988. Part 2, *Mythologies of the Primitive Planters: The Northern Americas.* New York: Harper & Row Perennial Library, 1989. Part 3, *Mythologies of the Primitive Planters: The Middle and Southern Americas.* New York: Harper & Row Perennial Library, 1989.

The Power of Myth with Bill Moyers. With Bill Moyers. Edited by Betty Sue Flowers. New York: Doubleday, 1988.

Transformations of Myth Through Time. New York: Harper & Row, 1990.

The Hero's Journey: Joseph Campbell on His Life and Work. Edited by Phil Cousineau. 1990. Reprint, Novato, CA: New World Library, 2003.*

Reflections on the Art of Living: A Joseph Campbell Companion. Edited by Diane K. Osbon. New York: HarperCollins, 1991.

Mythic Worlds, Modern Worlds: On the Art of James Joyce. Edited by Edmund L. Epstein. 1993. Reprint, Novato, CA: New World Library, 2003.*

Baksheesh & Brahman: Indian Journal 1954–1955. Edited by Robin Larsen, Stephen Larsen, and Antony Van Couvering. 1995. Reprint, Novato, CA: New World Library, 2002.*

The Mythic Dimension: Selected Essays 1959–1987. Edited by Antony Van Couvering. 1997. Reprint, Novato, CA: New World Library, 2007.*

Thou Art That. Edited by Eugene Kennedy. Novato, CA: New World Library, 2001.*

Sake & Satori: Asian Journals—Japan. Edited by David Kudler. Novato, CA: New World Library, 2002.*

Myths of Light. Edited by David Kudler. Novato, CA: New World Library, 2003.*

---

*   Published by New World Library as part of the Collected Works of Joseph Campbell.

Editor

Books edited and completed from the posthuma of Heinrich Zimmer:
Myths and Symbols in Indian Art and Civilization. Bollingen Series vi. New
  York: Pantheon, 1946.
The King and the Corpse. Bollingen Series xi. New York: Pantheon, 1948.
Philosophies of India. Bollingen Series xxvi. New York: Pantheon, 1951.
The Art of Indian Asia. Bollingen Series xxxix, 2 vols. New York: Pantheon,
  1955.

The Portable Arabian Nights. New York: Viking Press, 1951.
Papers from the Eranos Yearbooks. Bollingen Series xxx, 6 vols. Edited with
  R. F. C. Hull and Olga Froebe-Kapteyn, translated by Ralph Manheim.
  Princeton: Princeton University Press, 1954–1969.
Myth, Dreams and Religion: Eleven Visions of Connection. New York: E. P.
  Dutton, 1970.
The Portable Jung. By C. G. Jung. Translated by R. F. C. Hull. New York:
  Viking Press, 1971.
My Life and Lives. By Rato Khyongla Nawang Losang. New York: E. P. Dut-
  ton, 1977.

ABOUT THE AUTHOR

———————•———————

JOSEPH CAMPBELL was an American author and teacher best known for his work in the field of comparative mythology. Born in New York City in 1904, from early childhood he loved to read about American Indians and frequently visited the American Museum of Natural History, where he became captivated by the museum's collection of totem poles. From those days onward, Campbell's interest in mythology grew and deepened. He was educated at Columbia University, where he specialized in medieval literature, and, after earning a master's degree, continued his studies at universities in Paris and Munich. While abroad he was influenced by the art of Pablo Picasso and Henri Matisse, the novels of James Joyce and Thomas Mann, and the psychological studies of Sigmund Freud and Carl Jung. These encounters led to Campbell's theory that all myths and epics are linked in the human psyche and that they are cultural manifestations of the universal need to explain social, cosmological, and spiritual realities.

After a period in California, where he encountered John Steinbeck and the biologist Ed Ricketts, he taught at the Canterbury School, and then, in 1934, joined the literature department at Sarah Lawrence College, a post he retained for many years. During the 1940s and '50s, he helped Swami Nikhilananda to translate the Upaniṣads and

The Gospel of Sri Ramakrishna. He also edited works by the German scholar Heinrich Zimmer on Indian art, myths, and philosophy. In 1944, with Henry Morton Robinson, Campbell published *A Skeleton Key to Finnegans Wake.* His first original work, *The Hero with a Thousand Faces,* came out in 1949 and was immediately well received; in time, it became acclaimed as a classic. In this study of the "myth of the hero," Campbell asserted that there is a single pattern of heroic journey and that all cultures share this essential pattern in their various heroic myths. In his book he also outlined the basic conditions, stages, and results of the archetypal hero's journey.

Joseph Campbell died in 1987. In 1988, a series of television interviews, *Joseph Campbell and the Power of Myth with Bill Moyers,* introduced his views to millions of people.

ABOUT THE
JOSEPH CAMPBELL FOUNDATION

———————————•———————————

THE JOSEPH CAMPBELL FOUNDATION (JCF) is a nonprofit corporation that continues the work of Joseph Campbell, exploring the fields of mythology and comparative religion. The Foundation is guided by three principal goals:

First, the Foundation preserves, protects, and perpetuates Campbell's pioneering work. This includes cataloging and archiving his works, developing new publications based on his works, directing the sale and distribution of his published works, protecting copyrights to his works, and increasing awareness of his works by making them available in digital formats on JCF's Web site.

Second, the Foundation promotes the study of mythology and comparative religion. This involves implementing and/or supporting diverse mythological education programs, supporting and/or sponsoring events designed to increase public awareness, donating Campbell's archived works (principally to the Joseph Campbell and Marija Gimbutas Archive and Library), and utilizing JCF's Web site as a forum for relevant cross-cultural dialogue.

Third, the Foundation helps individuals enrich their lives by participating in a series of programs, including our global, Internet-based Associates program, our local international network of Mythological

Roundtables, and our periodic Joseph Campbell–related events and
activities.

For more information on Joseph Campbell
and the Joseph Campbell Foundation, contact:

Joseph Campbell Foundation
www.jcf.org
Post Office Box 1836
New York, NY 10026
E-mail: info@jcf.org